MW01411985

HAVANA FEAR

TIMOTHY FAGAN

To Susan,
Thank you for being the best barber around!

T. Fgn

Fireclay Books

This is a work of fiction. Names, characters, places, and incidents either are the product of the author's imagination or are used fictitiously. Any resemblance to actual persons, living or dead, events or locales is entirely coincidental.

Copyright © 2024 Timothy Fagan

All rights reserved. Published in the United States by Fireclay Books, Winchester, Massachusetts.

www.fireclaybooks.com

Cover design by damonza.com.

ISBN-13: 978-1-7324596-6-3 (paperback)

ISBN-13: 978-1-7324596-7-0 (ebook)

First Edition

5.4.3.2.1.7.16.24.1.2.3.4.5

To my mom.

CHAPTER ONE

Angel Cavada could feel the side-eye from his girlfriend, Marisol Borja, as they bumped along in a dirty taxi through the tropical afternoon heat.

Angel was as nervous as a cat in a doghouse. Their view out the opened windows transitioned from red clay farmland to suburbs, then to the city of Havana. They skirted a big, open square dominated by a tall concrete building dominated on one side by an enormous portrait of Che Guevara.

You're not in Cape Cod anymore, thought Angel.

As they progressed through the streets, crowds of men and women along the curbside gestured and shouted to flag down a ride.

When they were deeper in the city, Marisol leaned forward and spoke in rapid Spanish to their taxi driver, telling him to pull over.

"You okay?" Angel asked.

She made a face at him. "Angelito, do you never listen? I told you I always buy flowers when I arrive in Cuba. They brighten the *casa*. And they're good luck!"

Marisol climbed out of the taxi and gave Angel a tight smile.

"Can you behave while I'm gone? No more bananas, no more police trouble, *sí*?"

Well, that was a low blow, thought Angel, feeling embarrassment tingle his cheeks. Sure, he'd accidentally caused a long, tense run-in with Cuban customs officials at the airport upon arrival. But he didn't want to think about the "Banana Incident," as he was already calling it in his mind. Instead, he watched Marisol jaywalk across the street to a cobblestone plaza, her purse swinging at her shoulder.

Angel loved watching his girlfriend walk. He loved watching her do pretty much anything. Her skirt showcased her tanned legs, her Peloton calves, and her bubblegum pink shoes that were a little too high-heeled for practical traveling. Her cream-colored blouse was stuck to her back from sweat, and men turned to watch as she passed. Angel didn't blame them.

Angel knew he was screwing up everything today. And he knew the reason — his dead grandmother's diamond engagement ring, which was tucked away deep in his backpack, ready for a romantic wedding proposal. He needed to get his act together, pronto, and act like the kind of man Marisol would say yes to.

The Cuban taxi driver, a small man in his fifties with a Castro–style beard, turned up some classical guitar *trova* music on the radio and checked his phone.

Angel's knee was bouncing from nervous energy, so he held it still with one hand and tried to take in the surrounding city. It was his first time in Cuba, the land of his ancestors. Marisol had traveled here four times in the past year, filming a documentary about endangered orchids. This time she'd invited him along.

Peering through the traffic, Angel saw Marisol talking with a flower vendor—a tall, thin guy with a mustache and a straw hat. The vendor had little inventory, just five white plastic buckets with sparse flowers poking out of them.

Angel's backpack was in the seat next to him, so he double-checked that the engagement ring was still in its little pouch in the tiny interior pocket. A few days earlier, he'd shown the ring to Pepper Ryan, his closest buddy in the world. When he'd told Pepper his epic plan—the Malecón, the sunset, the marriage proposal—Pepper had looked shocked at first. Angel fell in love a lot, but never for very long.

Angel had spilled his guts, telling Pepper how he wanted things he would have laughed at before Marisol. Being with one woman forever. Having kids. He even admitted that he had an impulse to plant a garden in his backyard—an idea so foreign he'd wondered if he had a brain tumor. But suddenly, all those notions made sense to him as the path to happiness. Made him wonder what the hell he'd been thinking before.

Pepper had congratulated him with a bear hug, saying he could tell this time was different.

A snarl of Soviet–style cars and 1950s American cars crawled past his parked taxi, intermittently blocking his view. People in shorts, T-shirts, and straw hats walked the sidewalks all over the plaza and barged into the street traffic.

The taxi driver cleared his throat and spat out the window, his arm tapping the door frame to the music. Or was he tapping from impatience?

Hopefully, Marisol would return any second. Angel's view across the street was obstructed by a horse and cart clip-clopping past the taxi. The next time he craned his neck to glimpse her, he failed. He pulled his cell phone from his messenger bag and fired it up, but as he'd expected, it said "No Service." He'd have to buy a local SIM card first thing tomorrow.

The taxi driver glanced back at Angel. Marisol had been gone for ten minutes. What the heck was keeping her?

"Señor, espera aquí, por favor," said Angel, in his second-generation Spanish-American accent, gesturing for the driver to wait there.

The driver made a shooing motion—get the beautiful woman and hurry back.

Angel got out and crossed the street during a gap in traffic. He shaded his eyes against the afternoon glare, looking for Marisol.

The plaza was large, with quaint Spanish colonial buildings around a big old stone church. A string of street vendors lined its edges. Small palm trees in clay pots were scattered around the plaza, and a marble fountain rose in the middle. Crowds of people were walking around, but Marisol was nowhere in sight.

The spot where she'd been talking with the flower vendor was now vacant. He walked through the plaza in a small half-circle around the fountain, which was decorated with four lions vomiting water. Then he looped back the other way. No Marisol. Angel walked another lap deeper into the plaza, weaving through the thin crowd of vendors, tourists, and locals, and then came out the other side. Still no Marisol.

It made no sense.

Twenty minutes had passed since Marisol left the taxi. Had she gone into a restaurant to use the toilet? Or stopped at a store to buy something?

Then Angel remembered the taxi. She could have walked right past him in the throng. Had she returned to the taxi and found Angel gone, one more stupid screw-up by her boyfriend?

Angel hurried across the cobblestones toward the taxi. But then he saw an odd sight that made him stop short. It was a bubblegum pink high-heeled shoe, lying on its side, tucked against the steps of the white marble fountain. Marisol's?

Angel found that suddenly he couldn't breathe. He hurried to pick up the shoe. Its thin strap was broken, but the buckle was still attached. He was ninety-nine percent sure it was Marisol's. Angel's breath choked in his throat and he broke into a cold sweat, despite the muggy afternoon heat.

He hustled to the street and waited for a gap in the traffic. But when an opening came, he saw their goddamn taxi was gone too.

Angel felt a sudden coldness in his core. He waited there, head on a swivel, lost and alone in a strange country. The thought sent a tingling feeling up his spine and across his scalp, like icy water.

Angel's head was spinning. He stared at the broken shoe in his hand. Had Marisol been mugged?

Angel felt like he was going to throw up. His girlfriend had gone missing and their possessions had disappeared somewhere too. Even the backpack with his grandmother's heirloom engagement ring. Why'd he leave it in the stupid taxi?

His emotions swung between panic and anger as his imagination played out the range of disasters that might have happened to Marisol. He waited there uselessly, hoping Marisol and the taxi would reappear, but no such luck.

He didn't have any Cuban pesos yet to hire another taxi. He'd forgotten to buy local currency at the Havana airport, because he'd been too flustered by the Banana Incident at Cuban customs.

Angel knew the address of their apartment: Concordia 720. He sighed, then started walking in what he believed was the right direction. His mind raced with the same three questions, around and around:

Where's Marisol?

Is she hurt?

And what the holy hell am I going to do to find her?

Whatever it takes, Angel told himself, navigating through the pedestrians on the broken sidewalk. *Before you wreck the best damn thing that ever happened to you, as usual.*

CHAPTER TWO

Pepper Ryan stepped out of José Martí International Airport into a chaos of yelling people, colorful vintage cars, and blaring music.

He adjusted the duffel bag on his shoulder and looked in all directions. It was a Wednesday afternoon in mid-September, but Cuba was hotter and steamier than Cape Cod during a July heat wave.

His buddy Angel was nowhere in sight.

Earlier that morning, Pepper had been walking past the Lincoln Memorial reflecting pool in Washington, DC, when he got the call from Angel that blew up his big plans for the day. Angel had told him in a shaking voice that Marisol vanished in broad daylight in the heart of Havana, leaving behind only a broken high-heel shoe.

Pepper had been heading to a meeting at FBI headquarters with his department supervisor, Deputy Assistant Director Edwina Youngblood, to learn whether she was returning him to active duty as a special agent, or beginning the administrative process to kill his FBI career at the tender age of twenty-nine.

The uncertainty of his future weighed heavily on his mind, but he knew Angel desperately needed his skills as an investigator.

And if he found Marisol, he would prove to himself that he was still a good investigator.

Without a second thought, Pepper had left Youngblood a voicemail citing a family emergency, begging to postpone until Monday. Then he caught a connecting flight to Cuba through Tampa. Hopefully, he would dive right in, use his experience to find Marisol, then return to DC by Sunday afternoon to learn the fate of his FBI career. A reasonable plan, if all went well.

Angel had promised to meet Pepper curbside, so where was he? Men congregated around Pepper, inundating him with a riot of Spanish and broken English, offering rides to Havana, money changing, and anything else they thought might get his interest. Pepper tried to shoo them away, still looking around for Angel.

One young man who looked like a Latin version of Elvis Presley was waving, trying to catch Pepper's attention. He was wearing a white jumpsuit covered in sequins, with a gaudy bejeweled belt. He even had the trademark long black hair along with gold sunglasses.

Pepper laughed for the first time all day.

The young man gave Pepper a friendly smile and said, "Angel send me! Angel send me!"

"Jesus send me!" said an older man, and people around them laughed.

The young Elvis impersonator waved dismissively at the men surrounding Pepper. "Angel, he laughs like a madman, no? Angel is my *primo*. I am Hector Cavada ... I drive you to Angel!"

Two police officers, noticing the commotion around him, began walking his way, repositioning their automatic weapons on their slings.

"Okay, Hector, lead the way."

The young man guided Pepper through a tangle of cross-parked vehicles, continuing to wave off men who clamored to Pepper.

"We take my Caddy," Hector said proudly.

For good reason. It was a classic Cadillac convertible, in great shape. Maybe late 1950s. It had a baby blue exterior, with a white top that was folded down.

Man, this ride must have attracted the ladies back in the day, thought Pepper. *Maybe it still does.*

"Thanks for coming to get me," he said, climbing into the front passenger seat, dumping his duffel bag in back. At six foot two, he appreciated the extra legroom of cars from Detroit's golden age. "Seriously, I appreciate it. But where's Angel?"

Instead of answering, Hector turned the key, and its engine sputtered, then rumbled to life. Pepper smelled something that wasn't gasoline. Hector pushed an eight-track cassette into a tape deck roughly cut into the dashboard, and Elvis Presley started belting out "Jailhouse Rock." Hector stabbed a button to change the tune to "Viva Las Vegas." Then he began singing along in a velvety baritone.

All the while he navigated the big car through the cluttered parking lot and roared onto a highway.

"So, where's Angel?" Pepper asked again, shouting over the music and the wind roaring through the open windows.

"That is complicated," Hector yelled back. "Maybe Angel is at his casa now, we see."

Maybe we see? thought Pepper.

Hector went on. "Angel went to your embassy yesterday ... they were not so helpful. They ask, did Angel and his woman have a fight? They ask, does she have another lover in Cuba? Is there a reason she would plan her own disappearance? Angel, he said all of that was ridiculous. So this morning he made me drive him to the police station. I told him it was a bad idea, but he didn't listen. I waited outside the station a long time, very worried. Then I went for you."

"How long did you wait for Angel?"

"Hours and hours. Very bad, you know?"

Shit, thought Pepper. I was the one that told Angel to go there.

"Are you a big Elvis fan?" asked Hector.

"Sure, I like him," said Pepper offhandedly.

"This was his car," said Hector.

"What?"

"Elvis, he owned this car. He gave it to my grandfather, Santiago Cavada, you heard of him? He was number one drummer from Cuba. I tell you the whole story sometime."

"That's nice," said Pepper, still distracted by Angel's situation. He turned on his cell phone, hoping to check for voice messages. But his screen said, "Cannot Activate Cellular Network." Shit. He needed to get a local SIM card ASAP.

"Angel told me if anyone can find Marisol, it's you, yes? The best cop in America. He says you have caught psycho killers, you saved girls from kidnappers, all that stuff. He says you never give up."

"Angel talks too much."

Hector laughed. "And Angel says you are a great singer. Maybe I hear you sing sometime?"

Pepper laughed too. "Maybe. But you sound just like Elvis!"

"Thank you," said Hector, beaming. "My dream is to perform all of Elvis's songs for the crowds in Las Vegas, Nevada. Just like the King!" Hector sped up, passing a string of cars. "You bring lots of American cash to buy pesos?" he asked. "Your credit cards don't work here."

Pepper knew. Angel had told him to withdraw a pile of cash before getting on the plane to Cuba.

"Can we swing by a currency office to buy Cuban pesos?" asked Pepper.

"I got you," said Hector. "I know a woman. She can give you the best exchange rate."

"That's okay. I'd rather use an official money exchange."

"No, no," said Hector. "They rip you off. Twenty-five pesos for a dollar. I call my good friend. She will give you double, no problem."

Against Pepper's better judgment, he went with Hector's suggestion. Hector parked in front of a small store with handmade signs advertising soda and ice cream.

"Here's four hundred dollars," said Pepper, handing over a stack of American cash. But it was actually $460. Hector was Angel's cousin, but he was a stranger to Pepper. So he wanted to give the young Cuban a little test.

Hector disappeared into the store. A few minutes later, he returned and pulled a thick wad of multi-colored money from his pocket and handed it to Pepper.

"She paid sixty-five pesos for a dollar! You're lucky to know me, my friend! And you gave me sixty dollars too much, man. That's a lot of money ... you gotta be more careful!"

They drove down a narrow city street with balconied buildings that needed repairs and a paint job.

"You see La Guarida?" asked Hector, pointing at a small sign as they drove past. "Very famous *paladar*. What you say, a private restaurant? Obama ate there."

Pepper's stomach growled. "Lucky guy," he said, even though La Guarida looked like an abandoned building. Pepper hadn't eaten since the Tampa airport.

The next block of the street looked even more slummy. Amid the broken-down buildings were empty lots covered with rubble. Dogs stood in the street, staring down cars as they navigated around them.

Dystopian, Pepper thought, feeling uneasy.

"Not a fancy neighborhood of Havana," admitted Hector. "But it is not what you think. How you say ... don't judge the book by the cover?"

"No problem," said Pepper.

A few blocks later, Hector pulled over to the curb and parked in front of a narrow pale blue building with vines growing up its facade.

"This is Casa de Vides," he said. "It means 'house of vines.' you see them? This is Centro Havana, between Old Havana and Vedado. Not so many tourists here."

"Wonderful," said Pepper, barely listening. *Where the heck is Angel?*

The buildings were mostly in poor repair, but their doors and windows were open and people looked out, watching them, the men shirtless. And it was noisy. Shouted conversations, loud music. Car horns honking.

The light blue building they'd parked in front of looked well maintained, with ornamental bars on the tall street-level windows.

"It is a nice neo-colonial," said Hector. "Maybe 1940s."

Pepper tried the front door. It was locked. But maybe Angel was inside, anyway?

"I find your casa lady," promised Hector. He began shouting at the top of his lungs in Spanish, and in a minute an elderly woman appeared in the next doorway.

Hector launched into a loud conversation with her in rapid Spanish, gesturing at the casa, at Pepper, at the sky.

Pepper stayed silent and smiled at the woman, trying to look trustworthy.

"She looks after the place for the owner," translated Hector. "She knows Marisol, and she met Angel. She likes his big laugh. You need to give her your passport. She has to make a record of everyone who stays here. It's the law."

Pepper dug it out and handed it to her, smiling again. "Does she know if Angel or Marisol are inside?"

Another cascade in Spanish and the woman shrugged. She disappeared into her doorway with Pepper's passport, then reappeared a few minutes later and returned the passport with a ring of two keys.

"One's for the front door, the other's for a security gate inside," translated Hector. "She says these are the only extra keys, so don't lose them or she'll kill you, even though you're handsome."

After a few attempts Pepper got the front door unlocked. He waved to the woman, and he and Hector went inside. Halfway up a tall staircase, a heavy-duty metal gate blocked the stairs. Pepper opened it with the other key.

"She said to leave the street door unlocked when you are here. She needs to come in to turn on the water pump," said Hector.

"Water pump?" asked Pepper. "For this place or hers?"

Hector lifted his shoulder in a half shrug.

Pepper hustled up the rest of the stairs to the second floor, hoping to hear Angel's laugh.

Marisol had chosen a nice place. It had high ceilings, a tile floor, and tall wooden French doors that opened onto a balcony, letting in bright tropical sunshine. The apartment was decorated beautifully. Mid-century modern furniture with cushions. A vase of flowers on a table by the sofa. Plants everywhere. The apartment smelled like flowers. Two guitars hung on the wall over the sofa, displayed like art. The room looked like it had been furnished in the 1950s and left untouched, spotlessly clean, until today.

It also seemed to be empty.

"Angel?" yelled Pepper. "Hello?"

No answer. No one else was there.

Pepper checked every room in case Angel was asleep.

He discovered a large bedroom with two beds, which led into a smaller bedroom with a queen-sized bed. The apartment had no hallway—each room passed through to the next. Both bedrooms were empty. No Angel. No Marisol. And no luggage—what the hell was going on?

Pepper left his duffel bag in a corner of the room with two beds, then walked through the larger bedroom into a kitchen. At its far side was a small bathroom with an orange-painted sink. Pepper washed his face and sized himself up in the mirror. He looked even more tired than he felt. And he felt extremely tired. He dried his face with a crisp white towel.

Pepper found Hector on the balcony, smoking a cigarette.

"Can I borrow your phone for a second?" Pepper asked. "I'll pay any charges. I just need to check my messages."

Pepper hit +1, entered his own cell number, then interrupted his voice message by hitting the star key. He entered his password to access his voice mailbox.

A robotic voice said he had one message. Pepper's heart raced a bit.

His boss had left a message, delivered in a loud, clipped voice. "Good thing I checked my messages, Ryan, after you didn't show for our meeting. Take care of your family emergency. But if you're not here on Monday at eight a.m., I'll take that as your decision to resign from the FBI."

Great job, Pepper, once again.

Pepper was on a losing streak. In the past few months, he'd managed to screw up both his FBI career and a new relationship back home with a woman named Zula Eisenhower. After dating for a fun, dizzying month, Zula had asked Pepper if he'd be willing to transfer to the FBI's Boston field office, to be closer to where she was starting her first year of law school at Northeastern University in Boston.

And that's when Pepper screwed up, big time. He believed the FBI was likely to fire him soon, which was completely embarrassing. Instead of explaining his situation to Zula, he merely told her he needed some time to think about it. Like a complete idiot.

Two weeks later, the night before she left for law school, a tearful Zula broke up with him. She said to call if he ever got his head out of his ass and figured out what he really wanted in life.

Three weeks later, it still hurt, and the breakup was making him second-guess himself.

Pepper handed the cell phone back to Hector. "So, what the hell's going on? Where's Angel?"

"I told him not to go," Hector said with a frown.

"Not to go to the police station?"

"*Sí.* I hoped he was here now, waiting for you. But..."

Pepper's frustration was boiling over. "Hector, take me to the police station."

"But, Pepper—"

"Now, Hector."

To Pepper, it was a process of elimination. Angel hadn't been waiting at Casa de Vides. So either he was still at the police station for some crazy reason, or else maybe he'd gotten some hot lead there about Marisol and was following up on it alone.

On the drive to the police station, Hector tried to change Pepper's mind. "Is a difficult time. Many protests all summer. Police are out everywhere. You need to trust me. You have been in Havana for five minutes—you think you know Cuba?"

"Did Angel tell you I was a police officer back home in America?"

"Angel told me. You are not like Cuban police, I know. Is different here."

"I hear you, Hector," said Pepper. "Seriously. But I'm not a sit-around kind of guy."

Hector sighed. "Don't say I never told you."

CHAPTER THREE

"You've got to be shitting me," said Pepper, staring at the Zanja Police Station.

"I told you," said Hector.

The stone walls of the police station loomed like a medieval fortress amidst the crumbling buildings of Centro Havana. The brutal heat and the station's ominous appearance did little to ease his growing sense of unease about what he'd come here to do.

He almost changed his mind about going in. But did he really have a choice? Pepper didn't speak enough Spanish to ask around in Havana. And he needed to find Angel fast, then Marisol, and get himself on a plane.

Simple as that.

"Good luck, man," said Hector. "I will be here if you come out."

Pepper put his hand on the younger man's shoulder. "Hector, I need you to do me a favor."

"No, Pepper."

"I need you to come with me. To translate."

"No, no, no," repeated Hector, sounding terrified.

"My Spanish is mediocre at best," explained Pepper. "I need them to understand why I'm here."

"No Cuban goes inside Zanja unless he has to."

Pepper gave him a serious look. "That's just it. We have to, for Angel. Your cousin."

Eventually Hector caved, and they walked up a curved walkway to a black iron gate. The two officers with semiautomatic weapons and frowns were stationed there, and Hector talked to them in Spanish. The officer lifted a red phone next to the doorway and talked.

Pepper waited, his hands moist with sweat.

After the officer hung up, he said something to Hector. The other officer—a younger guy in his early twenties with a PNR shield sewn on his gray shirt—swung open the metal gate, which screeched like a warning.

The young officer led them inside to a dimly lit waiting room with a row of severe gray benches along one wall, like the lobby of a military complex. The room smelled of sweat and bleach.

The officer spoke to Hector again, who shrugged at Pepper. "He says I must stay here. He says an officer with good English will talk to you." Hector lowered himself onto the gray bench, his head leaning back on the stone wall.

"Cool," said Pepper brightly. "I'll meet you back here."

The officer opened a metal door and led Pepper through a maze of gray-painted hallways. At the end he ushered Pepper into a bullpen of scratched metal tables, metal chairs, and stone walls. A variety of uniformed and plainclothes men and women came and went. Working, sipping coffee, and joking with each other. This was an environment that Pepper knew.

The officer gestured to a single chair across from a cluttered desk. It held several precariously stacked piles of old-fashioned manila case files.

A man strolled over and sat down hard at the desk across from

Pepper. Unlike the previous officers, he wore brown dress pants and a white guayabera shirt. And a scowl.

The officer rattled off a quick stream of Spanish.

"*Hablo muy poco Español*," said Pepper. "*Habla Inglés?*"

The officer smiled, a thin crack. "I am Detective Juan Guiteras of the Policía Nacional de la Revolución. I speak enough English. The officer said you are looking for a missing friend? Or two missing friends?"

The detective dug a notebook from a drawer and looked expectantly at Pepper.

"My friend Angel Cavada came here this morning to report that his girlfriend was missing. And no one has seen him since."

"Yes, your friend spoke to me," Guiteras said. "And I'm still trying to understand." He studied Pepper. "If you tell me what you know, I will help you and your friend if I can. Is that fair?"

"Great," said Pepper.

Pepper told the detective that Marisol had gone missing on Monday afternoon, soon after arriving in Havana, when buying flowers. Angel had asked Pepper to come to Cuba, then had disappeared himself.

"And when did you arrive in Cuba?" asked the detective.

"Two hours ago," said Pepper.

The detective scratched a note in his book. "And back in America, what would the police do when someone cannot find his friend for two hours?"

The sneaky belligerence of the question jarred Pepper, but he tried to stay cool. "I'm not here to file a missing-person report for Angel. I just wanted to find out if he was still here, or else when he left. My phone doesn't work in Cuba. And his girlfriend, Marisol Borja, has been missing for two days. She left Angel in a taxi with their luggage and just disappeared. Angel was worried she'd been kidnapped."

The detective made a face. "Señor Ryan, what is your job in America?"

Pepper paused. "I work for the government."

"Ah. A civil servant. What specifically do you do?"

"I'm an employee of a federal agency," hedged Pepper.

Guiteras made a note in his book. "Your friend mentioned someone was coming to Cuba to help him find his girlfriend. An American police officer. Is there a reason you are hiding the fact you are a policeman?"

Shit.

"I used to be a police officer in Massachusetts. And I am on leave from my current employer right now."

"That is your Federal Bureau of Investigation, no? The world-famous FBI."

Shit. Angel must have told the detective everything about Pepper.

"You can imagine my surprise when I heard an American police officer was coming to Cuba to find a missing person."

Pepper sat up straight and locked eyes with the detective. "I'm only here to support Angel, as his friend."

"America tends not to respect our sovereignty. Like your embargo that's meant to hurt the Cuban people, which has failed."

Pepper wasn't walking into that trap.

"I'm fascinated with America," continued Guiteras after a pause. "The differences from Cuba. Tell me, what are the consequences if you lie to a police officer in America? Or if you interfere with a police investigation?" Guiteras made a face. "Those are serious offenses in Cuba too. How many times in the last two years has your friend Angel Cavada visited Cuba?"

"I think this is his first time."

"What kind of work does he do in America?"

"He owns a restaurant."

"Does your friend have a criminal record?"

That one knocked Pepper off balance. "No ... I don't think so. Is he still here in this police station?"

Guiteras didn't answer. He just changed topics. "And the missing woman, Marisol Borja. She makes documentary films?"

"Yes."

"What are her films about?"

Pepper mentioned the wolf film. "I don't know about her others," he admitted.

"What is she filming in Cuba?"

"It's a documentary about Cuban flowers. Some rare orchids."

"Is she a successful filmmaker? Would she be one of the best documentary filmmakers in America?"

Again Pepper was thrown. "Why would that matter?"

"Do you consider filmmakers to be artists? Like painters or dancers?"

"Um, sure."

"Do you have the video footage that Senorita Borja filmed the last time she came to Havana?"

This question truly confused Pepper. "No. I don't have it and haven't watched it. Why?"

Ignoring Pepper's question, the detective leaned forward. "Do you know if Angel Cavada is the beneficiary of life insurance in her name?"

Pepper was further surprised. "Absolutely not. Not that I've heard."

"Were they fighting? Could she have left him there on purpose?"

Pepper crossed his arms. "I asked Angel that. He said no."

"Does Angel have any other girlfriends?"

"No."

"Does Ms. Borja have any other boyfriends?"

"Not that I know of." Pepper felt himself getting annoyed by the rapid-fire series of questions, which he knew was part of the detective's strategy. Interview tactics 101.

"Are either of them married?"

"No."

Then he dropped a bomb. "Has Señor Cavada ever been the suspect in a disappearance or murder case before?"

"What? No! Why would he be a suspect? And is this a murder case?" Pepper felt ice in his chest. "Has Marisol's body been found?"

Guiteras waved a hand dismissively. "No, no, I am just trying to understand. Often when women disappear or are killed, the boyfriend or husband is a suspect. Isn't that true in America too?"

"Sometimes. But not in these circumstances."

"But what are these circumstances, hmm? That is what I'm trying to understand. It will save time if you tell me the truth. Has Angel Cavada visited Cuba under any other names or passports in the past two years? Specifically, last October, and in January, March, and August of this year?"

"No! What? I mean, not that I know of."

The detective raised an eyebrow. "Not that you know of? Okay. And it has been two days since Marisol Borja disappeared?"

"Yes."

"Well, I am confident we'd know by now if she was dead."

Pepper wasn't so sure. "What if her body was hidden somewhere? Or buried?"

Guiteras shook his head. "Trust me, that would not be the case."

"But she's not in police custody, right?"

Guiteras laughed, but his expression was hostile. Aggressive. "I can assure you, we do not have an open investigation of Marisol Borja. Why would the government care about a documentary film about orchids? Senorita Borja had the correct visa and permissions to make her film, so she would have no trouble with the police, *sí*?"

A woman in her early thirties, dressed in a snug light green pants suit, approached Guiteras and whispered in his ear. Guiteras stood. "I'll be right back. Junior Detective Valdés will keep you company." He smirked and left.

"Lola Valdés," she said, shaking Pepper's hand. Her small hand was cool and firm. "I apologize for Detective Guiteras." Detective Valdés appeared to be the opposite of her senior officer. She was a pretty woman with an easy, open smile. Her long hair was tied back in a ponytail. She grinned at Pepper. "If Juan worked for our Ministry of Tourism, he would do more damage than your government's embargo."

Pepper laughed.

"But Juan is usually less of a monster," she said. "He's working a high-profile serial killer case that's driving him crazy." She shrugged. "Can I get you something to drink? Coffee? Water?"

Pepper smiled at her. "It's been a long day. I'd love some coffee, thank you."

She adjusted her ponytail, smiled at him, and left.

Pepper stood and stretched, straightening his back. He glanced down and noticed the loose piles of case files on the desk. Then he focused on a name that made him hold his breath. One of the manila folders poking out from its ragged pile had a typed label that said "BORJA."

Damn! he thought. *The PNR had an open case for Marisol Borja.* "So he's an asshole and a liar," Pepper muttered. He got a bad idea and looked over his shoulder for Detective Guiteras or Detective Valdés. But neither were in sight, and no other officer was focused on him.

Pepper stretched forward and slipped the Borja file from the stack, praying that the stack wouldn't tip over and cause an avalanche of paper. It slid free easily.

It was a thin file, maybe a case report, not a full investigation file. Or a recent case with little paper trail yet.

As Pepper opened the file for a peek, he saw Detective Valdés walking back to the desk with two cups of coffee in her hand.

Instinctively, feeling stupid, Pepper slid the manila folder behind his back and under his shirt, tucking the folder into the top of his pants.

Screw Guiteras. The detective had lied about having an open case investigating Marisol—either her disappearance or her activity in Havana—and Pepper needed to know what was going on, with no more stonewalling. And Marisol's case file was the only way to get that information.

As long as the detectives didn't catch Pepper with the filched file ... he didn't want to imagine how ugly that would get.

Pepper sat down quickly, trying not to look like someone who'd just stolen a police file.

Detective Valdés handed Pepper a coffee and sat in the chair Guiteras had previously occupied. She crossed her legs and smiled at him. "Did Juan mention that we talked to Marisol Borja last month?"

Pepper uncomfortably felt the edges of the file against his back. "What about?"

"She called about a cousin who was murdered. I took the call, and she was very nice, probably because she didn't talk to Juan," Valdés laughed. "She asked why the PNR hadn't publicized the details of the murder in the newspapers and other media. In America, she said, many killers are caught by citizens offering information after the police televise all the details of their investigations." She looked questioningly at Pepper.

"Sometimes," he agreed. "Usually to warn the public or encourage witnesses and tips. But not all the facts. Marisol's a filmmaker ... so it makes sense she's a fan of making everything public."

Valdés smiled. She studied Pepper, then sipped her coffee. "So ... when did you—"

The return of Detective Guiteras interrupted her. "No coffee for me?" he asked Valdés in Spanish.

"Any more coffee, you might be a danger to public safety," she said in English. She got up, smiled at Pepper, and said, "Good luck with your time in Havana."

Guiteras scowled. "Junior Detective Valdés, isn't there somewhere you would rather be?"

She looked at Pepper with open appraisal and gave him a smile. "Not really."

Pepper barely smothered a laugh.

Guiteras glowered and gestured impatiently for Pepper to follow him.

Pepper stood gingerly, hoping the sweat on his back would keep the stolen police file stuck in place.

Detective Guiteras escorted Pepper back to the waiting room. Hector was still sitting on the depressing gray bench, his elbows pressed into his sides, like he was trying to make his body as small as possible. His lips were trembling and his face had gone pale.

"Please sit," Guiteras gestured to Pepper. "I will bring your friend." He exited back through the metal door.

Pepper sat down next to Hector, who raised an eyebrow but said nothing.

An hour and a half later, Detective Guiteras reappeared with Angel at his side.

Angel was a good-looking Cuban-American, about five foot nine, and usually had a big, open smile on his face. But not today. He looked like he'd been roughed up. His face was red on one side and his T-shirt was ripped.

Pepper felt a rush of anger and realized he'd unconsciously clenched his hands into fists. *What the hell happened to him?*

But Angel gave a little smile when he noticed who was waiting for him. "Hey, *mano*. Hey, cuz," Angel said, his voice cracking.

Pepper carefully stood to shake Angel's hand, getting a quizzical look from his buddy. But Pepper couldn't risk a hug, because it might dislodge the Marisol Borja police file hidden up the back of his shirt.

"What the hell happened to him?" Pepper asked Guiteras, his voice sounding loud and harsh in his own ears.

"*Se destimbaló*," shrugged the detective.

Pepper didn't understand the phrase in Spanish, but in police-speak, the shrug said Angel got what he deserved and what are you going to do about it? *Asshole.*

"I need to speak to you again, Señor Ryan." Guiteras led Pepper across the room from the others, out of earshot.

"I will forget for now that you lied to me about who you are, that you are an agent of the American FBI. And we will look into the disappearance of Señorita Borja. But you must promise me something. You will not investigate too, *sí*? Is very serious, interfering in a criminal investigation in Cuba. You can put yourself at great risk." The detective stared hard at Pepper as he talked. As if to decide, would this American do what he was told—sit on his hands, do nothing except wait?

"Okay," lied Pepper.

Guiteras smiled at Pepper, but his eyes were deadly serious. "Then welcome to Cuba, Señor Ryan."

CHAPTER FOUR

Pepper settled into the backseat of Hector's Cadillac. The faded leather felt warm against his skin as he pulled out the police report he'd "borrowed." The car engine growled steadily, carrying them away from the Zanja Police Station. And with each passing block, Pepper's resolve to unravel the mystery of Marisol's disappearance grew stronger.

"Pull over," he told Hector when the three of them were far enough away from the police station. *Would the police report hold the answer to what happened to Marisol?*

Hector found a place to park in front of an abandoned gas station.

"What's that?" Angel asked, pointing at the police report.

Pepper explained how he'd gotten it.

Hector gasped and grabbed his chest. "It is terrible, what you did! We will all be arrested!"

"I feel a little bad," shrugged Pepper. "But Guiteras lied when he said the PNR wasn't investigating Marisol. So as far as I'm concerned, the file was fair game. I hope it doesn't come back to bite me in the ass."

"Yeah," agreed Angel. "That Guiteras looked like he had strong teeth."

They crowded around as Pepper opened the folder.

A crime scene photo slid out into Pepper's lap, so he picked it up.

The color photo showed a woman's body, contorted and face down on the ground. Her back, and the ground surrounding her, were black with blood.

Shit. Pepper's heart dropped.

"Oh, God!" blurted Angel. His hand covered his mouth, and the blood drained from his face. Pepper put an arm around his buddy's shoulder.

"Look!" said Hector. "This isn't Marisol Borja! This is Carlina Borja, she was Cuba's most famous ballerina! She died this summer, it was a big story."

He pointed at the first typewritten page of the police report, and Pepper saw Hector was right. It said: *Victima: Carlina Borja.*

Pepper felt instant relief, then was ashamed a moment later. Someone had been murdered, after all.

"Marisol told me what happened to Carlina," Angel said in a weak voice. "She was Marisol's second or third cousin. Marisol met her on one of her trips to Cuba, not too long before, you know, this happened." Angel pointed a shaking finger at the photo. "Marisol was really broken up about it."

Wow, thought Pepper. Then a separate thought hit him like a sucker punch. *I stole the wrong damned police report!*

Hector cleared his throat. "Pepper, you know about the artists, *si*?"

"Angel mentioned them. Why?"

"Some of Cuba's most famous artists have been killed in Havana this year. Stabbed to death by a madman ... they are the most horrible murders in my lifetime. Like from one of your

Hollywood slasher movies. There are four I know about. Could Marisol be, you know, the next victim?"

His question crystalized the uneasy feeling in Pepper's gut. *What snake pit did I fall into?*

"But Marisol's American," said Angel. "And no one knew she'd be stopping there at that time to buy flowers. Shit, I only found out when she told the taxi to stop."

Hector thought awhile. "Maybe someone followed you from the airport?"

But Angel wasn't having it. "That's too crazy, too random."

"Either way, we need to learn more about those dead artists," said Pepper. "Their names and when they died. What kind of art they made. Hector, can you call around and get that info?"

Hector nodded. "Sí, I'll ask people. But not the police, no way."

"Fair enough, cuz," said Angel, unconsciously touching his own bruised cheek. "And I need to keep my eyes peeled for the damn taxi driver who took off with our luggage. Maybe he was part of what happened to Marisol. Either way, I want my shit back."

Finding the driver wouldn't be easy, thought Pepper. There had to be hundreds of taxi drivers in Havana. "Do you remember the taxi company's name?"

"Nope," said Angel, closing his eyes, massaging his temples.

"What'd the driver look like?"

"He was a Cuban guy, maybe fifty years old. Dark hair and a beard."

Hector made a face. "Him and thousands of others in Havana."

Pepper opened the Cadillac's large glove box, shoved in the police file, and clicked the lid closed. He'd really screwed up, impulsively swiping the police report. "I need to decide what to do with that file. But for now, let's go."

"Go where?" Hector asked weakly.

"Where this whole freaking mess started," said Pepper. "The plaza."

Twenty minutes later, the trio walked into the Plaza de San Francisco de Asís in Old Havana, where Marisol had vanished two days earlier.

The plaza was surrounded by well-restored historical buildings and was scattered with street vendors. Some had wheeled carts, but others had only a row of plastic buckets. Most of the vendors had brightly colored umbrellas to shade them from the hot September sun.

Pepper studied the old buildings, hoping to spot security cameras pointed at the plaza. But he didn't find any.

One woman wandered through the plaza, singing in a beautiful soprano voice.

"She sells peanuts," explained Hector. "And she is always singing. Everyone in Havana knows her."

Angel took out his phone and pulled up a photo of Marisol to show to people when they questioned them. It was a stunning photo, capturing Marisol's energy and sharp humor. She was half lit, half shaded, holding an orchid like a trophy and laughing.

Pepper remembered meeting her in July, how mature and intelligent she'd seemed, older than Angel's usual girlfriends. And he remembered how proud Angel had looked as she told Pepper about her new film project in Cuba.

"It's my favorite picture," said Angel. "It completely captures her fire and her smarts. Her cameraman down here took it the last time she filmed here, in August."

"What's his name?"

"Viktor Beriev. He's not Cuban, he's an ex-pat, from one of the old Soviet countries. He's known internationally for his photography portraits, but he does video too."

Angel didn't see the flower vendor who Marisol had talked to on Monday, so Pepper decided they should take a more systematic approach. They started in one corner and methodically questioned each vendor, showing them Marisol's picture on Angel's phone.

A woman displaying T-shirts and hats kept gesturing at her wares, while Hector tried to steer the conversation to whether she had seen Marisol on Monday afternoon. Getting impatient, Pepper handed the woman some Cuban money.

"Too much, Pepper!" protested Hector. "That was six hundred pesos!"

"I don't care. Ask her again about Marisol. Angel, show her the picture again."

The woman studied it, said something to Hector.

"She says the woman is beautiful, that she would remember her face. But she doesn't."

Frustrated, they moved on, questioning vendor after vendor to no avail. Pepper noticed two flower vendors, but Angel confirmed neither was the thin, mustached man Marisol had spoken to.

An hour later, they had talked to every vendor in the plaza. Pepper squatted down and picked up a few pebbles off the cobblestones.

"Help me out here," he said, placing the largest pebble on the ground. "This is the airport." He put a smaller pebble about a foot away. "This is the apartment, Casa de Vides." Handing Hector a third pebble, he asked, "Put this where the plaza's located."

Hector placed it about half a foot from the Casa de Vides pebble, farther from the airport.

Pepper frowned. "This plaza isn't really on the way from the airport. So why did Marisol have the taxi come here for flowers? Aren't there other spots on the way to buy flowers?"

Hector and Angel looked at each other and shrugged. "There are other places," said Hector. "But maybe she liked it here. Or she liked to buy flowers from the same guy. Like a tradition."

"But why wouldn't she have bought the flowers somewhere more convenient that first time she came to Cuba twenty months ago? If it's about tradition?"

"No idea, mano," said Angel, sounding depressed. "But it is weird."

Pepper thought it meant she had some history with this location, buying flowers or for some other reason. A chill went down his spine at the thought they might never find out why.

They were interviewing probably their thirteenth vendor when they had a hit. Hector asked the same questions while Angel showed Marisol's photo and described her pink high heels.

"*Zapatos rosados?*" asked the vendor, selling carved wood figurines.

Angel confirmed yes, pink shoes. High heels.

The man rummaged in his cart and pulled out a pink high-heeled shoe.

"Oh, shit," said Angel. "That's Marisol's other shoe!" He snatched the cotton candy pink shoe with the thick, clear heel and the brand name Stuart Weitzman printed across the insole.

Pepper studied the shoe, noting the strap on this one wasn't broken. Hector quizzed the man in rapid Spanish.

"He says he found the shoe on the ground two days ago, in the afternoon. Exactly when Marisol vanished," translated Hector.

"He picked it up, hoping to find the other shoe, but thought maybe alone it would still be worth something. He will sell it to us for three hundred pesos."

"Maybe she snagged her other shoe on the cobblestones and the strap broke?" offered Angel. "So, she took off this one, maybe threw it away because she was pissed off, then went somewhere to buy shoes?"

Pepper shook his head. "And then couldn't reconnect with you in forty-eight hours?"

They continued questioning vendors until a middle-aged man with a drooping mustache selling palm frond souvenirs gave a different answer. "Maybe yes," he said thoughtfully.

After a rapid exchange in Spanish, Hector turned to Pepper. "He remembers Marisol. She was beautiful and her clothes were too fancy to be Cuban. He thought she was European, maybe from Spain. She walked past him and he tried to get her to look at his items, but she said 'No, thank you' in excellent Spanish. She went straight to the flower vendor."

"The guy that Angel saw?"

"Yes. He said the man's usually here a few times a week but hasn't been back since Monday."

"Does he know what happened to Marisol?"

"He said he saw her talking to another man, in a black guayabera shirt. A strong Cuban man in his thirties, not dark, not light. He stood up very straight and had an attitude, like he might be in the military or the government. And he had tattoos all down one arm."

"Can he describe them?"

The man shook his head when Hector translated. "Just a bunch of dark tattoos. He was too far away to see what they were. Maybe thirty feet. He remembered that the beautiful woman was holding flowers."

"And he didn't see any trouble? No fighting, no yelling?"

"No. Just that they were talking intently about something. The man seemed to be angry. Then the vendor got a customer for his palm souvenirs, so he was distracted. When he looked back, they were gone."

They questioned the vendor extensively about what he saw, getting him to describe the man in the black shirt again. Just shorter than Angel, so probably around five foot eight.

Pepper's mind raced with possibilities. Was Marisol lured from the plaza and violently taken? For ransom? By a jealous local lover? Or was the black-shirted man a government agent, trying to stop her documentary? Pepper didn't know why a film about orchids would threaten the Cuban government, but when he located Marisol's cameraman, Viktor Beriev, he intended to find out.

CHAPTER FIVE

Back at Casa de Vides, Pepper huddled with Angel on the green couch in the living room to review the Carlina Borja police report. Detective Guiteras' mention of a series of artist murders during their conversation had been nagging at him. If there was a connection between Marisol's disappearance and these killings, the police report might contain crucial clues.

They'd opened the French doors to the balcony, hoping to invite in any breeze that would cut down the humidity. No luck so far. But the sounds of music, people shouting from windows, and the occasional honk of a car horn drifted in, providing a constant reminder of the foreign city just outside their walls.

"You want a pork empanada?" asked Angel, holding the bag out to Pepper. He'd directed Hector to stop for them on the drive back. "They're better than my mom makes. Just don't tell her."

Pepper took one and promised, "Only if she tortures it out of me."

They were alone, because Pepper had intentionally excluded Hector from this review by sending him out to pick up a local SIM card for Pepper's phone. Pepper didn't want Hector involved with the stolen police report any more than he already was.

"I guess I learned more Spanish in school than I thought," said Pepper as he began scanning the report.

"I can help you with any big words, *mano*," said Angel. "Like I do in English."

"You're the best," said Pepper, elbowing Angel in the ribs. Then they got down to business.

The police report said that Carlina Borja had been killed on a Friday night, four months ago. The report was dated two weeks after her death. So this would be the initial report of findings, which detectives would supplement in a larger open-case file over time as the investigation continued. Any tips received, any people interviewed, and any clues identified. Every result would be added to the file, which would grow until either the killer was arrested or until the case went cold and the file disappeared to a dusty shelf somewhere.

It began with a brief biography of Carlina Borja. She was born in Havana and lived in its La Rampa neighborhood, wherever that was. She was twenty-seven years old at the date of her death. And she was the prima ballerina of the Cuban National Ballet, reputedly the leading dancer of her generation in Latin America.

The report summarized the cause and manner of her death. Carlina Borja was found lying facedown on her bed, covered in blood, with a copy of Ernest Hemingway's *For Whom the Bell Tolls* lying open on her back.

"That's weird," commented Pepper.

"We read it in eleventh-grade English," said Angel. "Remember?"

Pepper did. A war drama with a messy bunch of characters. Pepper remembered he'd skimmed through it, because he had other distractions in his life—a girl and trouble on his high school hockey team. But he remembered his English teacher, Mr. Kernicki, had declared that *For Whom the Bell Tolls* was a profound, timeless classic and Hemingway's second greatest work, behind *The Old Man and the Sea.*

According to the coroner, Carlina Borja died of strangulation. Then after she died, her body was repeatedly stabbed in the back by a long, thin, blunt object, probably a knife.

"That's not what I heard," said Angel. "Everyone who told me about the deaths said the killer has been murdering artists by stabbing them. To me, it's even more freaky, stabbing her like that after she was already dead."

"Somebody was seriously pissed off," said Pepper.

Angel grunted. "Or seriously wackadoodle."

They moved on. The report also included a list of persons of interest in the investigation, which included eight names:

Gloria Borja
Vladimir Palenko
Edgar Sorana
Guillermo Infante
Heather Wilder (USE)
Viktor Beriev
Laurent Rappeneau
Quinto Chavez

"So these are ... suspects?" asked Angel.

"Some might be suspects or have a history of similar crimes," said Pepper. "Others could be key witnesses about the victim's whereabouts that night, or alibis for potential suspects. They might also be people close to the victim."

"There's Viktor Beriev!" noted Angel. "Marisol's cameraman."

Angel explained that Marisol often filmed as a two-person team—herself and a cameraman. So this guy Beriev would have been all over Havana with Marisol. He'd know where she'd gone and who she'd talked to.

"That guy gets around," said Pepper. "We need to have a chat with him as soon as possible. We need to figure out whether Marisol was targeted specifically. Maybe someone she pissed off while filming about the orchids. Or maybe someone with a more personal gripe. Angel, do you know if she dated anyone here in Cuba on her past trips?"

"No way, *mano*, she'd have told me. We've been dating since January. And exclusive since Valentine's Day."

Maybe, thought Pepper. "She ever mention anything about a stalker down here? Anything creepy like that?"

"No, nothing."

They went silent for a bit, both studying the list.

"I wonder what USE means?" asked Angel.

"Dunno," said Pepper. "Maybe some local cop shorthand?"

They kept studying the list. Then Angel sighed. "Be honest, *mano*. Do you think Marisol's dead, just like ..." He waved a finger at Carlina Borja's police report.

Pepper put an arm around Angel's shoulder. "I hope not, buddy. We've gotta assume she's alive, for her sake. You've got a local SIM card, right? You need to call and text Marisol every hour. Leave voice messages every time. A blitz. And check up on Marisol's social media sites. Facebook, Instagram, TikTok, all of it. Hopefully, you can tell when and where she logged in. What she last posted. Check for any activity at all, especially anything weird. She could signal for help."

Pepper didn't see any strong connection between Marisol's disappearance and Carlina Borja's murder, aside from both being artists and the overlap with Viktor Beriev. The other names on the police report's list were unfamiliar, leaving him to wonder if any of them would cross his path during his search for Marisol. An uneasy feeling crept down his back.

He made a mental note to circle back to the Hemingway book. It was a bizarre signature to put on the body of someone you'd just murdered. His experience investigating other murders suggested the book was a deeper message from the killer than the obvious: "Time's up, sucker!" Maybe some feud or grievance between the killer and the victim that the book somehow referred to. And was the same underlying situation connected to Marisol's disappearance?

Pepper lost that train of thought when the door downstairs banged open. The gate on the stairs creaked, and then Hector reappeared, a big smile on his face. He waved a small card at them. "I got it! Really good price too."

"Thanks, Hector," said Pepper, closing the police report file.

Angel had filled in Pepper a little about Hector when his cousin headed out to buy the SIM card for Pepper. Hector was in his early twenties. Like most Cuban men, he'd been conscripted into the Cuban military at eighteen years old and served his two years as an emergency room technician.

Since leaving the military, Hector's official job was as a nurse in a rehabilitation facility, for which he made the peso equivalent of forty-five dollars a month. He could make more if he accepted a position in another country, such as the Bahamas. But Hector made most of his money during nights and weekends, hiring out as a driver for tourists in his Cadillac, wearing an Elvis jumpsuit. Which made his outfits that week less eccentric.

"Hector, we need to talk to a guy named Viktor Beriev. He's a photographer and videographer who worked with Marisol."

Hector grinned. "I know him, sure, the Belarusian guy ... or is he Russian? He's kind of a celebrity." Angel thought about it. "I think I know where he'll be tonight. I'll take you, keep you out of trouble."

"Good man," said Pepper. "We appreciate the help, but we're not screwing up your life, are we? Making you miss work?"

Hector gave him a thin smile. "Is no problem," he said. "Cubans have a saying: We pretend to work, and the government pretends to pay us."

CHAPTER SIX

"Why here?" Pepper asked doubtfully as they waited in a jostling crowd outside a club with a small gray sign that said La Cueva. The Cave. A series of small red lanterns framed the entrance. Since that block didn't have streetlights, everyone looked strangely red-faced. It was 10:30 PM on Wednesday.

"Because Viktor Beriev is a regular," said Hector. "Many other artists. Many foreigners. This is the hot place tonight."

Pepper hoped the young Cuban was right. He was eager to question Beriev.

Pepper, Angel, and Hector shuffled forward behind a few other people waiting to get into La Cueva. Hector explained it was like a cross between a nightclub and a cabaret.

"Hi my friend, where you from?" asked a wiry little Cuban guy who approached them with a big smile.

"How are you, my friend?" asked another local, appearing on their other side.

Hector smiled but waved them away with a quick burst of Spanish. "They are *jineteros*," Hector explained to Pepper and Angel. "Your best friends, for a price!"

"Jineteros?" asked Pepper.

"You say ... jockey. They hustle *yumas* for money. Act like friends."

"Yumas?"

"That's you Americanos. They help you find anything you need. Cigars, girls, rum ..."

"Can they find Marisol?" grumbled Angel, waving off one of the more persistent jineteros.

"We find her, cousin," Hector promised. They stepped through the entrance. Hector talked with a woman, then asked Pepper to use some of his new Cuban pesos to pay their cover charge.

A skinny man with a shaved head led them through the crowd to a large half-circle booth. La Cueva was a cavernous room was full of shadows, candles, noise, and a decent-sized crowd of people drinking and eating. A cool place, he decided. But sinister around the edges.

When a waitress came to take drink orders, Pepper ordered the first Cuban drink that came to mind, a Cuba libre. A rum and coke. Since wasn't that what yumas would drink?

A band of seven musicians on a stage in the corner were playing upbeat Caribbean music. The music had a powerful rhythm and a sexy melody.

The club was filling quickly, and it had a chattering buzz. Laughter, loud voices. Excitement. Pepper cautiously sipped his Cuba libre.

"Listen to the hands on that guy," said Angel.

"Definitely! Ask him if he gives lessons!" Pepper elbowed Angel playfully. Angel played drums sometimes too, but this guy was world class.

"Hey, that's Beriev!" said Hector, pointing at a large man standing by the bar, talking to another man. He was a little over six feet tall and probably two hundred and seventy-five pounds.

He had a beer belly that stretched his tan guayabera shirt, a receding hairline, and a ponytail.

"I can invite him over!" Hector yelled, and he disappeared into the crowd.

Hector reappeared with Beriev and the man he'd been talking to. Beriev shook Pepper's hand and gave a thin smile. The big man's nose was bulbous, enlarged, and red, like W. C. Fields had. It gave Beriev a jovial look.

The second man who'd joined them was even more friendly looking. "I'm Ozzie Rappeneau!" he yelled with a broad grin, shaking their hands and slapping their shoulders. "I'm Canadian, but I know pretty much everybody in town, the fun people, anyway. But I'm super bummed about what happened to Mari!"

Ozzie was a handsome guy around the same age as Pepper and Angel, late twenties. He had a dark tan and a big, friendly smile with extra white teeth. He was about five foot ten and lanky, dressed in a designer shirt, jeans, and red Jordans.

At Hector's urging, both men took a seat at their table.

"How do you know Marisol?" Angel asked Ozzie, sounding wary or maybe jealous.

"She interviewed my dad in August about his big-ass flower garden, and we know the same people around town," said Ozzie with a half shrug. "So we've had drinks here and there. She's a smart, pretty lady—I'm sad to meet her boyfriend!" Ozzie laughed and grinned.

Angel laughed too. Ozzie seemed to have that effect on people.

"Is your dad Laurent Rappeneau?" Pepper remembered that name from the "persons of interest" list in the Carlina Borja police report.

"Yep! My dad's the top banana at a Canadian company that does business down here." The Canadian put his hand on Angel's shoulder. "Dude, anything I can do to help find Mari, you got it.

He's buddies with the hombres in charge, you know? I'll ask him to check around, see if anyone's heard the inside scoop about her."

Ozzie kept talking and laughing, driving the conversation. Beriev sat silently.

The waitress arrived with another round of drinks for the table, and her tray included drinks for Beriev and Ozzie.

The waitress sat down on Ozzie's lap while he pulled out a handful of Cuban pesos to pay her. "This one's on me!" he announced. "And I hope she stays there!"

The waitress giggled, accepting the money before slipping away into the crowd.

Beriev drank half of his cloudy, mixed drink in one gulp. The glass looked child-sized in his big hand. The man still hadn't said a word since sitting down.

"So, did you hear what happened to Marisol?" Pepper asked him.

"Ja. I heard she was buying flowers and then was gone. I heard her lover—"

"Me," said Angel. "Is there anyone you know of who might have kidnapped her off the street? Maybe anyone she'd pissed off when filming around town?"

Beriev studied Angel. "So you don't know much, but you're her boyfriend?"

"Hey Vik, go easy, eh?" laughed Ozzie. "Angel's gotta be in shock, after all the crap that went down."

"Ozzie, how'd you hear about it?" asked Pepper.

"I heard from Mari's buddy, Dayana. You know, that smoking hot actress, Dayana de Melina? Havana's a big city, but a small place. We're all super upset. Mari was a kick-ass filmmaker."

"She still is," said Angel.

"We must hope she's okay," said Beriev. "Her work is very fearless."

Hector had left their table, and Pepper saw him talking to the band. Then he climbed up on stage. The band started playing the Elvis Presley hit "A Little Less Conversation." And Hector grabbed a mike and began singing.

Beriev looked bewildered and annoyed. "He's with you? I'll let you enjoy the show."

He got up, but Pepper pulled him back. "Just a minute, please? I was hoping you could tell us. Did she upset anyone while filming? Or have any trouble here in Havana with anyone? Any businesses? Or the Cuban government?"

Beriev shrugged, still looking distracted. "We filmed all over Havana. She only hired me in August to take over as her cameraman. I've lived here for a dozen years and people know my work. She fired her cameraman, a Cuban with limited talent. I agreed to take over because I support her project."

Pepper thought. "That cameraman she fired ... could he have kidnapped her?"

"No, no...he was a shit. And he moved to Santiago de Cuba in July. The other side of Cuba, near your Guantanamo. A twelve-hour drive."

"Can you give us a list of places you guys filmed in August?" Pepper asked. "And the people she interviewed?"

Beriev shook his head. "I don't have the list."

On stage, Hector was gyrating his hips and playing air guitar as he sang. The crowd was getting riled up, clapping along.

Pepper tried to focus on his train of thought. "Do you have a copy of the footage from August?"

Beriev made a dismissive gesture. "No, no, Marisol protected her work like a jealous lover. And she edited in America between trips. She saved it all on portable hard drives. Video files are enormous."

"Another reason we gotta find our luggage," Angel said to Pepper. "Those portable drives are in her bag! She'll have backups in New York, but if we want to look for any clues, we need them back, pronto."

Pepper tried another angle with Beriev. "The footage you filmed in August. Did any of it make the Cuban government look bad?"

Beriev gave a dismissive wave of his hand. "Every search for truth makes them look bad, because the truth rarely matches their press releases. But that's the price of art, no?"

What could be so controversial about flowers? But if the problem wasn't Marisol's work, what was it? Pepper made a mental note to get a list of the people who knew when Marisol was scheduled to arrive. And who knew about her flower-buying habit.

"You should see Vik's portraits," interjected Ozzie. "He's like the Wayne Gretzky of photography. World-class stuff."

Beriev coughed out a laugh, then explained that he specialized in still photography. He'd been taking photographs around the city for an upcoming exhibition, which led to meeting Marisol.

"I do little video," sniffed Beriev. "Anyone can hold the camera and shoot for hours and hours. But in Cuba we do what we must to survive."

"Why'd you leave Belarus?" asked Angel. "Not enough of an art scene in Minsk?"

"No particular reason," said Beriev, waving a hand vaguely. "But I've been doing the best work of my career here in recent months. This is the work I'll be remembered for in generations to come, not my other work back home."

"Damn straight," said Ozzie, draining his glass and banging it on the table for emphasis. "I need a refill."

Pepper wondered if Beriev was a scattered artistic type or he was deliberately giving half-answers to their questions.

Hector finished his Elvis Presley song, and the crowd gave him a strong round of applause. "Thank you verrrry much," he said, in a perfect impersonation of the King. Hector hopped off the stage and trotted back to their table with a big grin. "Pretty good, right?" he grinned. "I told you!"

Pepper and Angel traded amused glances. "You rocked, cuz," said Angel. "But—"

"Hey!" blurted Ozzie. "There she is!"

Pepper looked around wildly. *Marisol's here? She's okay?* But the woman striding toward their table wasn't Marisol. She looked about five foot six. Fit but curvy. Her long hair fell across her shoulders and chest in a black swirl. Her face was exaggerated—mouth maybe bigger than beautiful, ears maybe a bit small. But high cheekbones, caramel skin. Her eyes were dark in the swirling lights.

She was wearing a red mini dress with black straps along with red high-heel shoes. The dress made her legs look impossibly long. She walked like an alpha female, and heads jerked around as she passed.

She's got angry eyes, though, noticed Pepper.

That was his only warning before she leaned across their table and gave him a good, hard slap across the face.

"Damn, Pepper!" laughed Ozzie, jumping to his feet. "You already know Dayana?"

She was shaking a finger. "I know who he is!" she said in English with a Spanish accent. "The American policeman! Or were they lying, what everyone said by the bar? He tells everyone he's in Havana to find Mari. You think you'll find her in a nightclub?"

"Hey!" objected Pepper. His cheek stung. "What the—"

"Mari told me about her yuma boyfriend Angel and his big friend Pepper. The macho policeman." She studied Pepper with a thin smile. "She didn't say you were lazy!"

"Whoa ... when did you last talk to her?" asked Pepper, gesturing for her to calm down.

"*Now* you investigate?" asked Dayana, not calming down at all. "I was crying and crying when I got the news. I thought el Segador took her—"

"No, no, Dayana," said Beriev. "It's not—"

"Don't shush me, Viktor, you're not the PNR. Mari was my friend, and Alicia Arenas, and Carlina Borja."

Alicia Arenas? wondered Pepper. *Another of the murdered artists?*

Beriev banged his glass on the table with mock outrage. "It's very Cuban, fearing to be stabbed to death by a ghost like el Segador."

The woman glared at Beriev, hands on her cute hips. "It's very Russian, drowning your talent in vodka."

Beriev chuckled. "Ouch! You know I'm from Belarus, dear. It's—"

"I have good reason to fear for Mari. Convince me I'm crazy!"

"El who?" interjected Angel.

"Mari could be dead!" she shouted. "Or she could be dying right now!"

Pepper locked eyes with her, and felt a spark of attraction to the intensity in her dark brown eyes and her raw beauty. "I h-hope not," he stammered. If his cheek wasn't already stinging, he'd be blushing like a damn schoolboy. "But I promise you, I'm fully committed to finding Marisol."

"By sitting here doing nothing?" she asked indignantly. "You should be ashamed of yourself!" She snatched up Pepper's drink off the table and dashed it in his face.

Damn! Pepper was suddenly blinded, and his eyes stung. By

the time he wiped his face with his shirt and got his vision back, she'd huffed away from their table and melted into the crowd.

Ozzie roared with laughter.

Beriev brushed drops from his drink off his tan guayabera shirt with a half-smile. "You angered the wrong woman!"

Pepper was still looking around to figure out where the mystery woman had gone. And where she'd come from. "Who the hell was that lunatic?" he asked Beriev.

"The glorious Dayana de Melina!" he said. "She's the leading actress of Cuban popular films in recent years. Like your Scarlett Johansson, or Gal Gadot."

"Except meaner," observed Angel, sipping his Bucanero beer. "But hey, Pepper's always had a way with women. Not a successful way, most of the time."

Pepper could finally see again. "Who's El Sacor?"

"El Segador," smiled Beriev. "It means The Reaper. A fiction, like your bogeyman."

"Like freaking Freddy Krueger!" added Ozzie.

"Ja, make believe," added Beriev. He snapped his fingers for the cocktail waitress.

"The dead bodies weren't make-believe," said Ozzie. "It's like —" But he stopped when the cocktail waitress arrived and plopped back into his lap.

Pepper saw that Dayana de Melina hadn't gone too far. She stood surrounded by a semicircle of four men. One, a Latino with a tall, fuzzy hairdo who was the shortest of the four, grabbed Dayana's arm.

"Shit, man," said Ozzie. He jumped up and hustled toward the actress. Pepper followed. Angel was a half-step behind.

Pepper stopped short when the guy holding Dayana's arm turned to face them. He had one side of his beard and mustache shaved off. The left side. The right side had a neatly tailored mustache and beard. What the hell?

Dayana pulled free of the guy with the bizarre grooming, then began gesturing and shouting at the four men in Spanish, too quickly for Pepper to understand.

"These friends of yours?" Pepper interrupted.

One of the four men, a muscular guy of average height in a black v-neck T-shirt, pointed a finger at Pepper and Angel. He said something angry in Spanish too fast for Pepper to understand. Then the guy stepped forward and poked Angel in the chest.

"*Tú eres el Segador?*" the man shouted, poking Angel again.

Pepper shoved the guy away hard, causing him to collide with two of his companions.

"No, this one would take your life for money," sneered the half-beard guy in excellent English, waving back his companions. "I told Mari the truth about the artists and she didn't believe it was possible! But I have proof!"

Who the hell's this clown? thought Pepper. *And what's he yapping about?*

"Behave, Guillermo," said Dayana, gesturing dismissively at the strange man.

But he wasn't done. "Dayana, you finally found your ride to America? Does he know the motherland will never let you go?"

Ozzie pushed forward. "You boys looking for a scrap? You wanna go?"

"And Marisol deserved better than you," the strange man said, pointing at Angel with a crazy grin. The bizarre facial hair didn't help. "*Eres un punto!* She had better, too, trust me. Trust me!"

"You fall asleep shaving?" asked Angel. "Which of your faces should I smack first?"

But Hector held Angel back.

Ozzie waved dismissively at the man. "Ignore that scumbag—my drink's melting."

But the man still wasn't done. He was puffing up like an angry bantam rooster. "I'm the scumbag? I have proof why the artists are dying. And I know about your father, the devil's visas! A capitalist conspiracy of—"

Ozzie gave him a hard shove, sending him into his companions, who barely kept their feet.

But Dayana stepped between the two groups of men, putting her arms out, separating them, her eyes flashing. She looked even more gorgeous now, Pepper thought.

She yelled some more Spanish at the Cuban men, then yelled at Pepper, Angel, and Ozzie in English. "Don't be like children! Back to your table!"

"Those guys aren't harassing you?" asked Pepper.

Dayana shook her head, looking disgusted at him. "When did you get to Havana, five minutes ago? You know nothing about Cubanos."

Then, surprisingly, everyone did what Dayana ordered. Or maybe Pepper shouldn't have been surprised.

With a flip of her hair, Cuba's leading actress sauntered away, and the crowd parted before her.

Damn ... thought Pepper. He shook his head, trying to clear it, and turned back to their table. But the primitive part of his brain was already hoping their paths would cross again.

CHAPTER SEVEN

"That went sideways fast," said Ozzie back at their table. "You guys are fun." He took a big gulp of his mojito.

Pepper monitored the crowd to see if the four troublemakers would reappear.

"This is no Miami," said Hector, sounding nervous. "Is a big problem, fighting in a club. I'll get the Cadillac. Meet me outside in five minutes, you promise?" He disappeared toward the door.

"Who were those assholes?" asked Angel.

"The crazy guy, he's Guillermo Infante," said Ozzie. "You hear of him?"

"No," lied Pepper. He'd seen Infante's name on the persons of interest list in the Carlina Borja murder report. But he didn't want to mention that here. He made a mental note to find out whether Infante was a suspect, or had a more innocent connection to the dead dancer.

"Infante's known as a poet," added Beriev. "But not for his poems, you understand? And the pushy guy's called Quinto Chavez. He's a jinetero, a hustler. And a criminal, I hear. He was probably showing off for Dayana, like most Cuban men do. And foreign men. Or maybe Quinto was trying to get you yumas away from her."

Quinto Chavez, thought Pepper. Another person of interest listed in the Carlina Borja police report!

"Viktor, can you help us tomorrow morning?" he asked. "We need to make a list of everywhere Marisol went in August, the last time she was here. Everyone she talked to. We need to retrace her steps, see if she had any trouble that might be related to her disappearance."

Beriev spread his hands helplessly. "Sorry, that is impossible. I'm preparing the most important exhibition of my career. It will be my legacy, and everything needs to come together perfectly. I can't let anything distract me."

"Do it for Mari," begged Ozzie.

Pepper spent a few more minutes trying to recruit Beriev, but the Belarusian dug in, refusing to change his mind.

Pepper and Angel exited La Cueva to the red glow of the sidewalk area.

Pepper was really pissed off by his failure to enlist Viktor Beriev's help. Ozzie, however, had been more helpful, repeating his promise to set up a meeting with his father, Laurent Rappeneau. That would also give Pepper a chance to learn why the PNR considered Rappeneau a person of interest in the Carlina Borja case and if Rappeneau believed Marisol had suffered the same fate as the four murdered artists.

They looked around for Hector's Cadillac, but it wasn't in sight yet. As they waited, the door to the club pushed open and five men spilled out onto the sidewalk.

Pepper recognized Quinto and two of the other guys from the pushing match in the club, plus two new guys. The poet with the defective facial grooming was not with them.

Looking cartoonish in the red light, Quinto spat something in Spanish at Angel. Too fast or too slang. Pepper missed all of it except the word "segador."

Pepper noticed a detail about Quinto that he hadn't picked up in the club's darkness. "You see his arm?" Pepper asked Angel, without taking his eyes off the hostile Cubans. One of Quinto's arms was covered in tattoos.

"Strong guy, sleeve of tattoos," muttered Angel. "You think he owns a black guayabera shirt?"

Exactly, thought Pepper. This had to be the guy the palm frond vendor saw talking to Marisol moments before she disappeared.

Hector and his old convertible were still nowhere in sight.

"You're Quinto, right?" Pepper asked him. "How about you tell me what happened to Marisol Borja at the plaza on Monday?"

Quinto laughed scornfully. "You think you're the PNR?"

"I know the PNR think you killed Carlina Borja. I saw the report." The police report didn't say that exactly, but Pepper wanted to see Quinto's reaction.

"¿Qué?" asked Quinto, looking momentarily confused. Then his face hardened.

"How long were you sleeping with Carlina before she died?" Pepper asked, more wild speculation.

Quinto snarled and leaped at Pepper, who grabbed him and spun, throwing Quinto against the wall of the club.

Pepper saw a blindside punch from one of the other Cubans bang into Angel's ear.

Two of the men came right at Pepper, but he dodged them, trying to get back-to-back with Angel.

Five against two.

So, step one, Pepper needed to improve the odds.

Quinto took a wild swing at Pepper, which he ducked, stepping into the jinetero, hitting him with a shoulder to the stomach. Pepper continued forward, lifting the man, who was already gasping for breath. He tossed him at the feet of one of his companions, who tripped over him and went down too.

A third jinetero danced forward, well balanced, hands up in a defensive posture. This guy had boxed some, for sure.

Pepper deflected the man's jabs, staying defensive while watching for other threats.

Angel blindsided Pepper's opponent with a straight right punch. The man stumbled and Pepper stepped in, catching him with an uppercut to the jaw.

Out of the corner of his eye, Pepper saw Hector's enormous Cadillac convertible jerk to a stop at the curb. Pepper pushed away another attacker, then grabbed Angel.

Quinto and the other man were almost back on their feet.

"Go, go, go," Pepper yelled to Angel, dragging him toward the Cadillac. They tumbled over the side into the backseat. Pepper lashed out a kick at one man as the car lurched away from the curb.

Someone on the sidewalk threw a bottle, striking Hector in the head. He howled in pain and surprise, and pawed at his forehead.

"¡Vamos!" urged Angel from the backseat.

"You guys are way loco," said Hector, hastily hitting the gas and steering the big car away down the one-way street. Blood was already dripping down his face.

Pepper heard revving engines, and two motorcycles came into view behind him, followed by the bouncing headlights of a car.

"Ah, shit!" said Angel. "Now they're freaking chasing us?"

"¡No me jodas!" spat Hector, speeding up the Cadillac.

The road was narrow, probably only wide enough for a car

and a half. The surface was cobblestones, and the car bounced and rattled along.

"You gotta go for it," said Pepper. "Floor it."

Hector made a sudden left turn, down an even narrower street, but he wasn't going any faster than before.

Pepper saw Hector try to wipe the blood from his eyes.

"I can't lose them!" Hector yelled.

"Hit the brakes!" yelled Pepper.

But Hector just kept driving, with a quick glance over at Pepper.

"Stop! Hit the brakes!"

This time Hector did. More gently than Pepper would have, but much quicker than their pursuers expected. One motorcycle had to veer off to avoid slamming into the rear end of the convertible, and that motorcycle's tire hit a curb. The rider flipped off and landed on the sidewalk, sliding about fifteen feet until he hit the wall of a building.

"Jesus!" yelled Angel.

Hector tried to wipe blood from his face, using his shirtsleeve.

"Quick, switch," said Pepper. He slid to the left and hefted Hector across his lap to the passenger side.

"No, no!" Hector protested. "Is not safe!"

One of their pursuers tumbled out of the car behind them and ran forward with a baseball bat in his hand.

Pepper stomped the gas pedal, but nothing happened except the engine revving loudly. Pepper slid the gearshift into drive and hit the gas again. This time the car jumped forward just before the bat-wielding man reached them.

The big Cadillac lurched away down the narrow road, drifting left and right, like a poorly balanced boat.

Pepper turned a hard right, and the Cadillac fishtailed wildly, barely avoiding a line of cars parked along the side of the road.

"Here they come, here they come!" yelled Angel from the backseat.

Pepper floored the gas pedal, and the Cadillac caught air as it passed through a small intersection.

"Fuck you!" Angel yelled behind them. He gave their pursuers the double middle finger.

Pepper turned a sharp left and saw a late-night group of pedestrians scatter from the middle of the roadway. He heard Hector swearing and praying in Spanish.

"Those guys are assholes!" Pepper yelled, driving through a red light, eyes darting left and right to make sure he would hit nothing.

Then he saw what he was looking for.

He turned a hard right, swerved around a parked truck, then took another hard right again, into a narrow lane.

He stabbed the gearshift into park, turned off the engine, and took his foot off the brake pedal, so the old Caddy's brake lights wouldn't betray them.

He heard the snarl of motorcycles racing past the lane. A moment later, the car rumbled past.

"¡Estúpido!" hissed Hector, still wiping his face with his sleeve.

"Hey, cuz, we lost them," said Angel. "Sorry about your head, but we dodged them."

"You're sorry? You crash my Caddy, or the police take it ... I'm dead. I'd rather be dead."

"Really sorry, man," said Pepper, suddenly feeling like a complete asshole. "It all happened so quick. And I'd have paid to get it fixed, if anything—"

"Paid to get it fixed? You think there's a Caddy dealership around the corner? I take six months to find a headlight. This car's worth more than I'll earn the rest of my life."

Hector got out the passenger side door, walked around the

front, then yanked open the driver's door. Pepper had already slid over to the passenger side.

"We appreciate all your help, cuz," said Angel. "We're not trying to cause you trouble—"

"No, no, I understand," interrupted Hector. "Big American Hollywood bullshit, *si*? Car chases, big crashes, no one ever gets hurt? But this is no movie ... The dead artists, they're really dead. Maybe your girlfriend too. I'm trying to help ... but when you guys fly home, I still need to live here!"

They sat hidden in the narrow, dark lane for a couple of minutes in brooding silence. Their pursuers were hopefully many blocks away by now.

Besides feeling like an asshole for hijacking Hector's car, Pepper was thinking about another thing Hector said.

Cars and motorcycles were like gold to Cubans. Did the jineteros chase them because of some perceived insult from the confrontation in the club? To Pepper, that seemed like a massive overreaction, although he didn't have a good handle on Cuban culture. So what actually caused the fight and the chase? Was it related to Marisol's disappearance?

Hector studied the darkness behind the Cadillac, and then in all other directions. Eventually, he turned on the ignition, revved the engine a few times, and delicately shifted into gear.

The three of them stayed quiet, all the way back to Casa de Vides.

They had no other leads to pursue that night. No freaking idea where to go to keep hunting for Marisol.

Pepper hoped tomorrow would be more productive. It had to be. Because his Sunday departure was coming mercilessly fast.

CHAPTER EIGHT

On Thursday morning, Hector drove Pepper and Angel across Havana in the vintage Cadillac, top down, Elvis–style. It was hot and sunny, with enough humidity for Pepper to bet it could only get worse.

An hour earlier, Hector had received a text from their new Canadian friend, Ozzie Rappeneau. His father had agreed to hear their story and see if he could help.

Pepper rode in the backseat, thinking hard about Marisol and what they knew so far. Which wasn't much. "What cell phone does Marisol have?" he yelled to Angel, to be heard over traffic.

"iPhone," Angel yelled back.

Marisol had her purse with her when she disappeared. So she'd had her phone, and possibly still did. Would its battery still have juice if she hadn't charged it?

Probably not.

So if it was on, even if she didn't answer calls, maybe that meant she was okay. That she could charge the phone wherever she was.

"Any chance you know her Apple password?" They could log

into her account online and check Find Your Phone. And hopefully, the phone was still with her.

Angel shook his head. "Sorry, *mano*."

"When we get back to the casa, go to the Apple website and try to log in as her. Try guessing her password until the damn thing locks you out."

"Got it."

Hector drove along the Malecón seawall, and Pepper saw Angel gloomily studying the promenade. "This is where I was going to propose to her," he said.

Pepper could hear the pain in his buddy's voice. He could imagine how Angel's dramatic proposal would have gone—his big mischievous grin as he pulled out the engagement ring. Marisol was a sophisticated woman, but she'd have been caught by surprise. She'd have been smiling and crying at the same time, trying to keep her composure. The proposal would be one of the great stories of their lives.

If Pepper could do anything about it, they would still get to that moment. "We'll find her, buddy," he said. "I promise."

When they reached Hemingway Marina, it was mostly empty. Its four fingers of canals divided by concrete docks held only a handful of boats tied to cleats.

Hector parked near a small building that looked like a marina office. Ozzie was waiting for them in the broken shade of a palm tree, waving with a big grin on his face.

"Ozzie's a good shit," said Angel. "So do me a favor, mano—don't blow up his dad's yacht."

Pepper punched Angel's shoulder. He hadn't *exactly* blown up anyone's yacht. A real psycho had done it two months ago, when trying to kill the president of the United States. "Hector, while Angel and I talk to Ozzie's dad, can you call every hospital in Havana? Start with the ones that usually treat foreigners. And give her name and a good description, in case she's unconscious and came in without ID."

As they joined Ozzie, he grinned. "I hear I missed a good donnybrook outside the club. I was pissed!"

Angel gave Ozzie a quick recap, and Ozzie shook his head quizzically. "Usually, the jineteros want to be buddy-buddy with tourists...then try to get their hand in your wallet. Come on, Dad's yacht's this way."

Ozzie led them to the largest yacht in the marina, a bright white vessel with an aggressive bow that made it look like it was racing forward even while tied to the dock.

"This baby cost seven million bucks," bragged Ozzie. "She does twenty-eight knots when you floor it."

They removed their shoes and followed Ozzie up the gangplank to an upper deck, where a man waited in the shade of an overhang.

He was a white man in his sixties, with a deep tan and a sleek head of salt-and-pepper hair. He was overweight, like a former athlete who now spent more time eating than working out.

"This is my dad, Laurent Rappeneau," said Ozzie, giving his father a half-hug. "He's CEO of Beaufort International. It's a great Canadian company. I'm a VP there too."

They all shook hands.

"Dad's an engineer by training," continued Ozzie. "But nothing to do with trains!"

Rappeneau gave a faint, pained smile, like he'd heard that line from Ozzie too many times before. Then he invited them all to take seats. The bridge had a mix of sofa seating and chairs.

Ozzie plopped down next to his dad.

"Oswald told me about your predicament," said Rappeneau.

Predicament. That was a weird word to use, thought Pepper.

"Beaufort International's a Canadian resource company," said

Rappeneau. "We're a world leader in mining and refining of nickel and cobalt, which are crucial for building electric vehicles. We sell natural resources all over the world, except the United States."

"That whole 'embargo' thing," piped in Ozzie.

"Our company's also the second largest independent energy producer in Cuba. We drill for oil along the north coast of Cuba. Long-reach directional drilling. And we process raw natural gas and generate electricity for sale to Cuba's national grid."

"We got a lot of gas," grinned Ozzie, holding his nose.

Mr. Rappeneau glanced at Ozzie, looking like he was going to comment but didn't.

Ozzie broke the awkward silence. "Well, it's five o'clock somewhere! Who's ready for a mojito?" He headed toward the door, then turned back. "Mari told me once she'd do anything to protect the artists here. I hope she didn't get herself in trouble, playing the hero." He shrugged and disappeared into the interior.

"Canada's a top import-export partner to Cuba," Rappeneau said. "So I talk to people high in the Cuban government, and they talk to me."

"Ozzie said Marisol interviewed you last month for her film?" Pepper asked.

Rappeneau nodded. "She wanted to learn about two rare species of Cuban orchids. The Botanical Garden is the best collection in Havana, but the garden at my home in Miramar's a close second."

"Did your son tell you how Marisol disappeared?"

"Yes, and I find it confusing." Rappeneau flicked something invisible off his pant leg. "Kidnappings happen every day in Mexico. But in Cuba? Rarely."

Ozzie returned, setting down a tray of glasses and a pitcher of mojitos.

Pepper held his tongue. His dad, a former chief of police back home in New Albion, used silence as part of his interview techniques, and Pepper tried to channel a little inner Dad.

"Oswald said you're a police officer back in the States?" Rappeneau made the statement a question.

The change of topic caught Pepper off guard. "I used to be ... in my hometown on Cape Cod. Now I work for the federal government."

"In what capacity?"

"Nothing right now, unfortunately," Pepper said, frowning. "I'm on medical leave. But we appreciate your time—can you help us figure out what happened to Marisol?"

Rappeneau hesitated. "How well do you know Cuba?" he asked. "I've been coming here for decades, and I'm still an outsider. I'm tolerated as long as I play nice and Cuba benefits from my presence. That's the first thing you need to understand."

"Got it," said Pepper.

"So I can't get involved publicly with your situation. We have a strong relationship with the Cuban government, and they want us to keep investing in their infrastructure, but we tread carefully. Unofficially, though ... I'll do what I can."

"Thank you," said Angel. He sounded hopeful.

Rappeneau leaned forward, locking eyes with Pepper. "I guess the first question is, why did she disappear?"

"We don't know," admitted Pepper. "If I worked on a case like this back home, I'd have started with a few obvious theories. That she ditched her boyfriend. Or someone kidnapped her."

"She didn't ditch me," said Angel.

"Have you heard about artists dying in Havana?" asked Pepper. "Rumors about a bogeyman?"

Rappeneau nodded, staying silent for a long pause. Then he shared what he'd heard from government sources about the dead artists and el Segador. It was a simple and horrifying story.

The first dead artist was a fiction writer named Alicia Arenas, who'd been a finalist for the Nobel prize in literature a couple of years earlier. Literary critics had christened her Cuba's own Ernest Hemingway. "So maybe it's ironic she died at Hemingway's estate on the outskirts of Havana, where she was doing a writing residency," said Rappeneau. "She was stabbed and thrown out of a tower. Really tragic."

Angel nodded. "Marisol was devastated when the news broke. She has a few of her books back home in New York."

Rappeneau moved on to the second death, which occurred the following January. The victim was Rolando Carreño, Cuba's leading sculptor and installation artist. He was stabbed to death too. They found his body near Havana in the village of Cojimar, spread-eagled across the top of one of his installations. Many considered it the best work of his career.

The third murder had happened in late March. The victim was a contemporary painter named Osanna Falcón. She was a professor at the Higher Art Institute in Havana. She was preparing a personal exposition that was going to tour fourteen countries. Then she was found stabbed to death like the others, inside Havana's Museum of Fine Arts.

"I knew Osanna," commented Ozzie. "Everybody was crushed."

Rappeneau glanced at his son, then continued. "The fourth artist to die was Carlina Borja, a prima ballerina of the Cuban National Ballet. She was found in her apartment, stabbed to death, of course."

"I've heard about her," said Pepper. "She apparently was a superstar. Did you know her?"

Rappeneau shook his head somberly. "No, but I shook her hand once, at a reception after her premiere performance last season. She was a sensational dancer. Really defied gravity ..."

Pepper kept his face neutral, but his mind started dancing like a ballerina. Why was Rappeneau listed as a person of interest in the Carlina Borja police report if he didn't know her? Or was he lying now? If so, why?

Rappeneau moved on. "Of course, people say the same person murdered all the artists. Everyone's calling the killer *el Segador*. It means 'The Reaper.'"

"So Marisol would have heard about all four victims?" Pepper asked.

Rappeneau nodded. "Definitely. When we chatted before she interviewed me, she mentioned Carlina Borja's murder. Coincidentally, they're relatives and the murder had just happened. But that's all we discussed. We focused on my orchid collection, which includes the rare variety featured in her project."

"I don't believe Marisol's disappearance had anything to do with that Reaper guy," said Angel. "Those dead artists were Cubans. Why would he go after some American filmmaker? And no way he knew she'd be at that plaza when she got there. Even I didn't know until she told the taxi to stop. It's way too farfetched."

Rappeneau unconsciously fixed the collar on his shirt. "There's a diplomat at the U.S. embassy, maybe number three in their pecking order these days. And she owes me a favor or two." He stood and casually stretched. "I think you guys need the help you can't get just walking in off the street. I'll be right back." He disappeared down some stairs into the yacht.

Ozzie refilled everyone's glasses from the mojito pitcher, except Pepper's. He hadn't taken a sip yet. He'd been too caught up in the conversation.

Ozzie's father reappeared in a few minutes, smiling. "She agreed to meet with you in an hour, but not at the embassy. Do you know the ferry that runs across Havana harbor to Casablanca?"

"We'll find it," said Angel.

"Her name's Heather Wilder. She's a foreign service officer in their consular section. She knows more about what goes on in Havana than any foreigner I know."

Heather Wilder! Pepper saw Angel give him a raised eyebrow, having made the same connection. She was another person of interest from Carlina Borja report. And that explained the mysterious "USE" next to her name in the report—it was the abbreviation for the U.S. embassy. There would be all kinds of diplomatic complications, trying to interview an embassy employee.

"She can help us find Marisol?" Pepper asked doubtfully. The embassy had been zero help to Angel when he initially reported Marisol missing. But Pepper was definitely curious to find out what the embassy official knew about Marisol's disappearance. And of course to ask how she knew Carlina Borja. Because there was probably a good reason she was listed as a person of interest in that police report.

Rappeneau put out a hand to shake goodbye. "Heather promised to be on the eleven o'clock ferry this morning to Casablanca. So don't miss it."

CHAPTER NINE

"Hey, the scene of the crime!" said Angel, as they drove past the Plaza de San Francisco de Asís, where Marisol had vanished three days earlier. He casually flipped a middle finger at the plaza as it disappeared behind them.

A little farther down the street, Hector pulled over to the curb and pointed at a two-story glass-walled building on Old Havana's waterfront. "Ferries leave from here to Regla and Casablanca," he said. "You want me to join you?"

Pepper thought he sounded half-hearted. Like Hector might want to sit this one out. "This is yuma trouble," he said. "Trust me, you don't want to get near it."

Hector pouted for half a second, then relented.

Pepper and Angel joined a brief line, paid one peso each, then went through a security checkpoint manned by police armed with machine guns. They emptied their pockets, and Angel had to go through a body search.

"And they didn't even cuddle afterward," groused Angel when finally they boarded the ferry.

"That is a lot of security for a fifteen-minute boat ride," said Pepper. "Maybe that's why Wilder picked it?"

Angel laughed. "Good thing I'm only armed with sharp wits."

They found a space on the outer deck by a railing that needed a coat of paint. There were around twenty other passengers, some on deck, some inside.

"Do you want to take the lead?" asked Pepper. Most people liked Angel at their first meeting. He was a pretty cheerful guy and his smile was infectious. And Marisol was his girlfriend.

Angel grinned. "Hit her with the old Cavada charm. Got it."

Pepper also wanted to keep as low a profile as possible. *I've got trouble enough waiting for me when I meet with Youngblood*, he thought. *Better if she doesn't get a call from the State Department complaining about me being down here in sunny Cuba.*

The ferry had just pulled away from the dock when a woman slipped into the space next to them at the rail. She was a tall woman in her late thirties, athletically built. A firm jaw dominated her face, which was framed by mid-length blonde hair.

She shook a paper bag of peanuts, then reached in and took one out, cracking its shell. "How about those Red Sox?" she asked in a quiet, flat voice.

"Can't hit, can't pitch," Angel said. "Otherwise, they're a hell of a ball club. Heather Wilder?"

"The one and only. And you're Pepper Ryan and Angel Cavada?" The woman smiled, but not with her eyes. "Laurent Rappeneau said you have a problem. I'm gone when the ferry hits Casablanca in …" She glanced at her watch. "Twelve minutes. So what can I do for you?"

Angel jumped right in. "My girlfriend went missing right after we got to Havana three days ago. Marisol Borja, she's American too. The police haven't been much help and—"

"I know all that. You filed a report at the embassy. My question is, what do you think I can do for you?"

Pepper was surprised. "We're hoping you can help. What do you usually do when an American goes missing in Cuba?"

The woman shrugged and offered her bag of peanuts to them. "Not a hell of a lot. Notify their family. Confirm that the Policía Nacional de la Revolución are aware of the missing person. Did she register with the State Department's STEP program?"

"What?" asked Angel.

"Our Smart Traveler Enrollment Program. It helps the embassy contact travelers if there is an emergency."

Was this woman an idiot, or just jerking them around? Pepper wondered. "She's not answering Angel's calls or texts," he said.

"You think she'll answer a call from your embassy?"

"Let me try a different approach," said Wilder. "Look around. What do you see?"

"Water," said Angel.

"And what don't you see? That you'd expect?"

"Other boats," said Pepper.

"Exactly," said Wilder. "Do you know why the police frisked us for a fifteen-minute ferry ride?"

Pepper shook his head.

"Cuban nationals have hijacked this ferry to Florida three times. They're so desperate, they make boats from whatever floats. I'm telling you, they'll do almost anything to get to the America dream. Literally anything."

"Cubans keep telling me Havana's mostly quiet and safe," said Pepper.

"I've worked here for two and a half years," said Wilder. "Havana's fairly stable on the surface. A low rate of violent crime. There's a heavy military and police presence, of course, so I guess it depends on your definition of safe."

"We're just trying to find Marisol," said Angel. "As quick as we can."

Wilder scoffed. "Typical Americans. You've been here for two days and you think you understand what's going on? Forget those constitutional rights you learned about back home in civics class.

Americans get arrested here all the time for activities that aren't illegal in the good old USA. The best thing you can do is go home, wait for news."

"Mr. Rappeneau said you might help us," said Angel.

"We're down to a dozen diplomats in Havana these days, after Havana Syndrome," said Wilder with a shrug. "We don't have a lot of time for extracurricular activities."

Pepper could see their destination, Casablanca, approaching. It looked like a village glued to the hillside over the water, with small buildings and scattered palm trees. He'd heard of Havana syndrome, a mysterious ailment that had attacked embassy staff in Havana. It started with an overwhelming sensation of buzzing in their ears, followed by headaches, dizziness, and brain damage. The cause was mysterious and heavily debated.

"Exactly," said Wilder. "So here's what I know about Marisol's situation. You and she arrived on Monday afternoon via José Martí. You were subjected to advanced screening and interrogation by customs officials because of a violation of Cuban law—"

"Jesus!" exclaimed Angel. "Where the hell'd you hear that?"

"… the exact nature of which I wasn't able to learn," she continued, ignoring his interruption. "So what happened there?"

"It was literally no big deal," grumbled Angel.

Wilder must be hinting she had unofficial sources within Cuban border control. Pepper fought back a laugh. Angel had mentioned, when alone with Pepper, a "Banana Incident" that happened when he'd arrived in Cuba. But he'd refused to tell him the full story. It sounded embarrassing and funny, so Pepper planned to get it out of his buddy, sooner than later.

"And Pepper Ryan, you arrived yesterday and have a ticket back to the U.S. on Sunday afternoon. You're both staying in Centro Havana, in a pretty raw neighborhood."

"Yes," confirmed Angel.

"Do you know the subject of Marisol's film?"

Angel nodded. "Sure, it's about some rare types of Cuban orchids that are going extinct. Why does that matter?"

Wilder laughed. "It matters because I'm trying to figure out whether you two are partially clueless or totally clueless."

"What?" asked Angel.

"Marisol Borja has filmed in Cuba four times in the past fourteen months, and every time she's been under watch. The Cuban government's spectacularly paranoid, but do you think they would spend the resources to watch every step of someone making a film about orchids?"

"That's what she was doing," said Angel, shaking his head. "I've seen some of the raw footage."

"She began with that project. But since last month her filming hasn't been about flowers."

What? wondered Pepper. "How do you know?" The ferry was approaching the Casablanca pier.

"Don't focus on that. Focus on *why* I know."

A few ideas leaped to Pepper's mind, but he didn't have time to sort through them.

Wilder continued. "If you piss off the PNR, do you know how much trouble you'll be in? There's not much my embassy can do for your dumb asses. Their country, their rules."

"We'll be careful," said Angel.

Wilder shook her head. "Cuba's a desperate place. Batista was a good old-fashioned dictator. Then he was pushed aside by Castro, who preferred the communist playbook. Cuba went from bad to worse."

"What's that have to do with Marisol?"

"Nothing. Or maybe everything."

Pepper sighed. "Laurent Rappeneau said you could help us. If that's true, can you please start?"

"Seriously," agreed Angel. "I'm going nuts with worry. I

thought you embassy folks are supposed to assist Americans abroad."

Wilder tossed a handful of peanut shells overboard. "We're here to promote peace, support prosperity, and protect American citizens while advancing our interests abroad. Not necessarily in that order."

"So?"

"So you're one misstep away from getting arrested," Wilder said. "If they think you're undermining the government, there's nothing we can do to protect you. What have you uncovered so far?"

Pepper hesitated, unsure how much to reveal.

"Just enough to be even more worried than I was on Monday," said Angel. "And trust me, we're not going to undermine the government."

"How do you know?" sniffed Wilder. "Do you know about the crime of '*desecato*'? All you have to do is disrespect a police officer or public official, and you can get sent to prison for a year. If you're charged with resisting an official in the exercise of their duties, you can get another year in prison."

Angel gave an exasperated sigh. "I'm not sure why Mr. Rappeneau set up this meeting. It seems like a gigantic waste of your time."

"You should stay away from him too. His help might do you more harm than good."

The boat was nearing the dock now. The engines howled as the pilot tapped them into reverse to slow the vessel.

"And a hurricane's headed this way," noted Wilder. "We announced this morning that all Americans should leave Cuba immediately, before the airports shut down."

Pepper and Angel exchanged looks, but said nothing.

The passengers began filing off the ferry.

"The point is," said Wilder, "things are more delicate now than for many years. You flip over too many rocks in Havana, one of them might be a landmine. An American landmine."

"So, shut up and go home?" asked Pepper. "That's your advice?"

"I understand how upset you must be. But you need to trust the local police to do their jobs. The same as you'd have wanted as a cop back home on Cape Cod. Or as a special agent with the FBI."

Shit, thought Pepper, while trying to keep any concern from showing on his face. *So much for keeping a low profile down here.* Still, it made sense that the embassy officer would research their backgrounds before meeting with them.

But Angel jumped in. "Doesn't it worry you that an American woman's missing in Havana? That she might be dead?"

"We worry about everything. That's our job. And we pay more attention to situations like that than you think. But we do it diplomatically. The opposite of your actions so far."

Wilder was annoying, but that didn't mean she was wrong. Should Pepper and Angel stand down and trust the local authorities to find Marisol? If they didn't, Pepper and Angel might do something that screwed up the police investigation, or pissed off Detective Guiteras enough for him to act on his earlier threats. A lose-lose situation.

Pepper stuck out a hand to Wilder to shake goodbye. "We'll see. And we appreciate your unofficial advice. But I think our next stop'll be to revisit the embassy and ask for more official help." He knew it was a risk, given his current seat in the penalty box with the FBI, but he couldn't let bureaucracy stand in the way of finding Marisol. If he had to piss off a few paper pushers to get the job done, so be it.

Wilder scoffed. "Do you really want us looking more closely

at you two? Whether you're violating U.S. law by being here? That can be a long, unpleasant experience."

"Hey, we're just here to show support for the Cuban people," said Angel.

That was the box on the paperwork they'd both checked to fit an allowed category for travel to Cuba despite the U.S. embargo.

Pepper stood his ground, meeting Wilder's gaze. "I'm here to find the truth about Marisol. If that means putting my career on the line, I'm cool with that. Her life may depend on it."

Wilder studied him thoughtfully, chewing her lip. "I enjoy doing favors," she said finally. "They make the world go around, especially here in Cuba. And lucky for you, I know a guy who can clue you in on what Ms. Borja's been up to."

Yes! thought Pepper. *This could be their big break.* "Who is he?"

"Show up to find out. He'll be at this address today at two o'clock." She handed Pepper a slip of paper.

"Why not just tell us yourself?" asked Angel.

Wilder looked at him like he was stupid. "Because I'm walking a thin line here, helping you with a local police matter. If you stepped in shit here based on information I gave you, can you imagine the international relations blowback? And I did some research on you. The smart money would be on you stepping in some significant shit."

Angel opened his mouth as if to object, then closed it. He grinned at Pepper and shrugged. *Fair enough ...*

"Of course, you'd be safer spending the afternoon like a real tourist. Suck down a few of the famous daiquiris at El Floridita. Grab some dinner at La Guarida—it's got great food, Obama ate there. Then catch a plane home tomorrow, ahead of that hurricane. But if you really want to understand what your girlfriend has been mixed up in here, and you're not worried about keeping your asses out of trouble? Go talk to the man."

Wilder disappeared into the stream of passengers exiting the ferry with a small, crooked smile on her face, like she was betting they would choose trouble.

CHAPTER TEN

When they pulled up to Casa de Vides, they saw Dayana de Melina sitting on the doorstep in yoga pants, a T-shirt, and a Los Angeles Dodgers baseball cap, looking casually gorgeous. She glanced pointedly at her watch.

"¡Una mango!" muttered Hector.

"Classic Pepper," Angel laughed. "He attracts them like flies. And he hasn't even sung for her yet."

"I couldn't sleep last night, I was so worried about Mari," she said when they joined her at the doorstep. "So I got your address from Ozzie." She held up a bag. "Chicken, rice and beans—good fuel for your work."

"You're a lifesaver," said Pepper, his stomach rumbling at the smell.

She flashed a big smile. "Was Ozzie's father helpful?"

"A little," said Pepper.

Dayana frowned. "Did Señor Rappeneau think el Segador took Mari?"

Pepper shook his head. "He didn't speculate much. He handed us off to someone else. So you came here to check on our progress?"

She laughed. "You think I have another agenda? Maybe to seduce a yuma?" She reached over and squeezed his biceps. "If I had a peso for every man who tried to seduce me, I could fly off to Hollywood."

"She's stunning," said Angel upstairs in the casa's living room when Dayana ducked into the bathroom.

"So was her slap," said Pepper. "I haven't stopped thinking about her since last night." He shook his head in bewilderment. "Now she shows up here, and no way it's for me, right? Was she that close to Marisol?"

Angel scratched his chin. "Marisol told me all about her. She's Marisol's closest pal in Havana. And if Dayana's *loco* enough to be into you, what's your problem with that? The lovely Zula? Don't forget, she dumped you—"

"Don't go there, buddy," said Pepper. He didn't want to rehash that disaster.

"Pepper runs deep," Angel explained to Hector. "And he's been through a lot lately. With work, and a girl who stomped on his heart back home."

"I know how you feel," Hector said to Pepper. "When I sing 'Heartbreak Hotel,' I cry every time."

They ate a lunch of breaded chicken, rice, beans, and tomato salad. All during it they updated Dayana on their efforts to find Marisol, including their next step: the anonymous meeting set up by Heather Wilder.

"I will come with you," said Dayana, lightly stroking her long neck, as if unconsciously tickling herself.

Pepper found himself wondering if she was ticklish and where.

"*Gracias*," said Angel. "We need all the local help we can get."

Hector looked uncomfortable, but he nodded vigorously, not taking his eyes off Dayana.

They drove to the address Wilder gave them, on a narrow lane in Old Havana. When Hector pulled to the curb, Dayana swore.

"What?" asked Pepper.

Dayana muttered in full-speed Spanish, sounding pissed off.

It turned out that the address was not for a building. They walked past a small sign that said *Rafael Trejo Boxing Gym*, through a little lobby, into the strangest boxing space Pepper had ever seen. The gym was located in a courtyard between two old apartment buildings, with plaster crumbling from their walls.

A boxing ring took up the middle of the space, with bleachers on one side. Athletes were everywhere, working out or sparring in pairs. Cuban music played from a radio.

A sweaty Detective Juan Guiteras, wearing blue Everlast shorts and a sleeveless yellow T-shirt, was talking to another man on the other side of the ring. Dayana muttered, *"Que idiota"* under her breath.

Pepper walked toward Guiteras, and the crowd of athletes parted in front of him. Then he realized Dayana's presence caused that effect. Everyone had stopped, even the two men sparring in the raised ring. The man talking to Guiteras walked away.

"The American tourists," said Guiteras, grinning humorlessly. "And Dayana de Melina! We have royalty among us."

"Save your nonsense, Juan," she said, low and hard.

He laughed. "What are you doing here?"

"I'm with them."

"With them? One of them or all of them?"

Dayana stepped forward, but Pepper restrained her. "Detective, can we talk?" he asked. "Our mutual acquaintance said you learned something important about Marisol. About her filming activities? That they might be a reason for her disappearance?"

Guiteras shrugged. "We have no evidence she was kidnapped

or hurt. Maybe Ms. Borja left the plaza of her own free will. She may have gone home to America. She may be somewhere in Havana with another man. But that is no crime either."

"She's not with another man," growled Angel.

Pepper made a calming gesture, aware of the gym's occupants watching them. "Tell us what you know, Detective. Please."

"I always enjoy yumas," said Guiteras, flashing his white teeth. "Never afraid to demand what they want. Or even to steal it."

Damn! Was Guiteras talking about the Carlina Borja murder file that Pepper borrowed? But Pepper didn't respond.

Guiteras, standing near a heavy bag, tapped a slow combination of punches. "Marisol Borja has been in this country for four visits in the past fourteen months." He repeated the combination, still slowly.

"We know all that," said Angel.

"And she received permission from all the correct government agencies for her filming, which is difficult to get in Cuba. She meticulously notified the Asociación Cubana del Audiovisual when she arrived and departed, and she made the required filings. All to film a documentary about rare Cuban orchids, *si?*"

"We know that," said Angel.

Pepper could tell that his friend was fighting back impatience.

"That is what her ACAV filings said. Rare ghost orchids. The threat of extinction, because of climate change caused by capitalism." Guiteras hit the heavy bag with three left hooks, making the bag jump. "And then the other mystery, an American policeman comes to Havana. I can't decide if you are playing games here, Señor Ryan, or if you think the Cuban police are incompetent. You should fly back to Disney World."

Pepper was getting pissed. Why did Wilder send them here, to get jerked around by Guiteras, who probably knew nothing important about Marisol, anyway?

"I need to go find my sparring partner and apologize for keeping him waiting," continued the detective. "I've nothing for you, unless you can give me something too."

"Like what?" asked Angel.

Guiteras stared at Pepper.

He means the Carlota Borja police report, thought Pepper. But there was no way he would admit to having taken it. "I'll spar with you," he offered instead. Maybe if they bonded caveman-style, the detective would act like less of an asshole?

"No!" said Dayana, her brown eyes flashing. "Enough macho bullshit."

"You joke?" Guiteras asked Pepper with a smile. "That's not what I meant."

Pepper grinned back. "Tell us the secret news you have about Marisol Borja. Then I'll spar with you."

Guiteras smiled. "Let's have our fun first. We'll be macho, like your Papa Hemingway. He understood men."

Against Dayana's protests, Pepper took off his shirt and quickly stretched. A small Cuban man who had to be eighty-five years old expertly wrapped Pepper's hands and tugged oversized sparring gloves on him. Pepper accepted a worn mouthpiece and tried not to think about how many fighters had used it before him. No one offered him padded headgear.

"Pay five pesos to Marco," said Guiteras, gesturing to the old man. "The facility fee."

Angel handed it over.

Then Pepper and Guiteras climbed into the gym's one ring. It had a gray canvas floor, frayed blue and white ropes.

Guiteras was probably five foot ten and one hundred eighty pounds. So Pepper had four inches of height and maybe forty pounds weight advantage. And they were only sparring. Pepper would be a good sport, play along. They needed better cooperation and respect from Guiteras, and this seemed to be the quickest way.

And maybe he'd impress Dayana at the same time? Pepper had boxed as a teenager and fought in a Golden Gloves tournament when he was nineteen. It'd been a good way to channel his teenage aggression. But he'd had even more fights as a hockey player, during his two seasons in the British Columbia Junior Hockey League before he went to college. Scrapping had been a core skill to survive that league.

So Pepper had enough basic fighting skills to spar with the detective. He took an orthodox boxing stance and brought his hands up in a conventional guard, right hand near his cheek, left hand up and out, elbows in.

He decided he would stay defensive. Throw some jabs for form's sake, move his feet, play along. Guiteras was testing him, so Pepper would step up. But he wouldn't hurt the smaller man, or even worse, embarrass him. That would be a quick way to end any cooperation by the detective.

Without a bell or any other official start, they began.

Pepper bounced and shuffled, sliding in a semicircle to the right. Guiteras matched him, grinning, his mouthpiece showing.

Then Pepper's head snapped back, twice in succession.

He hadn't seen Guiteras' jabs. They were impossibly fast. Guiteras had already danced back out of range before Pepper could counterpunch.

Pepper shook his head, brought his hands back up. The smaller man was crazy quick. Pepper kept his feet moving, his head moving. He tried a jab, caught Guiteras' gloves.

Pepper blocked Guiteras' next jab, but not the right hook that followed it, slamming into Pepper's ribs. His counterpunch hit nothing, then Guiteras backed out of range, bouncing lightly, gesturing for Pepper to attack.

Pepper feigned one, but not really committing to it, retreating into his guard in time to almost block Guiteras' next combination of punches.

"Come on, Pepper!" yelled Angel.

"Kick his ass!" yelled Dayana.

And then Pepper was sitting on the canvas, not sure how he got there.

He saw a middle-aged woman on an apartment balcony overlooking the boxing ring. Her arms were full of laundry, but she gave him an encouraging smile. Guiteras danced back, gesturing for him to get up.

Pepper slowly got to his feet, trying to suck the humid air into his lungs, to regroup. The left side of his jaw hurt from the blow that sent him down. So, Guiteras had caught him with a right hook. Good to know.

Pepper was getting his ass kicked. He shook his head, took his stance again. He needed to keep his guard up and keep his feet moving.

Thirty seconds later, Pepper hit the canvas again, sweat flying from his body. Probably another right hook, on the heels of a left jab. Again, the combination was too quick for Pepper to follow.

"Your hands are not as fast in the ring as they were at my desk," Guiteras said, barely understandable through his mouth guard.

Guiteras was a hell of a boxer. He was clowning around a bit, as Pepper got back to his feet, turned to yell something unintelligible through his mouth guard to a couple of fighters at ringside who were watching the yuma get a boxing lesson.

As Guiteras turned back, Pepper rushed him. Clinched the smaller man against the ropes, gave him three quick punches to the body, which Guiteras blocked. But Pepper's fourth punch was upstairs, a left hook, catching Guiteras on the side of the head. A pretty good shot.

Guiteras gave him a shove, trying to open up some space.

Pepper hooked his arms, spun the smaller man, and tried to throw him to the floor.

It was a move straight out of the B.C. Junior Hockey League. In a hockey fight, the basic strategy was to hold your opponent with one hand, try to drag him off balance, and pummel the living crap out of him with your other hand. And if you couldn't do that, you tried to wrestle him to the ice and hope the ref would step in quickly.

But Guiteras didn't fall. He twisted and broke free. Then his head and shoulders weaved like a pissed-off snake, and Pepper's flurry of follow-up punches all missed. Guiteras stepped to the side and counterpunched, catching Pepper on the side of the head, and Pepper went down for the third time, seeing stars.

Dayana leaped into the ring, pulling Guiteras away, hitting him and swearing in a furious stream of Spanish.

Then Angel appeared in the ring too, helping Pepper to his feet. Pepper shook his head, trying to clear it.

"I'm good," Pepper said, "Let's rumble." But Angel was pulling him to a corner, and the eighty-five-year-old man was taking off Pepper's gloves, saying something in Spanish that he didn't understand.

"Nice try, Pepper," said Angel in his ear. "But that asshole's a ringer."

Pepper climbed out through the ropes and stood without help on the cracked concrete floor, still breathing hard. He was dizzy, but his head was clear enough to be embarrassed.

Guiteras climbed down too. "Did you enjoy the exhibition?" he asked Dayana with a big smile. He looked as fresh as when they entered the ring.

"¡Idiota!" Dayana hissed at Guiteras.

He just shrugged and said, "It was a good session."

"Lots of fun," Pepper wheezed. "Let's do it again sometime."

"Tell us your big news about Mari," Dayana said. "Enough games, Juan!"

Guiteras grinned at her and squirted water into his mouth from an old water bottle wrapped in tape. Then he turned to face Pepper. "Marisol Borja filmed orchids on her first three trips to Havana. But I have information that on her last trip in August, she interviewed family members of the artists who died in recent months, and she filmed where their bodies were found."

"The serial killings?" gasped Angel.

Guiteras grimaced. "She began filming about the deceased artists without state permission. She put herself in danger, committing that crime."

The news hit Pepper almost as hard as Guiteras' punches. *Had Marisol realized the danger of her new project?*

There was a strong chance that Marisol disappeared because of her film work about the artists' deaths. The theory about a jilted ex-lover or other enemy in her personal life needed to go to the back burner. Pepper needed to rethink everything.

He took a deep breath and held it, trying to calm himself. The Cuban government would certainly try to stop an American documentary about the murders of Cuba's top artists, and the PNR's failure to catch el Segador. Or even worse, if Marisol's investigations had drawn the attention of the serial killer, would her body be found next?

"Time for you to go," said Guiteras, gesturing toward the gym's exit. "But I hope you understand me. If you continue investigating Marisol Borja's disappearance, then be prepared for the consequences."

CHAPTER ELEVEN

"You stupid men," grumbled Dayana. "I should have stopped you."

It was Thursday evening, and they were walking through Old Havana, except for Pepper, who was limping.

"And we need to get him some ice," Hector observed glumly. His day job was as a nurse, so he'd offered to check over Pepper. But Pepper had politely and firmly refused any medical attention, too embarrassed by the ass kicking he'd just received. He wanted everyone to move on.

His body was aching from the beating he'd taken in the boxing ring, but it was the bombshell about Marisol's secret new film project that truly left him disoriented.

It changed the known dangers that Marisol faced, because the Cuban regime would regard a documentary about a serial killer running wild in Havana as a direct criticism of their government.

As they walked, Pepper's mind raced with possibilities. Why had Marisol kept her investigation a secret, even from Angel? What had she uncovered that made her a target? The people listed in the Carlina Borja police report overlapped with people from Marisol's activities in Havana, and now those connections sent a chill down Pepper's spine. He needed to find Marisol's video footage from August, to see what she'd captured there. It could hold the key to identifying her antagonist and finding her.

"Juan can be a jerk," Dayana said, referring to Guiteras. "And he boxed for Cuba in the Olympics, about ten years ago. He won the middleweight silver medal."

Sonofabitch. She couldn't have shared that nugget of info about an hour ago? "How do you know him?" asked Pepper.

"We grew up in Manzanillo, a village to the east. He was two years older, and a cocky jerk then too."

"But you tagged him good once, Pepper," said Hector. "He looked surprised for a second before he knocked you down the third time."

"Thanks," said Pepper. His ears were still ringing.

He now thought that the most likely candidate to have grabbed Marisol was the PNR or some other part of the Cuban government. If that was the case, Pepper had no shot at locating her, dead or alive. And anything he did could also be seen as a threat to Cuban national security—so he could be next to be swallowed up by the regime. Left to rot in a Cuban prison? Or would a fisherman find his body floating in Havana Bay?

Hector paused at a street vendor to buy two bottles of water, then offered one to Pepper. "You look like you could use this," he said, offering one to Pepper.

Pepper took it with a nod of thanks and took a sip, but the water tasted bitter. Or maybe it was residual blood in his mouth from the fight. He spat out a mouthful of water on the sidewalk. He was already feeling a little more ready to get back into the hunt for Marisol. Danger be damned.

Angel finally broke his brooding silence. "This entire trip has been a nightmare. I love her so much, it's killing me, not knowing if she's alive or—"

"We'll find her, buddy," said Pepper, putting an arm around Angel's shoulder. "And we need to talk with Beriev again. He was Marisol's cameraman when she started filming about the artists' deaths. We can't take no for an answer."

Dayana pulled out her phone. "I'll text him. He'll always meet with me."

As they continued walking, the wind picked up, gusting enough to make walking a challenge. Pepper wondered if it was a first taste of Hurricane Gussie.

A minute later, Dayana's phone chirped. "Viktor says he can talk to me now for a few minutes. He's at the Fototeca de Cuba, preparing a photography exhibit. We can walk there from here."

"Talk to you?" asked Pepper.

She laughed. "Everyone has time for me. And the rest of you can surprise him."

As they walked, Dayana pulled Pepper by the shoulder, and they dropped behind Angel and Hector far enough that they couldn't be overheard.

"Juan has always been tough," Dayana mused, her gaze distant. "Even when we were kids, he had a way of getting under people's skin."

Pepper glanced at her. "So you knew him well?"

Dayana leaned closer to Pepper, her voice conspiratorial. "Growing up in the same village, it was hard not to notice Juan. But his world was sports, and my escape was acting."

As they strolled, Dayana talked about the limited resources near her village for learning to act and getting chances to perform. "And sometimes it felt like the whole world was conspiring to ensure I failed. It made me so angry! But I always knew acting was the way forward for me. It was the only life that made sense."

Pepper found himself drawn to the passion in her voice. The way her eyes shone as she spoke about her dreams, plus the frustration in her voice. He felt a connection with her, another person fighting against the odds to make her mark in the world.

"Law enforcement's all I ever knew, except music," he volunteered. "And playing hockey, but I wasn't good enough to make a living at that."

"You're the strangest lawman I've ever met," Dayana laughed. "You seem like more of a free spirit. That must be the musician inside you, trying to get out."

So Pepper shared with her his struggles as an FBI agent. The constraints of its enormous bureaucracy and risk-averse culture that conflicted sometimes with his own drive to get the job done.

Pepper was surprised how easily he spilled his guts to her. They were from opposite countries and wildly different professions, but they had a similar mindset—each determined to succeed on their own terms.

"It's always a fight, isn't it?" she asked quietly. "My dream is to go make big Hollywood films with the most famous directors in the world, the most famous actors. Really test myself. But I signed contracts with Cuban state agencies when I was too young to know better, so I'm stuck here on this little island, for now."

"I'm sorry," he said.

She gave a sad smile. "But people like us, we don't have the option to quit, right? We just get back up again, even when it's the dumbest choice in the world." Then she looked up at him and laughed. "Be careful, Pepper. If you keep looking at me like that, I might start thinking you're interested in more than finding Marisol."

Pepper felt his neck flush, but he grinned back at her. "And what if I am?"

She gave him a little shove, and her lips curled into a smile that made his heart stumble. "Then you'd better be prepared for the consequences, yuma," she said in a perfect grumbling imitation of Detective Guiteras' parting threat at the boxing gym.

Pepper laughed again. *What a little firecracker.*

The Fototeca de Cuba was lodged in a baby blue colonial building at the edge of a large square called Plaza Vieja. The Old Plaza.

"I like Viktor's neo-surrealist portraits," Dayana said as they waited outside the front door. "They're strange and beautiful. He combines images with his subjects, so the final photographs are optical illusions. They're very hard to describe. You can recognize the person photographed, but the overall effect transforms them into an unexpected image."

Beriev hurried out to meet Dayana, looking surprised to see she wasn't alone. He whipped out a gray handkerchief and blew his bulbous red nose. "Dear, why didn't you tell me this was business? It's an impossibly busy day. I'm arranging the most important exhibition of my career, and it opens next Friday."

"We wouldn't bother you if it wasn't life and death," said Pepper. "But we need to talk to you somewhere private. Right now."

Beriev looked back at the gallery, then led them to an entrance to a nearby building on the corner of the plaza.

Angel paid an admission fee for the group, and they took an elevator up. "Someone always watches in Cuba," muttered Beriev. "So where better to talk than a dark chamber? This is Havana's famous Camera Oscura."

They crowded into a cool, darkened room where an image of Old Havana's skyline was projected onto a circular table. Over the rattle of ancient air conditioning, Beriev started talking about the Camera Oscura's history and its connection to Leonardo Da Vinci, but Pepper sidled toward a door to a terrace and waved for everyone to follow him to the muggy outdoors. There was no time to waste.

As soon as they were away from the other tourists, Pepper moved close to Beriev and confronted him. "Why'd you lie to us about Marisol's work?" he asked. "We know she stopped filming about orchids. She was looking into the killings."

Beriev shrugged. "I don't work for you. If she didn't tell you, why would I?"

Maybe to save her damn life, Pepper thought, but didn't say out loud. "Do you remember where she filmed in August? Who she interviewed?"

Beriev sniffed. "Of course. I was her cameraman."

"But you don't have the footage?" Pepper asked.

"No, no, I downloaded it from my camera to her portable hard drive. She had the only copy."

Angel groaned. "She had the hard drives in her bag, which was stolen."

Pepper turned to Beriev. "What did the hard drive look like?"

"Just a little silver rectangle. But she put a monkey sticker on it. She did that to tell them apart. She had a bunch of them."

At least they'd confirmed the missing hard drive was real. He put his hand on Beriev's big shoulder. "Since we don't have that footage, we need your help to follow in her footsteps from August. Go to the same places and talk to the same people. Because something you filmed may be why she's missing."

Beriev frowned helplessly. "I wish you luck, but I have an impossible deadline for my exhibition. Totally impossible."

Angel snorted. "A photo exhibit matters more than finding Marisol? Are you kidding me? What's it about?"

Beriev crossed his arms. "The subject matter is totally confidential at this point. I'm sorry. If it helps, I don't believe the serial killer grabbed her. More likely the government, so—"

Dayana grabbed Beriev's sleeve. "Mari would want you to help them, and even more, she would want you to film it. Trust me, we will find Mari alive. Havana is a very safe city. Almost always."

"No way," said Pepper. *That'd be the opposite of low-key.* "We're not filming everywhere we go."

But she flashed her sweet smile at Pepper, then gave Beriev a full blast too, touching his arm.

There was no further debate.

CHAPTER TWELVE

Big and creepy was Pepper's first impression the next morning when he saw Havana's most famous burial ground, El Cementerio de Cristóbal Colón.

Or, as American tourists called it, the Christopher Columbus Cemetery. A stone wall surrounded the grounds, topped by a black wrought-iron fence with decorative spikes. Maybe ten feet tall. Enough to keep trespassers out, or the dead in?

They were there to talk to Gloria Borja, the mother of Cuba's famous ballerina. El Segador's victim number four. Marisol had interviewed Gloria at her daughter's grave a week after her murder.

Beriev had driven Pepper and Dayana there in a cramped Soviet–era Lada that he'd borrowed from a friend, because Hector was unavailable. Pepper had sent him and Angel to talk to some other relatives in the Cavada family tree about their interactions with Marisol on her most recent visits to Havana. Had she seemed worried about anything? Had she said she was in trouble with anyone? Since time was of the essence, they needed to pursue multiple paths simultaneously to find Marisol.

Beriev parked the Lada in a small lot by the entrance. Pepper looked around as they all got out, trying to see if anyone had followed them. He had seen no tail, and he didn't see anyone watching them now.

Dayana had come along to translate any of Gloria Borja's Spanish that was beyond Pepper's ability. Standing next to the car, she was wearing a T-shirt and jeans that fit her so wondrously that, in a less somber situation, Pepper would have tackled her on the spot.

"I'm excited to see a famous American detective in action!" She laughed and flashed her eyes at him, and he felt his heart skip a beat.

Against Pepper's better judgment, Beriev was going to film the interview. He hadn't remembered many details from Marisol's interviews with the dead dancer's mother. He'd been too focused on operating his video camera to the best of his artistic abilities. Or maybe he'd drunk too much vodka.

Pepper needed to learn whether the grieving mother had been harassed by Cuban law enforcement or anyone else after those interviews, or if she'd had any clues about Marisol's disappearance.

The three of them entered the iron gates and walked down a wide street past rows and rows of stone mausoleums and vaults, many decorated with statues, all bleached white by the Havana sun. The cemetery was alive with shadows, fingers of gray across the white surfaces.

"This is one of the most important cemeteries in the world," said Beriev. "For its history and its architecture. And of course, as a special place for the Cuban people."

"How many people are buried here?" Pepper asked.

The Belarusian's brow furrowed. "A million? More? It's over fifty acres. The mausoleums are like apartment buildings for the dead. You know Ibrahim Ferrer?"

Pepper had heard the name, but couldn't recall. He shook his head.

"Very famous Cuban singer...he's buried right over there. He was the singer for the Buena Vista Social Club. You know of them?"

"Of course." Pepper had heard their music when visiting Angel's family. Angel's mother would sing along as she cooked, rattling the pots and pans in time. Unforgettable.

"Looks like someone was just buried here," said Pepper, pointing to a mausoleum surrounded by flowers and a small crowd of people.

"No, no," said Beriev, shaking his head at Pepper's ignorance. "That's the tomb of Amelia Goyri, who they call La Milagrosa. She died in childbirth, and her baby died too. They were buried in two coffins, side by side. But when the coffins were dug up later, what did they find? The baby was lying on the mother's chest. A miracle! Catholics come here now, to pray for their own miracles."

"It's a minor miracle that you got Gloria Borja to speak to us so quickly," said Pepper.

"She was coming here this afternoon anyway," explained Beriev, lumbering along with a bag of video equipment over his shoulder. "To visit her daughter."

After a short walk Beriev stopped them beside a small white mausoleum with a few groups of flowers tucked in the metal railing around its perimeter.

"Here's the Borja family tomb," he said. He put down his bag and removed a video camera and began fussing with it. "And this beauty is my Canon C100 Mark 2. The best video camera in Havana."

Gloria Borja arrived ten minutes later. She was a tall, thin woman in her fifties with coffee-colored skin and an erect posture. Maybe she'd been a dancer like her daughter.

Beriev thanked her for talking with them and introduced Pepper and Dayana. The woman seemed star struck by Dayana.

"Did you hear about Marisol?" Pepper asked.

"Sí," said the woman. She spoke quickly in Spanish to Dayana, and Pepper only understood about half of it.

Dayana frowned. "She's too nervous to talk to you. She says she's sorry."

Shit. He locked eyes with the woman. "It's important for us to hear what you told Marisol about your daughter's death. We want to hear everything."

The woman hesitated. "Why do you want to talk about Carlina's death if you are not the police?" Her eyes glistened with tears, and her hands trembled. "I've already told the police everything I know. Reliving my memories of her ... it hurts me."

"I'm an officer back home in America."

She took a shaky breath. "But why do you care about Carlina?"

Pepper reached out and gently touched Gloria's arm. "I know the agony of losing someone you love to violence—criminals killed my brother. The emptiness and the anger. The endless questions. But maybe you can tell me something that helps me understand what happened to your daughter. Then we can find Marisol while she's still alive."

The woman began sobbing.

Beriev offered her a bottle of water.

She thanked him, uncapped it, and took a long swallow. Dayana chatted with her about Marisol, and they laughed. Then Beriev handed the woman a hairbrush and a small hand mirror. She checked herself in the mirror, sighed, then brushed her hair. Dayana took the water, the mirror, and the hairbrush from her.

Gloria seemed calmer now. More ready to talk.

So Pepper jumped right in, beginning by asking what she talked about with Marisol on camera.

It was what Pepper expected. Details of her daughter's upbringing, of her successful dance career. Her hopes and dreams, cut short by her horrific death.

Pepper and the woman stood next to the mausoleum. Beriev stood farther away, camera up and rolling continuously, panning back and forth. But he had a skill for being unobtrusive despite his bulky size. He blended into the background, and Pepper quickly forgot about him, focusing entirely on Gloria Borja and her answers.

She confirmed that Carlina didn't live with her, but they were close. Her daughter had always been very private, so she didn't know everything about Carlina's life. She knew Carlina worked too hard as a dancer, leading to a knee problem that eventually would have needed surgery.

"Did Carlina ever mention meeting or interacting with Marisol during any of Marisol's previous trips to Havana?"

"One time," said Gloria. "They met in April, because Marisol was attempting to meet her Cuban relatives."

"When Marisol interviewed you, did she ask about any conflicts your daughter had with other people, or any troubles in her life? Any ex-boyfriend or girlfriend? Had she borrowed money from someone?"

The theory was that the killer had some connection, however distant, to the murdered artists. This aligned with the statistical trend that most murder victims knew their killers.

"Yes," said Gloria. "She was dating a man when she died. Nothing too serious, I think. His name was Guillermo Infante."

Infante again! The feisty poet with the grooming problem from the club last night. And from the persons-of-interest list in the police report about Carlina's murder.

"Marisol interviewed Infante too, last month," offered Beriev from behind the camera.

"We need to talk to him again soon," Pepper said to Dayana.

Maybe she could ask him to meet, since apparently the actress was at the top of the celebrity food chain.

"Do you know if Carlina ever dated any of these men?" he asked. He told her three names that he hadn't been able to learn much about from the persons of interest list in the murder police report: Vladimir Palenko, Edgar Sorana, and Quinto Chavez.

Gloria looked at Pepper quizzically. "I don't know the first two. But like I said, Carlina could be very private, so ..." She shrugged. "But Quinto, he's my stepson! From my second marriage, after Carlina's father died." She made the sign of the cross.

Shit! Quinto was Carlina's stepbrother? Pepper had a sinking feeling in his gut. That also made the jinetero a cousin of Marisol's.

"Your stepson, he has tattoos all over one arm?"

"Yes," she nodded with a look suggesting she wasn't a fan of the tattoos.

That explained why the jineteros attacked them outside the nightclub. Pepper had unwittingly accused Quinto of sleeping with his own stepsister.

"Can you give me his phone number?" *I need to apologize,* Pepper thought.

But he also needed to ask Quinto what happened in the plaza when Marisol disappeared. Did they plan to meet there, or just unexpectedly bumped into each other? And if the witness was correct, what were Quinto and Marisol arguing about? Where did she disappear to, and was he involved?

Gloria entered her stepson's number in Pepper's phone.

Then he asked, "Did Carlina ever say she was worried about her safety in the weeks leading up to her death?"

"Yes," she nodded with certainty. "She told me that three artists featured with her in an American magazine were killed. She was scared about that."

Gloria began crying again, so Pepper paused the interview and Dayana offered her the bottle of water.

When she had gathered herself, Pepper asked, "Did Carlina talk about any upcoming projects or travel plans she was excited about?"

"No." Then Gloria thought further. "She said nothing, but I had a feeling she was involved in something big that she wasn't talking about." Her eyes took on a faraway look. "Carlina was always so driven, so passionate about dancing. When she danced, it was like watching music come alive." Her smile faded, and a single tear rolled down her cheek.

"The something big she was involved with ... do you have any guess what that was?"

She shook her head and shrugged helplessly.

Pepper believed her, but needed something more concrete to act on. "Had Carlina been in any trouble with the government?"

Gloria remained silent.

"It's okay," said Dayana. "It's public."

"Okay," said Gloria Borja. "My daughter took part in street protests, trying to push the government to increase food and power supplies. But she was never arrested."

Pepper continued on that line of questions, but the mother offered no other helpful information. Then he tried to refocus on gathering information that would explain Marisol's disappearance. "What can you tell me about Marisol's interview with you?"

Gloria thought about the question, then sighed. "She was very upset about Carlina. They only met a couple of times, but Marisol was upset like family should be. And she was frustrated by the PNR's efforts. She said the police easily should have captured el Segador after the first artist was killed, or the second, or the third. Eight months and nothing! She said Carlina's blood was on the PNR's hands."

Pepper knew firsthand that victims' families often felt that way about the police in America too, fair or not.

"After you talked with Marisol in August, did anyone bother you about it? Did anyone ask you about Marisol and what you talked about?"

"Yes," she said, sniffling. She explained that a PNR detective came to her apartment to return some of her daughter's items, things that had been in her pockets when she died. "He said I must tell him what I said to Marisol on camera. So I did."

"What did the detective say?"

"He was furious. He told me I committed crimes by giving an interview to Marisol, that I was a traitor to Cuba. I told him I had lost my only child, there was nothing more he could do to me. And I meant it."

Pepper paused, touched by what the woman had said. Then he asked, "Do you remember the detective's name?"

"No."

"Was it Juan Guiteras?"

The woman's eyes lit up. "Yes! That's the man!"

Asshole, thought Pepper. And really not surprising at all, from what Pepper had experienced.

"Did Carlina keep a diary, or a sketchbook, anything that might help me understand what was on her mind in the weeks before she died?"

Gloria thought about it. "She had a diary when she was a girl, and she has always been a packrat. But I looked all over her apartment after the police finished and found nothing like that. So if she did, maybe the police took them."

Hmm ... "If Carlina had things she wanted to keep private, where would they be? Did she have an office?"

"No, she was a dancer. She didn't have an office. If she had anything that she wanted to keep private, it would be at her apartment."

"I need to go there next," Pepper said. Where Carlina lived and where she died. And where Marisol interviewed Gloria less than two weeks later. Had Marisol filmed something there during the interview that had gotten her in trouble? "Can you please take me there now?"

"No," said Gloria. "It breaks my heart to go there. I need to clean it out, but it scares me. As long as I have her apartment, I have part of my daughter."

"It might be very important," said Pepper. "It might help us understand the terrible things that are happening in Havana."

Everything Carlina owned was in her apartment. So any clues about past relationships, or about anyone she feared, would be there, unless the PNR had seized it. Since Carlina was so private, maybe the police had missed wherever she'd hidden her most secret items. There was only one way to find out—go search her apartment.

The woman stood quietly, her head hanging down. But after a time she nodded slightly. "I will give you the key if you promise not to take or move anything."

"Thank you," said Pepper.

The woman said in an even quieter voice, "I will give you the key because you have given me new hope my daughter's killer will be punished."

"I don't think she completely understands that we're looking for Marisol, not the killer," Pepper said to Dayana in English.

Dayana began to say something to Gloria, but stopped when she saw the woman was crying again.

"Gracias, gracias," Gloria said to Pepper, looking him in the eye.

Pepper froze from embarrassment and awkwardness. "I'm so sorry about your daughter," he mumbled.

"You're right, Pepper," said Beriev, still filming. "She thinks

you are trying to catch the man who ended her daughter's life."
That was the first time he'd interjected his voice while filming.

"Dayana, explain to her that's not why I'm here," said Pepper, his voice breaking. Maybe his Spanish was worse than he thought. He didn't need rumors circulating around Havana that he was here investigating the artists' murders. He was already attracting enough negative attention looking for Marisol.

Dayana said something to Gloria in a gentle voice. She hugged the woman and whispered rapidly in her ear in Spanish.

Gloria hugged Pepper without saying another word. Then she slowly walked away through the mausoleums, her shoulders hunched with grief.

Pepper felt a lump in his throat. He knew he had to press on with his search for Marisol, but he felt a pang of guilt for dredging up such painful memories. He exhaled slowly. "Did she understand?"

"I told her you're not a policeman here, but you will try to find the man who killed her daughter. And that she shouldn't tell anyone that she talked to you or it can cause serious trouble."

Pepper felt his frustration boiling over. "What? She thinks I'm secretly investigating her daughter's murder?"

Pepper noticed that Beriev was still filming.

The lovely Cuban put her hand on Pepper's arm, squeezing hard. She looked up at him, her eyes glistening with new tears but with steely anger too. "If you could say no to that heartbroken mother, then I was wrong about what kind of man you are."

She started to say something more, but her voice caught in her throat. She turned away, but added, too quietly for Beriev's camera to pick up, "And wrong about us too."

CHAPTER THIRTEEN

They reached Carlina Borja's apartment building, a faded green building with curved balconies in the La Rampa neighborhood of Havana, a few blocks from the famous Hotel Nacional and the Malecón seawall.

The car ride had been quiet, but Pepper had taken the time to think. His mood had changed from anger to hurt and then to a new resolve. He was going to find out the whole truth about Marisol's disappearance, and hopefully that would include the truth about Carlina Borja's death, for her mother's sake.

The building entrance was unlocked, so Pepper, Dayana, and Beriev climbed to the fifth-floor apartment. Dayana handed over the key and Pepper tried it in the lock, but it didn't fit. Not even close.

Damn.

Had Gloria Borja given him the wrong key? Or had someone changed the lock?

Of course, Viktor Beriev had his camera filming the Great American Detective in action.

Pepper rattled the door, testing the strength of the knob and lock. It was old but solid, unfortunately.

Pepper owned a lock pick set and had used it a few times, with mixed success. But his picks were fifteen hundred miles away on Cape Cod. He had a knife he'd borrowed from Casa de Vides, since he felt better with a weapon. But its blade wasn't narrow enough to pick a lock.

He could probably kick in the door, but then neighbors would call the PNR, who would undoubtedly believe Pepper was investigating Carlina Borja's death. As promised by Detective Guiteras, Pepper would end up in Cuban jail—do not pass go, do not collect two hundred dollars.

But the thought of neighbors gave Pepper an idea.

He went to the apartment to the right of Carlina's and knocked. He heard a high-pitched voice before a woman around seventy years old opened the door. She had curled silver hair, wrinkles on her dark-skinned face, and ruby red lipstick. She was smoking a thin cigar. Salsa music played from somewhere behind her.

"¿Qué?" she grunted, blowing smoke in Pepper's face. Then she noticed Beriev a few feet to the side, with his camera filming. She tried to shut the door, but Pepper slipped his foot in the doorway.

"Turn that off!" Pepper snapped at Beriev. Then to the woman he said, "We know Carlina Borja's mother. She gave us the key to her daughter's apartment, but it doesn't work."

The woman pushed the door against Pepper's foot again. Maybe she wasn't understanding Pepper's mediocre Spanish.

Pepper held his ground, gently. "Can we please go to your balcony to look at Carlina's apartment?"

Then Dayana stepped into view and the woman blushed, her mouth falling open with recognition. Somehow, the cigar remained stuck to her lower lip. She straightened her house dress and patted her hair.

Dayana gave the woman a hug, somehow avoiding her

dangling cigar. Then they began chatting in Spanish, too fast and colloquial for Pepper to fully follow.

After a while the woman laughed and beamed at Pepper.

"She said yes?" asked Pepper.

Dayana smiled. "If you give her two hundred pesos and take a picture with her."

"A picture?"

"I told her you're a famous yuma actor and we want to film you on her beautiful balcony for a Hollywood movie set in Havana."

Ridiculous. But Pepper handed over the money. And using the woman's phone, Dayana took a picture of her hugging Pepper, with her cigar drooping from the corner of her mouth. Then Dayana took a selfie of her and the woman.

Eventually, Pepper stood on her balcony. Beriev was filming him again, and the woman watched closely from inside her apartment, puffing her cigar. Dayana stood nearby, grinning at Pepper's obvious embarrassment.

The balcony was long and curved, with a rough concrete floor and a low concrete wall, topped by an iron railing. A faded purple chair was flanked on both sides by a clutter of potted plants.

The woman yelled something to Pepper, blowing smoke through the open balcony door.

Dayana laughed. "She says you're very handsome, but don't crush her plants."

Pepper tiptoed through the clutter of plants in plastic pots to the railing closest to Carlina's balcony. A five-foot gap separated the two balconies. Or was it six feet? Or seven? Pepper tried to remember how far a man could broad-jump.

He looked down, saw the drop to the sidewalk. The apartment was on the fifth floor, so it was probably about fifty feet down. A deadly fall.

Pepper gave the iron railing of the balcony a good yank back and forth, and it felt rock solid. Was Carlina's too?

Pepper sighed. He had to get into that apartment in case it held clues that would lead him to Marisol. He couldn't walk away.

Pepper gingerly climbed onto the railing, with his left hand braced against the building's wall for balance.

He heard a gasp of astonishment from behind him, and the woman started praying in panicked Spanish, but Pepper concentrated.

Yes, probably about five feet.

His plan was to jump far enough to clear Carlina's railing and land on the concrete pad of her balcony. He might bang himself up, but he could live with that.

It looked completely doable, unless the gap was eight feet, in which case he would come up short, bounce off the low concrete wall of the balcony, then maybe bounce off some balconies below, as he plunged to the sidewalk.

Pepper swallowed. It was probably around six feet. Definitely over five.

He took a deep breath, squatted down, leaned forward, and leaped.

The railing stayed solid beneath his legs, almost completely. It flexed slightly from the thrust of his jump, costing him precious inches.

Oh shit, oh shit, he thought, soaring across the gap, fifty feet up in the air.

And he fell short, his chest and armpits slammed into the iron railing of Carlina's balcony, like getting hit by a metal length of rebar.

Pepper cried out from the painful impact, held on with one armpit and grabbed the railing with one hand. His other arm was already half numb from hitting a nerve against the railing. He held on, gasping from the pain and impact.

The woman was screaming on the balcony Pepper had leaped from, and he tried to tune her out. He flexed the hand of his numb arm, trying to restore feeling, while holding onto the railing with his other hand.

Excruciating seconds passed. Ten seconds, a minute?

He felt his grip on the railing weaken. He needed to pull himself up before his hand slipped and he fell fifty feet to the sidewalk.

Dayana was yelling at Pepper, but he blocked her out. He snaked his right arm up and over the railing. He now hung there by both armpits.

He scrambled his legs against the concrete side of the balcony, trying to find purchase. Nothing. He swung out a leg as far as he could, his foot scratching the wall. It found a gap. He couldn't see, but it had to be the gap between the bottom of the railing and the concrete floor. He pushed up, trying to create leverage to raise himself. His foot slipped and he almost fell.

But he pushed off again with his foot while levering his forearms against the top of the iron balcony railing, and this time he crept upward. He swung his other foot into the gap between the balcony's floor and its railing. His feet were crazy wide, almost doing the splits, and he was getting tired and needed to get up. He hauled himself high, inch by inch, walking his legs toward each other.

Finally, he toppled himself over the railing, his body smacking down on the concrete floor. He lay there for a full minute, gasping for breath, his eyes closed.

As Pepper lay there, catching his breath, he heard Dayana's laughter from the other balcony. He finally crawled to his feet and saw her grinning at him. She pumped a fist and whooped. Despite the pain, he couldn't help but smile back, feeling a warmth spread through his chest that hopefully wasn't the result of internal bleeding. Guys throughout history had taken idiotic risks to win approval from women, and most of them had been a lot less gorgeous than Dayana de Melina.

The neighbor was clapping and cheering too, a cloud of cigar smoke surrounding her head, and Beriev was still filming.

But the next time I star in a fake Hollywood movie, thought Pepper, *I'm asking for a stunt man.* He limped over to look through the glass sliding door into the dead ballerina's apartment.

The lights were off, and it looked like a typical living room.

Pepper took out the knife he'd brought. He pulled at the handle of the sliding door and slid the knife up into the gap he'd created. The flimsy lock popped open after a minute of digging around.

He was in.

Which was outstanding, because there was no way he would have jumped the gap back to the cigar lady's apartment. Not for a million pesos.

As Pepper entered Carlina's apartment, he heard a knock at the front door. Dayana slow-clapped for Pepper when he opened it.

"Now, *that* was sexy!" she said with a grin.

Beriev was behind her, camera on his shoulder, rolling. The woman stood next to him, puffing smoke excitedly.

"We need to make this quick," said Pepper. "Someone might have seen his flailing balcony leap and called the PNR. If so, better to be gone when they arrived.

Pepper started in the living room. Gloria had said her daughter was a packrat, and it showed in that room. Besides the usual furniture were stacks of paper and boxes along one wall. Pepper started there, quickly sifting through everything, not exactly sure what he was looking for. Something that proved

Carlina was in trouble before she died. Maybe even a threatening note with the person's name and address at the bottom, and a postscript that said, "BTW, I'm el Segador."

Pepper didn't find that, but he found an item almost as interesting in a red and white *Romeo y Julieta Reserva* cigar box. It was a brand-new Cuban passport, dated August 13th of that year, accompanied by paperwork from the Cuban Ministry of Foreign Affairs approving issuance of her passport.

"She must have been planning to go somewhere," Pepper said to Beriev, who zoomed his camera in on the open passport. Pepper remembered from the police report Carlina had died on August 20th, one week later.

Using his phone, Pepper took a picture of the inside page with her unsmiling photo, her name and the issuance and expiry dates. Then he took a picture of the first page of the government paperwork.

He was putting everything back in the cigar box when Dayana came into the living room and stumbled to the couch, her face pale. "I was going to search her bedroom, but I could see the blood from the doorway! I just couldn't go in." She shook her head, then slumped down on the couch.

Pepper headed into the bedroom, followed by Beriev with his camera up, missing nothing. Since Pepper had read the murder report, he knew that Carlina's mother had been worried and found her daughter's bloody body on the bed, face down. According to the coroner, her killer had strangled her to death, then had repeatedly stabbed her corpse in the back.

The PNR had removed the bedsheets as evidence, and the bloodstain on the mattress was a narrow oval, which made sense. Pepper knew that blood seeped when a person was stabbed after death. It didn't spurt as when the victim's heart was still pumping.

Pepper shook off the tragedy and gore of the scene and got to work. He was looking for anything that would help him understand what had happened to Marisol, which might be part of what happened to Carlina. So he was casting a wide net for clues. He looked under the bed. Nothing. He quickly searched the bedside table. Nothing. When he opened the closet door, he spotted something unusual.

"Viktor, get a close-up of this," Pepper said to the cameraman, who was now standing right beside him.

It was a mural of photographs. He recognized Carlina Borja in many of them, but there was a mix of other smiling faces.

"That's Ozzie's dad!" pointed out Pepper. The Canadian CEO, Laurent Rappeneau, was in a group picture with Carlina Borja and three other attractive women. All smiling and dressed up, like they were at a party.

"He throws parties at his house and on his boat," commented Beriev. "All artists in Havana know Laurent Rappeneau. He's a big fan of art and beauty."

One of the candid photos showed Carlina with Rappeneau, both of them in swimsuits. It looked like they were on Rappeneau's yacht. In another photo, Carlina was in a black dress with the Canadian CEO at a fancy table for two, with desserts and champagne.

Pepper felt himself getting annoyed. The pictures contradicted what Rappeneau had told Pepper on his yacht in Hemingway Marina when they met. *"I shook her hand once,"* he'd *said.* Why had he lied? And it made Pepper wonder again. Why was the Canadian CEO listed as a person of interest in the PNR police report of Carlina's murder?

Pepper used his phone to take pictures of the photos. "Rappeneau seems to really have a way with the ladies," he commented to Beriev.

The cameraman laughed and kept filming. "Money talks, especially in Communist regimes."

Pepper moved on to Carlina's dresser, searching it quickly but finding nothing helpful. Then he pulled the dresser away from the wall, in case Carlina had hidden anything behind it.

He found something that likely had been hidden accidentally. It was an envelope that looked like it had fallen off the back of the dresser and gotten stuck in the crack of one of the two cross pieces that attached the mirror to the back of the dresser.

Pepper opened the envelope, his pulse quickening.

It was a handwritten letter on small, hand-cut pieces of off-white paper.

Pepper looked at the last page and saw a nearly illegible signature. But to him, it looked a lot like a name he recognized: Guillermo Infante. The man who, according to Gloria Borja, had been dating her daughter shortly before her murder.

Pepper skimmed the letter, struggling in spots because of his mediocre Spanish and the poet's sloppy handwriting. It seemed to be a long-winded breakup letter, full of excuses and tangents. He accused Carlina of being a traitor, then pivoted and complimented her ethereal dancing. He clarified he couldn't be with Carlina, for all of those reasons, plus the moon and the stars. Or crap to that effect.

Two parts of the letter sent a chill down Pepper's spine. One said, if Pepper was translating correctly, "We should die together. A perfect mutual climax." Then near the end of the letter, Infante admitted he's also obsessed with an American woman, a love that he fears will similarly end in tragedy.

So Carlina Borja and Guillermo Infante had been troubled lovers too? The poet got around almost as much as Laurent Rappeneau. And who was the American obsession—Marisol? Was Infante hinting that the unnamed American was a potential target for violence, or was his statement just melodramatic outgassing?

What the hell did women see in the poet with the bizarre facial grooming? Pepper was going to have to talk to Infante soon, to get more clarity about his history with Carlina, and to ask where he was when the dancer died.

Pepper used his phone again to take pictures of each page of the letter, because he'd promised Carlina's mother not to take anything from the apartment. He would study the letter in more detail when time permitted.

Pepper pushed the dresser and mirror back to the wall, leaving the letter on top of the dresser. Then he finished searching the room, not to find anything else, but he had a nagging feeling that he was missing something...

He took out his phone and flipped through the pictures he took on Wednesday of the PNR murder file. He stopped at the photos taken in the bedroom. Moving to the corner of the room, he looked around, then looked at the photos. Something wasn't right.

Pepper almost gave up. Then he recalled something distinctive in the photo that included the dresser and mirror.

He studied his picture of the document that inventoried items in the bedroom crime scene. He zoomed in on one that said *"Premio Nacional de Danza."* A National Dance Award. A note briefly described it as a gold medal on an elaborate ribbon, like an Olympic medal. The report said her medal was hanging from the corner of her mirror when the police inventoried the apartment.

But today that medal wasn't there. Pepper got on his hands and knees to ensure he hadn't knocked it off when he moved the dresser. But he didn't find it.

Had the police taken it into protective custody because of its value, or its prestige as a top award by the Cuban government? Or had someone else entered the apartment during the past four weeks since the PNR processed the crime scene? But if the person had been a thief, he could choose other valuables in the apartment that would be easier to dispose of, like the jewelry in her dresser. Had the killer returned and taken the medal as a memento of the killing ... like a prize? Pepper wouldn't ask Detective Guiteras, but could he ask Detective Valdés if the PNR had taken custody of it, without admitting to stealing the police report? If he could let her know the medal was now missing, it might score a point for Pepper to get some other info from the nicer, better-looking detective.

Pepper moved back out into the living room. Could Marisol have filmed anything here that would make the Cuban government look bad in relation to the artists' murders? Or that pointed to the killer? The Cuban government and the unknown serial killer remained the two most likely culprits in Marisol's disappearance, neck and neck.

Pepper paused, thinking he'd heard something, and realized it was footsteps in the apartment above.

Viktor chuckled. "Footsteps of a dead dancer, eh? This place gives me the creeps."

The neighbor was now sitting on the couch next to Dayana, chatting spiritedly while holding a hand below an impossibly long ash dangling from the tip of her cigar. She seemed both fascinated by what Pepper was doing and excited to be talking with the famous actress.

Pepper went into the kitchen, followed by Beriev and his camera, and searched it quickly but thoroughly.

Dayana said to Pepper, "She saw men come to the apartment two times after the police finished, but she doesn't know who they were."

Or she knows, but wants more pesos, thought Pepper. He wondered if the men were from the Cuban government, and whether they left with the National Dance Award medal. He took another two hundred pesos from his pocket and counted it twice in front of the woman.

The woman spoke in her fast, thick Spanish, of which Pepper understood about half.

Dayana said, "She means it. She saw the men, but didn't know why they were here. She would tell you. She's a big fan of your Hollywood movies."

Pepper had never been in any movies, and never wanted to be, but he appreciated that the woman was running with Dayana's earlier lie.

"We should go now," said Beriev.

But Pepper wasn't finished yet. And he knew he wouldn't get a second chance to search this apartment.

"Do you know what a *tavo* is?" asked Beriev. "A *chiva*?"

Pepper shook his head, still trying to think about where else to search.

"It's a snitch. A natural outgrowth of the police state. No one completely trusts other people here. Information is a commodity. People snitch to gain credit with the government. Sometimes even for money. Someone will have called the police if they saw you jumping balconies, and someone sees everything in Havana."

Pepper definitely didn't want for any of the PNR, especially Detective Guiteras, to find him in the dead ballerina's apartment. "I need a minute. Can you turn off the camera?"

Pepper went to Dayana, put a hand on her shoulder and softly asked, "Are you all right?"

Dayana took a deep breath, and her eyes glistened with tears. "It was the blood," she explained. "Where I grew up, I saw too much of it." In English, she told Pepper how her father and mother drank too much rum and would fight, and it often ended in bloodshed. "They never touched me. I think they believed my looks would lift us all out of the gutter. But to see my parents, my home, the blood ..." She shuddered. "I felt powerless and ashamed. And I decided I'd do whatever it takes to protect myself and the people I cared about, and never look back."

The woman from the next-door apartment was nodding along, apparently not understanding Dayana's English, but reading her sadness anyway. She put an arm around Dayana's shoulder, almost dislodging her cigar ash onto Dayana's head. Miraculously, the long curve of ash held.

"I'm sorry," said Pepper. "I want to hear more about your childhood. You've been through so much."

Dayana took a deep breath and exhaled quickly. "But Viktor is right. We should go."

Pepper helped her to her feet and felt her shiver at his touch. He almost kissed her at that moment, right in front of the cigar-puffing neighbor and Beriev's camera. Instead, he checked himself and said lightly, "And I can tell you about a love letter I found from Guillermo Infante."

"A love letter?"

Pepper laughed. "A letter only a bad poet could write. Full of emotional angst and bullshit. I have a PNR police report for Carlina's murder that lists Infante as a 'person of interest.' Maybe he's a crazy ex-lover. Can you help me meet with him as soon as possible?"

"Police report?" exclaimed Dayana. Her eyes grew larger. "Luis shared it with you? What else does it say—do they think Guillermo is el Segador? Oh my God, he said at the club he knew things about Mari's disappearance!"

"He's a person of interest, but that includes people like witnesses and acquaintances too."

"I need to read that!" said Dayana. "If el Segador took Mari..."

"Not a good idea," said Pepper. "Trust me. There are some very bloody photos."

Dayana pressed her lips together and shuddered. "Then I'll leave all that to you."

Pepper herded everyone out the door. The neighbor, slowest to leave, grinned conspiratorially at him, puffing her cigar. Pepper figured she was going to be telling stories about her adventure with Dayana de Melina and a crazy American movie star for a long time.

As Pepper locked the doorknob from the inside and pulled it firmly closed, he heard a police siren screaming faintly in the distance but growing louder.

CHAPTER FOURTEEN

Hector parked across the street from the Inglaterra Hotel in the heart of Old Havana, sang the last verse to "Heartbreak Hotel," then turned off the engine.

"You're a singer and you've seen the world," Hector said to Pepper. "Do I have what it takes to make it in Vegas?"

"You're the best damn Elvis I've ever met," Pepper said honestly, because Hector was the first. "Vegas won't know what hit it."

Hector grinned with pleasure, then pointed at the Inglaterra. "She is the oldest hotel in Cuba," he said. "Built in 1875."

It looked straight out of central casting for a tourist hotel in Cuba. Classic. Colonial. Pepper and Angel were highjacking a lunch date that Dayana had successfully scheduled with Guillermo Infante.

The lover-boy poet was going to be pissed off when Pepper and Angel arrived instead of Dayana. She had begged off joining them because of a meeting about a film role that she couldn't reschedule.

Beriev had also left to return his friend's Lada and get back to work on his all-important photography exhibition. Angel stayed with the Cadillac, because Pepper expected Infante would speak more freely to the two Americans.

A long open-air terrace lined the front of the Inglaterra Hotel, full of cafe tables. People drank coffee, or mojitos. The heavy smell of cigar smoke drifted to the sidewalk from several tables. Some people were eating, but most were socializing and drinking.

Pepper scanned the terrace but didn't see the odd poet. Pepper needed to find out the truth from Infante—what was his relationship with Marisol? With Carlota Borja? And what was the big news about Marisol and a major conspiracy that he'd insinuated at the nightclub? And if there was extra time at the end, he wanted to ask the man—what was up with the bizarro half-faced beard?

"Do you think he'll show?" asked Angel, clearing his throat. "The guy's a wacko, but he might tell us exactly what we've been looking for."

Angel's nervousness was clear to Pepper. He saw a boy was standing on the sidewalk, eating a banana, which reminded Pepper of a way to distract his buddy. "While we're waiting, why don't you tell me that Banana Incident story?" he asked. "The suspense is killing me."

Angel let out a high-pitched laugh and gave Pepper an elbow to the ribs. "Over my dead body," he grumbled.

Although Infante hadn't arrived yet, Pepper saw the not-so-helpful representative of the U.S. embassy, Heather Wilder, sitting in a cream-colored suit at a table at the far end of the terrace, alone. Wilder was puffing on a Churchill–sized cigar, looking out at the long row of classic cars parked at an angle across the street.

Half a sandwich was on a plate in front of her, accompanied by a bowl of olives and a half-empty martini glass. She looked like she was watching people go by, talking, arguing, enjoying the sunny day. Maybe waiting for someone?

Hopefully not waiting for Pepper...

"I'll be right back," he said.

He went the other way down the terrace, checking each table for Guillermo Infante. A dozen small groups there were drinking, chatting, hugging. But not the squirrely little poet. Was it cultural for Cubans to be fashionably late for appointments? How about odd Cuban poets?

Pepper went back and found that Angel had migrated down the terrace and joined Wilder at her table. Pepper took a seat at the table as well, facing the sidewalk, so he would see Infante when he arrived. The table was made of pretty hand-painted tiles. Wilder carefully placed her cigar in a big ashtray, and smoke floated around the table, spicy yet smooth.

"Ryan, what happened to your handsome face?" she said, peering closely at him. Her lip quivered from surprise. Or from amusement?

"The little meeting you set up, that's what. Did I already thank you for your help? I take it back."

She laughed. "But I bet you learned some things, too. Have a Montecristo?"

"No, thanks," Pepper said. "I'll leave the smoke blowing to the experts."

Wilder laughed again. "They say La Bodeguita del Medio has the best mojitos in Cuba, maybe the world. But I prefer the ones they serve here. And with a Montecristo number two for company? Heaven on earth."

"They must pay you diplomats well."

She popped an olive in her mouth. "Compared to back home, everything's cheap in Cuba, with the right connections. Even humble State Department bureaucrats live large in Havana."

"Cubans can't afford the Inglaterra," said Angel. "Not earning fifty dollars a month."

"True," laughed Wilder, taking a sip of her martini. "But I love it here. It reminds of what Havana has been and what it can be again someday."

For tourists and elites? thought Pepper.

A Cuban man walked up to them. "Friends, where are you from?" But Wilder shooed him away with a quick Spanish retort.

A gathering of younger Cubans in the park across the street was playing salsa music over a loudspeaker, which gave the terrace a perfect level of background music. It would have been a wonderful day in Havana if they weren't seated with Heather Wilder.

"Have you seen Guillermo Infante today?" Pepper asked her.

"The poet? Not yet. But he's a regular here, trying to sponge lunch off anyone who's amused by him. What nuggets of intelligence are you hoping to extract from him?"

"Anything he knows about Marisol," said Pepper. He didn't want to get into details with Wilder, because he didn't trust her.

The embassy officer chuckled. "And the FBI knows you're here investigating a missing-woman case? Because it puts me in an awkward position, knowing that a rogue FBI agent's running around Havana."

Pepper tried to shrug casually. "I'm currently off duty."

"I hope so," she said. "My section head sent a secure message to DC this morning, asking why an FBI special agent was in Havana."

Shit.

She shrugged innocently. "I couldn't stop him, sorry. Maybe if you fly home today—no blood, no foul?"

Pepper had a sudden case of heartburn, but tried to hide it. "Thanks for the heads-up. We've got to go find Infante."

She chuckled. "I hope you won't cause a scene. Beat him up, in front of all these tourists."

"Why would we?" asked Angel.

"Oh," she said. "You didn't know?"

"Know what?" asked Pepper.

"That Guillermo Infante has a history of canoodling with Marisol Borja?"

"What?" Angel asked in a husky voice.

Wilder laughed. "It wasn't much of a secret. They dated for a while during her earlier trips here."

Oh shit, thought Pepper. That news would freak out Angel, and it threw more complexity into Pepper's search for Marisol. Was Infante involved with Marisol before she started dating Angel back in the USA, or was there some overlap … ?

Wilder puffed her cigar, leaning back to blow a stream of smoke over Pepper's head. "I thought maybe Infante was angling for a U.S. visa, maybe a quickie marriage. Or sponsorship for some other visa category. There's been an uptick of high-profile Cuban artists emigrating to America—not that Infante is high profile, except in his own head."

This was a lot for Pepper to digest. Was it true? He was still aching all over from the way she set him up for trouble with Guiteras at the boxing gym. Had she done that to discourage Pepper from searching for Marisol, and maybe to set Detective Guiteras even more firmly against them? And how had her station chief learned about Pepper, if not from Wilder?

Whatever, he thought. He was here to pick Paredes' mind, not get tangled up by Wilder's mind games.

"You boys really should go home," she advised. "Leave Marisol Borja to the lawful local authorities."

"And if she's been in their custody all along?" asked Angel.

Wilder scratched her chin. "If I hear that, my embassy will do what it can. And trust me, that'll be more than you can do."

"Enjoy your smoke," said Pepper, and they left her, heading back to the other end of the terrace, looking for Infante. They now had even more questions for the odd poet.

Pepper felt blindsided by the news that Marisol and Infante had a romantic connection during her earlier trips to Cuba. Was Infante a crazy ex-boyfriend, capable of taking revenge against Marisol for moving on? And maybe even had a hand in Carlina Borja's murder?

But Pepper had been misled about what Marisol was filming in Cuba, so what else did he think was true? What else was he misunderstanding?

"I'm gonna kill that poet," Angel growled as they scanned the other end of the terrace.

"Wilder might have been lying," Pepper reminded him.

"She better be," said Angel. "That's one cold-hearted lady. It's like she gets off on spreading misery. She looked me in the eye back there, and I felt like I was being measured up as a snack by a great white shark."

They spotted Guillermo Infante seated at the far end of the terrace. He was wearing a multicolored scarf despite the midday heat and humidity.

Pepper and Angel joined his table without a word.

"This is a bad time," Infante said, brushing invisible dirt from his sleeve. "I have a date."

"Dayana sends her regrets—and a hug," said Pepper. "Which I'll skip."

The poet blinked at them, pulling himself up tall in his chair. He pulled out his phone, maybe reacting to the buzz of a text. He glanced at it, smiled mysteriously, and texted back. Then he returned the phone to his pocket.

"What's this about you and Marisol?" Angel asked Infante. "Is it true?"

Infante adjusted his scarf and raised a hand, trying to get the attention of a nearby waiter. But failed. He shrugged at Angel. "I don't know what you're talking about."

"Did you date Marisol Borja?" Angel clarified, his voice low and shaking. Pepper knew that voice. It usually came out shortly before Angel's fists.

The poet stared at Angel, then smiled. "The heart is a—"

Angel gave Infante a savage kick under the table. "The heart's a muscle that pumps blood through your body. So if you get punched in the nose, the heart keeps pumping, and you get blood all over your ridiculous face."

A waiter arrived, but any words of welcome froze in his mouth when he sensed the tension among the three men. He hurried away without a word.

"Too bad," said Angel. "I really wanted to try a mojito. But I probably would have accidentally spilled it on your head."

"Angel ..." warned Pepper. They needed the squirrely poet's cooperation. "Let's put that aside for now. Tell us what you meant at the club Wednesday night."

The poet waved a hand at another waiter. "Why should I tell you anything? You're putting my life in danger, asking me these questions in public. Do you know who's involved? The stakes?"

"So we'll all try to keep our voices down," said Pepper. "You said you told Mari the truth about the artists. That she didn't believe it was possible. You said you have proof. Tell us the whole thing, because strangely, I believe you. I think she should have listened to you."

Pepper was laying it on thick, but Infante nodded back. The poet smiled, distorting his half-beard and half-mustache. What the hell did women see in this guy?

"It was too much for Marisol to believe—sex, money, and power. I'll tell you the whole thing, but first I need to visit the men's room. When the waiter comes, get me an Aperol Spritz and a menu. You're buying." The poet stood, adjusted his scarf and his hair, then strutted off into the lobby toward the men's room.

"Buddy, you need to back off a bit," Pepper said to Angel. "We need to hear what he knows about Marisol and the dead artists. I'm going to ambush him about that breakup letter he sent to Carlina Borja, maybe surprise him into telling us something helpful. And at the club he was throwing around insinuations about Ozzie's dad too. Do you remember what else he said?"

Angel scoffed. "He called Dayana a whore and insulted America, but he was so damn flowery about it, it's hard to be sure." Angel waved at a waiter, who came their way. "But after we pump him about that, we're getting back to whether he was dating Marisol, and pin down a timeline. Maybe it happened on her first visit, but by Valentine's Day we were exclusive. And no way she was running around on me with *him*."

The waiter hovered a safe distance from the table, so Angel ordered the poet's drink, and Cokes for the two of them. A couple of minutes later, the waiter dropped off the three drinks and menus.

"We should grab a sandwich with him," commented Angel. "I'm starved."

"If Infante ever comes back," said Pepper. He had a bad feeling, so he got up and went into the hotel and asked directions to the men's room. Which he found empty.

"He bugged out," said Pepper when he returned to the table.

"Oh, I'm gonna kill him," growled Angel, causing their waiter to back away from their table again. "I'm gonna rip that half-beard off his squirrely little face."

Pepper's phone buzzed. It was Detective Valdés.

"My favorite PNR detective by far," Pepper said. "What can I do for you?"

"Are you okay, Pepper?" she asked, her voice heavy with worry.

What? "Sure," he said. "We're just about to get lunch at the Inglaterra."

"Forget that," she said. "We need to talk at your casa right now." No Ministry of Tourism bubbliness in her voice this time—was she upset about the police report Pepper had stolen?

But Pepper wanted to be friendly with Valdés. She was a hell of a lot easier to work with than Guiteras. And a lot better-looking. "If you want to join us here, we'll buy you lunch."

"Maybe another time," she said. "I'm standing in your casa, and you need to come immediately. Someone broke in and tore your casa apart."

CHAPTER FIFTEEN

Pepper and Angel hurried up the steps to the Casa de Vides' living room. They stopped, frozen with shock.

Someone really trashed the place.

Detective Lola Valdés, in a tan, well-tailored pants suit, was talking with the casa lady from downstairs. A uniformed police officer stood next to them.

Pepper couldn't believe what he was seeing. Someone had broken and flipped over furniture. Cut open cushions. They'd pulled the two guitars off the wall and snapped one in half. The room stank of stale coffee, which the intruder had poured on the living room area rug.

On the wall where the guitars had hung, someone had written with a black marker in English: *"Yumas go home or die!"*

"What the hell!" gasped Angel.

Pepper was too speechless to respond. He felt sick to his stomach. Holding up a finger to Valdés, he wordlessly asked her to give him a minute. He needed to check on his stolen police report without drawing the detective's attention.

She nodded.

Feeling numb, Pepper checked his bedroom and found it

similarly trashed. The intruder had emptied Pepper's duffel bag and strewn his clothes and toiletries around the room. Including the suit he'd packed for his FBI meeting. *Shit.*

Then Pepper hustled into the kitchen, his heart beating hard. He looked over his shoulder to make sure he was alone, then opened the oven and reached deep inside. His heart thumped when he realized that the stolen police report folder was still where he'd hidden it, tucked against the ceiling of the oven, wedged under the top heating element.

"Good thing neither of us bakes," said Angel at Pepper's shoulder, startling him.

"Quick, stuff this in your pants, under your shirt," said Pepper. "I'm screwed if they find it."

"So, plant it on your best friend instead?" Angel grumbled. "Classic." But he quickly did what Pepper asked.

Going back to the living room, they found Hector had parked the Caddy and joined them. All the blood was drained from the young man's face. "I told you we should be careful," he said. "Was this to scare you, or to find something?"

"Or both?" guessed Pepper. He tried to suppress his rising anger and think straight. Maybe someone thought they had the footage from Marisol's footage from August. Or maybe they were trying to get the police report Pepper had stolen. For either of those scenarios, the number one candidate was the same person: Juan Guiteras. The detective had all but accused Pepper of stealing it when they'd faced off at the boxing gym.

But if the motive was to intimidate them, Pepper had to admit there were plenty of other people that he and Angel had pissed off since arriving in Havana. Practically everyone they'd met.

Angel picked up the two halves of the broken guitar, which were loosely connected by its twisted strings. "There goes the security deposit," said Angel. "But at least they couldn't mess with my luggage—somebody else already stole it." He stacked the guitar pieces in the corner.

Then another idea occurred to Pepper. "Hector, can you call Beriev? Let him know what happened here, and to be careful?" Whoever trashed this place might think Beriev's home was the next best place to search for the Monkey hard drive footage.

"The plot sickens," Angel joked, with little humor.

Detective Valdés said, "Come look at this." She led them all into the kitchen. "We think the intruder entered by this back door," she said. She opened a narrow door that Pepper had assumed was a broom closet, but when he poked his head in, he found a thin, twisting staircase.

"I should've noticed this on Wednesday," he muttered. A second exit was invaluable as a fire exit, but was also vulnerable to intruders. Whoever trashed the apartment might have taken this route, arriving and departing with no witnesses.

Pepper and Angel followed the rickety stairway down one floor and arrived at an impossibly narrow corridor, probably just a hallway constructed to fill the gap between the two buildings. Pepper's shoulders touched both walls at the same time.

He saw doors along the hallway, leading into the neighboring building. He and Angel tried them, and they were all locked. At the end of the makeshift hallway, Pepper found another narrow stairway that twisted downward to the street level, emptying into a back alley.

"We'd better try to lock that door upstairs tonight," Angel suggested glumly. "Or at least get something to block it." He ducked into the bathroom and Pepper heard water running.

Pepper's phone rang. It was Ozzie Rappeneau.

"Hey!" said the Canadian. "Just checking in. My dad wondered if Marisol turned up yet."

"Nope," said Pepper. "But we had another run-in with

Guillermo Infante, and someone broke into our apartment and tore it apart."

"Crap on a cracker!" said Ozzie. "But no leads about Mari?"

"Not really. We've been talking to people, but so far it's like chasing a ghost."

"Dad's actually pretty pissed off, because he heard gossip that Mari changed film projects. She interviewed him in August and he donated a hundred grand for her movie, because he's such a big nut about flowers. So he's pissed to hear she's spending it on a movie about murdered artists."

"Why's he mad?" asked Pepper, although he had a good guess.

"Bad for business, having his name on that kind of project. Might piss off the big shots here in Cuba, you know? But I say good for Mari. The dead artists matter more than some stupid flowers..."

Pepper thought about it. Was the money a donation to support the arts, or was a quid pro quo expected from Marisol? He needed to learn more about the story behind the hundred grand.

"So, what's your next move?" asked Ozzie. "And how can I help?"

Pepper thought a bit, then said, "Can you spend some time figuring out all connections between the dead artists? Other than them being successful artists and stabbed to death? Did they all know each other?"

"Sure, I'll ask my dad. And I'll think about it too. I know some of them hung out together. But other than that magazine article, nothing really comes to mind, you know?"

"The *Vanity Fair* article?" guessed Pepper.

"Good, you knew about that? They did a piece late last November about Cuba's ten biggest artists of the twenty-first century. Less than two months later, one of those featured artists, a writer, was murdered. And then three more artists from the article got murdered in May, July, and August. It's like el Segador's using that damn article as his kill list."

Maybe the article took shots at the Cuban government, or speculated that the artists would be more successful if they left Cuba.

It also made Pepper wonder: who were the other six artists in that article, and were they still alive? "Can you find me a copy of that article?"

"You got it, man," said Ozzie, and hung up.

"Let's sit," said Detective Lola Valdés, back upstairs in the kitchen. She tightened her ponytail and gave the two friends a sympathetic smile.

Pepper noticed that Angel was sitting up ramrod straight, thanks to the police folder shoved down the back of his pants.

The uniformed policeman had herded the casa lady and Hector out into the living room, and Pepper could hear furniture being tipped back over.

"She called the police emergency number," said Valdés. "She thought maybe you yumas got drunk and started tearing up the place."

"We're completely sober, unfortunately," muttered Angel.

Valdés chuckled. "I have some questions for the two of you. When did you leave here this morning?"

They gave her all the basic information she asked for, but avoided volunteering much about the people they'd each talked to that morning—the Borja relatives and other people who knew Marisol, to learn whether they'd heard from her.

Surprisingly, she didn't push them about their activities, but she might be avoiding any information she wouldn't want to pass on to Guiteras.

"Did the intruder steal Marisol Borja's video footage from August?" she asked.

"I talked about that with Detective Guiteras," Angel said. "That external hard drive was in Marisol's luggage, which the taxi driver stole around the time she disappeared on Monday."

She made eye contact with Pepper. "You Americans have a saying: scratch my back, I'll scratch yours?"

Pepper had a quick mental image of what the detective's back would look like beneath her duty blouse. He blushed. "We do. What would you like?"

"I need that hard drive. Detective Guiteras is impatient about it, and he doesn't believe you. And I want to see the look on his face when I bring it to him."

"We'll do what we can," promised Pepper. "But while we're scratching backs, could you get me something?"

"Yes?"

"I think Marisol's disappearance is tied to the four artist deaths. Can you get me a copy of the police reports, so I can understand how she might tie in to the cases?"

Valdés laughed loudly and flashed her big white smile. She was probably in her early thirties, but when she laughed, she looked like a teenager. "You're the funniest man I've met in a long time. Four police reports or three?"

Pepper coughed. "If you could, ah, give me all four reports, that'd be a big help."

She grinned. "Then you will owe me a big one, I think. Good."

Angel kicked Pepper under the table.

"Thank you, Detective," said Pepper.

"Call me Lola," she said, and smiled again.

Pepper shifted his legs out of Angel's reach, and a moment later his buddy kicked the table leg and yelped.

"Any hope that the PNR will find Angel and Marisol's stolen luggage?" he asked. Pepper was okay with the police getting the external hard drive if he got the police reports in trade, but how was he going to find the luggage while searching for Marisol?

Valdés frowned, almost as cutely as she smiled. "Probably not," she admitted. "But I will be cheering for you. And if you fail, consider hiring someone to help you."

"Like ... a private detective?"

She laughed again. "No, no, your Elvis friend in the other room can point you to the right people to hire. We call them jineteros. They find anything for *yumas*, for a price. No one loves money more than Communists."

Pepper only knew one group of jineteros—Quinto and his buddies from the nightclub. Would hiring them be more trouble than they were worth?

When Valdés headed downstairs to leave, Angel pushed Pepper to follow with him. The detective's vehicle was parked right in front of the casa—a small, plain unmarked car by a manufacturer Pepper didn't recognize. It was the color of melted vanilla ice cream.

"Is this a Geely?" Angel asked incredulously, peering into the car's backseat. "I've never seen one in real life before! A real Beijing special!"

Angel's excitement baffled Pepper. He opened the driver's door for Valdés, then touched her arm. "Hey, what's the deal with Guiteras? Does he hate all Americans, or just me?"

Angel was behind the detective, still peering into the odd little car. He seemed fascinated.

The detective turned to Pepper, standing about six inches away. At six two, Pepper was probably about eight inches taller. She looked up at him, shielding her eyes against the sun, and gave a sweet frown. "Juan can be pigheaded at times. The artist murders—I think these cases are eating him alive. But he's a very patriotic Cuban. I'm sure he believes everything he learned in school about evil imperialist yumas. Or maybe he's just jealous."

"Jealous?"

Valdés touched Pepper's arm. "You're in law enforcement back home...you figure it out."

She slid into the front seat and Angel stepped away from the car as Pepper shut the driver's door.

"Thanks, Detective," said Pepper, giving her one of his best smiles.

"Call me Lola," she said, smiling back. Then she raised her eyebrows at him, gave a little wave, and drove away.

"Call me Lola. . ." imitated Angel. "I think she wants to frisk you thoroughly, mano. But I'm glad she didn't see what I did."

"What you did?"

"I tossed the police report into her backseat. She'll find it and she'll know it was from us, but she'll have what bureaucrats love worldwide—plausible deniability." Angel laughed, the first full belly laugh he'd heard from Angel since Pepper had arrived in Cuba. The laugh that defined Angel as well as anything about him, but which had been in hiding because of the Marisol crisis.

"Angel!" Pepper was dumbfounded. He'd been thinking about finding the right time to fess up to Valdés and return the report. If she didn't arrest him on the spot, maybe it would help build trust with her.

"You're welcome," said Angel. "I even took it in the bathroom and wiped off your grubby fingerprints."

Pepper hoped the detective wouldn't react the wrong way when she found the report...like they thought she was an idiot who could be fooled by such a basic stunt.

Finally, Pepper shook his head and laughed. Angel meant well, and he was just trying to protect Pepper, even if his particular methods were nuts.

Pepper put his arm around his buddy's shoulder. "Let's go talk to Hector. We need to go hire us an entrepreneurial Communist."

CHAPTER SIXTEEN

Barbara Buckley, the supervisor of the New Albion Police Department's dispatch desk on Cape Cod, answered Pepper's call on the second ring.

"Pepper Ryan!" she said. "What pile of shit do you find yourself stuck in, this fine fall morning?"

"Barbara!" he complained. "Why would you assume that?" Even though she was right. Pepper was desperate, calling her for special help. He estimated about a fifty-fifty chance he'd get it.

Barbara was a longtime employee of the town force. Pepper's dad had hired her back when he was chief of police. He could picture Barbara, curly gray hair, in her wheelchair, with a cigarette between her lips. Either lit or unlit, depending on her location. A bag of Dunkin' donuts would be within reach.

"Pepper, this is my day off. I've got a bridge game in ten minutes. Speak."

"I was hoping you could do me a little favor."

"A little favor?" she laughed, which turned into a cough. "Is this a little favor that'll get me fired? Or get someone blown up?"

Pepper winced. "Of course not! I need cell phone GPS data

and location history for a woman who's missing. Who could I call but my favorite girl?"

Barbara harrumphed. "Your favorite girl, Zula, is up to her cute ass in law school. So you're bugging me instead? Aren't there any gullible career women at the FBI to do your grunt work?"

Pepper definitely didn't want to talk to her about Zula or the FBI right now. "Barbara, it's not an FBI case. It's about Angel's girlfriend. She's been missing since Monday. She disappeared right off the street with no witnesses. Angel's freaking out."

Pepper gave her Marisol's full name, home address in Brooklyn, and her AT&T cell phone number. "Do you have a contact at AT&T to make an off-the-record request for her phone's GPS data and location history?"

"What kind of criminal mischief was this girlfriend up to?"

"No, she's not a suspect in anything," emphasized Pepper. "She's a missing person, so I really need to skip the time and hassle to get a warrant."

"My AT&T pal is friendly because I haven't gotten him in trouble with screwball requests."

"Thanks, Barbara, you're the best! And one other favor, can you keep this a secret?"

"You mean if the General knew, he'd tell you to go soak your head? Pepper, I'm not promising anything. Nothing. Nada."

"The General" was everyone's nickname for New Albion's Chief of Police Donald Eisenhower, except to his face. "I'm ah ... I've gotta jump into a big meeting."

"Your big FBI meeting? To find out if you still have a job?"

"It is a very bad idea," said Hector, as he and Pepper drove across Havana.

"It'll be fine," Pepper said, hoping he was right. He'd phoned

Quinto Chavez, who'd, after some wary, verbal sparring, had finally agreed to meet with Pepper. Whether he would tell Pepper anything that helped him find Marisol remained to be seen.

Pepper had asked Angel to stay at Casa de Vides, to keep working the phones in the network of his Cuban relatives and to try the local hospitals for the third time. They had their hands full trying to find Marisol, and time was short.

Soon after, Pepper and Hector parked at a broken curb in the Jesús María neighborhood near the address Quinto had given Pepper. Jesús María was close to the historic heart of Havana, but according to Hector, it had fallen by the wayside in recent decades. Crumbling housing and not much economic activity.

Quinto's address was a building in rough condition, second from the corner. Four stories high. The top three floors were in terrible repair, and their butterscotch and gray facades and colonial stone balconies blended with the neighborhood. But the building's ground floor was painted purple, with a modern white-trimmed window and a white door. Three garbage bins almost blocked the door.

Pepper watched the building and the street, assessing the situation. Men and women were hanging around in small groups, standing on the sidewalk or huddled in doorways. Farther down the street near the next corner, a long, wide line of people filled the broken sidewalk, waiting in a queue for something.

"Is a government store," explained Hector. "Everyone waits six, maybe eight hours." He explained that each of them would get a small allotment of heavily subsidized meat, rice, beans, and other food. "The people resell on the black market as much as they can spare."

Then Hector explained that the jineteros's hustle was next level, because they tapped into the tourist trade. "Every tourist is rich, to Cubans," noted Hector. He explained that the only trick was to figure out what would get the tourists to hand over their US dollars or Euros: maybe cigars, or rum, or women. The jineteros would supply anything for a price.

Pepper smiled. "And that's why we're here."

When Pepper and Hector approached the purple building with the white door, Hector kept looking around in all directions, like he expected an ambush. Hector had explained that jineteros' hustles were mainly financial, so why was the young Cuban so nervous? Maybe because the first time Pepper encountered them, it'd devolved into a street fight and car chase?

A skinny boy sat on the purple building's front step, eating a plantain. When Pepper and Hector approached, the boy jumped up, flicked his plantain skin into the street, and disappeared through the white door, closing it firmly behind him.

They stood there for a full two minutes, with Hector shuffling his feet nervously.

"We should go," said Hector, but before Pepper could answer, the door opened and the boy nonchalantly waved them in.

The inside of the first floor was a big, open space, like a car garage with all the equipment and cars missing. There were a few old couches and crates arranged around the space as tables, but it was otherwise empty, except for seven unhappy men.

Each of the men, except one, held a weapon. A few had machetes, two held baseball bats, and one was lightly swinging a length of chain.

Quinto stood empty-handed in front of them like the alpha of the group. The jinetero leader had a black-and-blue bruise on the side of his face, and he also had a bulge under the front of his shirt. A handgun?

Pepper also recognized two other Cuban men from the fight outside the club.

"Thanks for meeting with us," said Pepper.

Behind Quinto, a tall guy with tape over the bridge of his nose slapped his baseball bat in the palm of his hand. He growled something at Quinto.

Quinto turned to him and growled something in Spanish that Pepper didn't understand. The tall guy hefted his bat, glaring at Quinto. He looked like he was about to rebel. One of the other men took him by the arm and pulled him back.

Quinto's face shook with barely controlled anger. "You're loco to be here, after what you did," said Quinto. "He wants to break your nose with his bat, and then get violent."

"That's why I'm here. I wanted to apologize for what I said outside the club. I didn't know you and Carlina Borja were family." It was softer than saying, *sorry I accused you of sleeping with your stepsister*.

Quinto shrugged. "You came all the way here to apologize? I accept."

"A few other things too," said Pepper. "You talked to Marisol Borja on Monday at the Plaza de San Francisco de Asís, right before she went missing. Do you know what happened to her?"

Quinto studied Pepper. He looked at the other jineteros, communicating silently with them. Half of them were glaring at Pepper. The other half looked like they didn't understand enough English to be following the conversation. Then Quinto laughed. "So you came here to buy information?"

Pepper sighed. He pulled out some peso notes that he'd tucked in a pocket, anticipating this development. He held them up. "If you have information worth buying?"

Quinto stepped forward and snatched the money from Pepper's hand. It was 1,500 pesos, worth around $25 American dollars. About half a month's salary in Cuba...

"Why did Marisol ask you to meet her there?" asked Pepper.

Quinto shook his head. "It was a coincidence. I saw the yuma cousin of my stepsister who passed away. So she is family, and we said hello."

"One vendor told me he saw you arguing."

The jinetero with the length of chain rattled it at his side, and Pepper saw Hector tense up. But Quinto said something sharp to the chain rattler, and he stopped.

"He was mistaken," said Quinto. "I asked Marisol to do me a favor. Maybe I took her by surprise. She was in a hurry and she said no, but I tried to convince her."

"What kind of favor?"

Quinto shrugged. "It was just business."

"And then she left the plaza with you?"

Quinto looked genuinely surprised. "No! I asked her to think about it, and we said goodbye."

"So you don't know what happened to her, right after you talked?"

Quinto shrugged. "Why would I lie? I saw nothing."

Hmmm. Pepper didn't think Quinto was lying, but he probably wasn't telling everything he knew, either.

"We're worried about Marisol," tried Hector. "Like you said, she's your family. Is there nothing else you can tell us?"

Quinto shrugged again. "When I left her, she was okay. The rest is a mystery."

Pepper fought down his frustration. "Okay, well, think about it. If you remember anything else that would help, call me."

The skinny boy trotted back into the room, went to Quinto, and whispered in his ear. Then the boy disappeared back through the front door.

"Did anyone follow you here?" Quinto asked accusingly.

Pepper looked at Hector, who looked back, shaking his head, his face turning pale. "I didn't see anyone," said Pepper. "And I was looking."

One of the other men swore in Spanish, but Quinto silenced him with a gesture. "Okay, okay. Tell me about your other problem."

Other problem? wondered Pepper, laughing on the inside. *Where to start?*

But Quinto continued quickly. "I hear Marisol and her yuma boyfriend had their luggage stolen on Monday too."

"Yeah? Where'd you hear that?" asked Pepper.

Quinto shrugged and held his hands wide. "Our business is getting things for tourists. Maybe you should hire us to find the bags."

Pepper liked that idea. He wanted to watch the footage Marisol filmed in August—it might hold the key to Marisol's disappearance. And after he watched it, he could hand it to Detective Valdés, hopefully in exchange for more case information from her. He needed all the goodwill as he could get within the PNR. Not to mention, it would be great to recover Angel's dead grandmother's engagement ring. Angel's mother would kill him when she found out he'd lost it. And it wouldn't hurt to get back some spare underwear and deodorant for Angel...

Pepper took out two twenties, and a ten, then held them up. "I'll pay you fifty American dollars now, and a hundred more when you bring me their four bags with all their belongings." He knew that a hundred fifty dollars was three months' pay for a typical Cuban.

One of the other men, holding a machete, snarled something unintelligible to Pepper.

"He still wants to chop you up," said Quinto. "Feed you to the fish in Havana Bay. We could find your bags anyway, sell everything in them to pay for the damage you did to our motorbikes."

Pepper put out his hands in a peaceful gesture. "Nothing in the bags is worth a hundred and fifty bucks," he lied. "But I want them all back, with everything inside. If anything's gone, so is your money."

Quito crossed his arms. "Maybe we find your bags, but it is not so easy. And lots of expenses, you know? People don't talk for free, not even to us. We can do our best effort for two hundred dollars. If you pay me now, we start right away."

Pepper noticed that the semicircle of men was slowly inching closer to him and Hector. "I didn't bring that much money here, but I have it. Here's fifty." Pepper held up two American twenties and a ten. He waved them gently. "If you want the rest, get me the bags and the taxi driver's name and address."

Pepper smiled, thinking about the not-so-gentle conversation Angel hoped to have with the taxi driver. Was the man involved in Marisol's disappearance, or was he just an opportunistic thief? And if the latter, had he at least seen what happened to Marisol?

"And if you get me the luggage by tomorrow, I'll give you an extra fifty dollars as a bonus," Pepper said. His remaining time in Cuba was incredibly short—it would be money well spent.

Quinto looked around at his companions, then nodded sharply. "Deal."

The jinetero pocketed the fifty dollars. "What did they look like, the taxi and the driver? Was it—"

The skinny lookout boy burst through the front door. With a sidelong glance at Pepper and Hector, he darted to Quinto and whispered in his ear.

"*Vamos*!" said Quinto, making a gesture toward the back of the building. Two of the men ran and pushed aside a pile of junk, exposing a narrow doorway.

"Hey!" yelled Pepper. "You need to—"

The seven jineteros and the boy disappeared through the door, pulling it shut behind them.

Pepper ran to the door and gave it a tug, but it was locked.

The front door banged open again, letting in a horizontal streak of sunlight. A man stood in the doorway. It was backlit so Pepper couldn't see his face, but he didn't need to. He could tell by the man's outline that it was Detective Juan Guiteras.

CHAPTER SEVENTEEN

How on God's green earth did the detective know where Pepper was? Because Pepper didn't believe in coincidences, not with Guiteras.

"You promised not to investigate during your time in Havana," said the detective, "So, let me guess—you came here to buy Montecristo number twos?"

Pepper said nothing.

"Or maybe you are interfering with my cases and I need to arrest you both?" mused Detective Guiteras.

Pepper waved a hand. "Not sure what you're doing here, but Hector was just taking me to sample a few of Havana's best mojitos." He walked toward the exit, and Hector followed close behind him.

But Guiteras blocked their path. "Is my English not clear enough? I know you are still investigating the disappearance of Marisol Borja. After I clearly warned you to stop. Where's her photographer, Viktor Beriev?"

"What?" asked Pepper. "No idea. Why do you want to talk to him?" Although if Pepper had to guess, Beriev was probably at the photo gallery fiddling with his big exhibition. But Pepper's jaw still ached from the boxing gym, and a couple of his teeth still felt loose. So why help the Cuban detective?

"He is a prime suspect in the artist murders, so that makes him a suspect in the disappearance of Senorita Borja," said Guiteras. "Did he tell you where he was on the afternoon she disappeared? Or on the nights that the four artists died?"

Beriev? "Why, is he a suspect?"

Guiteras shrugged. "In each case he claims he was home alone, working on his art or drunk. So no alibi at all. And he fits the profile for el Segador—an English–speaking man, probably a foreigner, who knew all the victims personally."

Pepper could guess, but he asked, "Why?"

"A man, because it is very rare for women to be serial killers in any country," said Guiteras. "A foreigner because Cubans are not serial killers. And because the killer left an English–language copy of the Hemingway novel *To Whom the Bell Tolls* with each victim. Cubans are fond of Papa Hemingway, but a Cuban killer so inclined? Trust me, there are many of our own writers whose work would better serve that purpose, for Cubans."

That made sense to Pepper, as a semi-biased, semi-educated guess. "Why do you think the killer knew the victims personally?"

Guiteras gestured dramatically. "He knew the best places to find them alone. Where they lived, where they worked. Their schedules."

Maybe, thought Pepper. The Belarusian definitely had a guarded style. Getting information out of him about his personal life or his past was like pulling teeth from a turtle. The only thing Beriev talked about freely was his art. But the idea of him being a killer or a kidnapper seemed damned thin. And how would he have known Marisol would stop at that plaza at that exact time on Monday afternoon?

Pepper heard the buzz of Guiteras' phone. The detective checked its screen and grimaced. "No more interfering," said the detective. "And no more warnings." Then he turned and left the building.

Hector let out a sigh of relief that echoed around the big, empty room.

"Exactly," said Pepper.

Pepper and Hector drove back toward Centro Havana, with Elvis' "Suspicious Minds" playing loudly enough to make the Cadillac's speakers crackle.

"That is a dangerous man," Hector yelled over the music.

"Definitely an asshole," Pepper yelled back. He wondered why Guiteras had a hard-on for Viktor Beriev. Was he really a prime suspect in the artist murders, or did the PNR have some other problem with the Belarusian photographer, such as his camera work for Marisol's unauthorized el Segador film?

Pepper guessed that all artists in Cuba started with two strikes against them, since their art could always be a threat to the regime.

Then Hector turned down the music. "And now he is following us," he said, glancing repeatedly at his rearview mirror.

Pepper turned and took in the traffic behind them. Havana's typical motley mix of vehicles. "Which car?"

"The silver one—a Peugeot, very nice. For a newer car."

Pepper thought about it. "Do the police have Peugeots here?"

Hector made a face. "They have anything they take."

"Maybe he wants us to see him. To be intimidated."

"Okay, it is working," grumbled Hector.

Pepper told Hector to turn left at the next intersection, and then turn left three more times. Completely circling the block.

Pepper looked back. The silver Peugeot was now right behind them.

"Either Cuban police are the worst tailers in the world," said Pepper. "Or he wants us to know we're being watched."

Hector looked nervous. "What should we do? And don't say another car chase!"

Pepper looked around to get his bearings. They were in Old Havana, approaching a building with a sign that said El Floridita. Pepper knew it was famous as the birthplace of the frozen rum drink called the daiquiri, as well as one of Ernest Hemmingway's favorite drinking holes. As a busy tourist trap, El Floridita would offer a conveniently public place to bring this low-speed pursuit to an end. "Park there," said Pepper, gesturing at a row of parking spaces next to El Floridita, most of which were empty.

"Serious?" Hector's hand was shaking on the wheel.

"Whichever spot you like," said Pepper. "That should be Cuba's tourism slogan. Come to Havana—lots of free parking."

"Señor Pepper, you're loco."

Once Hector parked, the Peugeot pulled in tight behind the Cadillac, blocking them in. Ignoring the other empty parking spots.

"I told you," said Hector. The young man took his shaking hands off the steering wheel and hugged himself.

The Peugeot's windows were darkly tinted, so Pepper couldn't see inside. Was Guiteras waiting for backup?

"What do we do?" Hector asked.

"We wait too."

And they did. But the Peugeot stayed where it was, and no one got out.

"Maybe we get out and run for it?" suggested Hector.

Pepper laughed. "I'd rather go have a daiquiri."

"They are good," admitted Hector. "Small, but they kick your *culo*."

"*Culo?*"

"Is how we call your ass."

"Sometimes culos need a good kicking," said Pepper.

His boss would have said that was exactly the wrong attitude. Was Pepper wired wrong for proper law enforcement, as Youngblood had said?

Pepper couldn't deny he was impulsive and headstrong. And he knew those qualities meant he might never be a model law enforcement officer. But was he ready to move on? Or was he capable of trying to change...to become more disciplined and more responsible?

Two months had gone by since his misadventures on Cape Cod that had saved the president's life, and even though Pepper thought he'd learned from those experiences, deep down he knew that he'd do it all again, the same way, if that's what it took to save the president's life.

So, yeah. Maybe Pepper was wired wrong.

He wanted to live up to Youngblood's expectations for him, but he would have to start after he got back to America, because the assholes in the Peugeot were pissing him off. "Speaking of culos to kick, wait here," he said.

"Pepper! Is a bad idea! Just—"

But Pepper was already out of the Cadillac and approached the Peugeot. He smacked a flat hand on Guiteras' window four times in quick succession. Intentionally obnoxious.

After a long pause the driver's window motored down, but the driver wasn't Juan Guiteras. It was Lola Valdés, the far nicer PNR detective, alone in her car.

She grinned at Pepper. "Hop in," she said.

"I was just working on getting you that August footage," he said when he was seated. "Your pal Guiteras interrupted me."

She laughed. "He blames you for a lot of his troubles."

"He's hated me since before we met. He probably blames me for that hurricane headed this way too."

She laughed. "I think he's jealous of you and Dayana de Melina."

"What?"

"Or should I tell him you're gay?"

"No ..."

She made a face. "Then he will keep presuming and keep hating you."

"Fair enough." With some people, Pepper was more comfortable being hated.

"But I myself would rather get along." She slid some manila folders from the crack between her seat and the gearshift and handed them to him. "You didn't get these from me."

"Get what from you?" asked Pepper.

"Exactly. And let your cute friend know I saw his silly little sleight of hand, tossing the Carlina Borja file in my backseat. Does he think I was staring at your blue eyes so hard, I was blind? Please ..."

Cute friend? thought Pepper.

"And when you find that August footage, you will give it to me, not Luis, *si*?"

"Gladly."

Valdés slid sideways in her seat, her eyes fixed on Pepper. "And while I'm being so generous, I have a piece of reliable gossip for you," she said, her voice low and serious. "Laurent Rappeneau tipped off someone high in the Cuban government about Marisol Borja a week after she left Cuba. He told them she'd abandoned her orchid documentary and started looking into the serial killings."

Pepper was shocked to silence, trying to process the bombshell information. Finally he said, "Why would Rappeneau do that?"

Valdés shrugged. "Maybe to curry favor with the Cuban

government. But there's another possibility." She paused, choosing her words carefully. "Rappeneau's a wealthy and influential foreigner here. I've received tips suggesting he might be using his status to cover up his involvement in criminal activities in Cuba. Nothing concrete, but it's worth considering."

A realization dawned on Pepper. "Rappeneau's son Ozzie told me his dad donated a hundred grand in August to Marisol's film project. Maybe Rappeneau was trying to keep her quiet about some of his dirty laundry that she'd dug up."

Valdés nodded. "And maybe later he decided the bribe wasn't enough."

How far would the Canadian CEO go to silence Marisol? Try to get her banned from Cuba by ratting her out to the government? Would he go as far as snatching her off the street? Pepper's mind raced with the possibilities.

"Maybe you should go try to find out tonight," suggested Valdés. "Rappeneau's throwing one of his big parties at his house in Miramar. VIPs only, the cream of the one percent in Havana. Maybe his son would add you to the guest list. You could dig around for anything that ties him to Marisol's disappearance, or to anything else illegal."

Pepper thought about the suggestion. "Don't take this the wrong way, but what's in all this for you? You're taking a lot of chances here. Don't tell me you're this generous to every yuma cop who rolls into town."

She shrugged prettily. "Like I said, Laurent Rappeneau's an influential foreigner here. He has friends in the highest places. So what do you think would happen to a junior detective who starts digging into him without hard evidence first?"

That made good sense to Pepper.

"But listen," Valdés said, her tone urgent. "If you find any hard evidence of Rappeneau's criminal dealings tonight, bring it to me. Not to Luis. Okay?"

Pepper met her gaze. "If I find anything solid, I'll call you first."

"*Perfecto*," smiled Valdés. "I hope you discover tonight what happened to your friend Marisol." Then she wrinkled her nose. "Now go shower for that party, yuma—you need it!"

CHAPTER EIGHTEEN

After such a fun day, what else was there to do but crash a party full of Cuba's elite? He called Dayana to beg her to accompany him, but as he began explaining how she could help, she cut him off.

"It's a date," she said. "Now goodbye, I need to do my hair!"

Hector was still rattled from earlier, so Pepper gave him a break. He picked up Dayana in a taxi, which they took through a tunnel to Havana's historic Miramar neighborhood. They passed its famous clock tower, then the fortress-like Russian embassy. Its concrete tower looked like Russia was pointing a middle finger at Miami.

Laurent Rappeneau's address was a mile farther. The taxi dropped them off just before nine, at the end of a long driveway.

It was the largest art deco house Pepper had ever seen, highlighted by floodlights hidden among grand palm trees. He whistled. "What's a place like this cost?"

"His company rents it," said Dayana. "They don't let foreigners buy property in Cuba. That would be an embarrassment for the Revolution."

Pepper was wearing the blue suit and white dress shirt he'd

brought from home for his DC meeting. No tie, because it was still too damned hot and humid.

Dayana was wearing a short red dress that would have brightened up the Oscars' red carpet. She looked stunning. Hopefully stunning enough to get them both into Rappeneau's party, despite not being on the guest list. Pepper was wearing the suit he expected to get fired in on Monday back in DC.

Pepper had phoned Ozzie to wangle an invitation, but the Canadian playboy hadn't picked up. Dayana had said not to worry. She had an open invitation to Rappeneau's parties, and she would sneak in Pepper as her companion. But he would owe her one ...

She didn't say one what. So Pepper briefly allowed his dirty imagination to run wild.

This party—a large gathering of Havana's government, business, and arts elite—was probably the wrong time and place, but Pepper couldn't wait. The clock was ticking; the hurricane was getting closer.

"This place would impress Angel," he commented. His buddy had been desperate to join them, but Pepper wanted to corner Rappeneau one on one. He thought the Canadian would be more candid that way. So Angel was phoning a long list of the people Marisol knew in Havana, carefully assembled by Dayana and Beriev. Maybe someone had heard something through the Havana grapevine.

A tall woman in a black dress and three security guards in black garb were screening arriving men and women at the front door. The woman didn't even check her list when she saw Dayana. She just gave a big smile and ushered her through the door. Pepper glided along at Dayana's side.

"Don't tell anyone, but these rubies aren't real," she giggled in his ear. She was wearing a spectacular necklace that perfectly matched the shine of her big eyes. "I wore them in my most famous film role. I played an innocent young bride named Maria who ended up killing her husband on their wedding night, to avenge her brother's murder." She laughed. "I wanted to keep the nightgown I wore in that scene. It was the skimpiest little thing, but it was stained with fake blood! So I kept this necklace instead, to remember the thrill of playing Maria."

"It looks beautiful with your dress," approved Pepper. "But I bet it'd go even better with that nightgown. Minus the fake blood."

She laughed, then whispered, "I still feel like an intruder at these kinds of parties. My father was a drunk, and we were the poorest family in a poor village. The girls made fun of my ragged clothes, my men's sneakers. Of course, now I hope those girls see my films and burn with jealousy!" She hooked her hand around Pepper's arm and squeezed.

They stood together in the grand front hall, soaking in the opulent scene. Polished marble floors. Crystal chandeliers. Elegantly dressed men and women crowded the room, smelling of expensive perfume and cigar smoke.

Dayana squeezed his arm. "The usual VIPs," she whispered, her warm breath tickling Pepper's ear. "Some top-shelf politicians. Some businessmen. And their wives and girlfriends. Mostly girlfriends. And of course some artists to liven things up."

The guests were chatting in small groups. Servers circulated with silver trays of food and drinks.

"Hey, there's Ozzie," said Pepper.

The Canadian playboy stood at a long bar, with two young women on each arm. He was telling a story, his eyes roving among them. He touched one woman's arm, then another's back. All four women broke into laughter at something he said.

"The kid's got moves," noted Pepper.

Dayana laughed. "He's got money. But yes, Ozzie is fun to be around. Somehow he's like a boy, and very genuine. That can be refreshing."

A trio of female flamenco dancers carved a rhythmic path through the crowd, with flashing eyes and passionate twirls.

"Lovely," Dayana said with an approving smile. "Do you like to dance?"

"Only with someone who really loves me," Pepper said. "So they don't laugh too hard at my dance moves."

Dayana elbowed him, laughing.

A large man raised a camera and took several shots of the dancers. "It's Viktor!" said Dayana, waving to him. "People beg him to make portraits of them. He applies special filters that give the portraits a neo-surrealist style—he's one of the best in the world. But for a party like this, Laurent pays Viktor to circulate and take candid shots."

Pepper had thought about what Detective Guiteras had said, about Beriev being a prime suspect in the artist killings. Pepper didn't give his theory much credence. Maybe the detective had been blowing smoke up his ass. "Your childhood pal Guiteras wants to pin the artist murders on Viktor."

Pepper thought she would laugh, but she regarded Beriev with concern. "Really? I always heard he left Belarus one step ahead of some criminal trouble. Do you think he could commit murder?"

"I doubt it. Do you?"

Dayana thought. "Only if it made more people know about his art!" She laughed.

Pepper's phone buzzed in his pocket. He recognized the number—Barbara Buckley's. He answered the call, and she jumped right in with no pleasantries. "What the hell, Pepper? You don't answer your phone? I got some info for you, but maybe not what Angel wants to hear."

Pepper raised a "wait a sec" finger to Dayana. "Go ahead, Barbara."

"So, you're not gonna believe this. The data for Angel's

friend's phone is coming back from a cell tower in Havana, Cuba! Crazy, right?"

"Crazy," said Pepper.

"And her phone was active there as recently as yesterday morning."

"Okay, that's great! Did AT&T say a specific location in Havana?"

Buckley gave a belly laugh that turned into a coughing fit. "Not a chance. Cuba's cellular network's from the last century. But what's it matter, anyway? You ain't going to Cuba to find her!"

"Sure, that'd be nuts," agreed Pepper.

"Maybe Angel's girl ran off on him. Too bad! So when are you getting back from DC? I hear Zula's coming home next weekend."

"We'll see," said Pepper.

We'll see if I'm in a Cuban prison by then...

But at least Marisol's phone was functioning yesterday. Someone must have charged the battery. Maybe that meant she was still alive and in Havana.

Dayana poked Pepper in the ribs and pointed. The little poet with the big mouth and the bizarre half-beard, Guillermo Infante, was holding court near one of the more opulent pieces of art, a shiny metal conquistador. Maybe gold? Infante was waving his hands dismissively and talking nonstop, and a small group with admiring smiles gathered around him.

"Thanks, you're the best!" said Pepper. "But I'm chasing something down right now, gotta go!"

Barbara laughed again. "Yeah, what's her name?" And she hung up.

"Was that your girlfriend?" Dayana asked playfully.

Pepper made a face. "I'm completely single these days, unfortunately!"

She gave him a skeptical look. "You should watch Guillermo

flirt and take notes. Besides, no one's more popular at a Miramar cocktail party than a die-hard communist."

"Yeah? Let's go interrupt his flow." Pepper wanted to know why Infante snuck away at the Inglaterra Hotel. And what bombshell information did he think he had about Marisol?

Infante was telling a dramatic story in loud Spanish, illustrated with broad gestures of his hands, but Pepper interrupted him.

"Hey, friend," he said. "You ran out on your free lunch. From what I hear, that's not your style."

Infante and his little group fell silent. They watched Pepper with disapproving expressions, mixed with curious glances at Dayana. Why was the famous actress with this rude yuma?

"Guillermo, I was worried about you when I heard what happened," Dayana said, with huskiness in her voice.

To impressive effect. "Ah, *gracias*, little bird," said Infante. "Tragically, I was needed elsewhere. And that other American—he was drunk or insane. My leg still has a bruise! But I'd be happy to chat over lunch soon, with both of you." And Infante turned back to his group.

"I don't have time for soon," said Pepper, circling around Infante to face him. "Do you know what happened to Marisol? Where she is?"

Infante laughed nervously and crossed his arms. "Why does everyone think I know anything?"

"Because you said you did. And I know you and Marisol dated for a while. Like you dated the dancer Carlina Borja, before she died."

"Sadly, I had to let both of them go. Long before their tragedies."

Dayana looked confused. "You let them go? Why?"

Infante puffed out his chest. "Because I don't associate with traitors."

Pepper hadn't seen that coming. "Traitors?"

"I have evidence that Carlina pursued ways to leave Cuba to continue her art in other places, especially America. Just like the other three artists who died. Some might say they got justice for betraying Cuba."

What the hell was he talking about? wondered Pepper.

"But Marisol's not from Cuba," objected Dayana.

Infante scoffed. "Cuban-American. Her blood is Cuban, but her heart and mind belong to America. She should have stayed there. But I have nothing else to say right now." The little man turned his half-bearded face away from them.

Not good enough, thought Pepper. "Call me in the morning," he said. "Or I'll send Angel looking for you." Pepper had a pen but no paper, so he took out a five hundred peso note and wrote his local SIM phone number on it, then forced it into Infante's hand.

Infante turned pale and said something in quick Spanish to his group, but Pepper noticed that Infante smoothly pocketed the money.

Dayana put her hands on her hips, as if she wanted to question Infante further, but Pepper pulled her away.

"He won't tell us anything juicy in front of all those people," Pepper said as they walked away. "We need to find our host, but I need to find a bathroom first. Meet you in two minutes?"

Pepper didn't need to use the bathroom. It had occurred to him he might learn more by digging around in Rappeneau's house than he would learn from the man himself.

He slipped away down a hallway as if looking for a bathroom. He kept going until he reached a pair of tall double doors at the end of the hall. They were unlocked, so Pepper quickly entered, not looking back. Then he locked the doors behind himself.

He was in what looked like Rappeneau's office. Big shiny wood desk. Thick area rug. French doors looked out toward what was probably the back lawn, but light blue curtains blocked most of their glass. Bookshelves held a handful of books, but mostly framed photographs of Rappeneau, grinning and shaking hands with people Pepper didn't recognize. Very important people, no doubt.

The desk drawers were locked. Pepper didn't have any tools to pick the locks, and he didn't want to damage the desk, so he moved on. Where would he hide secrets if he were Rappeneau?

Pepper felt around the bookcase for hidden compartments or doors, but found none. Apparently, Rappeneau didn't watch enough spy movies.

He noticed an eight-by-ten framed photo of father and son Rappeneau. They were both in tuxedos, and they were sharing a private laugh with the father's arm on the son's shoulder. Pepper picked up the photo to look at it more carefully, and his fingers felt an unexpected bulge on the back side of the frame. He spun it around and saw a small white envelope tucked behind the velvet leg.

The front of the envelope had Laurent Rappeneau's name and Miramar address. It was unsealed, and Pepper opened it, finding a small, hand-cut piece of off-white paper.

At that moment, Pepper heard someone try the doorknob to the office. It rattled but stayed closed. Someone else looking for the bathroom? Or had someone seen Pepper come in there and brought security?

Pepper scanned the letter quickly. It was typewritten in all caps English, and unsigned.

YOUR BOURGEOIS PLAY WILL END WHEN I EXPOSE THE SICK TRUTH. YOU GET ONE CHANCE TO BUY

MY COLD HARD EVIDENCE OR PAY THE ULTIMATE PRICE. YOUR FREEDOM, FOR $800,000 USD.

BE READY, THERE IS NOWHERE TO ESCAPE YOURSELF.

A weird, anonymous extortion letter, concluded Pepper. Normally, his first question would be, who sent it? But not this time.

Pepper had seen the same hand-cut, off-white paper recently used for one of the cheesiest, most overwritten breakup letters he'd ever had the misfortune to read. And in that case the writer had proudly signed his name.

Guillermo Infante.

Pepper slipped the extortion letter and envelope into his pocket. He didn't know whether it tied in to Marisol's disappearance or the artist murders, other than that two of the same sketchy people were involved—Infante and Rappeneau. He'd have to think about it more when he had time.

The doorknob rattled again, this time more insistently, and someone banged a fist on the door four times. Either someone really had to pee, or Rappeneau's security was waiting on the other side of that door.

Pepper hurried the other way, to the French doors facing the back lawn. He quickly unlatched them and pulled aside the curtains to peek out. No security guard with a headset and a machine gun. No chained-up tiger. He spotted other guests nearby, but why would they care when Pepper strolled out into their midst? They were all too important to notice him, right?

Pepper took a deep breath and went through the doors. To go find Dayana, and then the extortion victim himself, Laurent Rappeneau.

CHAPTER NINETEEN

"Poor Guillermo is pretty scared of your friend Angel," Dayana observed, when Pepper pulled her away from three men gathered around her.

Maybe for good reason, thought Pepper. The strange poet was a remarkably busy man, leaving a trail of broken romances, an extortion attempt, and other drama all over Havana. "If we find her, Marisol's gonna have some questions to answer about Infante. If Angel doesn't wring his neck first."

"*When* we find her," corrected Dayana. "And Angel needs to get himself under control. He started stirring up trouble here before he even got out of the airport, right? Who the hell smuggles *bananas* into *Cuba*? It's completely ridiculous. And then the fighting at La Cueva. And now he wants to beat up Guillermo?" She laughed. "You yumas are born troublemakers."

"Angel's been a little freaked out," admitted Pepper. "But he loves Marisol, and this whole situation's driving him crazy with worry."

Dayana hooked her slim arm through Pepper's. "He's lucky to have a loyal friend like you."

They circled the other way through the big room, looking for the host of the big party. Dayana caused a ripple as she circulated through the crowd. Guys' heads lifted, turned, and followed her. Women's eyes narrowed, and they watched her more closely.

Pepper had only seen a woman like Dayana a handful of times. The sort of woman that changes the energy in a room. Turned guys into slobbering idiots or peacocking assholes. Turned women into insecure, mean girls. Pepper chuckled.

"What's so funny?" asked Dayana.

"You."

"So now you are making fun of me?" She gave him a mock glare.

Pepper laughed again, took her hand as they walked, but said nothing.

They didn't see Rappeneau inside, so they walked through tall patio doors onto a broad terrace. It overlooked the gardens and a strategically lit swimming pool. A five-musician group was playing salsa music from a small stage on the lawn, and couples were dancing under the three-quarter moon.

This was a heck of a sight, thought Pepper. A real spectacle. In a couple of days he'd be on his plane out of Cuba, and he'd never be back again. He squeezed Dayana's hand.

"I've never been to America," said Dayana. "But every Cuban has seen the movies and TV shows."

"And you hope to make movies there someday? Beriev says you're a world-class talent."

"I want to see how far I can climb as an actor."

"I hope you do," said Pepper. "I think you'd take Hollywood by storm."

"You're a good man," she said, squeezing his hand.

Pepper laughed. "Are you hitting on me again?"

"Again?" she protested, her big brown eyes dancing with indignation. But then she laughed too.

A strong, moist wind hit them, maybe a first taste of Hurricane

Gussie that was still tracking toward Cuba. The wind tossed Dayana's hair around her face like dark flames. The band began a lively, rhythmic tune, and she asked, her eyes shining, "Do you know how to mambo?"

"No. Besides, we really need to find Rappeneau."

She shook her head at him and smiled. "Rappeneau can wait five minutes. This is an important part of your effort to understand Cuba." She tossed her hair and led him to the dance floor. "Just listen to the trumpet," she whispered in his ear. "And keep your eyes on my hips."

That was all the encouragement Pepper needed.

Dayana took his hand and effortlessly moved in a quick-quick-slow combination of steps, swinging her hips to the trumpet, leading Pepper through the dance.

Pepper was a good student, and he followed her instructions. Listened to the trumpet, which rang through the song like a wild yowl. And his eyes never left her elegant, powerful, and sinuous hips.

She laughed with pleasure. "This is what it means to be Cuban!" she shouted, and Pepper grinned, pulling her near, and then their bodies moved in sync. Some irresistible force pulled their bodies closer and closer together as they danced. Pepper lost track of time and thoughts for a while, and he somehow spun her at exactly the right moment. Then she curled back in his arms, like he had a clue what he was doing. She was such a talented dancer that she made the dance easy for him.

He dipped her when the song ended, and he didn't know if that was a legit mambo move, but she smiled up at him, her eyes laughing and the ruby necklace shining in the night. When he pulled her back up, he stepped in and kissed her. She kissed him back, a sweaty kiss that she broke with a smile.

"I think I will teach you to dance very easily," she said. "You're strong and have good balance."

"My college hockey coach might disagree, but thank you."

She laughed. "And Mari told me you are a beautiful singer. I think the band would let you join them to sing me a song. I'd be flattered."

Pepper smiled back, but shook his head. "I wish we had time, seriously, but we need to find Rappeneau."

Dayana pouted, her eyes twinkling with mischief. "Was Mari wrong?"

Then a woman in a flowery dress fell into the pool, sending up a splash of water and drawing a burst of laughter from the crowd. A man in a black suit jumped in to rescue her.

Pepper saw the American embassy official, Heather Wilder, standing near the pool with a wineglass in one hand and a small plate of appetizers in the other, watching the shenanigans with visible distaste.

When she saw Pepper and Dayana, she waved, so they left the dance area and approached her. Pepper introduced Dayana.

"We've met before," said Wilder with a little smile.

A waiter walked past with a tray of small dishes of food, so Pepper took a dainty fork and two dishes with what turned out to be crispy beef prepared in a marinade of lime, garlic, and salt.

"It's *vaca frita*," said Dayana. "But an elegant presentation for VIPs."

It was absolutely delicious, especially since Pepper hadn't had a full meal all day. He didn't know what he should do next, find Rappeneau or stalk the waiter with the dishes of crispy beef.

"I wish it had been in better circumstances," Wilder said to Dayana. Then to Pepper, she explained. "I was trying to help her get a work visa for a film project in California, but she hit a dead end on the Cuban side. Her passport application was rejected." Wilder rolled her eyes.

Dayana looked around, as if to see whether anyone had overheard. "Leaving is always delicate in Cuba," she said. "And I couldn't push too hard, because if my government blacklisted me, I couldn't make films here either." A hint of annoyance crossed her face, but she chased it away with a smile. "But isn't this a beautiful party?"

"Hey, there's our elusive host," Pepper said, pointing across the lawn.

Wilder chuckled. "Go get him, Ryan!"

Rappeneau was wearing a yellow shirt and a pale blue silk suit that probably cost more than Pepper's pickup truck back home. He was listening to a large Latino man in a khaki suit, nodding, his face frozen with politeness.

So maybe Pepper was helping him out by interrupting.

"Mr. Rappeneau? We need to talk," said Pepper.

The rotund Cuban in the beige suit looked immediately annoyed. He moved to block Pepper from Rappeneau and continued talking in Spanish, more loudly now.

Rappeneau put a hand on the man's shoulder and said something in Spanish. The man gave Pepper another look, this time his annoyance mixed with curiosity.

"Come see my gardens," said Rappeneau. "Señorita de Melina, you're a vision! Would you do me a favor? Rescue Oswald from whatever ladies have cornered him. I need him to do something for me when I get back."

Rappeneau was obviously used to getting his way. He led Pepper down a winding cobblestone path lined with old-fashioned globe lights, like he'd imported them from a quaint Spanish town. Their yellow glow highlighted trees, bushes, and flowers, all carefully cultivated and arranged.

"What can I help you with?" Rappeneau asked when they'd rounded a curve in the path and were alone.

"Why did you lie to me about knowing Carlina Borja?" Pepper asked, going right to the heart of the matter.

"What?" scoffed Rappeneau.

"I saw pictures of you with her."

Rappeneau's smile didn't reach his eyes. "I must say, you Yanks have a knack for getting straight to the point. But I don't quite understand what you're implying. Carlina Borja was a talented dancer, and her loss is a tragedy for the dance community worldwide."

"I'm sure. But the pictures were on your yacht, out to dinner—just the two of you, very cozy."

Rappeneau stopped walking. "I'm photographed all the time, with all kinds of people. At cultural events, at parties, wherever. I support the arts here and back home in Toronto."

"Thank you for your service," Pepper said dryly. "But where were you on the night Carlina died?"

Rappeneau's jaw clenched, and a vein in his forehead throbbed. "I don't like your tone, Ryan. I've done nothing but help you, and now you're accusing me of what, exactly? Being involved in a young woman's murder?"

Pepper shrugged. "I'm just trying to understand why you lied to me about your relationship with her. And you made a hundred thousand dollar donation to Marisol to help finance her documentary," Pepper said. "Did you date her too?"

"What?" gasped Rappeneau. "How could I say no to a brilliant filmmaker, working on a project about the same endangered orchids I have in my gardens? Of course I gave her money."

"So it wasn't a payoff, like the eight hundred thousand dollars? There wasn't anything incriminating you wanted her to leave out of her film?"

Pepper took out the extortion note and showed it to Rappeneau.

Rappeneau's cheeks reddened, and his eyes narrowed. "I don't know what game you're playing. But I have friends in high places here, and they won't be pleased to hear you're harassing me. And where the *fuck* did you—"

"Sir?" A deep voice cut through the semi-darkness. "Is everything cool?"

Pepper saw two large white guys in red blazers on the path, studying them. Canadian private security?

Rappeneau tugged his shirt and shot his cuffs. "Yes, McDonald. But this man was just leaving." He snatched the extortion letter out of Pepper's hand, stepped around his security men, and hurried away towards the house.

Pepper noted the tension in his shoulders and the hurried pace of his steps. The Canadian businessman was hiding something, but what, and was it merely scandalous, or also illegal?

"Mr. Rappeneau!" said Pepper, moving to follow him, but the two security guards blocked his path.

"Time to go," said McDonald. He was taller by a couple of inches and at least fifty pounds heavier. His partner was even bigger. They both wore black polo shirts, black pants, and heavy black boots.

"If he's McDonald, who're you?" Pepper asked the bigger guy. "The Burger King?"

They grabbed Pepper at the same moment and hustled him up the path back toward the house, half carrying Pepper, half dragging him. Like taking out smelly garbage was a job they'd get done quickly and efficiently.

"Hey, I can walk!" Pepper protested, earning him a business-like smack to the side of the head.

Heads turned as they reached to the lawn, and chatter rose. Probably speculating what had happened—was the yuma drunk? Had they caught him acting scandalously in the gardens with Dayana de Melina?

Pepper saw Heather Wilder watching with a smirk on her face. She'd gotten rid of her plate and glass, and she had her phone up, pointed at Pepper. Recording every moment of his embarrassing exit.

The two security giants and Pepper reached a brown door set in a high stone wall. The larger man kept his big hand locked on Pepper's neck and the other hand squeezing his arm. Then McDonald took out a key and unlocked the gate, pushing it open.

"You can walk or you can fly," Burger King said in Pepper's ear. "Do me a favor and pick flying."

"Do me a favor and pop a breath mint," said Pepper, stomping the man's high ankle above his boot. Pepper swung his shoulder, breaking free of the man's grip. He stepped through the gate, but a gigantic, heavy boot caught him in the ass and Pepper fell forward, landing and skidding in the dark street.

Fuck, that hurt.

The two men stayed inside the gate. Burger King was favoring his stomped ankle, but looked as if he was trying not to.

"Can you at least call me a damn taxi?" asked Pepper.

"Fair enough," said McDonald. "You're a damn taxi."

The heavy brown door thudded shut.

CHAPTER TWENTY

"So, what the hell can we do now?" asked Angel.

After a long walk and a short taxi ride, Pepper was back at Casa de Vides, sprawled in the living room with Angel and Hector. Angel looked upset. Hector looked defeated. Pepper felt both.

But time was short, so he brought out the police reports Detective Valdés had so kindly slipped to him, and they got to work.

They spent an hour reading the reports and studying the pictures in silence. Then they compared notes, including everything they could remember from the Carlina Borja report.

All the victims were artists. In fact, all were the most celebrated Cuban artists in their field. The four murders occurred in January, May, July, and August. So, the time between killings was shrinking.

"Looks like el Segador is getting more confident," suggested Angel.

"Or more excited," said Pepper. He knew both possibilities were not unusual for serial killers.

"The causes of death were all different," pointed out Hector.

The writer, Alicia Arenas, died by blunt trauma—her fall from the tower and her impact on the concrete walkway.

The sculptor, Rolando Carreño, was poisoned.

The painter, Osanna Falcón, died from a blow to the back of the head.

And the dancer, Carlina Borja, was strangled.

"But then comes the weirdest part," said Angel. "The killer stabbed each of their bodies in the back, over and over—after they were already freaking dead!"

"I agree with the psych profile," said Hector. "The stabbings, it's like the killer has personal anger toward the victims."

Pepper placed the pictures of the three victims side by side. Absolutely brutal and absolutely similar. "I agree," said Pepper.

"The book thing's bizarre too," commented Angel. Each victim was found with a copy of Hemingway's *For Whom the Bell Tolls* resting on their bloody back. But the reports didn't speculate about what the books signified.

"It's got to be a statement by the killer," speculated Pepper. He knew that Hemingway got his book title from a famous English poem by John Dunne. Pepper remembered from a long-ago English literature class that there were debates about what Dunne meant by the phrase. Some thought it had to do with the interconnectedness of all people. Others thought it was a warning to the reader not to forget their own mortality. But leaving a book with that title on the body of someone you'd just killed? To Pepper, the act felt more like gloating. Or hubris.

"Holy shit," said Pepper. He was reading the murder file of Alicia Arenas, the writer. Her body was found in January at the foot of a tower at the Ernest Hemingway estate outside of Havana, where she was doing a writing residency. She was el Segador's first victim. The ones who first discovered her body, an estimated thirteen hours after the woman's death, were Viktor Beriev and Dayana de Melina. They had arrived together to meet with

Arenas about a possible film adaption of one of her novels. Instead, they'd found her dead.

"That must have been traumatic," said Angel, after Pepper shared the information.

"Like a nightmare," he agreed. He could only imagine their shock upon finding the writer's broken and bloody body. "Can you make a note? We need to hear all about it from Dayana and Viktor, next time we see them. And also put down that if I go to check out any more of the crime scenes, I want to start with that Alicia Arenas scene."

"Why there?" asked Hector, sounding curious.

"Because nobody starts out as an expert, including serial killers," explained Pepper. "So maybe el Segador made a rookie mistake and maybe the PNR missed it, since they haven't busted him yet."

Angel dutifully wrote both notes down on a yellow pad, which held their growing list of observations, questions, and follow-ups.

Pepper moved on to the "Persons of Interest" lists in each file, which turned out to be similar to what he'd seen in the Carlina Borja file. For each victim there were a couple of extra names, but the core list remained the same:

Guillermo Infante
Heather Wilder (USE)
Viktor Beriev
Laurent Rappeneau
Quinto Chavez

"So looking at these names, and the fact that the victims were all top artists, obviously all of these killings tie together," said Angel. "But how do they tell us anything that'll help us find Marisol?"

Angel was right.

The police reports helped them start to understand the serial killings, like Marisol had begun to do for her film. But had el Segador grabbed Marisol?

If not, the last hour might have been a complete waste of time.

Pepper closed the files with a heavy sigh. "It's almost midnight," he said. "We don't have any leads to track down tonight. The best thing we can all do is get a good night's sleep."

"Mano, she's been gone five days!" said Angel, his voice shaking. "She could be dying somewhere right now."

"Buddy, we could drive around and pretend we're doing something productive, but we wouldn't be. First thing in the morning, we'll hit it hard again. We're going to find her."

Hector's phone buzzed, and he frowned, then texted back, slumped low on his chair.

"Is everything okay?" Pepper asked him.

"My mother," said Hector with a sigh. "She thinks my yuma cousin is a bad influence."

"Smart mother," said Pepper.

Hector unzipped his Elvis jumpsuit a few inches and fanned his chest. "Some days I feel no matter if I stay here or run away to Las Vegas, I'll always be a failure. So why bother?"

"Sorry I'm making things worse for you, cuz," said Angel. "But we'll find Marisol, and then if I can do to help you get to Vegas, just ask. Money, whatever ..."

Silence fell over them. Finally, Angel said, "And that gives me one of my brilliant ideas. How about we bribe him?"

"What?" asked Pepper. "Bribe who?"

"That asshole Guiteras. He's got all the cards. He knows more about Marisol's disappearance than we do, and he's the lead detective on the murdered artist cases. So I'm saying we need him to stop harassing us and show us his damn cards. If money'll do it, let's offer him all the cash we've got, and a promise to get him more. Whatever it takes."

The idea stunned Pepper. The detective acted like a no-nonsense Cuban police officer. Was that actually a front? Was he being so difficult because he was waiting for a sneaky big payday from rich Americans?

"Maybe," said Hector to Angel. "Bribery is everywhere in our government, you know. But Cuban laws say it's seriously illegal. You don't want to know how many years of prison you would get if Guiteras reports you."

So, thought Pepper, two crappy choices. Try the bribe and risk enraging Guiteras, or likely keep running around blind to most of the information they needed. And he couldn't think of any other good options.

Perfect.

"We're definitely floundering on our own," Pepper said. "And time's running out. I vote we roll the dice and call Guiteras in the morning and try to set up a meeting."

"Me too," said Angel.

Hector gave a loud, long sigh. "I will drive you to a meeting with him, but I will stay in my car. I am not too religious, you know, but I will pray for you."

"Say, there's one other important thing we can take care of tonight," said Pepper. He went into the kitchen and returned with three beers.

"Yes?" asked Hector, taking one and holding it against his cheek to enjoy the coldness.

"Yes," said Pepper in a solemn voice. "Angel has been holding onto a big, terrible secret, and I think it would be good for him to spill it."

Angel looked confused. "Mano, are you drunk already?"

"You know what I'm talking about. The Banana Incident!"

Angel groaned. "You kicking me while I'm down? No way I'm talking about that!"

"What about Angel's banana?" Hector asked warily.

After further pressure and joking, Angel relented and told the story. He even got into it, using different voices, dramatizing it.

No one told a funny story better than Angel. It was the first time since Pepper had arrived in Cuba that he saw his old buddy relax.

Angel began by explaining that the Banana Incident had happened at the airport after his and Marisol's plane landed in Cuba.

A pretty, young woman in a serious blue blazer searched their bags at Customs, especially a duffel bag that Marisol had labeled MEDICINAS, ASEO Y COMIDA in big lettering, because it was full of medicine, toiletries, and packaged food that she was donating to people she knew in Havana.

All of that was cool with Customs. The trouble started when the woman searched Angel's backpack. He had tucked away his dead grandmother's engagement ring in a small velvet pouch, semi-hidden in a tiny inside pocket of the backpack, in case Marisol started poking around in his bag for gum or a snack during their trip.

"Engagement ring?" Hector interrupted excitedly.

"Absolutely. I was going to pop the question to Marisol at sunset down by the Malecón."

"*Muy* romantic," Hector said with an approving nod.

Then Angel explained he was acting jittery as he watched the Customs woman do a proctological search of his backpack, and the Customs woman noticed it too.

When she asked Angel, "*¿Qué es esto?*" while pulling her arm from his backpack, Angel dreaded seeing the velvet ring pouch and his big surprise ruined. His heart had freaking stopped. But the Customs woman was holding a banana he'd forgotten was in there.

Relieved, Angel had jokingly replied, "¿*Un teléfono?*"

Pepper burst out laughing. Classic Angel. Pepper could picture the moment in exact, stupid detail.

Angel continued, describing how the Customs woman escorted them to a small windowless room, where a series of stick-up-their-butts Cuban customs and immigration officials questioned them for thirty minutes, while examining their passports, visas, and baggage over and over. They grilled Angel and Marisol about their places of birth, their families' heritage, and the purpose of their travel to Cuba. They especially focused on Marisol and skeptically scrutinized the special visa she'd gotten to permit filming her documentary about Cuban orchids. Angel replayed it all, giving each official a ridiculous voice, until Pepper's stomach hurt from laughing.

Eventually, the officials released Angel and Marisol after a stern warning not to import fresh fruits in the future without a special permit from Cuba's National Plant Health Protection Organization.

"Kind of low on the dumbassery scale, but high on the funny scale," Pepper said approvingly as he tried to catch his breath. "And don't you feel better, having gotten it off your chest?"

"Don't fucking tell *anyone*," warned Angel. "I'm a prominent businessman back home. I've got a reputation to maintain."

They had a second beer, sitting in comfortable silence, with the occasional exchange of insults and wisecracks. Even Hector got in a few good one-liners. It was a much-needed break from the chaos, Pepper thought, as he finished his beer and headed to bed.

Hector announced he would stay and sleep on the sofa, declining the extra bed in Pepper's room. "If el Segador comes up the stairs, my screams will wake you."

The night air hung over Pepper as he lay in bed at two o'clock, unable to sleep.

In part, because the bedroom's air was incredibly humid. Casa de Vides didn't have air conditioning, but an old ceiling fan pushed the heavy air around the bedroom, like stirring soup.

And despite the late hour, Cuban music was playing somewhere in the building, loud enough for Pepper to hear the drums, trumpet, and saxophone partying in 4/4 time. A woman sang in Spanish about love, or a tragic loss, or something equally hard.

But mainly Pepper couldn't sleep because his brain was spinning like a washer machine. He couldn't stop thinking about everything he'd experienced in Cuba over the past three days, and everything he'd learned about Marisol's disappearance. It ran over and over in his head, like scenes from multiple movies, all playing at the same time.

It didn't help that Pepper's flight back to the US was less than forty-eight hours away. And Angel understood that if Pepper missed it, it'd be career suicide.

So in a day and a half, Pepper would be forced to leave the entire mess in Havana to the local authorities to solve. If Pepper flew home tomorrow with Marisol still missing, how could he ever look Angel in the eye again?

Almost worse, Pepper had a nagging feeling that he'd overlooked a crucial detail in Marisol's disappearance. The feeling was causing a tingle down the back of his neck, like an itch.

I'm missing something super important.

Pepper's stomach rumbled loudly from hunger. He had eaten little on this trip, because he'd been too focused on finding Marisol. Stupid. If he didn't keep his energy up, what good would he be? Pepper wondered what food was in the kitchen for a midnight snack. He only remembered seeing some fruit.

A thought triggered in Pepper's mind, like a puzzle piece snapping into place. *Damn!* He had to be wrong, but if he wasn't? He felt his pulse speeding, and adrenaline flushed through his body.

He needed to go ask Dayana de Melina an important question. A question he shouldn't ask over the phone. She had mentioned something that seemed unimportant...but Pepper now thought it was crucial to ask where she'd learned it. He realized he was suddenly drenched in sweat.

He got up and went to the next bedroom, entering quietly to find Angel was still awake too.

"Grab your pants and wake Hector," Pepper said.

"What's up?"

"Somebody's about to look like a real asshole. And I hope it's not me." Pepper shared the idea that'd occurred to him, and what he wanted to do about it. His big question for Dayana.

"You're definitely nuts, mano," said Angel. "But screw it, let's go."

CHAPTER TWENTY-ONE

"Is this a yuma booty call?" yawned Hector, steering around a dog standing in the middle of the intersection.

The three were driving across dark, slumbering Havana at two-thirty on Saturday morning. There were almost no other cars on the road.

As they rode, Pepper worked through a couple of plantains he'd found in the kitchen. Fuel for the hunt.

They had dropped off Dayana de Melina yesterday, so they knew where she lived. They soon reached her apartment building in the Colón neighborhood. Most of the buildings looked dilapidated, but Dayana's was the nicest on her street. Its dirty white exterior, lined with a row of swaying palm trees, glowed faintly in the moonlight.

Dayana had told Pepper that she lived on the top floor, with a view of the capitol building in the distance. But Pepper didn't know her apartment number.

"She's going to be angry," suggested Hector. "Maybe we wait until morning?"

"Pepper's experienced at making women angry," said Angel. "He can handle it."

Pepper laughed. "Hector, you stand guard down here. Call us if the police show up, or anyone else."

"No, no, I should come with you," Hector protested.

Maybe he wanted to tell people he'd set foot in the famous Dayana de Melina's apartment.

Pepper put a hand on Hector's shoulder. "We need you down here. Phone us if the police arrive, or anyone else."

Hector looked worried. "There is going to be trouble?"

"I hope so."

Pepper had Dayana's phone number from earlier, so he called it as he and Angel walked to the front entrance of her building.

She picked up on the fourth ring.

"Si?" she asked, sounding part asleep, part confused, and part alarmed.

"Sorry to wake you, but we need to talk."

"What is it?" she asked. "Did you find Marisol?"

"No."

Then, in a huskier voice, she said, "Is this about … something else?"

"I'll explain when I see you," said Pepper.

The front door was locked. Pepper rattled the door as a test and found it was loose in the frame. He handed the phone to Angel, put one foot against the doorframe and gave a big pull, popping the door open.

"I can meet you for breakfast," she offered.

"No, we need to talk now."

As the call went on, Pepper and Angel climbed the worn, cracked marble stairs to the top floor. They pushed through a heavy metal door and walked down the hallway, looking for any marker showing which apartment was Dayana's. No luck.

Dayana said, "It's too late for me to go out. Ask what you want over the phone. I need to get back to sleep. I'm not even dressed."

Pepper was pissed off and frustrated. Too many things in

Havana hadn't been what they first seemed. He'd misjudged people. Misunderstood situations. It felt like too much of Havana was smoke and mirrors.

"Then put on a bathrobe," Pepper said. "Because I'm at your apartment door."

Pepper and Angel waited in the hallway until a door flew open forty feet away. Dayana stood in the doorway with her face full of anger and her legs planted wide. She was wearing sweatpants and a T-shirt. Her hair was messy, she wore no makeup, and she still looked spectacular.

She glared at Pepper. "Men at my door at night always have the same question," she said. "My answer is usually no."

Pepper smiled. "That explains the sweatpants. But I'm here about Marisol. Can we come in, so we don't wake your neighbors?"

Dayana thought about it, but finally ushered them into her apartment.

The small living room area had a leather-covered sofa and two sleek armchairs. Books were piled along one wall, and a sweater lay forgotten on the floor. She didn't invite them to sit.

"So ... ?" she prompted, waving a hand.

"So how'd you hear about Angel's banana incident?" asked Pepper. "About how he got into trouble at the Havana airport?"

Dayana looked flummoxed. "You came here at three a.m. to talk about bananas?"

"Only because it's important."

"I don't remember what you're talking about. What bananas?"

"At Rappeneau's party, you made fun of Angel for smuggling bananas into Cuba. Where'd you hear that story?"

She paused, looking confused. "Your friends, I think."

"Which friends?"

"Maybe Viktor and Ozzie were laughing about it yesterday. I

don't remember. It's the typical dumb mistake Americans make when they come here."

"Was Beriev telling the story or Ozzie?"

Dayana gave a beautiful half shrug. "Maybe Beriev. But I'm still half asleep." She yawned into the back of her hand.

Pepper turned to Angel. "Did you tell that story to Beriev or Ozzie? Or anyone other than me and Hector tonight?"

"No."

"And you definitely didn't tell Dayana?"

"No way. That banana incident was hella embarrassing."

Dayana said nothing. She looked like a cross between bewildered and annoyed.

"Absolutely embarrassing," said Pepper. "But pretty funny too. Would you like to hear it?" he said to Dayana.

"Tomorrow," she said. "You boys need to go to your own beds now. Maybe you'll be less crazy after you sleep."

But Pepper'd had enough.

"No, it's just too funny a story to wait," he said. "Marisol would tell it best, since she was there when it happened and she tells stories for a living, as a filmmaker. Why don't we let her tell it?"

"What?" asked Dayana.

She looked totally puzzled. But everyone in Cuba said she was the best actor of her era.

"Marisol!" called Pepper. "Come out, you're busted!"

Everyone stood silent.

At the far end of the apartment, a door opened.

And Marisol Borja stepped into the hallway. Pepper had met her on Cape Cod in July, and she looked the same. She was a tall, slim woman with dark skin, brown eyes, and long black hair braided like a rope. A natural beauty. She was wearing green shorts and a plain white T-shirt.

She looked relaxed. She had a partial grin on her face.

Nothing like how you should look when caught in a serious, unforgivable lie.

When Marisol saw Angel standing behind Pepper, she pushed out her lower lip in a pout. "Angelito, you didn't bring me flowers?"

Pepper went from angry, to white-hot furious. *What the hell!* Marisol was completely unharmed—so why did that piss off Pepper even more?

No one had kidnapped Marisol, and el Segador hadn't murdered her. She was alive, and Pepper knew she was responsible for everything he'd gone through in Cuba.

A small table near the door had a potted orchid on it. Angel picked up the orchid and threw it across the room.

Dayana, still standing near the door, looked terrified.

"What the hell's going on?" raged Angel, his nostrils flaring. "Was this some kind of sick joke?"

"Angelito, I can explain," Marisol said, her hand to her throat.

"Fantastic!" Angel growled. "I can't wait!"

Marisol wrung her hands and stared at Angel. "You should sit."

He laughed harshly. "I'm too mad to sit. Let's hear it."

Marisol paused, as if gathering herself. Then she said in a quiet voice, "It was the only way."

Pepper, Angel, and Dayana waited, but Marisol said nothing more.

"Well, that clears it up!" exclaimed Angel, making a big sweeping gesture with his arms. He was visibly sweating now. "You abandoned me at that plaza. I thought you were kidnapped or dead in a ditch, but it was the only way. Thanks, sweetheart!"

Marisol gave Angel one of those loaded looks that pass between couples in public. "Angelito!"

Pepper stared at her, his mouth falling open. *Who the hell does she think she is?*

"We both deserve a better explanation," Pepper growled. His body was tense and his pulse was racing. "You brought Angel to Cuba, then disappeared, leaving him stranded. So walk us through why that wasn't batshit crazy."

Marisol blinked at him. "You don't understand yet?"

"Yeah, no shit," said Angel, his hands clenching and unclenching. "So your disappearance was a hoax? You sent me up, dragged Pepper into it? That's a hell of a complicated way to break up with me, unless this is some kind of cruel reality show."

"Okay," said Marisol. "Okay." Then, in a calm, measured voice, Marisol explained herself.

CHAPTER TWENTY-TWO

The reason, Marisol claimed, was the murdered Cuban artists. The killings that started nine months ago. Four of Cuba's greatest artists were dead so far, including two artists Marisol knew personally.

"We got all that," said Angel, his voice trembling.

Marisol continued in the same cool voice. In her view, the Cuban police had done almost nothing to catch the killer. The fourth killing occurred in August, just before she arrived—a relative she considered a friend.

"Carlina Borja," said Angel, sighing in exasperation. "We fucking *know* all this."

Marisol stared him down. "I arrived in Havana a week after her death, and I was devastated. I'm a filmmaker, and in all my projects, I get to the truth. So I decided that dying artists were a more important film topic than dying ghost orchids.

"Back in August, I began interviewing family members of the victims, and other people connected to Havana's arts community. I quickly learned I didn't have the investigative skills to catch the serial killer. I didn't even know where to start."

Marisol glanced at Pepper, then continued.

"Angelito, I thought of your stories about Pepper. Then I saw him in action, when the president's family came to Cape Cod. During all the chaos that unfolded around Pepper, he was brave and relentless. Like a wrecking ball when chasing criminals. And I thought, if only Cuban police were like Pepper."

"That's not exactly what happened on Cape Cod," said Pepper. But it had been a messy situation.

Marisol waved a hand. "I thought Pepper would be the perfect man to catch Havana's serial killer. So I faked my disappearance, Angelito, knowing you would call Pepper to help you. And I knew when you both looked for me, you'd learn about the four murdered artists. I hoped you would pursue el Segador to find me alive, or at least to bring my killer to justice."

Poor Angel, Pepper thought. He must be devastated. His girlfriend—almost his fiancée—had used them both like pawns on a chessboard. So much for her loving Angel and him trusting her . . . all the essential stuff a relationship needs to survive.

Pepper had seen firsthand how frequently his buddy fell in love. But Angel had fallen hardest for Marisol, really throwing himself into the relationship, to make her happy however he could. Only to get completely burned.

"Hey, at least she came clean," Pepper said to Angel. "There should be a flight out to Fort Lauderdale this afternoon. I wonder if we can get seats."

Marisol tried to take his hand, but Angel backed away. "Don't take this so personally," said Marisol with a frown. "I did this because you and I have so much faith in Pepper."

"You and I?" Angel laughed. "I'm joining Pepper on that first flight out."

Marisol's eyes welled with tears. "I'm so sorry," she said. "I was desperate and scared, and ... a terrible, terrible girlfriend."

Angel looked at her like she was a stranger. "You left me in the gutter of a foreign city with no luggage. I thought you'd been abducted and maybe killed. Let's come up with a stronger word than terrible."

Marisol's hands were shaking as she waved them. "You should be mad. But I felt it was the right thing to do! Wonderful, talented people—friends of mine—were getting killed. And more will die until someone stops the killer."

Despite his anger, that statement registered with Pepper. "The murders are horrible, no argument," he said, lowering his voice and trying to sound reasonable. "But the Cuban police will catch him. I'm sure it's their top priority."

"Juan claims it's been their top priority for more than a year," said Dayana. "But what have they done if el Segador is still killing?"

Pepper knew of American serial killers who evaded law enforcement for decades, like John Wayne Gacy and the Green River Killer. Sometimes, DNA testing identified a killer years later. In other cases, serial killers continued building their body count until they made a dumb mistake, or the police got a lucky break.

Hopefully, the Cuban police would catch el Segador soon. The situation was tragic and brutal. But bottom line, this wasn't Pepper's country, his city, or his responsibility. Pepper had heard that message ever since he arrived.

Marisol stared imploringly at Pepper. "I believed in my heart if you came here, you'd catch el Segador. I believed you have a special talent to stop evil people. And tell me the truth. If I asked you, explained everything in advance, would you have come to Cuba?"

"That's crazy!" interjected Angel.

Yet Pepper said nothing, knowing his answer would have been no.

Marisol put her hands on her hips. "I did it to save the next victims. For that I don't apologize."

Pepper knew his buddy had been about to propose to Marisol. That was tragic, or maybe it represented a silver lining—that he hadn't proposed before she pulled her disappearing trick.

"We need to talk in private," Angel said to Marisol in a quiet voice. The two of them went into her bedroom, and Angel slammed the door.

Pepper looked at Dayana, who was still standing by the kitchen, out of the line of fire. She looked pale but unapologetic.

He felt his pulse speeding and heat flush through his body. He was pissed at her, not to mention hurt. She'd been a big part of Marisol's scam. She'd played Pepper, lying to him extensively. Every captivating glance with those big brown eyes, every spectacular smile, all designed to hook in Pepper. Everything since Wednesday night, all of it an actor playing a part. Pepper needed to rethink all his interactions with her. And all of his feelings.

A sudden realization hit him—even in this moment of betrayal, he couldn't deny the pull he felt toward Dayana. The way she stood her ground, the mix of strength and vulnerability in her eyes—they stirred something deep within him and that made Pepper feel even more frustrated and angry.

Her big brown eyes were studying him now. "And what will you do?" she asked quietly.

"When Angel's finished, I'm heading back to bed for a few hours," Pepper said, trying to sound calm. "Then I'll try to grab a seat on a flight out this afternoon. If nothing's available, I'll ask Hector to give me a tour of Havana. Check out at that fort I keep seeing across the water, then go to El Floridita and get roaring drunk. Then I'll fly home tomorrow on my original flight."

But Pepper didn't mean home. He meant Washington, DC. This bogus side trip to Cuba had increased the chances of him getting fired by the FBI. And it had all been a hoax.

"But what about el Segador?" Dayana asked in a near whisper.

Pepper shrugged. "Everyone's been lying to me since I got to Havana, including you, right? All your flirting and laughing, part of the role Marisol had you play, right?"

Dayana glared at him. "That's not true!"

Pepper threw up his hands in an "I give up" gesture. "If I'd uncovered anything useful, I'd have shared it with your schoolyard buddy, Guiteras, before I fly out. But I didn't. So I'll let him do his job. The serial killer's not my problem."

Dayana started crying. "But he's my problem," she blurted. "I'm his next target!" Then she snatched a magazine from the kitchen counter and flung it at Pepper. It bounced off his chest and hit the floor.

Pepper picked it up. It was the *Vanity Fair* edition with the story about Cuba's most important artists, the one Ozzie Rappeneau told him about. Pepper knew because it said so right on the cover. And from the big cover shot of Dayana.

Shit.

It was a stunning picture of her. Eyes on fire, hair blowing in the wind. Maybe a still shot from one of her movies.

"You have to understand," she said in a shaking voice. "I'm trapped here in Cuba. They won't let me go. So maybe you can forgive me for using my acting skills to get your help. And you surprised me, how you made me feel. How much alike we are, even though we're from different countries. And none of *that* was a lie."

Pepper hadn't thought of actors as being within the scope of "artists" who would be targeted by el Segador. But of course, it made sense now that he saw the magazine. So Dayana was on the shadowy serial killer's short list.

Pepper walked to a sofa and slumped down. He flipped through the magazine until he found the Cuba article. It covered ten Cuban artists in a variety of disciplines. Dayana was the fifth artist featured.

Pepper checked the cover for the date and did the math in his head. The first artist was murdered three months after the Cuban artist issue was published. If some homicidal psycho was selecting his victims using that magazine article, then Dayana had every reason to be afraid.

"Okay, I get it," Pepper said. "I understand why you helped Marisol. And maybe in some crazy way, it even makes sense what Marisol did. But your entire plan was completely mistaken. The best people to catch el Segador are the PNR. They have the resources, the local knowledge, and the authority."

"But they haven't caught him," said Dayana, her voice trembling with fear.

For once, Pepper knew she wasn't acting. He sat silently, thinking hard. He stared out the window, but because the lights were on inside, all he saw was his own reflection. The Pepper in the window looked glum—he only had unacceptable options too.

It was all completely crazy. The only thing nuttier would be for Pepper to spend the next day and a half trying to catch a serial killer before his flight home.

"What else do you see about the article?" asked Dayana.

Pepper flipped through it again.

Shit.

The first four artists featured were the first four killed. In that order.

Pepper flipped to the next artist in the article and saw Dayana's smiling face.

Double shit.

Pepper had every reason to believe Dayana would be el Segador's next target.

Pepper leaned his head against the window, his mind racing.

Detective Guiteras had made clear the nasty price of interfering with a police investigation in Cuba. If he pissed off Guiteras any further, Pepper could end up in a Cuban prison. Maybe for years.

Besides, the PNR knew everything Pepper knew, and far more. He was not the kind of egomaniac to believe only he could stop the killer. What could Pepper do that the PNR couldn't?

Pepper reminded himself that he hadn't come to Havana to catch a serial killer. He'd come to help find Marisol, and Pepper had accomplished that. Job done. So, Pepper should hop the next plane back to the USA.

"That's why I had to help trick you," Dayana said quietly. "For me. And for the other artists who'll soon die."

Over the years, Pepper's law enforcement bosses had criticized him for being too impetuous. He tended to leap wildly before he looked. Ready, fire, him. Was he going to fall into that old pattern again?

And would it even be possible for Pepper to catch a serial killer in Havana in the next day and a half? But if he went home on the first flight out, how would it be until he got news that another artist had been murdered in Havana?

Would it be Dayana?

Leaving was indefensible. But so was staying.

Pepper found himself walking over to Dayana. He put his arms around her shoulders and hugged her close.

"I'll stay until Sunday," he heard himself say.

She looked up at him, her eyes full of tears, but her face held a note of hope. She tilted her head and rose toward him, and Pepper kissed her. Then he kissed her again, harder. And somehow it was better than their amazing kiss after dancing at Rappeneau's party. Which Pepper would have doubted was possible.

He gently brushed Dayana's hair away from her face. "I can't stay past Sunday or I'll get my ass fired," he explained quietly.

"But I'll investigate for the next day and a half, and I'll hand over anything I learn to the PNR. Maybe it'll help them catch el Segador soon."

Dayana gave Pepper a long hug, and he felt her tears wet his chest. "Maybe so," she whispered. "Or maybe you will kill him first."

CHAPTER TWENTY-THREE

"Stop here," Pepper said.

Viktor Beriev halted at the driveway entrance to Ernest Hemingway's Lookout Farm estate. It was on a tropical hill on the outskirts of Havana. Ernest Hemingway lived, loved, and wrote there for many of the prime years of his life. It was now a museum to the famous American writer owned by the Cuban government.

As Pepper knew from the police report, Alicia Arenas' body had been found here the next morning by Dayana and Beriev, when they'd arrived to meet with her about a potential film adaptation of Arenas' most famous book, *City of Clouds*.

Instead, they'd found her dead body.

So who better to accompany Pepper to see the place? He'd wanted to see for himself where the spree began. But could he learn anything almost nine months after the murder?

Pepper's first question was, did el Segador made a rookie mistake here that the PNR had missed? The killer was less experienced in January, and less confident. Maybe he'd unknowingly slipped up in a way that pointed to his identity.

Pepper's second question was more of a statement—he felt

there was a squishiness to Alicia Arenas' time of death. There was a broad estimate from six to ten o'clock that Saturday night, resulting from a blend of the autopsy findings and the crime scene investigation. But the time of death for the other three artists' deaths was a two-hour window. Which obviously had big implications for the strength of witness statements and suspect alibis. So why the discrepancy for the first murder?

Also, the first murder was unique because Pepper had access to the two people who discovered the victim's body—Viktor Beriev and Dayana de Melina. He would like to hear their experience right at the place where it happened.

So he'd ridden southeast of Havana for half an hour with Dayana and Beriev in a cramped Soviet-era Lada that Beriev had borrowed from a friend.

"What are you wondering about, to come all the way out here?" asked Dayana. She sounded somewhere between fascinated and amused.

Pepper shook his head. "And spoil my mysterious image? No, you'll just have to watch and be amazed. My first act of investigative wonder will be to take a quick look at the gate."

Pepper studied the gate from the backseat of the compact car.

It was a horizontal metal pole, painted red, that swung on a post to block the driveway. It was currently open, but the police report stated that this gate was locked at sundown every day, by the museum director himself. And on days that the museum director was away, by the head groundskeeper.

It looked sturdy enough and well enough designed to do its job—to keep vehicles from driving onto the estate at night. The Hemingway collection of books, paintings, and other historical items was probably a tempting target for burglars. The police report said that after the gate was locked, the museum director activated primitive motion detectors for the road. Any significant motion activated a loud alarm, although the system did not notify the police.

The police report concluded that Alicia Arenas was murdered around 6PM on a Saturday evening, which meant the killer could have arrived and departed by car. But Pepper had nagging doubts about some statements in the police report that supported that conclusion. For him, the time of death was a litmus test—has the PNR done a solid job investigating this crime scene? Had they made mistakes that cast the net for Alicia Arenas' killer in the wrong direction? Followed by a tiny voice, way in the back of Pepper's head asking the obnoxious, paranoid question: had the PNR made no progress on catching el Segador because they had some dirty reason not to, such as corruption or a tangle of the regime's politics?

Yep, obnoxious and paranoid. But the tiny voice wouldn't shut up.

"Okay," Pepper said. "In we go."

Beriev pulled up the dusty road to an off-white stucco villa with a dramatic tower and parked in a dirt lot near the farmhouse villa. The warm breeze carried hints of decaying mangos and the smoke of cooking fires.

"This is Finca Vigía," said Beriev. "Hemingway lived here when he wrote *For Whom the Bell Tolls* and also *The Old Man and the Sea*. When he died, the Cuban government seized the farm and everything in it. His widow was eventually permitted to retrieve some paintings and manuscripts, but Cuba kept everything else."

"Alicia was doing a residency here," added Dayana. "Writing her next novel up in the White Tower. She stayed in a cottage just down the hill. It gives me chills coming back to where we found her."

Pepper saw Dayana shudder in the front passenger seat. He felt a surge of protectiveness and wanted to wrap his arms around her and promise that he'd bring Alicia's killer to justice. But he settled for a gentle squeeze of her shoulder. "I'm sorry to put you through it again."

"It's fine," she said, in a voice that suggested it wasn't.

"So, what first?" asked Beriev.

Pepper jumped right in. "My first question is: why did the killer come here that evening?"

"What?" asked Dayana.

Beriev laughed. "I can make two guesses. The killer came here to kill Alicia. Or else, the killer came here for some other reason, such as robbery, and ended up killing Alicia when he found her in the tower."

"I agree," said Pepper. "And since four artists have been killed, I lean toward all the deaths being premeditated. Can you show me where you found her?"

They were walking to the house when they heard a shout from behind them. A small man in a pale blue suit, white shoes, and a straw Panama hat was hurrying toward them.

"He probably wants our entry fee," grumbled Beriev.

But the man had a big smile on his face. "Dayana de Melina, *bienvenida!*"

Dayana introduced him to Pepper as Carlos Hernandez, the museum's director. She had met him once before, on the morning the tragedy was discovered. She asked Hernandez whether he minded if she showed Pepper the scene of the tragic event.

"Anything, anything," he promised. He escorted them toward the house, trying to engage Dayana in flirtatious small talk.

Beriev shook his head at Pepper with a wry grin, like he'd seen it too many times before.

Hernandez brought them down a path around the corner of a building. Pepper looked up and saw the workshop tower looming above him. According to the police report, that had to be where Alicia Arenas fell from. Probably was pushed from.

Hernandez reached a concrete walkway skirting the tall tower, and he looked up to the height the author had fallen from. He took off his straw hat, sighed fatalistically, and made a vague sign of the cross with one finger.

"It was a terrible time," the man said, shaking his head at Pepper.

"I'll bet," Pepper said. He turned to Beriev and Dayana. "Can you guys tell me how you found her?"

Dayana crossed her arms and shivered despite the warm day. "Alicia asked me to visit her to discuss her most famous book, *City in the Clouds*. She knew I adored it and wanted to discuss having me play the female lead in a film adaptation. She thought the project was more likely to happen if she could attach my name to it. I called Viktor and asked him to come with me, as a favor, to take pictures of me and Alicia together. Early publicity."

"She is hard to say no to, if you haven't noticed," laughed Beriev. "So I put down my breakfast and joined her."

"We arrived around eight. We drove up in Viktor's friend's car, which he borrowed and parked in the same spot we did today. I knew Alicia liked to write early in the morning, even before sunup, so we came right to the tower where she would be working. But when we came around the corner . . . !" She stopped, biting her lip, and tears began flooding from her eyes.

Beriev put an arm around Dayana before the museum director could, and Dayana rested her head against his big chest. "Her body was right here," Beriev said. "It was terrible, the red blood everywhere, against the white stone, and. She was lying on her back, with her legs hanging off the walkway, all twisted up where she hit. Her face was to the side, and it was already as white as the stone walkway. Her one eye was open and—"

Dayana began sobbing louder, and Beriev squeezed her. "Well, there was blood everywhere. And the weird thing—the book resting on her back. Dayana threw herself on Alicia's body and she was crying so hard. And checking to make sure Alicia was dead, I thought. But it was obvious to me." He shook his head and closed his eyes. "There was no question, her body was cold as stone. She had been dead for hours."

"When I pulled myself together, I called Juan," said Dayana in a thin voice. "He was the only detective I knew, and I had his number. And I knew with my fame and the protests I'd been part of . . ." She shook her head. "I didn't want my presence to distract from the search for the killer. I knew Juan would take charge of the horrible scene, that he would get our statements taken and get us out of there before any more photographers arrived. And I was covered in blood, like a character from one of my movies."

Beriev nodded. "I'll say this for him. Guiteras arrived in record time, and he took charge of everything. Made sure we could give our statements, then go home. He was very professional. And protective of Dayana."

"Did you take any photos yourself, before Guiteras arrived?" Pepper asked Beriev.

"No," said Beriev, glancing at the museum director. "We walked back to the car and waited. Dayana got blood on the seats."

"It was a terrible time," Hernandez added, twisting his hat in his hands. "And we do not know if our copy of *For Whom the Bell Tolls* will ever be restored to us."

From the police report, Pepper knew that a bound galley copy of the novel was found resting on the corpse's back. The publisher made bound galley copies to be sent to book reviewers, journalists, and booksellers to generate interest in an upcoming publication.

The book had been taken from Hemingway's desk in the white tower, where it had been staged on his desk with other items. And then placed on Alicia Arenas' back below the tower, like some twisted statement by the killer.

"Have you read it?" Dayana asked Pepper. "Cubans still read it in English class."

"I have," Pepper said. Although he remembered leaning on the Cliff Notes too.

"It's very beautiful and sad," said Beriev.

Dayana smiled wistfully. "When I was a teenager, I dreamed of playing Maria in a Hollywood version of the novel someday." She laughed. "But no one makes movies from the classics these days."

Besides the killer's strange use of that book, Pepper was also interested in the knife used to stab Arenas repeatedly after she died. The police report said it wasn't found at the crime scene. So, presumably, the killer took the knife away after the murder. But did the killer bring a knife? In other words, did the killer go there to kill? Or did he find the knife there? The police report said that no other items were believed to have been moved or taken during the murder.

The Alicia Arenas police report stated that the estate had an inventory of over twenty-seven thousand personal items of Ernest Hemingway. Were any of his knives missing? "The police said none of the knives from the Hemingway estate were missing?"

"That is true," Hernandez said.

The police report was dated ten days after the murder. "How did you double-check that none of the twenty-seven thousand items were missing?" asked Pepper. "That must have taken weeks or months."

"We are here every day, and we are professionals," Hernandez declared. "We are in charge of every part of the Hemingway legacy at Finca Vigía, and we take that responsibility seriously."

Pretty defensive, thought Pepper. "Were you surprised that museum staff didn't find her body first?"

Hernandez's mouth opened and closed like a fish. "It was Sunday. The museum was closed, and no one was here to find her. I live in the village nearby, but I was at a Ministry of Culture event in Havana. With my wife. We stayed in a hotel in town. But when they called me, I came immediately, of course. The blood!" The man looked like he was hoping for a comforting hug from Dayana, so Pepper reached over and squeezed his shoulder.

Hernandez wiggled loose, clearing his throat.

"Have any other crimes been committed here?" Pepper asked him.

The man looked indignant. "Never, nothing! Maybe children from the villages steal mangoes from our trees down the hill, but other than that? Never, nothing."

Pepper thought. "And you discovered nothing was stolen the day of the murder?"

Hernandez paused, then said, "Nothing."

Hmmm, thought Pepper.

"And how about after the murder? Has anything been stolen since?"

A longer pause by the director, who was visibly sweating now. He put his Panama hat back on his head. "We have thousands of items from Papa Hemingway, over nine thousand books. Over three thousand photographs, many other possessions. And we protect them all carefully."

"But some of them have gone missing since the murder?" tried Pepper.

Hernandez looked like he was going to throw up. "Only a handful of items. We cannot say when, because this was discovered missing six months after the terrible murder. During the annual audit."

"What were the items?"

The man shrugged. "Mostly books from Papa Hemingway's personal collection. We are currently doing another full inventory, because maybe the first time there were mistakes made."

"How many books?"

The man swallowed. "Twenty-three."

That's a handful? "And anything other than books?"

Hernandez said weakly, "An African letter opener, a souvenir from one of Papa's trips to Africa. Of course, we never want an item to go missing, but it wasn't of any great historical significance. The house is full of more meaningful items."

"Where was it kept and when it was last seen?"

"We kept it on the desk up there. In the tower."

CHAPTER TWENTY-FOUR

The four of them climbed a cramped and shaky spiral staircase to the musty top floor of the White Tower.

Taking center stage was a desk with a typewriter, a cup full of pens and pencils, a newspaper, and a few books. Nearby, closer to a window, stood a telescope on a tripod.

"We put it there," pointed Hernandez. "Among the other items on the desk, for tourists to see. But we rarely allowed tourists up here anyway. It is too dangerous."

"What did the letter opener look like?" asked Pepper.

The man shrugged again. "It was an African folk art letter opener, with an ornamental handle—the figure of a woman. Its only real value was that Papa owned it."

"Do you have a picture of it?"

"Of course!" Hernandez sniffed. "We have pictures of every item in the estate."

"Can you show it to us?" asked Pepper.

"It would be such a kind favor, Carlos," added Dayana, giving him what Pepper thought of as her moderate blast of smile and wide eyes. More than enough for most mere mortals.

"I will be right back," said the museum director.

If the missing letter opener was what the killer used to stab Alicia Arena's dead body, it suggested at least that part of the crime was not premeditated. The killer had pushed or thrown her from the tower to her death, then had grabbed the letter opener off the desk and used it to stab her corpse repeatedly in the back.

So maybe the first part wasn't premeditated either. Maybe there had been an argument or a fight. The killer won, and Arenas ended up going over the railing to her death.

But Pepper's theory was not even half-baked, so he didn't share it.

He meandered around the tower room, taking it in. "So, this is where the great man wrote."

Dayana shook her head. "Actually, his wife built it for him as a writing studio, but he preferred to work at a standing desk in his bedroom. But he came here sometimes. The Hollywood actress Ava Gardner used to come stay here as a guest. Hemingway would come here and use this telescope to watch her swim naked in his pool."

Pepper wondered if most people's lives were doomed to be mundane, compared to men like Ernest Hemingway. He stepped out to the landing and saw an empty swimming pool a short walk away, with Havana in the distance. Then he looked straight down. Alicia Arenas had died instantly after a fall of about thirty-five feet. Blunt trauma to her head. Broken neck, among other injuries. Pepper felt a momentary dizziness, standing in that spot.

"If there's nothing else to see?" asked Beriev, brushing past Pepper and beginning down the spiral stairs. "I'm not a fan of heights."

Pepper started to follow him, but Dayana grabbed his hand, stopping him on the metal landing. She stepped in front of him by the railing.

"I had nightmares for weeks," she said in a thin voice. "I dreamed it was me who was thrown off this tower. Then I can see someone standing over my body, stabbing my already dead body. But I couldn't see the killer's face. Why would someone do that?"

"Do what, kill her?"

"I guess that too. But I mean, why stab a person after you'd already killed them?"

Pepper had learned about this during his law enforcement training, and the theory had been included in the police report of Arenas' death. "It happens, but not a lot. Usually, those killers had a personal relationship with the victim and had strong animosity toward them. It's an act of vengeance, or taking something back."

Dayana crossed her arms and shivered. "El Segador must be a lunatic. And it almost paralyzes me, knowing the madman wants to kill me next. Promise you'll stop him, whatever it takes."

"I'll do everything I can."

"Until you go home on Sunday," she said accusingly.

"Hopefully, we catch him before that."

"Hopefully." She studied him. "But Juan and his officers have been trying for nine months and have made no progress. It scares me. What will happen after you go?"

Pepper took both of her hands. "Then maybe you should go too."

"Go?" she asked, her voice trembling. "To America?"

"Why not?"

Dayana shook her head. "I've tried. My government refused to give me a passport. I couldn't even start the process."

"Sometimes that can become a point in your favor, being oppressed in your own country. Their refusal to give you a passport might help you get an emergency visa."

Dayana hugged him, and her embrace lingered. "I don't want to leave my home forever," she whispered in his ear. "But I don't want to die, either. And I wonder how far I can go with my talents, you know? I want to see if I can succeed internationally. Work with new directors and actors. Really push myself."

"Why did they deny your passport?"

Dayana released him and made a face. "I took part in some political protests last year against the government, trying to get them to fix our food and power shortages. The people in charge don't suffer, the entire problem's foolish. So I was photographed protesting. Other artists protested too, but they didn't get the same attention. Alicia was there with me, but she got permission to emigrate to America the same week my request was denied!"

"That's the price of being Cuba's top actor, I guess," said Pepper. "Your face ends up out in front for whatever people are trying to sell."

"I believed in the protest," she explained. "But it's not fair, the way I'm being punished, when thousands of people marched in the streets. It was so amazing—but they are making an example of me. And Cuba loses status when its top artists leave for America. It hurts the Revolution." Then Dayana said in a small voice, "Could you please hold me for a minute?"

Pepper obliged.

Dayana shuddered. Her eyes were closed. "It terrifies me, just thinking about it. A crazy person threw Alicia off this tower. Then went to her dead body and stabbed her in the back, over and over. Who would do that, except a madman? And now the madman wants to kill me next? It feels like it can't be real, but he's already killed three more artists from that stupid magazine article. I can't sleep, I can't eat. I'm terrified."

She turned in his arms and embraced him harder, then tilted up her head to lock eyes. "I meant what I said last night—you need to kill him if you get the chance. A lunatic doesn't stop. He can't be scared away. He'll keep coming for me, and the other artists, unless he dies first."

"I'll protect you while I'm here, but I have to leave tomorrow. You should try to leave Cuba when I do. We'll talk to Wilder together."

"I would feel like I'm running away ... but what else can I do to protect myself?"

A tear was resting halfway down Dayana's cheek, so Pepper gently wiped it away with his finger. "You can always come back after the police catch el Segador."

"Most Cubans don't. It's complicated, with the government, with family."

"Well, that'd be up to you."

She hugged Pepper even tighter, then whispered in his ear. "But if you get the chance to kill him, you promise me you will?"

"I'll defend you and myself if it comes to that."

"And you've killed before, Marisol told me. You're a man who can do the hardest things, when facing evil."

Pepper didn't respond, because he didn't like to talk about the men he'd killed. Both of them had absolutely deserved it, and both had in their own way taken part of Pepper's happiness and sanity with them when they died at his hands. It was a hell of a price that he'd paid, even when justified, and he couldn't make easy promises to do it again.

Dayana stepped forward and kissed him. A quick, hard kiss.

Nothing like how Zula kissed, Pepper stupidly thought, right in the middle of it. *Idiot.* This wasn't the time to think about how Zula kissed, or how she'd unceremoniously dumped him. Was he subconsciously afraid to get hurt by a woman again so soon?

She frowned up at him. "What are you thinking of?" she asked. "Are you scared?"

Before Pepper could make up a lie, they heard a shout from below and stepped apart to look. Beriev was on the ground level, waving up at them in an agitated way. "I'm late, so if you want a ride back to the city, let's go." He turned and trudged toward the parking lot.

Dayana chuckled. "He has a crush on me, I think. I posed for him once, so he could make one of his crazy neo-surrealist portraits of me. And he keeps asking me to pose nude. Do you think I should?"

"Now, *that* would be totally surreal."

Dayana laughed and punched his shoulder.

They reached the museum director's office at the moment he burst out his door, almost flattening them.

"I found it," he announced, flourishing a photograph and handing it to Dayana.

Pepper studied it too. It was more of a stiletto than a letter opener. A real weapon. A measuring ruler lay beside it in the photo, so Pepper could see the letter opener was ten inches long. African folk-art style, he guessed. It was thin, with a black handle topped by the profile of a woman.

"Probably a souvenir from one of Papa's many trips," Hernandez said. "He was a packrat, thank goodness."

"When did you discover it was missing?" Pepper asked.

"Three months ago, during the annual audit," the man said decisively. "Six months after the terrible day."

Pepper thought this was likely the weapon used to stab Alicia's corpse. And possibly the other dead artists too.

Using his phone, Pepper took a close-up photo of the picture of the letter opener.

The revelation of the missing items sent Pepper's mind racing. The opener could easily have been the murder weapon. And his gut told him there was a connection between the stolen books and Alicia's death, but he needed more information to make sense of it.

"Thank you," he said to Hernandez. "There's one other thing I was wondering."

"Si?"

"Who locked the gate by the road on the evening of the murder, with you away in Havana?"

The man paused.

"The head groundskeeper locks the gate when I'm away," he said, as if quoting a memo. "Locks it at sundown, unlocks it at dawn."

"And you confirmed he locked the gate at sunset on the Saturday of the murder? And opened it the next morning?"

"Of course."

"Can I talk to him?" asked Pepper.

Hernandez looked back and forth between Pepper and Dayana. "I'm sorry. He doesn't work here anymore."

"Why not?"

The man bristled. "I can't discuss personnel matters. They're confidential by law."

"When did he leave?"

The man waved dismissively. "Many months ago. We replaced him easily."

"How many months ago?"

Hernandez said nothing.

"I can ask Detective Guiteras to ask you these same questions and more. How long ago?"

The man's mustache shook. "Eight months." A month after the murder. "You believe the groundskeeper killed Señorita Arenas?" he asked.

"No," said Pepper. "I believe the killer arrived after sundown, killed Alicia Arenas, then left during the night." Which in Pepper's mind explained the discrepancy in the police report between the official time of death—approximately six o'clock—not reconciling with the coroner's later view that the time of death might well have been closer to nine.

The man was shaking harder now. His mind was probably spinning with fears of the blame that might attach to him. The legal risk. The professional damage. "I was in Havana all night. With my wife."

"Then I'm sure you have nothing to worry about. But if I were you, I would call Detective Guiteras to correct a mistake in the police report. That you are no longer certain that the gatekeeper locked the gate at sunset on the day of the murder, and activated the motion alarms on the driveway."

"I will have to think," Hernandez said.

"Don't think too long, because I'll be sharing my opinion with the PNR shortly. And did you contact Detective Guiteras when you learned the letter opener and the books were missing?"

He shrugged helplessly. "No, of course not. It was six months later. No one instructed us to contact him."

"You should call him immediately," said Pepper.

The museum director looked down at his white shoes and swallowed miserably.

Pepper sat in the backseat of the Lada on the drive back, scrunched up like a folding lawn chair. He felt like his mind was moving twice as fast as the little Lada, as he tried to process what he'd learned at the Hemingway estate.

The official timeline of Alicia Arenas' murder was incorrect, and an African letter opener, believed to be the weapon used to stab the victims, had gone missing, along with two dozen valuable Hemingway books. Had Alicia Arenas sold those books to raise money for her visa application, possibly through her stepbrother, Quinto Chavez? And did that point Pepper toward the identity of the serial killer?

Then a crazy thought came to Pepper, just before they reached Centro Havana: set a trap for el Segador.

Get the killer to come to him. Probably a *loco* long shot, but it could be attempted in Pepper's brief window of remaining time.

Pepper told his idea to Dayana and Beriev. He focused on Dayana, because she was the key to the plan. She would be the bait in the trap, which was a dangerous risk. Maybe even a reckless risk.

But Dayana understood the plan right away, risks and all. She liked it; she was in. She even grinned at Pepper, her hair blowing around her face as they drove toward Centro Havana. Dayana looked like she was having a good time, talking about being used to lure a serial killer, and again Pepper saw the steel in her gaze.

What a woman.

Pepper hoped neither of them would soon regret it.

CHAPTER TWENTY-FIVE

They regrouped with the others back at Casa de Vides and began making calls to spread the phony rumor immediately. The tale had all the juicy elements necessary to race through their entire social network in Havana like a dropped flame through a rum factory.

The story was just believable enough, given that the serial killer wouldn't have very long to think about it. Hopefully, he'd decide he needed to silence Dayana de Melina and her yuma lawman and steal the hard proof of his identity before she handed over her evidence to the PNR.

When Pepper called Ozzie to spread the fake news about Dayana, the younger Rappeneau was full of apologies about Pepper getting tossed out of the party.

"Arguing with my dad's like jerking off a snake," said Ozzie. "Confusing and dangerous."

Pepper told Ozzie the fake story, trying to keep it simple and believable. But he started by announcing he'd found Marisol alive and well.

"Whoa, dude, that's amazing!" Ozzie exclaimed. "Where was she?"

Pepper explained that he couldn't say because of the next news. He told Ozzie that during their search for Marisol and a visit that morning to the Hemingway estate where Alicia Arenas was killed, Dayana came into possession of hard evidence that proved el Segador's true identity.

"Seriously?" gasped Ozzie. "The bogeyman fucked up?"

"Big time," agreed Pepper. "Definitive proof." He explained she was going to the PNR police to tell them everything she knew, just as soon as the authorities approved the papers for her to leave Cuba for America, for her own safety. The Cuban government needed to grant her a passport, and the U.S. embassy had to grant her an emergency visa.

"That's wild!" exclaimed Ozzie. "Dayana's such a badass! Do you need help to protect her from getting stabbed in the meanwhile? My dad's got plenty of muscle heads. You've met 'em!"

Pepper laughed. "I can look after her. Don't tell anyone, but I'll hide her away at the Hotel Nacional. Hopefully, she'll sit down with the PNR detectives later this afternoon, after everything's approved by the bureaucrats."

"I hope she leaves Cuba," said Ozzie. "My dad's been trying to help her do that for months. She's the best damn actress I ever saw and obviously hot as shit. She could make it in movies anywhere."

"He's already been trying to help her?"

"Absolutely! And she's not the only artist he's tried to help get off this rock. He's got tons of cash and connections, and he's happy to use them."

Pepper wondered if Rappeneau's involvement with the arts was benevolence or something more sinister. "Why would he help Cubans defect?"

Ozzie laughed. "Because lots of them want to! And Dad sure knows how to pick 'em. He got divorced about ten years ago from

Mom, and he's been on a rampage ever since. Lining them up and mowing them down. I love girls too, obviously. But Dad's setting some kind of record."

Pepper felt bad for Ozzie. He seemed like a good guy, quite different from his father.

Thirty minutes later, Angel left with Marisol and Hector and checked into a standard hotel room at the Hotel Nacional de Cuba. No reservation, but no problem with Angel's fistful of American dollars.

Pepper, Dayana, and Beriev were last to leave Casa de Vides for the hotel. But they needed to make one quick stop—an important meeting Pepper had set up—on the way to their hotel trap.

"I'm too busy for this," said Heather Wilder. "But Ryan, you're so damned entertaining, I couldn't say no."

Pepper and Dayana joined her where she was sitting on the Malecon's seawall, in a long green dress and sunglasses, three blocks down from the U.S. embassy. Beriev waited at the curb nearby, his engine running.

Wilder held a coffee cup in one hand and three square pastries in the other. She was hunched over against the gusting wind. Pepper wondered if the cup actually held coffee, or was a spy-vs.-spy recording device.

"We didn't know who else to call," admitted Pepper, taking a seat on the rough stone seawall. Dayana sat on the embassy officer's other side and gave her a hug. Havana Bay was choppy with waves, and only one boat was fighting its way across the skyline.

Pepper looked at his watch. It was two o'clock. He needed this conversation to finish quickly.

He laid out the entire story for Wilder. He told her they'd found Marisol, and she was completely unharmed. "And thank you for the help you gave," said Pepper, trying not to lay it on too thick.

"Great news!" Wilder said, but her face was less excited than her voice. "I told you she'd be fine."

Pepper told Wilder about the legitimate clues he'd discovered at the Hemingway estate, including that an African letter opener had been stolen and likely was used by el Segador during each of his crimes. Also, almost two dozen valuable books were missing from Hemingway's collection.

"African letter opener?" whistled Wilder. "Our killer has a flair for the dramatic. But I can guess about the books."

"Really?"

Wilder smiled. "Alicia Arenas had tried for months to get a visa to the U.S. Like I said, it's expensive. It's a process, and money turns the wheels, you know? She talked to me about ways she might raise the money, and then in December, the money came through. She refused to tell me where she got it, but it was a huge amount of money for a Cuban to have. Like, more money than she would have earned in ten lifetimes."

"So you think she stole the Hemingway books when she was doing her writing residency, then sold them?"

Wilder shrugged. "She probably found someone else to sell them. Probably overseas."

Pepper immediately guessed who that might be. Someone she could trust, and someone with black market connections. Someone like her stepbrother, Quinto Chavez.

That might explain how he ended up on the persons of interest list in her killing. Yet why was he also on the police reports' lists for the other artist murders?

Then Pepper moved on to the Big Lie part of his story, telling Wilder that Dayana had found even more explosive material that morning at the Hemingway estate—hard proof about the identity of the person who had been killing Cuba's top artists.

"Yeah?" Wilder asked skeptically, studying Dayana. "So who's el Segador?" She popped one of the small pastries in her mouth. "And what's the proof?"

Pepper waved her off. "She's not telling anyone except the police," he said. "She doesn't want the killer to hear about any of this until she's handed over the evidence to the PNR and she's safely out of harm's way."

"So, then, you're telling me this, because . . . ?"

Dayana turned and looked Wilder right in the eye. "I'm afraid for my life, and I believe I'll be in even more danger after I share what I have with the PNR. After that happens, I'm hoping I can get asylum at your embassy. And then an emergency visa to America." She touched Wilder's sleeve. "I would only leave Cuba until the killer is imprisoned," she added, almost too softly to be heard over the wind.

Dayana's phone rang. She looked at the screen, apologized, and move away to talk. Wilder fell silent, watching Dayana. When Dayana finished, she walked back as the sun came from behind a cloud, and Pepper's pulse raced. She looked so perfect it was hard to believe she wasn't on a movie screen.

"I'm sorry about that," Dayana said as she sat back on the seawall. "But I have amazing news. The hard proof I have—about who's the killer? Someone heard I'm going to the PNR. He wants to give me more evidence about the killer, to turn over to the police. Very strong evidence, he said."

"Who said?" asked Wilder.

Dayana wrinkled her nose and shook her head. "I promised to leave him out of it. But he says he will give me the evidence this afternoon. He said it would convict el Segador even without my proof." She looked at Pepper triumphantly, and he could read her silent message to him: *We won't be bluffing anymore.*

But for Wilder's benefit, Pepper said, "Even better. But that puts Dayana even more at risk. I'm flying home tomorrow, and I want her to go with me. Can you help? Please?"

Wilder studied Pepper, then Dayana. "Maybe there's a way for me to make this happen. I can see the news stories back home—Cuba's leading actress seeks asylum when Cuba can't protect her from Havana's ghostly serial killer."

Then she sipped her coffee, so Pepper decided it probably wasn't a microphone.

"It gives me chills," admitted Dayana. "When you say it like that."

"Someone's been killing Cuba's best artists for almost a year, and the police have no solid suspects until you hand over that evidence," said Wilder. "If I were you, I'd have chills too."

"No solid suspects we know of," corrected Pepper.

Wilder laughed. "If the Cuban police had ID'd the killer, he'd be in custody. They would interview him, Guantanamo–style. A method they've perfected over the decades, with none of our Miranda rights, no lawyer, no right to remain silent. They would extract a confession one drop of blood at a time. And in the meantime, the killings would have ended."

"So you'll help me?" Dayana pleaded, studying Wilder's face.

"Give me some time," she said. "I'll see what I can work out. And what Uncle Sam will demand in return."

"Demand?" asked Dayana.

"The U.S. government can do almost anything, but it has to make sense for us too. And you'll also have to reveal all the details, including who is the killer and what proof you have."

She turned to Pepper. "Where will you keep her safe in the meantime?"

"I have a place," said Pepper. "Not too far away."

"Good. Where's that?"

"Better we don't say," shrugged Pepper, glancing toward the Hotel Nacional. "The fewer people who know, the safer she'll be."

Wilder studied them both again, then shrugged. "I'll call you," she said. "Let's hope you're both still alive when I do."

Fifteen minutes later, Dayana de Melina checked into the Hotel Nacional. Like Angel, she had no reservation, but that was no problem at all.

The desk manager, a small man in his fifties with dandruff on the shoulders of his blue blazer, shooed away the desk clerk. He announced he was a devoted fan of her films and upgraded her to the Presidential Suite. "The bed where Winston Churchill slept," he confided to her. "And Leonardo DiCaprio."

Dayana and Pepper took the elevator up one floor to the suite. It had two bedrooms, a dining room, a sitting room, and an office. The red velvet curtains and mahogany furniture were classic 1930s Cuban, like the suite had been preserved in time. It also smelled musty.

The rumor they'd carefully spread said Dayana was guarded only by Pepper. But that was just part of the trap, because Angel, Hector, Marisol, and Beriev soon moved from Angel's room to Dayana's suite, each bearing weapons ranging from a baseball bat (Angel), to pepper spray (Hector), to a machete (Marisol). And Beriev had a stun gun which looked like it had never been used, but no one took him up on his offer to demonstrate it. Beriev also had his video camera, fully charged to record their hopeful takedown of el Segador.

"This is the hotel where those old-time Mob guys like Lucky Luciano and Meyer Lansky had their summit meeting—before Castro ruined the party," said Marisol. "Now it's run by the Cuban government, like most of the hotels here."

"Nice joint, for a trap," Angel said approvingly, standing by an enormous window, looking out over the Malecón and Havana Bay. Pepper joined him, so they could speak confidentially.

"Good news," Pepper said in a low voice. "Our scheme shook the tree in a way we didn't predict." He explained that after they left Wilder, Dayana told him who had called her—the odd poet, Guillermo Infante. The poet asked Dayana to come to his apartment. He said he heard through the grapevine that she knew who el Segador was. "He said he has undeniable proof of the killer's identity too, and he wanted her to hand it over to the PNR at the same time. Like most Cubans, he's allergic to cops."

"Might help turn our bluff into a winning hand, if the little bastard isn't lying," said Angel. "And my money is, he's lying."

"Either way, he'll have to wait. The trap is set here and we need to be ready for the killer to show up."

"But will he?" asked Angel, sounding doubtful.

Marisol walked over to Angel and gave him a hug. "El Segador?" she asked. "Assuming he hears our rumor, his two choices are to run or to come here and eliminate the threat."

Pepper shrugged. "If you told me I had a fifty percent chance of catching a serial killer today, I'd take those odds." That reminded him. For the third time, he confirmed the balcony doors and the front door were locked.

All they could do was wait. Pepper and Dayana went to the living room, carrying on the fiction that Pepper was there protecting her alone, and everyone else split up into the master and second bedrooms. Marisol and Angel took the master, and Pepper hoped they'd take the time to talk some more about Marisol's faked disappearance. Angel had a new reserve with Marisol, a stiffness, telling Pepper that his buddy hadn't forgiven and forgotten her fake disappearance trick.

In the living room, Pepper wandered over to the window

again, looking down on the harbor, dealing with his own heavy thoughts.

"What's wrong?" Dayana asked, putting a hand on his arm.

"I have to leave Cuba tomorrow, no matter what," he reminded her. "Or my career will be shot. I'm worried about what to do if this trap doesn't work."

She stepped back and studied him. "You'll choose your job over my life? I hoped you'd change your mind when the time comes."

"That's not fair," he protested, although he had been wracking his brain for solutions that would do just that.

"I assumed you cared about me," she said, with a cool steel in her voice. She turned away from him, her shoulders shaking with emotion.

Pepper reached for her, but she shrugged him away.

"I'll find a way to protect myself," she said quietly. "I always have." Then she went and lay down on the sofa, facing away from him, and wouldn't talk.

Feeling like an asshole, Pepper stayed by the window, waiting until five o'clock for the next phase of the trap to begin.

When it was time, he rode down in the elevator and publicly departed via the grand entrance, through the thin crowd of tourists checking out the iconic hotel. If someone was watching, they would see the yuma lawman leaving the hotel—apparently leaving his charge unprotected.

Pepper took the long walk out to the street, then circled the property. He found it was more awkward and time consuming to cut back to the hotel's side door than he'd expected. The landscaping seemed designed to discourage sneaky arrivals.

He finally entered by the side door, sweating heavily, and took the stairs up two at a time. He'd been gone for twenty minutes, longer than planned.

He reached the presidential suite to find its door wide open and shouts coming from inside.

Pepper burst into the presidential suite, his heart pounding.

He found Quinto Chavez and four of his jinetero buddies facing off against Angel, Hector, and Beriev. The men were shouting back and forth, their voices rising with each passing second.

Dayana was standing in the doorway to the master bedroom with the door mostly shut, as if she was going to slam it the moment trouble escalated.

"Kneel down, hands behind your heads!" Angel yelled, waving his baseball bat.

Quinto didn't yield. "I know Dayana has evidence of who killed Carlina and the others. She needs to tell us."

"You need to go," said Beriev. He pulled himself up to full height and girth, which was considerably larger than Quinto or his companions.

"El Segador will have learned she's here," implored Quinto. "He will come to eliminate Dayana's evidence. And her too!"

Angel stepped forward. His eyes narrowed. "If you don't leave, the next victim's going to be you!"

The threat heightened the tension in the room. Quinto's men advanced, their hands in pockets and under shirts for hidden weapons.

Pepper's mind raced, trying to figure out how to defuse the situation. They hadn't known who would show up, so contingency planning had been generic and thin. Grab whoever showed, sort it out later.

Then a loud whistle shattered the room, and everyone froze.

Detective Lola Valdés was standing in the open doorway, one

hand to her lips to form her piercing whistle. Her other hand was holding a handgun. Somehow, it seemed like she was pointing it at all of them at once.

"Enough!" she shouted, her voice cutting through the chaos. "Everyone, stand down. Now!"

The men hesitated, their eyes darting between Valdés and each other. Slowly, they lowered their hands, the threat of immediate violence dissipating.

Valdés advanced into the room, her gaze sweeping over everyone present. "I am Detective Valdés of the Policía Nacional de la Revolución. I'll shoot the next man who moves without permission."

Pepper watched dumbfounded as Valdés took instant control of the situation. "That lady's smile has teeth," he thought, impressed.

Everyone complied with her authority simultaneously, draining the tension from the room.

Someone knocked at the open door, and Valdés whirled, pointing her handgun at the new arrival.

The front desk manager blanched. He raised both hands tentatively. "There was talk downstairs. The police are here, that there is trouble. Can I ask what is going on?"

Valdés holstered her handgun, her expression softening slightly. "Police, yes. Trouble, no," she said, showing the hotel manager her laminated PNR identification card embossed with a miniature Cuban flag. The manager nodded, satisfied with her explanation.

What a shit show, thought Pepper. The trap was absolutely blown, no question. If el Segador had been about to pounce, this circus would have spooked him.

He glanced at his watch. It was time to go collect Guillermo Infante's ironclad evidence. The proof that would turn the situation from a failed bluff to a winning hand. Unless the flaky poet was full of shit.

He pulled Valdés aside. "I promised to pass along anything I learned about the artist murders, so here you go." He told her what he'd uncovered at the Hemingway estate, how the museum director had covered up their failure to close the gate the evening Alicia Arenas was murdered, so the official timeline of the crime was incorrect. "You might want to rethink the alibis of your suspects for a broader range past sunset."

He also told her about the discovery during the audit that an African letter opener had disappeared from the tower, along with some valuable books from the main house. "I saw a picture of the letter opener—it's basically a knife, and I'll bet it's the weapon used to stab each of the dead artists."

Valdés' mouth fell open in surprise. "Thank you. And I have something for you. You asked me to find out why Dayana's passport application was rejected." Pepper stiffened at this news. "I have a childhood friend who works at the Dirección de Inmigración y Extranjería. He said the official reason was her participation in protests that undermined the Cuban government. And the unofficial reason was that it would hurt Cuba's prestige to lose her. But there was a more interesting part to it."

"Yes?"

"The person who wrote to the division describing Dayana's unpatriotic behavior was my colleague Juan Guiteras."

"Seriously?" Pepper felt his anger instantly rising. He grew up with Dayana, yet he threw her under the bus? Pepper had already thought Guiteras was an asshole, but this was next-level assholery. Pepper had suspected Guiteras had feelings for Dayana, but his act seemed like controlling, even stalker behavior, hidden behind a thin excuse of patriotism.

"It was very unusual," added Valdés. "I believe he allowed his personal feelings for Señorita de Melina to cloud his professional judgment. I plan to talk to him about it when I get a chance."

Pepper laughed sympathetically. "Good luck with that conversation! Speaking of Dayana, can you stay here with her for an hour? I need to go somewhere, and there's nobody else I trust to keep her safe while I'm gone. And can you politely get rid of Quinto and his pals?"

She looked at him questioningly. "You need to go somewhere? Tell me."

Pepper smiled. "It'll be better as a surprise when I get back. Hopefully, the best surprise of your career."

"You know how to tease a woman," she smiled back. "I can only stay for an hour, so hurry back."

Pepper grabbed Angel and Hector, told the others he'd be back, and a moment later they were trotting down the stairs to retrieve the Cadillac.

Pepper didn't want to leave Dayana after setting her in the killer's crosshairs, but the poet's evidence might give them everything they'd been looking for. Real evidence, real leverage.

If the squirrely poet could be trusted, thought Pepper. With every step, Pepper's doubts grew. If Infante had lied to Dayana or exaggerated the extent of his proof, Pepper was going to lose it. He already felt himself getting agitated, just thinking about the possibility.

Angel glanced at Pepper as they climbed into the Cadillac. "You're thinking what I'm thinking?" he said. "If that clown's wasting our time again, you know, just looking for attention, I'm gonna shave the other side of his face with a dry razor blade."

Pepper laughed. "And I'll hold him down."

CHAPTER TWENTY-SIX

"Guillermo Infante hates you," Pepper said to Angel, when they and Hector reached the poet's apartment building. "So I'll take the lead, okay?"

They knocked on Infante's second-floor apartment door. They stood, shuffling their feet in the hallway for the longest time, but the door stayed shut.

"He's probably just jealous of my superior grooming skills," Angel muttered. "The egotistic weasel."

Pepper knocked again, harder. Again, no response. "This guy's getting on my last fucking nerve," he said, trying the doorknob.

It opened. Pepper pushed it wider and yelled the poet's name. Again, no response.

"Maybe we wait in the hall?" suggested Hector.

"To hell with that," said Pepper, walking in. They'd wait inside, and when the weird poet showed up, they'd grab the evidence, if the guy really had any. Then they'd hurry back to the hotel.

Pepper had taken three steps into the apartment when he saw the blood. And the dead body. Guillermo Infante was propped up in a chair with a book open in front of him, as if he was reading. But his pale, waxy face was tilted to one side, showing only the cheek that was clean shaven, making him look younger.

A large heart was drawn on the floor around his chair, in blood. The rancid sweet smell of death crept into Pepper's nostrils, and he involuntarily took a step back.

"For freak's sake!" said Angel, stopping.

Pepper put a hand over his nose to ward off the coppery stench. "Whatever evidence Infante had, the killer got to him first."

Hector was pale and he looked like he was going to throw up. "I should have waited in the car," he said in a faint voice. "We must go."

Angel nodded in agreement. "If we get caught here, we're screwed."

But Pepper was a lifetime law enforcement officer, from a family of law enforcement officers. "We need to call 911," he said. "The PNR needs to process this scene right away. Infante phoned Dayana a little after two, so this is a fresh murder scene. Somebody in the building or out front might have seen the killer, and if we don't call this in, that witness may be long gone when someone else finds the body."

"That is a *terrible* idea," insisted Hector.

"Maybe," conceded Pepper. "But it's the right thing to do, for Infante and all the victims."

Hector shook his head like Pepper was crazy, but said, "It is not 911 in Cuba. For emergencies, you phone 106."

That seemed pretty random. "That must be tough to remember, in the middle of an emergency."

Hector shrugged. "Most Cubans don't call the police, so it doesn't matter." He sighed, then pulled out his phone and dialed. After a long pause, he began talking, sounding stiff and nervous.

When Hector hung up, his face was pale. "The police said I should wait in the hall until officers arrive."

Pepper's mind raced as he tried to piece together the implications of Infante's murder. If el Segador murdered the poet to silence him, it meant Infante's evidence was legitimate and threatened to expose the killer's identity.

How did the killer know about Infante's evidence in the first place?

But maybe more important, was Infante's evidence still available?

Pepper guessed they had five to ten minutes until the police arrived, but in a foreign country, it might take longer. "You guys wait in the hall," Pepper said. "If they arrive, yell."

Pepper quickly searched the living room. He checked through drawers, piles of books, inside the refrigerator, and everywhere else that Guillermo might have placed evidence of the serial killer's identity. Of course, the poet might have left his evidence right on the counter, and el Segador might have taken it after murdering the poet.

But Pepper found nothing, and the clock was ticking.

Knowing it was a risky move, Pepper walked over to the poet's body in the chair. He got up close, careful not to smear the heart-shaped blood mark on the floor.

He carefully studied Infante's corpse. The dead poet was wearing green pants and a long-sleeve shirt. Pepper looked at the open book in his hands, and saw it was one of Ernest Hemingway's most famous books, *For Whom the Bell Tolls*.

Well, that message from the killer is super clear, thought Pepper. *Bad news, little poet—it tolls for thee.*

Pepper wondered again what was behind the killer's Hemingway fixation, leaving the same book with each of his victims. It seemed like a bizarre calling card.

Pepper scrutinized Infante's face. It was hard to look at the pale corpse and remember the boisterous, tipsy poet. Not so loud anymore. Not the life of any party, ever again. He was wearing the small round glasses that John Lennon had made popular for leftist intellectuals the world over.

Pepper gently took the glasses off the man's face and looked through them. They were prescription-less.

"Do Cubans have better eyesight than Americans?" asked Pepper.

"What?" asked Hector from the hall.

"Back home, maybe seventy percent of people wear glasses or contact lenses. In Cuba, almost no one does. How come they all have better eyesight?"

Angel laughed. "Or maybe they have uncorrected vision. That would explain the car accidents."

Pepper gently put the glasses back on Infante's face. He felt bad that he hadn't liked the poet the few times he'd met him. The man had seemed arrogant and flaky. Pepper hadn't read his poetry, but Infante had given off the impression that he was a national treasure. Maybe poets lived in their own heads so much that they built little kingdoms there, not caring about the real world, or what lesser people thought.

Or maybe Infante had just been a narcissist.

Pepper recalled that Infante wasn't included in the *Vanity Fair* article about Cuba's top artists. So either el Segador was broadening his hit list, or he learned Infante had evidence to expose his identity and decided to eliminate that threat.

Using his good left hand, Pepper gingerly searched both of the poet's front pants pockets and then his rear pockets. He found nothing that seemed like a clue—just some Cuban pesos, the man's ID card, and a soiled handkerchief.

Pepper knew he was leaving fingerprints on those items, but he planned to be long gone from Cuba before the PNR processed them.

Pepper heard voices in the hallway, and Angel called out Pepper's name. As he hustled to the front door, he noticed the entryway floor mat was slightly raised and askew. He walked over, lifted the corner, and found a thin stack of documents. The perfect place for Infante to hide them, if he'd unexpectedly needed to answer the door but didn't want sensitive papers in his hands.

The top document looked like a memo in English. He saw the name of Carlina Borja, the dead dancer, at the top of it. Pepper shoved the thin stack of documents into the back of his pants waistband, untucking his shirt to cover them. Then he smoothed down the floor mat. He heard Angel call his name again, more anxiously. Pepper quickly exited the apartment, glancing at his watch. The police response had taken four minutes.

"They're on the stairs," said Angel.

Pepper could hear heavy footsteps from the stairwell. And the first officer to reach the hallway was Detective Juan Guiteras.

Guiteras smiled at them without an ounce of warmth. He was wearing a light black suit, a blue shirt, and no tie. "I would be crazy not to arrest you."

"We phoned in the murder," said Pepper. "You can't possibly think I'm el Segador?"

Guiteras grunted. "Then tell me why you are here."

Pepper told him a reasonable version of the truth. The poet had called Dayana, claiming to have evidence of the serial killer's identity. Infante was trying to help her because she was rumored to be a future target of the killer. And the three of them came to collect that evidence in Dayana's place. Pepper added that he'd been planning to turn over any evidence to the PNR immediately. He brought up Infante's reputation as a blowhard and a flake, so Pepper hadn't wanted to bother the police until he had legitimate evidence in hand.

"How well did you know the victim?" Guiteras asked.

Pepper explained that he'd met Guillermo Infante on Wednesday night at the La Cueva club. He had also spoken to him briefly at a party at Laurent Rappeneau's home last night.

"I received information you had a confrontation with him at that club," continued Guiteras. "Which led to a fight and then a car chase."

Pepper didn't respond. *Where had Guiteras heard all of that?* Of course, there had been plenty of potential snitches at a club that large and public.

"Infante wasn't part of any fight or car chase," said Pepper. *At least not directly.* "But someone in this building or the neighborhood might have seen the killer. I'm not telling you how to do your job, but the more time you spend on us, the more likely you'll miss your witnesses."

Guiteras bristled. "You think our investigative methods are primitive, that we are all incompetent or corrupt, *sí?*"

Pepper didn't answer. But he was glad he hadn't offered Guiteras a bribe when he was desperate to find Marisol. He now believed Guiteras would have arrested him on the spot. The guy was a super patriot, a professional, and he definitely didn't like Pepper.

Guiteras went on. "I am grateful you are not telling me how to do my job. I don't have time to give you another boxing lesson. We will check the scene for fingerprints, hair, bodily fluids, and then we will decide if you are suspects."

More heavy steps pounded up the stairs, and four uniformed PNR officers came into the hallway.

Detective Guiteras pointed at one of them. "This is Officer

Ortiz. He speaks good English. He will take a separate statement from each of you. I will be busy locating your friend Viktor Beriev and determining his alibi for the time of this murder. You may be interested to know I recently received word from authorities in Belarus that they wish to talk to him about crimes that occurred in Minsk in the months before Beriev left for Cuba."

Pepper was surprised, but didn't want to show it. "Good luck with that."

"He is the one who will need luck," said Guiteras. "If he lied to get his entry visas, he will be deported back to Belarus, and his property will be confiscated, including his art."

"I don't know anything about Belarus, but his alibi for Guillermo Infante's murder is rock solid. He was with me and Dayana all day. We were out at the Hemingway estate. Infante phoned Dayana a little after two o'clock, and Viktor was with me right until I came here. So there's no way he's your killer. I can vouch for him, one hundred percent."

Guiteras looked surprised and maybe disappointed. "Include those specific times and details about Viktor Beriev's whereabouts in your statement, and we will see."

"You're welcome," said Pepper.

"I'm welcome?" A vein on the detective's neck began pulsating like an angry worm. "You are going to give this officer your complete and honest statement. When you return to your apartment, you are officially ordered to stay there. A police car will be stationed outside your door to make sure that you comply. And then tomorrow you will have two choices. A police car will escort you to the airport to leave Cuba, or I will escort you to Combinado del Este prison myself. It's a quick drive, like falling into hell. Your choice."

CHAPTER TWENTY-SEVEN

Quinto and his jinetero pals were gone when Pepper, Angel, and Hector returned to the hotel suite.

"I think I made them uncomfortable," smiled Detective Valdés. "Which was intentional." She said she was on shift and needed to go, but made sure Pepper had her cell phone number. "Anything you need," she said.

"We'll be fine," said Dayana, taking Pepper's arm.

Valdés studied her. "You are lucky to have his help, aren't you? And I think you like it even better that he's American."

Dayana's eyes tightened and her nostrils flared. "I like that he's dangerous."

The two women stared at each other, neither turning away, until Pepper gave a big fake cough. Then Valdés said a businesslike goodbye and Pepper showed her out.

"I would be careful," she said, stepping into the hallway.

"I'll double-check all the locks," he promised.

"Not about the killer," said Valdés. "About the actress. I think maybe she is using you to get to America."

"She's trying to stay alive," said Pepper. But the detective's comment momentarily made him wonder about his new, raw feelings for Dayana as he strolled back to her.

Their el Segador trap had been unsuccessful, so there was no reason to keep an army of people in the suite on standby. Hector headed downstairs to sleep in the room Angel had paid for. Beriev headed home. Leaving Angel, Marisol, Pepper, and Dayana in the suite.

"Do you think Guiteras knows yet that we didn't head back to the casa?" asked Angel.

"Somehow he knows every move I make," said Pepper. "But this time I hope he knows and I hope he's pissed off about it. Screw Guiteras."

They ordered room service for dinner, which arrived without incident. No killer disguised as a hotel employee. No one smashing in a window, gun blazing. They were probably safe for the night.

"I am going to ask the hotel to find me a guitar," Dayana said.

"You play guitar?" Pepper asked, surprised.

"No," she said. "But you do!" She laughed.

Marisol and Dayana lightly explained that they had some things to do, and disappeared into the master bedroom without any more explanation.

"Girl talk," guessed Angel. "Probably about you. Did you know Marisol has video of Dayana slapping you at the nightclub when you met?"

"What?"

"Absolutely. Marisol had Dayana wear a buttonhole camera. And remember how Dayana convinced Beriev to record your interviews when you were following in Marisol's footprints from August?"

"Yeah."

"Marisol told her to do that. All fodder for her eventual documentary."

Damn. "When else has she been wearing that buttonhole camera?" During their talks when Pepper had felt a connection with her, an attraction?

"Why?" asked Angel. "You guys been getting cozy behind my back?"

Pepper said nothing. Dayana was stunning, sure. But she'd been part of Marisol's deception, and Pepper was still wary about her for that.

"You'd be nuts not to get to know her better," persisted Angel. "She's a total smoke show. And if you're stupid enough to be feeling guilty, don't forget, Zula dumped you—"

"Buddy, I'm out of here tomorrow. And we've got our hands full already. So I'm glad I'm not on any secret sex tapes."

Angel grinned. "No disrespect to Marisol, but Dayana might be the most beautiful woman I've ever seen in real life. Like, not in a movie or on social media. She's beautiful enough to make any guy stupid. Probably happens everywhere she goes, every day. But I think for some weird reason she likes you, mano, just saying." Angel laughed again, the full, happy belly laugh that meant he was in good spirits.

Pepper shrugged. "Hopefully, Marisol puts in a good word for me. But while they're busy, come have a look at something."

Pepper led Angel into the second bedroom and lifted the mattress by the window to retrieve the package of documents he'd found at Infante's apartment. It was another of Pepper's crimes in Cuba, taking the package from a crime scene. Better to allow Dayana and Marisol to have honest deniability if Pepper's rash act ever blew up in his face.

Pepper told Angel where he'd found the package, and they laid out all the documents on one of the twin beds.

Pepper confirmed the impression he'd formed at the crime scene—it was a stack of memos, in English, apparently written by

Heather Wilder, because her name was at the top of each. Each memo was addressed "To File, Confidential."

The package contained four sets of five memos, one set for each dead artist, with their name in the subject line.

Pepper scanned one set quickly while Angel flipped through another.

"It reads like some kind of governmental bullshit," said Angel.

His buddy was right.

Despite the lack of official letterhead, they read exactly like you would expect State Department memos to read. Full of jargon and run-on sentences. Full of qualifiers and smoke blowing. But the substance was there as he waded through the rest of it:

How respected globally the artists were, their upcoming international exhibitions or performances, and their influence on other artists worldwide.

A long summary of their specific habits, insecurities, and weaknesses.

Their health issues and medical vulnerabilities.

Their level of support for Cuba's communist regime

Their financial net worth, including the value of their current and future revenues. Also, their value to the Cuban government from tax revenue, tourism draw, and cultural prestige.

"Holy shit," said Angel. "So, Wilder took the time to build dossiers on all the dead artists? Why would she do that? The memos aren't dated—I wonder if they were from before or after the artist died?"

"This set has some writing on it," said Pepper, moving to the memos about Carlina Borja.

Someone had annotated the memos with blue handwriting. Some underlinings. And some comments, like "sick!" and "capitalist BS!" One of which, at the end of the psychological profile, said, "Had her killed!!" "Killed" was underlined twice.

Pepper showed the writing to Angel. "I've seen the

handwriting once before, on a badly written breakup letter," he said. "Guillermo Infante wrote these notes."

Angel thought about that. "Maybe he wasn't as loony as he acted. So what do we do with these?"

"Let's put them back under the mattress for tonight. I need to sleep on it."

Angel groaned.

They experienced an awkward moment when Angel and Marisol said good night and headed to the master bedroom room.

"You take the other bedroom," said Pepper. He would sleep on the couch in the living room. Which would be good if el Segador was crazy enough to break in during the night.

Dayana laughed. "Don't be foolish. The other bedroom has two beds. Are you scared of me?"

Scared of myself, he thought.

"Can I ask you a question?" Dayana asked a little later. She was lying on her old-fashioned twin bed, four feet away from Pepper, and the curve of her hip caught the thin glow of the nightstand lamp. She was wearing a white v-neck T-shirt that was short enough to show a peek of red panties.

"Anything," said Pepper. He could smell her sweet floral scent.

"Why did you lie to me about not having a girlfriend?"

"What?" he exclaimed.

"You said at Laurent's party, you were 'unfortunately single.' But Marisol told me you are crazy about a lovely girl from your hometown. That you are dating."

Pepper didn't want to talk about Zula, but didn't want Dayana to think he was sneaky, either. "I was dating someone at the end of the summer, but she dumped me."

Dayana made a sad noise. "Why would she do that?"

"She wanted me to move my job to be nearer to her. But it's not that easy." Pepper swallowed hard, remembering the hurt look on Zula's face when he didn't jump at her invitation to join her in Boston. And his stupidity for not swallowing his pride and telling her about being on the shit list at the FBI, with no likelihood of getting a transfer anytime soon. A pink slip, more likely.

"Why not?"

To hell with it. Pepper told her the whole story. His success that summer which had resulted in his injury, and that his FBI career was likely about to be cut short.

He even told her about Zula. How they'd begun dating, how it was like being caught in a rainstorm. A mix of exciting and nerve-wracking. But Zula was going away to start law school that fall. She'd asked Pepper if he would transfer to the FBI's Boston office, close to where she would be living.

Like an idiot, Pepper hadn't given her a complete answer. The truth was, his FBI job was in limbo and headed toward the trash heap. But he didn't tell her that or explain himself coherently. He'd basically gone silent.

"So she dumped me," Pepper admitted. "She told me to call her if I ever figured myself out."

"Ouch," said Dayana.

He sighed. "So everything in my life is imploding. First Zula. And on Monday, probably my career too."

"I'm sorry I mentioned her, but I will say this. If she wanted to be with you, she would have fought harder. But let's talk about something else. Tell me, what do you think of Havana?"

Pepper thought over his answer. "I've only been here for a few days. My first impression wasn't good. So many buildings are crumbling . . . it was a shock. But now that I've been here a few days, I'd say one of the most beautiful places I've ever been. But also one of the saddest."

Dayana sat silently.

"No offense," said Pepper. "But this totalitarian regime is everywhere. The iron fist on jobs and the economy. The long lines of people waiting to get food and resell it on the black market. I see the guarded conversations when people talk on the streets. Everyone has this careful look when talking about the government, or any other topic that someone might report on them. And most of the people I've met are friendly, but they're also trying to hustle me, constantly."

Dayana's face turned hard. "You think I'm hustling you now?"

"No!" laughed Pepper. "But you did before, helping Marisol trick Angel and me."

"I didn't know you then!"

"I get it. You were helping your friend."

Dayana looked crestfallen. "I'm sorry for what I did, my part in her ... tricks. I hope some good comes from you being here."

"I'm leaving tomorrow."

"I know. And I feel bad for helping trick you. If your embassy fixes a way for me to go to America with you, I will make you forget the American girl."

Pepper's dirty mind raced.

Dayana was watching him, her eyes impossibly large. Impossibly brown. If she went to Hollywood, Pepper thought, she could be the next Ana de Armas. And if he got fired on Monday, maybe he'd go to California and keep her company. Make sure she wasn't lonely. Pepper grinned at her.

"Excuse me," she said, rising and disappearing toward the living room. A minute later, Dayana came back with a guitar in hand. "Look what the hotel loaned me! You're welcome!" She handed it to him and flipped back her hair, smiling. "Play me one of your songs."

"What? No!" Pepper objected.

"Marisol told me how beautifully you sing. To be honest, I can't picture it. Show me."

"How about in the morning?" he tried.

She pouted playfully. "If you want to get to bed, just sing to me. Marisol said you write your own songs."

Pepper strummed the guitar, and it sounded like a cat being strangled. He started absentmindedly tuning it.

"So what will you play in a bedroom at night to please a Cuban woman?" she asked. She was back on the second bed, her legs curled under her, and her thin white T-shirt ended halfway down her hips.

She was captivating.

Pepper suddenly knew which song to play. It was a song he'd wrote last spring when he was living in Nashville. It never really felt finished. But now Dayana was giving him some ideas that he might improve it on the fly.

Like how earlier that day her hair had fallen over her face. Then she'd pulled it back, giving him a piercing look. Eyes that were intense but warm. Maybe she'd learned that move as an actor, but damn, it worked.

She was a beautiful, mysterious woman who had a gravitational pull on him. Maybe every guy felt that way about her.

Either way, he wanted to play her that song. It was like he'd written it for her months before they'd met.

"Okay," he said, strumming a chord to make sure the guitar was in tune. "I've been working on a song, and I'm going to add in a few new ideas. It's called 'You Mystify Me.'"

She sat up tall and clapped, and the sight of her on that bed in her little white T-shirt and red panties almost made him snap the guitar neck.

He cleared his throat, then began playing the intro, finding the chords, finding the pace and feel. It was a Nashville country song, fairly up-tempo, with a touch of pop.

She probably never listens to this stuff, Pepper thought, but he pushed the negativity out of his mind and focused. When he reached the first verse, he began singing.

This was the first time he'd played this song for anyone. He revised the lyrics as he sang, reshaping them to reflect the inspiration of this beautiful Cuban woman.

Dayana's face went through phases as she listened to the first verse and the chorus. Softening, tightening. Lips parting, then arms crossed.

Did she hate the song? Think it was ridiculous? Pepper knew it was nothing like popular Cuban music.

But during the second verse, Dayana began dancing in place on the bed, swaying, with her arms above her head. Then she jumped in, harmonizing during the chorus the second time around.

*Heaven knows
where this thing goes.
Heaven knows
where this thing goes—
Girl, you mystify me.
Yeah, you mystify me!*

Dayana's harmony was so spot on, Pepper got chills as he sang too.

When Pepper finished the song, she applauded wildly. "That was so beautiful. When I get to America, I'll make you play it to me every night." She grinned at Pepper, then yawned and stretched. Pepper saw her T-shirt rise, then fall. She blinked her impossibly large eyes at him, like a cat in the semi-darkness.

And like he'd sang, Pepper wondered how this thing was

going to go, because at least from his side, he was definitely falling for her.

"Thank you," Dayana said.

Pepper had to think to make sure he hadn't said out loud what he'd been thinking. "For what?"

She laughed. "For everything. For making me feel safe here, when I know someone is out there ..." She shivered. "You are a strong man, Pepper Ryan, and you have a good heart. I heard it in your song. I hope you can protect that part of you, no matter what crimes you fight."

"Me too," he said.

"Can I ask you something?" she asked.

"Anything."

Pepper waited in the darkness, his imagination racing through a bunch of possibilities, some making his cheeks warm.

"Do people trust you with their secrets?" she finally asked.

Damn. That wasn't one of his guesses. "What?"

"Their secrets. Do you find people confide in you, the things they don't tell anyone else?"

"Sometimes. It's lonely, right? Too many secrets? So people eventually spill the beans to someone."

"The beans ... ? That's funny! Can I tell you a secret?"

Dayana was first and foremost an actress. According to Beriev, she was one hell of an actress. So was she acting now? "Sure."

After another pause, she said, "I don't think I can sleep. Part of me is thinking about el Segador and the dangerous, crazy things that have happened since you arrived in Havana. I've never been so scared. But another part of me is thinking about how to get you to come over to my bed and kiss me good night."

Pepper laughed. *What a line.* But he was powerless to resist it. So, he didn't.

CHAPTER TWENTY-EIGHT

"So ... ?" Angel asked the next morning when he and Pepper were alone at the dining room table, drinking coffee and eating pastries and fruit from room service. Dayana and Marisol were still asleep.

Pepper yawned, long and loud. "So, what?"

"Mano, you're killing me. Did you and Dayana get it on? Get down and dirty?"

"Angel! A gentleman never—"

"Go fuck yourself, Pepper. I heard you playing the guitar last night, and I know what that means. That's the express train to bootyville."

"Not always," said Pepper.

The truth was that Pepper had slept poorly, because after some enthusiastic kisses and a JV–level session of roaming hands, Dayana had pulled back.

She'd said she was so afraid of el Segador, she couldn't focus on Pepper and her feelings for him. Their first time couldn't be in the middle of this nightmare.

Then she'd whispered in his ear what she planned to do with him when she got away from Havana and the serial killer. She described some particular acts she had in mind, and by the fourth one, Pepper was quivering with desire.

And then she'd thanked him for understanding, kissed him one more time with finality, and slipped back to her own twin bed.

So the answer was, *No. Not Freaking Yet.*

Someone began knocking on the suite's door, too firmly to be housekeepers.

"The crazy train begins again, right on schedule," said Angel. He went to answer the door.

He yelled, "It's Heather Wilder, the nice lady from the embassy."

Pepper could hear the thick sarcasm in Angel's voice. He had obviously not forgotten her artist dossiers. Pepper groaned.

"Are we receiving?" asked Angel, looking pointedly at Pepper, then toward the bedroom. Angel laughed, then let Wilder in.

Unlike Pepper, the embassy official looked fresh and rested in a cream-colored blouse with matching pants. "I have bad news and good news," she said when seated on the living room couch.

"I'll get you some coffee," said Angel, hustling out of the room.

"If you have rolls or pastries, bring them too," she called after him.

Dayana came out of the bedroom, and Pepper did a double-take. She'd borrowed his dress shirt and was wearing it as a dress. And she'd found a belt somewhere, which made the outfit look even more sexy. She greeted Wilder.

"Ah-hah," Wilder said. "Both of you need to hear this."

She started with the bad news. Her sources within the PNR—excellent sources—told her that Luis Guiteras had just gotten approval from his supervisors to arrest Pepper and Dayana. Both of them would face a long list of charges, all centered on obstruction of justice and committing acts that undermined the Cuban government.

Shit, thought Pepper. What the hell were they going to do?

"And if he finds you two sharing this hotel suite, he might pile on some more charges," Wilder added with a chuckle.

"Why would he arrest me?" asked Dayana. She sounded genuinely confused.

Wilder shrugged. "You know Cuba. Detective Guiteras has a lot of power as the head of the el Segador investigation. Unfortunately, he's bringing it down on both of you."

Pepper's heart tightened. Getting arrested in Cuba would be the start of a long nightmare.

"But I have good news too—there's a good chance Uncle Sam might help you. I'm trying to get approval to shelter you both at the embassy. We can get Pepper on a plane home, and maybe we can work out a legal way for Dayana to go too. Maybe even before that hurricane shuts down air travel, if we hustle."

"How would it work?" Pepper asked.

Wilder waved a hand. "We'll figure it out when you're safe at the embassy. Maybe a helicopter to Guantanamo, then a military flight back to the States? And then you can leave the artist murders for the Cuban cops to sort out."

"I always thought immigration was tougher than that, for Cubans especially," said Pepper.

"That's part of the embargo myths, that Cubans cannot get into the U.S.," said Wilder. "We issue about twenty thousand visas to Cubans every year. But the desperate ones on the rafts built out of soda bottles, they get all the press."

Twenty thousand a year? The number surprised Pepper.

"So if a Cuban artist wanted to apply to immigrate to America, how difficult would that be?"

"Not so difficult," said Wilder. "It mostly takes patience and money."

"And what if time's a problem?" asked Pepper. "If an artist can't wait?"

Wilder shook her head. "If an artist sneaks in, they won't be able to work freely, so what does that get them? Trust me, this is what I do best. There'll be some costs involved, but I'm sure Dayana's American friends will step up, right? We'll work all that out later. For now, I'll go to the embassy to get everything set up."

"How long will that take?" Pepper asked.

Wilder shrugged. "Maybe two hours?"

"We'll be ready to go," said Dayana. "Thank you!"

But Pepper remembered Dayana didn't know about the artist dossiers. Wilder might be cooking up a different plan for them, one that involved cells at Guantanamo's detention camp, or shallow graves in the hills.

In his gut, Pepper didn't trust Wilder. She was up to something sneaky, and she might even be the serial killer. All of the murders had happened during her brief service at the embassy in Havana. She definitely moved in Havana's arts and social circle. And those creepy dossiers ...

"So we're good?" asked Wilder, smiling. To Dayana she said, "Once you get a taste of the first world, you'll never look back."

Angel returned from the kitchen, carrying Wilder's cup of coffee. "One cream, one sugar," he announced, but caught his foot on the area rug's edge and stumbled forward.

Pepper saw the disaster unfold, as in slow motion.

Angel's hand came up, the coffee arcing toward Wilder. She had just enough time to pull back slightly before it splashed across her midsection.

"Fuck!" she cried. She danced around, pulling her blouse away from her stomach as the coffee spread and dripped on her legs and the floor.

"God, I'm sorry!" blurted Angel. He looked horrified.

Dayana ran and returned with a towel, looking embarrassed as she held it out to Wilder. "Let's get you to the bathroom," Dayana said.

They disappeared into the master bedroom to clean her up.

"Are you drunk?" Pepper asked Angel.

He didn't answer. He immediately snatched Wilder's purse and hustled away after the two women.

What a screw-up, thought Pepper. Wilder was a sanctimonious bureaucrat at best. And maybe had murdered five artists, at worst. But if she wasn't the psycho serial killer, Pepper could put aside his personal distaste for her, for Dayana's sake. Would Angel's blunder impact whether she would help them?

Wilder and Dayana returned with Marisol, who was blinking sleep from her eyes. Wilder was wearing a different blouse, which Marisol must have loaned her.

"It was the least I could do," she said, glaring at Angel, who had rejoined them, wringing his hands apologetically. He limply deposited Wilder's purse on the coffee table.

"I'll pay to get it cleaned," Angel offered.

"That blouse was Valentino," Wilder said. "So it's as dead as Guillermo Infante. I'll add it to the tab." She snatched up her purse, glaring again at Angel.

"Sorry that Angel's such a clumsy bastard," said Pepper. "We'll be waiting to hear from you."

After Wilder left, the four of them gathered in the living room, watching Angel try to mop up the rest of the spilled coffee. "So we ask for a late checkout, then get you guys to the embassy, right?" he asked.

"I don't feel I can leave Cuba yet," shared Marisol. "El Segador will keep murdering artists after Dayana leaves. If only Guillermo lived to give us his proof ..."

Pepper didn't volunteer about the dossiers, because they weren't definitive. Just a definitive lead.

Dayana sighed. "I would feel bad running away, like a coward. But what else can I do?"

"You ladies talk it out," suggested Angel. "Mano, can you come with me for a sec?"

In Pepper's bedroom, Angel took out a key ring with two door keys and what looked like a fob. It had a small silhouette of a black cat on it, like a logo, and a small display with a digital number on it. As Pepper studied it, the number changed.

"Buddy, what the hell'd you do?" Pepper asked.

"This might've fallen out of Wilder's purse, after all the coffee commotion," said Angel.

"Fell out?"

"Yep, right in my hand."

"Angel, are you nuts?"

"Those dossiers are creepy and way over the top, but maybe Wilder wrote them after the murders to brief the State Department. Or maybe they were background material to help get approval for special visas."

Pepper thought about it. They needed to decide before Wilder phoned in a couple of hours. If they went to the U.S. embassy, would they get shelter and a way out? Or would they be stepping into el Segador's grip?

Angel explained further. "Anything that proves Wilder's part of the killings would be either at the embassy or her house. We're not breaking into the freaking embassy ... so I grabbed her keys. And whatever security thing this fob is." Angel shrugged. "Why not use the time we have to poke around? Maybe we'll find that African letter opener. Or something else that shows there's blood on her hands. And if you find nothing, that tells us something too, right?"

Pepper didn't tell Marisol or Dayana that he was leaving the hotel, or where he was going.

Nor did he call the other hotel room for Hector to give him a ride. If the Cuban police spotted Pepper and arrested him, he didn't want Hector to end up in legal trouble too. Pepper knew his attempt to break into a U.S. embassy officer's home might end up with him getting grabbed.

So, Pepper grabbed a taxi from the front of the hotel and told the driver to head to Miramar, where Wilder lived.

Getting her home address had been simpler than Pepper thought. Angel had called Ozzie, shot the shit for a minute, then asked for the home address, saying they wanted to send her a gift for having helped so much during the past week. Ozzie had pulled the address from his dad's list of VIP party invitees. Apparently, Ozzie never suspected a thing.

Pepper directed the driver to take him down Miramar's major boulevard, Fifth Avenue, and he climbed out a few blocks from Wilder's address. He walked the rest of the way.

Wilder's street was not as fancy as Rappeneau's, but it was still upper crust for Havana. She lived in a two-story stucco house painted a faded pink. It had an open front porch that leaned significantly to the left.

The house's front door was unlocked. A child opened the ground-floor apartment door, poked her head out in the hallway, and saw Pepper. She stuck out her tongue at him, then quickly closed the door.

Pepper climbed the stairs to Wilder's second-floor apartment. *This could be over before it starts*, he thought, but the key slid easily into the door lock and turned like butter.

Pepper took a deep breath and pushed the door open.

He spied an alarm panel on the wall to the right. It had a small silhouette of a black cat on it, like the security code fob Angel had stolen. Pepper checked the six-digit number currently blinking on the fob. The number disappeared, replaced by another number. So Pepper probably had a full thirty seconds before it changed again.

Pepper carefully punched in the new six-digit number on the alarm panel and waited for the house alarm to turn off.

It didn't.

For his FBI job, Pepper had an RSA SecurID fob, similar to this Blackcat fob, that he used when logging into his work computer. That fob worked by combining his own personal pin code with the fob's randomly generated number.

Maybe the code on this Blackcat fob needed to be combined with Wilder's own pin code. Pepper frantically punched in the number again.

The alarm blinked on, its beep getting steadily louder.

"Shit," said Pepper. Then time ran out and an ear-splitting klaxon horn sounded, over and over, with a robotic male voice barking: *"Warning! Intruder detected! Exit the premises immediately!"*

The robotic voice repeated the threat in Spanish. Then in English, again. Then in Spanish.

And so damn loudly!

Pepper's heart began racing, and he almost turned to flee the building. But he knew he would not get this chance again.

He ran into the apartment, scanning it wildly. The alarm probably interfaced with the U.S. embassy's security team. Pepper was a fifteen-minute drive from the embassy. But if many of their staff lived in the Miramar neighborhood, they might have security personnel nearby. He probably could only risk a minute or two.

So Pepper combed the apartment on fast forward, looking for anything that proved a connection between Heather Wilder and the artist killings.

Wilder had a full bookcase in her living room, so he checked it quickly. She had titles in Spanish and English, all neatly arranged and color coded. Pepper got excited when he saw a row of eighteen books by Ernest Hemingway, a matching set of hardcovers with colorful leather covers. At a glance, they looked similar to the novel that Pepper had seen resting in Guillermo Infante's dead hands. Pepper scanned the row of books and didn't see the one at the poet's crime scene, *For Whom the Bell Tolls*.

That's something, he thought.

He decided he might have one more minute to nose around. *Go, go, go,* he told himself.

He spent half a minute in her bedroom, but saw nothing. He checked a second bedroom with a desk set up like an office. The desk was the messiest place in the apartment, completely covered in papers, books, and magazines.

This was where Wilder really let her hair down, Pepper thought.

But the apparently missing Hemingway book, *For Whom the Bell Tolls,* was not on her desk.

He tried to read the papers scattered around the desk, but nothing registered. Then Pepper saw a smile he recognized, half buried under a book and some loose papers.

Pepper pulled it free of the heap. It was the *Vanity Fair* magazine with Dayana on the cover, flashing a smile that could launch ships. Her second best smile, as Pepper had learned last night. He hurriedly flipped through it and saw someone had written in it in various places with a pen.

He rolled up the magazine, shoved it in his pocket, and darted for the entrance. Time was more than up. He had to get out of there immediately.

Pepper closed the door behind him, only locking the handle's knob. He thumped down the stairs, past the wide-eyed young girl in the hallway, so fast she didn't even have time to stick her tongue out again.

No one was on the street yet. No police cars and no embassy security force. So Pepper got the heck out of there, strolling as vigorously as he could without looking like he'd just broken into the home of an American diplomat.

He made it back to Fifth Avenue without incident, and after a few anxious minutes, he flagged down a taxi. Letting his heart rate slow, Pepper slumped in the taxi's backseat and pulled the magazine out of his pocket.

It was the same edition he'd seen before at Dayana's apartment, but with notes written in the margin next to every artist's profile. Tiny notes in English, almost too small to read. The notes included dates and comments about contact with the artists. Also, observations about what the artists had said to Wilder, presumably, or how they'd acted.

More chilling, a black X was drawn through the sections of the article covering the first four artists. The four who'd been murdered.

Pepper noticed that he was passing the Christopher Columbus Cemetery, and immediately was pulled back to the interview with Carlina Borja's mother. Seeing the pain in her face, only a month after her daughter's tragic death. It had propelled Pepper forward to find out the truth, and he felt like he hadn't stopped yet.

Pepper heard an engine growl behind him and looked over his shoulder. He saw a vehicle half a block back. It wasn't a typical beat-up Russian–bloc car or yellow taxi. It was a brand-new black Ranger Rover, approaching fast.

CHAPTER TWENTY-NINE

After the first few times that people came after him in Havana, Pepper had suspended his ability to believe in coincidences.

Pepper took stock of his situation. He told the taxi to turn left, then right, then left. The Range Rover continued behind them. Practically riding their bumper. Pepper couldn't see the assholes in it because of the tinted windshield.

Pepper was alone and had no weapons. His only means of outrunning the Range Rover was an ancient yellow taxi, which was struggling to keep up with traffic. So he wasn't outrunning anyone.

Who was following him? Maybe someone he had pissed off, or someone who didn't want him to do something?

Did the PNR have Range Rovers? Did the U.S. embassy? Pepper thought he'd seen multiple black SUVs parked at Rappeneau's house.

Should he go back to the hotel? Or would that bring trouble down on his friends?

Pepper decided that he wanted to deal with the Range Rover himself. He had to confirm who was following him and—

depending on who that was—either confront them or try to lose them.

Pepper asked the driver to change destinations, to a place in Centro Havana every taxi driver would know. The first neutral place that popped into Pepper's mind.

A few minutes later, Pepper saw the small, wine-colored sign hanging on a building ahead, for La Guarida, the famous *paladar*, or private restaurant. Hector had pointed it out to Pepper on the afternoon he'd arrived in Havana. Obama had eaten there, Hector had said, but Pepper couldn't recall if the president had made the restaurant famous, or if it had already made its name before Obama arrived.

The restaurant's giant, ornate gray doors were open. Pepper guessed it was around one o'clock on Sunday. Maybe they'd have a lunch crowd that he could use to his advantage.

The Range Rover was now fifty feet behind Pepper, getting closer.

Pepper hurriedly paid the driver and entered La Guarida's building. At first he didn't see a restaurant. Instead he found himself in a grand colonial mansion that had fallen into disrepair. It had a tile floor and in one corner was an ornate marble staircase. The newel post was topped by the statue of a woman with her head knocked off. The wall was a scarred brown and yellow.

A small red car was parked in the lobby, partially blocking a long hallway with doors on each side, and a tangle of clotheslines, old bikes, stacked boxes, and other signs that at least this level of the building was an active apartment building.

Pepper hurried up the stairway. Looking back, he saw three men enter the building. They were backlit, so he couldn't see their faces, but their outlines were large and tall.

Pepper had an immediate thought: maybe Rappeneau's security goons, McDonald and Burger King? Plus a third guy ...

Maybe Ozzie Rappeneau wasn't as dumb as he seemed.

Maybe he'd mentioned Angel's request for Wilder's home address to his dad. But why would that be enough for Rappeneau to unleash his Canuck goon squad? Pepper knew he hadn't gotten to the bottom of the ties between Rappeneau and Wilder yet.

Pepper reached a second-floor landing, a wide-open space strung with clotheslines sagging with sheets. He looked around, trying to come up with a plan. The stairway kept going up. Maybe to the restaurant? But there was also a long hallway lined with what looked like apartments. He hurried down that hallway, hoping to find a rear staircase leading to a rear exit.

If not, he was cornered.

And Pepper didn't have any weapons. It would be a lovely day to have a baseball bat, or anything to swing to keep the three men at bay. Unless they had guns.

Every second doorway had a face in it. Their residents waved to get his attention, pointing back, pointing up. Pepper guessed that many tourists who came down that hallway were looking for La Guarida, and these residents were steering him to the restaurant.

Pepper hurried past them and reached the end of the hallway. He didn't see a door to a rear staircase. He was going to be cornered. He would have to turn and find out why the three men were following him. Probably to injure, kill, or snatch him, Pepper decided. And he didn't like his odds, three against one.

A gray-haired man in a sleeveless white T-shirt was leaning in the doorway of a nearby apartment. He grinned at Pepper, his hands on his hips. Watching the lost yumas was probably a form of entertainment for the residents.

Pepper turned a hard right past the old man, entering his apartment. The man's eyebrows shot up and he shouted with surprise. Pepper stood in a combination living room-kitchen. He looked around wildly, searching for something he could use as a weapon.

On the stove was a cast iron frying pan. *Bingo.*

Pepper snatched it up and headed back toward the door, thrusting a thick handful of Cuban pesos at the old man. The man stopped his loud protests to count the money.

Pepper stepped through the door just before two large men reached it. McDonald and Burger King. Both men were holding handguns down at their sides, but neither was ready for Pepper to appear.

He backhanded the frying pan across the side of Burger King's head, sending the man crashing against the scarred wall. Then Pepper rushed McDonald, getting close inside as his gun hand came up and fired. Pepper was already chest to chest with the man inside the firing line.

McDonald was smaller than Burger King, but not by much. And he was thick and strong. He wrapped his other arm around Pepper's back, and Pepper saw the handgun come up. Pepper raised the frying pan defensively, and the man's next shot deflected off the pan and punched through the wall.

Pepper got a leg behind the man and rammed him with his full weight, tripping him backward onto the hallway floor. The man fired again, hitting the ceiling.

Pepper swung the frying pan and connected with his forehead, who immediately slumped back, unconscious.

As Pepper turned, Burger King howled with anger and got up on one knee, shaking his head. Pepper swung the frying pan again, catching him on the jaw. Lights out at the Burger King. His body hit the wall and landed on his companion.

But where was unnamed asshole number three?

The old man was standing in his doorway again, not yelling or reacting to the sudden conflict that had broken out. He looked both stunned and hugely entertained.

Pepper guessed that the third Rappeneau goon had taken a different direction. Maybe he'd continued up the marble stairs to the next floor, where Pepper now assumed the restaurant was located.

Pepper pocketed both men's handguns. One was a Smith & Wesson and the other a Sig Sauer. What had been their plan? To shoot Pepper? Or had they brought handguns to force Pepper to go with them, and the gunplay had happened reflexively when Pepper startled them?

The downed men were both unconscious, but breathing.

Pepper pulled the shoes off both men and tossed them into the old man's apartment. He emptied their pockets of wallets and a set of car keys.

He pocketed the keys.

Taking the wad of Cuban pesos, he was about to hand it all to the old man for his trouble when he noticed his own handwriting on one of them.

Holy shit.

He flattened out the bill and saw he was right. It was the five hundred peso note on which he'd handwritten his phone number at Rappeneau's party, then given to Guillermo Infante. The bill had a red smear covering the last two digits he'd written. A red smear.

Blood?

No matter. It was definitely the peso note he'd given to Infante. And there was no reason to speculate how it ended up in Burger King's wallet. The only explanation that made sense was that Burger King had taken it after he'd killed Infante.

Pepper carefully put the bill with the blood smear back into the man's wallet and pocketed both wallets. He didn't have evidence bags, but no worries—he wasn't building a legal case, anyway. He was simply trying to nail down the truth and stop the killer.

Pepper shoved the rest of the pesos into the old man's hand. Pepper put a finger to his lips, pantomiming that this should be their secret. He gestured for the man to go back into his apartment and lock the door. The old man grinned conspiratorially.

Then Pepper waved the frying pan in a friendly manner and trotted away down the hall. Pepper was going to keep the pan, because he might need to use it on the third man if their paths crossed. Besides, it probably had the first two men's DNA on it, so maybe Pepper would turn it over to Detective Valdés.

He retraced his path down the hallway with one hand on the Sig Sauer in his pocket, ready to draw it if he encountered the third man.

As Pepper reached the big foyer to the second floor, he heard footsteps slapping down the marble stairs. Pepper ducked behind a stone column and drew the Sig Sauer.

The third man reached the landing and thumped away down the long hallway.

As soon as he was out of sight, Pepper trotted back down to the first floor and exited the building.

A large bus was parked in the narrow street, blocking traffic in both directions. A stream of tourists was exiting the bus and filing into the La Guarida building. One thin middle-aged woman said to Pepper in a Tennessee twang, "Did you enjoy it?" Then she paused and looked down at Pepper's left hand. He realized her eye had been drawn to his new frying pan.

"Best in town," he said, hustling away. He yelled back over his shoulder, "Obama ate here!"

Ahead of the bus, parked half on the sidewalk, was a black Range Rover with a spare tire mounted on the back. Pepper took out the key fob he'd taken from the men, clicked it, and the headlights flashed. So Pepper hopped in and drove away.

Despite the chaos, it had been a pretty successful outing. He'd picked up some very interesting evidence—as well as the handguns and a sweet ride. Not to mention his sturdy new frying pan ...

Pepper parked the Range Rover in a small lot with a handful of other cars, two blocks from the Hotel Nacional. He pulled in between an enormous truck and an old yellow bus. The truck looked like it had been welded together from multiple parts. The bus, with weeds surrounding it, looked like it hadn't moved in years. This spot should be hidden from anyone on the street.

Pepper backed into the space until the Range Rover's rear bumper tapped the low stone wall behind it. Oops. He'd definitely scratched it.

So, he pulled forward a few feet and backed up harder this time, and the Range Rover made a satisfying crunch as it hit the low stone wall. Hopefully, that would piss off Laurent Rappeneau if he eventually recovered his SUV.

He checked the glove box, looking for any other evidence against Rappeneau's goons, but only found another Sig Sauer and a box of ammunition. He stuffed one of the Sig Sauers, the Smith & Wesson, and the box of ammunition into the seatback pocket behind the driver's seat. But he kept the other Sig Sauer, because he'd had the kind of week that he felt happier armed.

Pepper locked the doors and kept the keys. He had a feeling he'd need wheels again before his Havana troubles ended.

CHAPTER THIRTY

Pepper entered the hotel suite to find Angel, Marisol, and Dayana waiting anxiously in the living room.

Dayana stood quickly. "I was so worried about you," she said.

"What's with the frying pan?" Marisol asked, pointing.

Angel laughed. "With Pepper, it's better not to ask."

Hector rolled his eyes and shook his head.

Pepper quickly gave them a recap of what he'd found at Wilder's house. The gap in her Hemingway novel collection. And the marked-up copy of the *Vanity Fair* article.

He laid it on the coffee table and they gathered around, trying to read the tiny notes handwritten in each artist's section of the article.

They were basically summaries about the artists. Who they were, where they lived, where they worked, and their typical daily schedules. Other notes detailed the contacts someone had had with the artists, presumably Wilder. When and where she'd talked to them, what the artists had said. What they thought about America and if they were seeking to leave Cuba.

"Well, that break-in went better than I expected," said Marisol.

Pepper laughed. "On the way back, some of Rappeneau's security guys followed me," he said. "I ducked into a building in Centro to shake them. The one with that restaurant, La Guarida."

"La Guarida?" exclaimed Dayana. "They filmed a famous Cuban movie there in the nineties, did you know? *Fresa y Chocolate*. It means Strawberry and Chocolate. It's an important film for Cubans, very famous, and two of my acting coaches had parts in it. Did you lose the security men in the restaurant?"

Pepper didn't want to get into details. "I never got to the restaurant. Just the lobby and the second floor. Then one apartment."

"An apartment?" asked Marisol, sounding suspicious. "What were you doing there?"

"Trying to get out of trouble."

Unsuccessfully, as usual, he thought.

Dayana shook her head. "You find trouble in the strangest places."

You don't know the half of it, sweetheart, Pepper thought. He excused himself for a minute. Going into his bedroom alone, he sat on his twin bed and scrutinized his attackers' wallets.

The IDs confirmed one man was actually named McDonald, but disappointingly, the larger man, formerly known as Burger King, was named Cockett.

Cockett claimed on his ID that he weighed two-forty, which Pepper would bet was a lie by about forty pounds.

Both of the driver's licenses were from Ontario.

But otherwise, he found nothing helpful.

Pepper went and lay down on his little twin bed to think about what the hell to do next. On the positive side, he felt like he was finally making progress on the artist murders. The Cuban money covered in blood that he'd found in Cockett's wallet was damning evidence against Rappeneau and his Canadian goons, and all the evidence he'd gathered against

Wilder suggested she was up to her designer blouse in the murders too.

But everything else was on the negative side. The PNR's hardass detective, Juan Guiteras, was going to arrest him as soon as he found him. Pepper's best way out of that trouble that also helped Dayana—the U.S. embassy—came from Heather Wilder, a woman who likely had a greater incentive to make Pepper and Dayana disappear than to help them.

Pepper had one other option to escape arrest by the PNR, but it seemed too simple to succeed. It was almost 2:30PM on Sunday now, and Pepper's original plane ticket out of Cuba was for that afternoon at five-thirty. Should he simply go to the airport and try to board his plane? He could picture the relief he'd feel as his plane lifted off from Cuban soil. Not to mention that the only way for him to make his FBI meeting tomorrow would be to catch his flight out this afternoon. Edwina Youngblood had been crystal clear: if he missed his meeting tomorrow, his FBI career was done and dusted. No doubt about it.

But then he'd be leaving Dayana to survive el Segador on her own. Could he ever forgive himself if he flew home today, and in a few days or weeks, heard Dayana was dead? Because that was a pretty realistic possibility too.

For the first time in days, Pepper calmed down and decided what to do. He was tired and fed up. He stood to go back to the living room, to tell everyone he was heading out, and why.

Pepper felt his stomach tighten with apprehension, imagining how they would react. Especially Dayana.

Less than an hour later, Dayana de Melina was crying at the tall door of Laurent Rappeneau's Miramar house when one of his security detail answered her frantic ringing of the doorbell. Rappeneau joined them at the door and quickly ushered her in.

"I didn't know who to trust," she said, her voice catching with emotion. "I had to come here."

"I'm glad you did," Rappeneau said. He made her a cup of tea himself and then brought her back to his private office, which looked out through the French doors over his enormous backyard.

"Don't interrupt," he told the security man, who was hovering by the office door, gawking at Dayana. "No calls, no visitors." He gently but firmly closed the door.

Dayana sat on a beautiful red sofa, sipping the tea. She had almost stopped crying now.

So she told him everything. Pepper Ryan had abandoned her. He had given her a hug and a hundred dollars, then caught a taxi to the airport. He had made her all kinds of promises last night, how he was going to protect her from el Segador, how he was going to take her away to America. But they'd heard that the PNR was going to arrest them both. Pepper didn't trust the U.S. embassy, particularly Heather Wilder. He had to look after himself, and she had to go to the PNR with everything she'd learned about the serial killings and ask for mercy, for protection.

They hadn't really learned anything solid. It had been a bluff by Pepper to draw out the killer. And it had failed miserably.

Now he was gone, and she had nowhere to turn.

As she told the tale, she began crying again. Tears slid one by one down her cheeks.

"I need your help," she whispered.

"Do you have your phone on you?" he asked.

She looked surprised and wary, but nodded. "In my purse."

"Do you trust me?" he asked.

She paused, then nodded again.

Rappeneau smiled at her, then took her purse and left the office. He came back a minute later, empty-handed.

"In order for you and I to put our heads together, we need to speak freely. Those damn phones—everyone's always listening these days." He made a vague gesture up toward the sky.

She looked uncertain but said, "Okay."

Rappeneau joined her on the couch again, this time sitting closer. He smiled at her encouragingly.

"I stayed with him last night," she blurted out in a thin voice. "I was terrified to be alone. Then this morning he acted like it was nothing!"

"Typical American," said Rappeneau.

"Exactly! Detective Guiteras ordered him to stay in his casa under house arrest, but he took me to a hotel instead, then he snuck out and caused all kinds of trouble. He even said your security people followed him, so he flipped out and beat them up. It made no sense."

Rappeneau patted her hands. "He sounds goddamn unhinged."

"He was! And all the things he promised me last night in bed —that we would be safe at the embassy, that I could go to Hollywood ..." She began sobbing so hard that she couldn't continue.

"I always knew he was an asshole," said Rappeneau. "But Oswald asked me to help him, so I tried." He shook his head in disgust. "You're safer with him gone."

She looked up at Rappeneau with her big, wet eyes. "The woman from the American embassy, Heather Wilder, she promised to help me go to America with Pepper. But she said it would be very expensive. And Pepper only left me a hundred dollars, like I was a whore!"

She got to her feet, her hands fluttering, and began pacing the room. Then she gently rested her forehead against the French doors leading to the backyard, turned away from Rappeneau, as her shoulders shook.

"You're going to be okay," Rappeneau said.

She wheeled, her face full of terror. "I'm next on el Segador's list! I'll be dead if I don't leave Cuba!"

"No, you're going to be okay," he repeated. Then he explained what he knew about the process and expense of getting a Cuban citizen out of the country. Lots of paperwork and permissions. It took a considerable amount of money.

But she'd come to the right person, Rappeneau assured her. He knew exactly what he was doing, and he was close to Heather Wilder, which would put Dayana at the head of the immigration queue.

He smiled at her affectionately. "And don't worry, I'll pay the sixty thousand dollars. I'll even kick in some extra money for you. To get you started off right in America."

Dayana stared at him wide-eyed, with tear tracks streaking her cheeks, her chest heaving from labored breaths. She slowly came to the couch and sat down next to Rappeneau. "You would do that for me?"

He reached for her hands and squeezed them reassuringly. "Friends help friends. Are you willing to be my friend?"

She swallowed. "I can be your friend," she said timidly.

"Let's be clear," he said. "Because you shouldn't suffer any more unpleasant surprises. The deal is, you'll live here as my girlfriend for one week. Seven days and seven nights. The real thing, you know?"

"Your girlfriend?" She sounded surprised but not completely upset.

He gave her a flirty smile. "I'll pay Heather Wilder the sixty grand to expedite your paperwork, push it through the bureaucracy. And I'll give you another forty grand. My security detail will protect you here for the next seven days. And I'll protect you for seven nights. Then you'll be off to America, and you'll never have to worry about el Segador again."

Dayana looked hopeful, mixed with nervousness and uncertainty. "And what will you want me to do?"

Rappeneau took her hands again. "You're the most beautiful woman I've seen in many years. We'll have a wonderful, romantic fling, with champagne and chocolates and whatever else you want. I promise you'll love it."

Dayana stayed silent for a long time, her head down. Finally, she asked, "How do I know all this will work?"

Rappeneau gave her his charming, power CEO smile. "Because it's already worked before. A dozen times in the past two years, for many Cuban women. I scratched their backs, they scratched mine. Everyone's happy. And Heather Wilder uses my money and her paperwork to move you to the front of the line to enter America legally. The land of opportunity. And think about it—does anyone else care what happens to you?"

That was more than enough of Rappeneau's bullshit for Pepper.

He stood up from behind the bushes outside the office and stepped through the French doors that Dayana had unlocked minutes earlier. His new Sig Sauer handgun was pointed right at Rappeneau's big mouth.

"I care," Pepper said. "And I'm missing my damn flight to prove it. So thanks for making that worthwhile."

CHAPTER THIRTY-ONE

"What the devil?" gasped Rappeneau. "How did *you* get in here?"

Pepper kept walking, his handgun still pointed. It was zeroed in on a deep wrinkle that had formed between Rappeneau's eyes.

"Through the back gate you tossed me out last time," said Pepper. "What's with your security, anyway? Some of your goons out on sick leave?"

Rappeneau opened his mouth to shout for help, but Pepper had closed the distance and caught him with a punch square to the chin. The Canadian CEO fell back, unconscious.

"You get that punch on tape?" grinned Pepper, pocketing the handgun. The punch had a little extra mustard on it, because he hadn't enjoyed hearing the rich older man putting his greasy squeeze on Dayana. And Pepper was already pissed about missing his flight back to the U.S., which meant missing his FBI meeting, which meant blowing his damned career. That was his decision, but Rappeneau deserved to share a big part of the blame.

Dayana gave Pepper a broad smile, then tapped the buttonhole camera on her blouse. "You waited long enough," she chided him. "Good thing I'm a great actor!"

"And good thing his eyes don't have to be open to unlock this," said Pepper, fishing Rappeneau's iPhone out of the man's pocket. He held the phone in front of Rappeneau's slack face, flicked the screen, and it opened.

Pepper quickly found Heather Wilder in Rappeneau's contacts and sent her a brief text on the Canadian's behalf.

"Now we wait," Pepper said, going to the office door and confirming that Rappeneau had already locked it.

"He told his security not to interrupt us," Dayana said with a demure smile.

"They're probably used to his private meetings with beautiful Cuban women," Pepper replied harshly.

They heard the doorbell ring thirty minutes later. Rappeneau must keep Heather Wilder on a short leash.

Dayana untucked her blouse, then rushed out to get her.

"Laurent's on the phone," she said breathlessly, pulling Wilder's arm as the embassy officer stepped through the front door past a security guard. "He told me to bring you back." She froze the security guy with a brilliant smile. "And he said to tell you to be ready. Another VIP's coming soon!" She hauled Wilder toward Rappeneau's office before either Wilder or the guard could object.

The two women entered the office, and as soon as Wilder had cleared the doorway, Dayana tripped her and gave her a shove. Pepper was quickly on her, covering her mouth with duct tape and heavily taping her hands behind her.

Grinning, Dayana had already shut and locked the door again.

Pepper hauled Wilder to the couch, where Rappeneau was leaning against a cushion, still unconscious. Pepper hoped he hadn't hit the Canadian too hard, but most people took a while to recover from being knocked out. Real life wasn't like in movies, where people bounced back to their feet a minute later. But at least Rappeneau was breathing, long and slow.

Pepper focused on Wilder instead. "I won't bother explaining to you what's going on, since you're a smart lady."

Pepper took out his phone and called Lola Valdés. "Detective, there's an emergency at Laurent Rappeneau's house in Miramar," he said. "Call me back when you're on your way and I'll explain."

And that's exactly what happened. Valdés called back ten minutes later.

Wasting no time, Pepper summarized the evidence against Rappeneau and Wilder. That the two had been running a visa scheme for sex and money. Pepper said he had video and audio evidence of Rappeneau confessing to the scheme. Plus, Pepper had evidence that Rappeneau's men killed the poet, Guillermo Infante, especially the five hundred peso bill with Pepper's phone number and blood on it.

"We have Laurent Rappeneau on tape saying he and Heather Wilder have run the sex for visas scheme a dozen times in the past two years, but as far as I know, the only times their scheme ended in murder was with Cuba's top artists. You'll have to get them to explain that."

"That's on tape?" exclaimed Valdés.

"You bet. And you'll want to arrest two of Rappeneau's Canadian security goons, named Cockett and McDonald, and check them for traces of Guillermo Infante's blood. It's hard to create that messy of a murder scene without getting at least microscopic traces of blood on them. I assume you guys can test for trace evidence? I'll bet they'll sing for you, the whole truth and nothing but the truth, to stay out of Cuban prison."

"Of course," Valdés said, and Pepper could hear the smile in her voice.

"Cockett and McDonald shouldn't be too hard to round up. Either they're resting upstairs in Rappeneau's house, or they're being treated at a hospital near Centro Havana. They had an accident a couple of hours ago."

"An accident?"

"Yep. They accidentally tried to kill the wrong person."

Pepper saw Heather Wilder's eyes bulge.

"So, el Segador was a team effort," Pepper concluded for Valdés. "All five of the artist killings might have been carried out by Rappeneau's security goons. Maybe to silence artists who Rappeneau and Wilder had approached with their U.S. visa scheme, but hadn't been willing to play ball. Or maybe some artists had tried to extort money from Rappeneau for their silence—I'll bet that's what happened with Guillermo Infante. Or maybe some killings were done to scare other artists, so they'd agree to have sex with Rappeneau in exchange for him paying Wilder tens of thousands of dollars."

"So, it was all about sex, money, and capitalism?" asked Lola Valdés.

"Good old-fashioned sex and greed, and whatever political lens you want to use," said Pepper. "The scheme needed both of them. Wilder could push through a variety of visas applications. Rappeneau had the money needed to move those applications quickly through the U.S. bureaucracy. And he was happy to spend it, to get him in bed with beautiful Cuban women."

"Hmm. You have the embassy officer there with you?" asked Valdés. "Heather Wilder?"

Pepper could guess what she was thinking. "No doubt she'll start screaming about diplomatic immunity as soon as you pull the tape off her mouth. Maybe it's above your pay grade, how she gets handled. But either way, there won't be any more artist killings. And Laurent Rappeneau and his Maple Leaf goons can't claim any immunity—"

"We will see," said Valdés. "We'll be there in eight minutes."

Pepper checked Rappeneau's desk, where he'd written a quick summary of everything he'd figured out, together with his hard evidence.

The marked-up *Vanity Fair* article.

The SD card from the buttonhole video camera that held the recording of Rappeneau's confession to Dayana, while thinking with his little head.

The bloodstained five hundred peso bill.

Valdés would have to sort out the legalities of using the evidence in the Cuban courts, but Pepper guessed that murder suspects in Cuba had considerably fewer rights to remain silent.

"We did it," he said to Dayana, taking her hand. "We stopped the artist killings and the victims will finally get justice."

Dayana nodded and hugged him. "And what happens now, with us?" she whispered in his ear.

"I want us to be together," he whispered back. "I want to show you my country, and you deserve your shot at Hollywood." He kissed her once, and her kiss back was hungry.

Pepper double-checked the thick rounds of tape on Rappeneau's and Wilder's hands and feet. He heard banging and shouting at the front door.

He grabbed her hand. "Time for us to exit stage left."

CHAPTER THIRTY-TWO

Pepper didn't want to get sucked into the PNR's long and tedious process to arrest the guilty parties and secure the evidence, especially while Juan Guiteras was still looking to arrest him and Dayana. So they would slip away while the PNR took over the situation.

Pepper trusted Detective Lola Valdés to handle the arrests and evidence. He was going to lurk in the backyard outside the French doors only long enough to make sure the Canadian goon squad didn't interfere with her.

His money was on Valdés.

But then he heard another voice he knew, belonging to someone he'd hoped to never hear again—Juan Guiteras. The detective was shouting at someone, probably the Canuck schmuck who'd opened the door. Pepper wanted to see Guiteras' face when he saw Laurent Rappeneau and Heather Wilder bound up with everything except a bow, including the evidence of their crimes.

You're welcome, asshole. And make sure Lola gets a big cut of the credit.

Pepper sent Dayana to wait for him at the backyard's gate, while he remained to peek around a curtain that shielded the nearly closed French doors. Guiteras and Valdés burst into the study. Both detectives took in the bound suspects, then moved to the desk, studying the evidence where Pepper had laid it out.

Then they started arguing in Spanish so fast that Pepper only understood half of it. And that half wasn't good.

Guiteras evidently believed that it wasn't a righteous bust. He had good reason to know these two were not the serial killers. He mentioned Viktor Beriev, twice.

Valdés emphatically disagreed, but Guiteras ended the argument by drawing a long stiletto knife and walking toward Rappeneau and Wilder on the couch.

Pepper held his breath, not believing what he was seeing.

Guiteras used his knife to cut the duct tape binding them.

That was the second most unbelievable thing Guiteras could have done with the knife. A knife, Pepper noticed, that was a damn good match for the weapon used by el Segador to stab the dead artists repeatedly. If it turned out that the African letter opener wasn't the actual weapon ...

But this was not the time to chew on all of that. Rappeneau would soon tell Guiteras how and when Pepper had left the scene.

Pepper slipped across the back lawn, staying out of sight of the study's window. He joined Dayana by the back gate. Together, they escaped Rappeneau's home, with Pepper's triumphant arrest of Rappeneau and Wilder crumbling in his mouth like ashes.

Despite getting away, Pepper needed to come up with another plan—somewhere to hide out from Guiteras and the PNR and figure out what the unexpected release of Rappeneau and Wilder meant. And where Pepper could plan how to get their butts out of Cuba as fast as humanly possible.

If that was even possible, anymore.

It's hard to run and hide when nowhere's safe.

Pepper decided, then texted to Angel and the others, and everyone else went along with the plan. They arrived at the Fototeca de Cuba gallery in the Plaza Vieja around four-thirty. Luckily, the gallery was closed on that Sunday, so no one was there except Viktor Beriev, who had been working on his upcoming photography exhibit.

For an anxious few minutes, they waited for Victor Beriev to unlock the door. Then he let them in. It was Pepper, Angel, Dayana and Marisol. And, of course, Hector. The gang was all there.

Despite its colonial exterior, the inside of the gallery was simple modernity. Gray tile floors, white walls. As close to a blank canvas as an artist could get.

Pepper wasn't in the right head space to tour an art exhibit, but he had to admit, Viktor Beriev's neo-surrealist portraits were powerful, deep, and disturbing. Especially disturbing.

"He's way ahead of his peers worldwide with his techniques," Marisol explained. Basically, Beriev took a photo and then changed the image in whatever bizarre ways that he thought would reveal the person as they truly were. "He pokes the viewer's subconscious. Sprinkles in some absurdity. Stirs in the illogical."

"Okay ..." said Angel.

Marisol gave him a glare. "The point is, the result looks like a dream within a dream within a dream. But it's actually a more truthful view of the person photographed than the original photo. They call him neo-surrealist, but I think he's something even beyond that."

The pictures were wild, but the most surreal part for Pepper was the labels beneath the photography.

Alicia Arenas.

Carlina Borja.

And the two other dead artists, Rolando Carreño and Osanna Falcón.

The other portraits were of people whose names Pepper didn't know, except one: Dayana de Melina.

It was a portrait of her whirling toward the camera, her eyes wide but missing. They were black holes from which hundreds of small butterflies were pouring. The butterflies surrounded her like ropes, binding her or supporting her, and her head was thrown back in an expression of passion, or terror, or both.

To Pepper, it was totally bizarre. Recognizable as Dayana despite the ink-pool eyes and the butterflies. But he didn't agree that the portrait somehow illustrated the woman better than a photo.

Maybe he was just creeped out.

"You said you wouldn't include mine!" Dayana complained, sounding angry. "You're brilliant, Viktor, but that portrait? It makes me look like butterflies are using my skull as a nest!"

Pepper felt his body tensing as he got angry on her behalf. *What am I,* he thought, *a man in love? Or just an idiot?*

Beriev laughed and blushed. "You look fierce and lovely, which is how I have always seen you," he mumbled. "If I'll be remembered after I'm gone, it'll be for this collection of my work. Maybe your portrait most of all."

Dayana stuck out her tongue at him.

"This one of Carlina Borja—did you make it before she died or after?" Marisol asked.

It showed Carlina's entire body as a stretched silver and orange blur from the right side of the frame to the left, like a violent smudge of powerful, kinetic grace.

"She sat for the camera session two weeks before she died," he said sadly. "But I finished this after."

Pepper looked nervously at the gallery's front windows, afraid to find Guiteras' ugly face there, grinning at him. "Is there a room where we can all talk out of sight?" he asked. He hoped it wouldn't occur to Detective Guiteras to search for them there, but he might come looking for Beriev and get lucky. He seemed equally focused on the Belarusian. Pepper couldn't understand why, after all the evidence he had turned over.

Pepper needed to tell everyone his plan, but he didn't have one yet.

The simplest part was, Angel and Marisol should head straight to José Martí International Airport for the next flight out of the country, wherever that was going. But Dayana didn't have a passport, so she would not be allowed to leave the country by plane. And for all he knew, Beriev and Hector would be in trouble if left behind.

Pepper's phone rang. It was Ozzie Rappeneau's number, but he answered it anyway.

"Dude, I just talked to my dad," Ozzie yelled. "What were you, high?"

What could Pepper say? "Seriously, I'm sorry it played out like this."

Ozzie laughed bitterly. "He said that you tied up him and that American embassy woman. That you were batshit crazy, but Detective Guiteras showed up and set them free. And the detective promised Dad he'll arrest you for what you did, and dammit, you deserve it. You need psychological help."

"You should know. I gave the PNR clear evidence that your dad and Heather Wilder were running a 'sex for U.S. visas' scheme. It led to those artists getting murdered, including Guillermo Infante, who was trying to extort him about it."

"You are definitely high," disagreed Ozzie. "Sure, Dad's into the ladies, big time. But two of those artists that got killed were men. You thought he was getting sex from them too? Next time I see you, I'm going to kick your ass. And at least I don't have to worry about you running back to the States."

"Why's that?"

Ozzie laughed. "The Havana airport just freaking closed. That hurricane's too close, and you're stuck here. So I'll see ya!"

Shit!

Pepper ended the call and sat down, shaken by the call. The airport was closed. There was no way out of Cuba?

It was one thing to hide from Guiteras and the PNR for an hour or two, but with the airport closed, Guiteras would have plenty of time to organize officers, communicate with the authorities at the airport, and put in place a dragnet that would be impossible for Pepper to slip through. He was trapped.

"What's wrong, mano?" asked Angel.

Pepper told everyone what he had heard, but then his phone rang again, interrupting.

Double shit. He recognized the phone number. It was Juan Guiteras.

"Where are you?" Guiteras asked in a calm but firm voice. "I'm coming to collect you."

"Collect me? And where would you take me?"

"The airport," said Guiteras.

Pepper laughed mockingly. "The airport's closed. Why the hell did you let Rappeneau and Wilder go? You realize you just put Dayana's life at risk again?"

In the ensuing pause, Pepper pictured Guiteras getting angry. But when Guiteras spoke, he sounded reasonably calm. "We appreciate the evidence for the Infante murder," he said. "But there are differences between that crime scene and the other four murders. So the case against Rappeneau and Wilder is not as airtight as you seem to believe."

"You couldn't hold them for Infante's murder while you

gathered the proof you needed for the other four cases? What's your excuse for that?"

Guiteras didn't answer his question. "Where are you?" he demanded. "And where is Dayana?"

Pepper had absolutely no reason to trust Guiteras at this point. Nope! "We're getting drunk at el Floridita. These daiquiris are kicking my *culo*! No, actually, I'm at the Plaza de la Revolucion, checking out the cool old cars. No, wait, I'm confused. I'm driving to Guantánamo. Sorry, gotta get both hands back on the wheel!"

Guiteras laughed. "See you soon," he said, sounding smug and confident, then hung up.

Pepper turned off his phone. He didn't want to get any more bad news.

Then he filled in everyone about the shocking calls from Ozzie and Guiteras.

"Maybe Guiteras is handcuffed by the politics," suggested Angel. "Rappeneau and Wilder might be too powerful to face justice in Cuba, but at least he's getting them to leave the country. So no more artists will get killed."

Pepper frowned. He just didn't see it. Guiteras was a hardass. He wasn't some nuanced bureaucrat. No, if he was letting the scumbags go, he wasn't worried about the lesser of two evils.

Was Cuba trying to avoid an international scandal with Canada and the U.S.? Or were Rappeneau and Wilder paying for police protection? Was Guiteras crooked, and did that explain why he had been targeting Pepper and his friends for the past week? Most likely, Guiteras had gotten an offer he couldn't refuse. Enough money to change his life. Maybe enough to propose to Dayana, offer her a life of style and comfort.

Maybe in Guiteras' twisted mind, that was the right thing to do.

Was it plausible for Guiteras to help Rappeneau leave the

country, escape punishment for multiple murders, as soon as the weather permits? And to help ensure that Wilder's role was covered up, so she could quietly leave Cuba, too? In other words, he would help scumbag killers walk away free?

And the worst part was, Pepper couldn't think of anything he could do about it...

"And don't forget about Rappeneau's goon squad," said Hector. "They will be looking too. Maybe Rappeneau thinks if he takes you out before he goes, then he wins."

"Right, what's one more murder?" agreed Pepper. "And once he leaves Cuba, he gets away clean."

Pepper laughed out loud. He was a wanted fugitive in a foreign city. He had few friends and fewer resources. The only question seemed to be—who'd find him at the photography gallery first, the Cuban cops or the Canadian goons?

Guiteras would, guessed Pepper. The detective seemed to always locate Pepper way too quickly, wearing his trademark smirk.

It suddenly occurred to Pepper that he should get to the bottom of that curious trend. It might get him a little wiggle room to maneuver. He was going to try an old trick, but a reliable one. Would it work?

"You guys relax here," said Pepper. "I'll be right back."

CHAPTER THIRTY-THREE

Angel didn't like the look on Pepper's face when he returned fifteen minutes later. His best buddy looked like crap. His face was drained of color and he looked shaken.

Which made sense. None of them could get out of Cuba immediately, and that prick Guiteras had a hard-on for Pepper.

Pepper slumped to the floor, his back against the wall. "I just called my boss at the FBI," he said. "Let's just say I'm not up for employee of the month, calling her at home on a Sunday. But she got a handle on the situation quickly. She contacted the chargé d'affaires at the U.S. embassy in Havana. The top guy."

That confused Angel. "The ambassador?"

Pepper shook his head. "We haven't had a Cuban ambassador since Castro took over. But the guy in charge told my boss he'd be happy to help us. He said they've already relieved Heather Wilder of her duties, and she's going to be sent back to the U.S. So, bottom line, we can all go to the embassy and request temporary refuge. Dayana and the rest of you non-Americans can ask for a referral to the U.S. Refugee Admissions Program."

Beriev waved a hand dismissively. "I don't need to go to your embassy," he said. "I'm a citizen of Belarus and my work is here. If the flying monkeys from the PNR harass me, it won't be the first time."

Angel laughed. He got a kick out of the big Belarusian.

Pepper just stared at Beriev, looking troubled. Then he shrugged. "The rest of us, then. We leave in one hour. They said it's only an eleven-minute drive from here."

"And on the bright side, we don't have to pack," Angel quipped. Pepper had cooked up a good plan, and Angel was already feeling better.

"How about you, Hector?" said Pepper. "You told me you want to get to Las Vegas. Do you still feel that way?"

Hector, wearing bejeweled sunglasses and a black sequined jumpsuit, was sitting with his back to the wall, legs out in front of him. He paused for only a moment before shaking his head. "I can't. Not like this."

"Then you should stay here with Viktor, at least until after we go," said Pepper. "Getting into the embassy is going to be risky, and I don't want you to end up as collateral damage."

Hector shook his head, looking sad. "At least I will drive you there. But first I should text my mother, tell her I love her, just in case." He exhaled. "She will never let me see any yuma cousins again."

Angel walked over to Hector and affectionately tousled his long Elvis hair.

"How about you?" Pepper asked Dayana, who was sitting nearby, slumped in her chair. "Are you in?"

Angel thought Dayana also looked close to tears.

She made a helpless gesture. "If Juan set the killers free, my life here is as dangerous as before. I'll leave Cuba if you can arrange it, at least for a while."

Pepper went to her, squatted, and whispered something in her ear. Then Pepper gave her a kiss.

I called it! thought Angel, mentally raising a fist to celebrate. *Good for you, mano!*

Then Pepper stood. "Hector, can we talk in the other room?"

Pepper and Hector left.

This was one of Angel's favorite things about Pepper. He knew his buddy was going to boost Hector's spirits, give him some hope, and stiffen up the young man's backbone for this next gamble.

Marisol squatted next to Angel and squeezed his hand. "Angelito, I'm worried about this plan."

Angel didn't squeeze back. He gave her a small smile and said, "Pepper knows what he's doing."

She studied him. "Do you always go along with whatever he tells you to do?"

Angel combed his hair with his hand. "I'd trust him with my life."

"That's good, because you are."

Pepper and Hector returned after ten minutes.

Hector looked pale, and Pepper looked flustered.

"Everything okay?" Angel asked as a nervous feeling grew in his stomach.

Hector looked like he was going to throw up. "I am ashamed to say no. Elvis would expect me to be a better man."

"Hector has some things to say, but they need to stay between him and me for a little while longer," said Pepper. "Because the plan has changed—we're leaving immediately."

Detective Juan Guiteras was being driven by a uniformed officer to Zanja police station for an emergency meeting with several layers of his superiors in the Policía Nacional Revolucionaria, as well as comrades from the Ministry of the Interior, when he received a text on his personal cell phone:

"*P & D going to yuma embassy in caddy passing Nacional one hour.*"

Guiteras' pulse raced. He told the uniformed PNR patrolman to alter their destination and began making calls for support.

Twenty minutes later, he received a second text from the same person:

"*Plan change, going now!*"

Angel felt like he was going to have a heart attack.

If he ever got back home, he was going to eat better. And exercise more. Because being Pepper's best buddy was hazardous to his health.

Hector had collected his Cadillac and repositioned it at the edge of Plaza Vieja, and now they were one minute into the eleven-minute drive to the U.S. embassy. To safety, they hoped.

As instructed, Hector had manually fastened the white roof in place and rolled up the windows to make it harder for people to see inside the Cadillac, although Angel could tell Hector wasn't happy about it, among his other worries. His cousin loved his ride and knew that Elvis's old car looked best with its top down.

Marisol was up front in the passenger seat next to Hector. She was acting like she didn't have a care in the world, smiling and filming video with her iPhone as they drove. As instructed.

Angel hadn't stopped caring about Marisol, but he was still messed up from the brutal trick she'd pulled to lure Pepper to Cuba. She was beautiful, smart, and lots of other great things, but could he ever trust her again? He planned to have one hell of a talk with her when this thing was over.

The only silver lining, thought Angel, *was she pulled her disappearing stunt before I proposed.*

But it killed him he'd lost his dead maternal grandmother's ring. The family heirloom was beyond priceless to him. His mom was going to be sad and furious when she heard.

Angel shook his head and fought to refocus on the situation. Lots of things could go wrong, and likely would. He began craning his neck in all directions, looking for police vehicles.

Marisol shook her head at him. "You're acting like a fugitive," she scolded. She probably wished Beriev and his camera were along for the ride, but Beriev had insisted again that he would stay behind. "This footage is going to have more bounce than Blair Witch Project," Marisol muttered.

"Hopefully minus the bloody killings," Angel said, but no one laughed.

They were taking a route that he was familiar with—approaching their recent hideaway, the Hotel Nacional.

Angel was going to make a crack about the thread count of the Hotel Nacional's towels, but he swallowed it when he saw a marked police car turn from a side street and pull up immediately behind the Cadillac.

"I see it, I see it," Hector said, his voice trembling, but trying to stay cool. He slumped a bit more in his seat, but otherwise kept driving. Then he fiddled with his eight-track player and Elvis Presley's' "Heartbreak Hotel" began blaring from the speakers.

Marisol began singing along.

Another police car pulled out in front of the Cadillac, so now they were sandwiched between two police cars.

"*Coño, coño, coño ...*" grumbled Hector.

Angel saw a third police car come alongside the Cadillac, with its windows down. It hit its siren, and the man in the passenger seat gestured for Hector to pull over.

It was Detective Juan Guiteras.

The devil himself, thought Angel.

There was absolutely nowhere for them to go, other than to follow the detective's instruction.

The police car ahead of them turned into the long driveway to the Hotel Nacional. Hector followed obediently. When the lead police car stopped, Hector did too. The other two police cars stopped behind the Cadillac.

All had their lights flashing, and the one next to the Cadillac had its siren screaming.

Then the siren turned off in the third police car, and Guiteras climbed out.

Angel noticed that Marisol still had her phone out, and she angled it behind her, as if to catch footage of the PNR detective as he calmly walked to the Cadillac. Guiteras came up on the passenger side and snatched the phone from Marisol's hand. He dropped it on the asphalt and stomped on it several times.

"Good thing us yumas are all rich," said Angel.

Four uniformed police officers gathered around the Cadillac.

"Where are Pepper Ryan and Dayana de Melina?" asked Guiteras.

The obvious question, because only Hector, Angel and Marisol were riding in the Cadillac. Hector up front, and Angel and Marisol in the backseat.

Hector made a broad gesture. "It's just us," he said.

"Don't tell me they are hiding in your trunk?" Guiteras shook his head like the situation was ludicrous. "You've done well so far. Now open your trunk," he ordered Hector.

But Hector didn't move.

Guiteras barked at one of the other officers, who approached the driver's side, leaned in, and pulled the latch to the trunk.

The trunk popped open, and one officer grabbed the lid to pull it all the way up. The officers crowded in, pointing their weapons at the trunk. But no one shouted, no one began pulling people from the trunk.

Because it was empty.

"You guys think I was smuggling bananas again?" asked Angel.

"Where are they?" shouted Guiteras.

"We don't have any," said Angel. "I've switched to plantains ever since I got here."

Guiteras' mouth opened and closed, and his face turned red. "Where are Pepper Ryan and Dayana de Melina?" he shouted, and his spit flew in Angel's face.

"Who can say?" asked Angel, wiping his face with his forearm. "Young lovers in a romantic city like Havana? They could be anywhere, as long as they're together, right?"

The truth was, he didn't know where Pepper and Dayana went. Pepper had asked Angel, Marisol, and Hector to act as a decoy. Pepper hadn't explained how, but he said Guiteras was nearby, ready to arrest Pepper and Dayana. So Pepper had thrown out a decoy. Get Guiteras moving in the wrong direction, and then Pepper and Dayana could slip out of the net. Because Pepper had the beginning of a plan to bring this whole Havana nightmare to a crashing end.

Without understanding all the details, Angel had trusted his buddy, and the decoy seemed to have worked.

But then Guiteras gave Angel a horrible smile. "You are all under arrest."

"For what?" objected Marisol. "We were headed to see el Morro."

Angel knew that the Castillo del Morro was a historic fortress guarding the entrance to the Havana harbor. It was a mandatory stop for tourists, especially for the historic reenactment of soldiers ceremoniously firing off a cannon at nine o'clock, which in colonial times had warned everyone within earshot that Havana's gates were closing for the night. It had been on Angel's sightseeing list before this entire damn trip had derailed almost immediately on Monday afternoon.

Guiteras laughed at Marisol, loud and hard. "Hector, you didn't tell your friends?"

Angel's heart sank. "Tell us what?" he asked.

"Your cousin told me of your plan to flee to the embassy. How do you think we intercepted you?"

"No freaking way," Angel said. There was no possibility that his own cousin ratted them out. *Or was that what Hector had been kicking himself about, back at the photo gallery?*

Hector hung his head and denied nothing.

Angel leaned forward and slapped his cousin hard on the back of the head.

"All of you are obstructing justice," said Guiteras. "And all of you have taken actions that promote social indiscipline and harm the prestige of Cuba."

"We did nothing wrong!" protested Marisol. "And Angel and I are American citizens!"

"You will learn how little that matters," said the detective. He turned to Hector. "And you, my friend, will face even more serious charges. And in connection with your crimes, I am officially seizing this ridiculous American car." He crossed his arms. "Maybe it will be disassembled and its pieces used to repair the cars of more patriotic Cubans. Or maybe it will be rebuilt for farm work."

Hector looked like he was going to throw up. His eyes darted around, and he was pale and shaking. He looked like he was about to start the engine of his precious Cadillac and drive away. But he stayed frozen in place.

The officers grabbed all three of them. They were handcuffed and searched. Then they were loaded in a PNR van waiting down the street.

"Your friend Pepper Ryan will join you shortly," said Guiteras before he slammed the van door shut.

It was pitch black in the back of the windowless van.

"We'll be okay," Angel said to Marisol and Hector.

Hector was making little noises, somewhere between moaning and crying.

"Hopefully, our decoy trick will give the rest of them room to maneuver," Angel said. "Because if Pepper doesn't pull off his big plan ..."

Angel left that statement unfinished, because they were all thinking similar, terrible thoughts about what awaited each of them if Pepper failed.

CHAPTER THIRTY-FOUR

Pepper didn't want to get arrested or worse, and he figured the last place anyone would look for them was a tourist trap. So he, Dayana, and Beriev were now at El Floridita, Havana's legendary bar and restaurant, with frozen daiquiris in front of them, just like the horde around them.

A life-sized bronze statue of Ernest Hemingway leaned against the bar, arrogantly grinning at Pepper, as if asking: are you man enough to fight?

Pepper hoped so.

He needed to arrange one last face-to-face with Guiteras in order to get to the full truth about the artist killings and related crimes. Because with Rappeneau and Wilder back on the street, justice was not even close to being served. Sometimes, survival required doubling down and risking it all.

Pepper's plan was still half-baked, but he'd asked Beriev to bring his equipment bag with his video camera and all of his supporting cables and accessories. There'd be no justice without irrefutable proof.

If ever.

Pepper took a taste of his drink, trying to look like just another tourist. He had to admit that the daiquiris were damned good. He could see what the fuss was all about. They were smaller than Pepper had pictured, but he limited himself to one. Tonight he needed a steady *culo*.

After a waiter dropped off three Cuban sandwiches at their table, Pepper quietly explained that for a while he'd suspected someone in his inner circle was informing Detective Juan Guiteras of his every move. That explained the detective's uncanny ability to track him down.

So Pepper lied to everyone at the photo gallery about arranging safe harbor at the U.S. embassy, and Hector betrayed himself by immediately texting someone. When Pepper dragged him in the other room and demanded to see the text he'd sent, Hector had confessed. When Pepper made him go to the police station on Wednesday, Guiteras had threatened him with criminal charges if he didn't report Pepper's movements to the PNR. So, how could Hector say no?

Pepper had been furious, but after thinking about it, he was just as mad at himself for not predicting Guiteras' move. After calming down, he'd decided that since Hector had already texted Guiteras about the fictional embassy plan, Hector, Angel, and Marisol should drive the Cadillac to the U.S. embassy as decoys. Meanwhile Pepper, Dayana, and Beriev would regroup and make a new plan that would hopefully bring the chaos to an end.

"I dragged Hector into that police station," admitted Pepper. "So Guiteras strong-arming him was my fault. I didn't understand the risk."

Pepper took a big bite of his sandwich. He was hungry, and the ham, pickles and especially the spicy mustard went straight from his taste buds to his soul. If Dayana didn't finish her sandwich before he did, he'd probably steal the rest of hers.

"Juan can be a bully," said Dayana with a hard look on her face. She was wearing a baseball cap she'd found in the staff area of the gallery, and she had pulled her hair up under the hat. It only made her look one percent less gorgeous, and she was drawing looks from the surrounding tourists, mostly men but some women, too.

I don't blame them a bit, thought Pepper. But out loud, he said, "It turns out, Hector tipped off Guiteras about everywhere I went, all week. That's how he cornered me at Quinto's hangout. And that's how he arrived at Guillermo Infante's apartment so quickly, after I phoned in the dead body."

"The little traitor," Beriev growled, signaling to a large red-tuxedoed bartender with a bald head that his glass was empty again.

"I hear you," said Pepper. "But I'm going home soon and Hector's gotta live here. It is what it is."

"So why did Hector drive the others to the embassy?" asked Dayana. "When Juan realizes your trick, he's going to be furious."

"I asked him to," said Pepper. "It was a chance to redeem himself."

Another daiquiri arrived for Beriev.

As Pepper sipped his drink, he tried to summarize in his mind the key points of the investigation and figure out how the entire crazy puzzle fit together.

To Pepper, the primary suspects were clear: Laurent Rappeneau, Heather Wilder, and Juan Guiteras. But if he was wrong about Guiteras, then he should include as a suspect the person the detective kept saying was the PNR's primary suspect: the Belarusian photographer Victor Beriev, sitting two feet away from Pepper, slurping his frozen daiquiri with a blissful look on his face. Pepper had to admit, Beriev had connections to all the murdered artists socially and through his photography.

Pepper felt he had a good handle on the serial killer's methods, which included using the *Vanity Fair* article featuring Cuba's top artists as a "kill list," with the victims being murdered in the same order they appeared in the magazine.

Although each artist had suffered a different cause of death, Pepper guessed that the missing African letter opener from the Hemingway estate had been used to stab each artist's corpse, likely out of rage or revenge. It was the grisly detail that became the serial killer's signature move.

However, the clue Pepper felt strongest about was the bloodstained five hundred peso bill with Pepper's handwriting that he'd found in Cockett's wallet. It was a clear link between the Canadian goon squad and the murdered poet, Guillermo Infante. Which put Rappeneau at the top of Pepper's suspect list.

Heather Wilder's copy of the *Vanity Fair* article, filled with cryptic notes and markings, as well as her missing copy of Hemingway's *For Whom the Bell Tolls*, implicated her further as a likely co-conspirator in a "U.S. visas for sex and money" scheme with the Canadian CEO.

One clue still teased Pepper—what was el Segador trying to say by leaving a copy of Hemingway's novel at each crime scene? Was there some deeper message? If so, Pepper hadn't been able to decipher it.

Pepper cautiously sipped his drink and checked his phone to make sure he hadn't missed a text from Angel. He was supposed to contact Pepper when he reached the embassy, or—if something went wrong on the way—as soon as he got clear of the trouble.

But that text didn't come.

"I wish I knew why Juan let the killers go free," said Dayana. "It makes no sense."

"Totally," said Pepper. "There's no doubt Rappeneau and Wilder were selling U.S. visas for sex and money, and we gave the PNR plenty of evidence that they killed Infante to cover up what they were doing. I have two guesses about Guiteras."

Pepper paused while a group of tourists at the next table got up and bumped and squeezed their way past them. One man was gawking at Dayana and tripped over a stool, literally falling for her.

"Two theories," said Pepper, fighting back a grin. He leaned closer to his companions. "First, maybe Guiteras is dirty, taking payouts to look the other way and give them protection when needed."

"No," objected Dayana. "Not Juan!"

Pepper shrugged. "Or second, maybe he was handcuffed by the international politics of the situation. He knew a U.S. diplomat and a Canadian CEO were essentially untouchable." In other words, he didn't have the guts to do his job, thought Pepper. He didn't know which theory disgusted him more—Guiteras being dirty or gutless.

"Any message from Angel?" asked Beriev as he finished another daiquiri.

"Not yet," Pepper said glumly.

Guiteras must have arrested them. Had he underestimated the risk they'd face from the angry detective?

"So, what can we do?" asked Dayana, sounding hopeless. Her daiquiri was almost untouched.

"Keep drinking?" suggested Beriev.

Pepper laughed. "I think I have a plan."

Pepper could only think of one plan that would get justice for the murdered artists, Angel and the others released, and Dayana clear of danger. Pepper needed to get hard proof of what he now believed: the artist killings resulted from a three-way conspiracy among Rappeneau, Wilder, and Guiteras. And the best source for that evidence was the PNR's lead asshole, Detective Juan Guiteras.

"Are you willing to help me try to end this *el Segador* mess?" Pepper asked Dayana and Beriev.

Beriev pushed away his empty glass. "I'm your guy."

Dayana studied Pepper, then said, "I'm in too."

"It'll be dangerous," warned Pepper.

"What's art without risk?" grinned Beriev.

Pepper stood up. "Then let's go for a ride."

Beriev made a sour face. "I don't think I can drive," he slurred.

"No worries, we'll take my car," said Pepper. "But don't forget your camera. It's the key to the entire plan." He gestured to the Belarusian's camera bag under their table.

Pepper found the Range Rover still hidden where he'd left it.

"Where did you get this?" asked Dayana.

"Spoils of war," said Pepper.

Beriev nodded approvingly.

In the privacy of the SUV, Pepper shared his plan with Dayana and Beriev. They talked it back and forth, from different angles, until they agreed.

Then Pepper drove them toward Christopher Columbus Cemetery.

At one point, they approached a police car parked sideways in the road, its lights flashing, and Pepper thought his plan was already dead. But a miserable police officer was merely redirecting traffic around a power pole that had fallen in the pre-hurricane's heavy winds, bringing down a tangle of power lines on the road. The surrounding buildings were dark. Pepper detoured around the trouble and was soon back on course.

He reached the cemetery just as the sun hit the horizon. It was eight o'clock. The cemetery's high gates were already locked shut for the night and the area was abandoned, except for them.

Pepper followed the wall encircling the cemetery, finding a less noticeable place to park. At this spot, the stone wall was about five feet high, topped with another five feet of wrought iron.

Pepper figured they'd be able to climb it easily if starting from the top of the Range Rover. But he hoped Beriev wasn't so drunk that he'd break his neck.

"I thought the weather would be worse by now," said Dayana. She was right that the wind seemed to be dying down somewhat.

"Our first break," said Pepper, but he was thinking, if the wind dies even further, that might just be the calm before the storm. Because Hurricane Gussie was close.

Beriev was in the back of the Range Rover, humming to himself and fiddling with his camera equipment. He fitted what he called a dead kitten on the built-in microphone, to reduce audio distortion caused by wind. He adjusted the lenses in anticipation of the lighting getting worse by the minute. They would have the faint light that came after sunset, and then they would depend on the moon for light.

"Where did you get these?" Beriev chuckled, holding up the two handguns Pepper had stowed in the rear seatback pocket after the La Guarida fight.

"They came as a package deal with the car," said Pepper. "I have a third handgun, too. Hopefully, I won't need it, but..."

"I'll take one," said Dayana. "Since I'm on top of el Segador's list."

Pepper didn't love that idea. "Have you ever fired a gun?"

Dayana laughed. "My father didn't have sons. When he was sober enough to hunt for boar and *jutías* in the Sierra Maestra mountains, he brought me. I began firing his shotgun and his Makarov pistol as a young teenager."

She kept surprising him. He couldn't picture her trudging through a tropical forest as a teenager, hunting for her family's next meal. "What are *jutías*?"

"They are between a rabbit and a rat. We call it 'poor man's meat.'" She laughed again. "Not recommended for yumas like you."

"My camera's the only weapon I need," said Beriev.

"Take the other gun anyway," Dayana suggested to him. "I'll feel better knowing you have it, if there's trouble."

"She's right," said Pepper. "Better to have it and not need it than..."

"Okay, okay," said Beriev. "I'll take it to make Dayana feel better."

It was time for Dayana's acting job.

Pepper took a deep breath, dialed Juan Guiteras' number, hit speaker phone, and handed it to Dayana.

Dayana didn't give Guiteras a chance to say hello, or "fuck you," or however the detective typically answered his phone.

"Pepper went to the bathroom, and he left his phone, so I needed to tell you how mad I am at you!" she said, at a loud volume. "Juan, you are such an asshole!"

"Dayana?" Guiteras asked. "Are you drunk?"

"I'm mad, Juan. I'm very mad. Pepper told me you blocked my passport application," she said, sounding hysterical and hurt. "I told him that's impossible. You know about my dreams, the movies I need to make, to see how far I can go as an actor. Tell me he was lying."

Guiteras said nothing.

"You snake," she said more quietly. "You traitor..."

"You were the traitor," he said. "Betraying Cuba with your protests."

"Bullshit! You couldn't have me, so you wouldn't let me go!"

"I think you are drunk." Guiteras sounded amused.

Dayana glanced at Pepper and Beriev, took a deep breath, then said, "I want to offer you a deal. I'll do something you want if you will unblock my passport. Please, let me go."

"I'm listening."

"I believe you are right about Laurent Rappeneau and Heather Wilder. And I believe you are right about Viktor Beriev, too. I saw something in his loft that almost scared me to death. It was the African letter opener, the one stolen from the Hemingway estate. I know it was the same one. The director showed me a picture."

Why was Dayana improvising? Pepper wondered. Did she think she needed to lull Guiteras into thinking he wasn't being set up? The detective was so cagey, Pepper hoped Dayana wouldn't overplay her hand. But she was an actor, he reminded himself. And a damn good one.

"Where is Viktor Beriev now?" asked Guiteras.

"Who knows?" asked Dayana. "As long as he's far away from me." She winked at Beriev, and he stuck out his tongue at her.

"Dayana, what is it you think you can offer me?"

"Pepper," said Dayana. "I can give him to you. But you need to explain yourself. Why you released Laurent Rappeneau and Heather Wilder when my life is in danger. And most of all, you need to fix my passport."

Guiteras considered the offer, then said, "Maybe you and I can make a deal. Let's get together and talk about it, you, me, and the yuma. I will explain why I had to release the Canadian and the embassy lady. Where are you?"

"It doesn't matter. We're leaving the second Pepper gets back from peeing. I'll tell him we need to go to Carlina Borja's grave—a nice, private place to talk," suggested Dayana. "I'll tell him I need to pray there, to decide what to do about all this. Meet us there in fifteen minutes. You and I can help each other out, like when we were children."

"The Cementerio de Cristóbal Colón?" Guiteras said skeptically. "The gates will be locked soon, if they are not already."

Dayana laughed. "The gates won't stop Pepper from taking me where I ask. You're going to let them stop you?"

Guiteras didn't respond.

"It will just be us and a million dead people," she laughed. "You can explain yourself, and you can do whatever you're planning. Maybe beat up poor Pepper again. You animal!" She gave Pepper an apologetic shrug. "He's coming back," she hissed. "Fifteen minutes. Be there, Juan, for my sake!" She disconnected the call, grinning at Pepper and Beriev.

"Now, *that* was fun!" she laughed, and when they began clapping, she gave them a mocking little bow.

CHAPTER THIRTY-FIVE

Pepper waited with Dayana in the twilight after sunset, sitting on an iron railing around the Borja family mausoleum.

In the near darkness, El Cementerio de Cristóbal Colón felt like the scene of a bad dream. Elongated shadows stretched across the mausoleums and statues. Howls of wind from Hurricane Gussie came and went in heavy gusts, echoing among the stone structures. An early crescent moon added a thin, silvery light.

Pepper's heart was pounding in quick time, and his senses felt hyper-focused and crisp. He'd set up his plan as best he could. Dayana was right about the location—it was deserted and secluded. The kind of place to get Juan Guiteras talking. Victor Beriev was hiding off to the right, scrunched down low in the darkness beside another large mausoleum, to record what unfolded.

Viktor's video camera was set for low-light recording. He had a microphone on the camera, and he'd also velcroed a small, wireless microphone to the fence that encircled the Borja mausoleum.

"What if Juan's right?" Dayana whispered. "About Viktor. If—"

She paused when they both heard a scrape from across the cemetery, but the noise stopped.

Pepper felt a chill down his spine. "Why would you say that now?"

She squeezed his arm. "The things Juan has been saying about him, it made me think. Viktor's obsessed with whether his work will be remembered. He's jealous of Cuba artists who get more recognition than him. And when I saw those weird portraits of the four dead artists ..." She shuddered. "And the one of me. I felt like I was already a victim too, right beside my friends, you know?"

"I get that was upsetting, but it doesn't prove anything." Pepper was unsure what to think. Beriev was a quirky artist, but a serial killer? Pepper thought the facts still pointed more to Rappeneau, Wilder, and maybe Guiteras. Pepper had seen Guiteras pull a stiletto knife when he cut Rappeneau and Wilder free. He knew that Dayana grew up with Guiteras—could that be blinding her to the possibility that he was a killer?

A beam of a flashlight carved through the near darkness. Someone was approaching. The person stopped, shining the flashlight in different directions, as if searching.

Pepper's neck tingled with anticipation. The truth of the whole damned mess lay just ahead—the murders, the corruption, and the lies.

The beam of light reflected off a wall of stone, illuminating the person's face for a split second. It was Guiteras.

Pepper tried to swallow, but his mouth was too dry. "Stop right there," he yelled hoarsely.

Guiteras stopped. "Where's Dayana?"

Pepper pulled Dayana to her feet from where she had been sitting on the low railing.

"Let her go," yelled Guiteras. "You're under arrest."

The detective had pulled his handgun and was pointing it at

him. He slid behind Dayana, using her as a shield. "I sure hope he cares about you," Pepper whispered in her ear.

Dayana gave him an elbow in the ribs.

Guiteras paced toward them, still pointing the handgun, so Pepper pulled the Sig Sauer from his pocket and pointed it at Dayana's neck. "I said, stop!" Pepper yelled.

"Yes, yes," said Guiteras, stopping. He put away his handgun and raised his two hands in front of him, showing they were empty. "So we will add assault and kidnapping to your crimes. Okay, what now?"

Pepper lowered the Sig Sauer to his side, so it wasn't pointed at Dayana. "Now you talk. Why'd you let Rappeneau and Wilder go? How much did they pay you to let them walk? Or were you a partner in their visa scheme the whole time?"

Guiteras laughed harshly. "You know less about Cuba than the day you arrived. And less than that about my murders."

"Are you saying you're the serial killer?" Pepper asked. His voice was steady, but inside, uncertainty gnawed at him.

"Watch out, Juan!" Dayana yelled to Guiteras. "Viktor Beriev is hiding nearby, and I think he's el Segador!"

"What?" yelled Beriev.

Shit, thought Pepper. *What the hell was Dayana improvising now?*

"He has that African letter opener in his camera bag. I saw it in the car!" Dayana yelled.

Pepper saw Beriev dig deeply in his camera bag. He eventually pulled out a long, thin blade that glinted in the moonlight.

Damn! thought Pepper. *Dayana was right!*

Beriev froze, then shoved the letter opener back in the bag. When his hand came out again, it was holding a handgun. The weapon Pepper had encouraged the photographer to take.

Guiteras drew his handgun, which reminded Pepper it made sense for him to raise his Sig Sauer.

Viktor Beriev stepped toward Pepper. "I didn't kill anyone!"

"Shoot him!" Dayana yelled, gesticulating wildly at Beriev. She let loose a long, shrill scream that echoed through the cemetery. Then she broke and ran from Pepper's side.

Which probably made sense, he decided. No point being a front-row spectator at a gunfight.

"Drop it!" Guiteras ordered Beriev, his voice filled with rage. His gaze snapped to Pepper, his lip curling. "And you too, Ryan. Just holding that weapon will send you to prison, which you deserve anyway for interfering. Your vigilante shit put Dayana's life in danger."

Pepper's jaw clenched, and he didn't drop the Sig Sauer. "I wish I could, but bottom line? I think you're a dirty cop, covering up for Rappeneau and Wilder. How much did you cost?"

The twilight seemed to dim faster as the three men stood their ground in a rough triangle, their weapons pointed at each other, while accusations flew back and forth.

Guiteras laughed, moving his handgun closer to Pepper's direction. "This is what your Hollywood calls a Mexican standoff, *sí?*"

"Pretty much," said Pepper.

"Do you know the difference between a Mexican standoff and a Cuban standoff?" Guiteras asked.

"Tell me."

"In a Cuban standoff, only Juan survives!"

The detective's gun shifted slightly to aim at him, so he threw himself sideways. He heard a handgun fire, and then his ribs struck a low, thick stone railing. Pepper rolled away, his side burning with pain.

He heard the crack of another shot fired, then the thud of a bullet hitting stone. More shots followed, back and forth, from different handguns, deafeningly loud, echoing across the cemetery. Pepper peeked out the other side of the mausoleum and saw Guiteras and Beriev firing at each other, both from behind mausoleums.

Where was Dayana? Pepper hoped she was well clear of the crazy crossfire.

Guiteras or Beriev, thought Pepper. Who was the serial killer? Pepper liked hard evidence—something you could hold up in court and say, "ta da," like the letter opener from Beriev's bag. But sometimes it came down to things people said. Things they admitted or said by mistake. Like something that only el Segador would know.

Then it hit him, stopping him mid-crawl. Someone had!

Pepper's mind raced, trying to reassess the clues he'd gathered over the past five days. Everything he'd found, everything people had said.

A discrepancy was poking at Pepper like a chicken bone caught in his throat, but he couldn't quite shake it loose. And then he remembered what it was.

Everyone in Havana talked about el Segador's brutal murder of the artists—stabbing the victims repeatedly in the back until they died. It was the stuff of nightmares. But Pepper knew from reading the police reports each artist was already dead by the time they were stabbed in the back. That strange detail hadn't been publicized by the police, and so everyone repeated the other story, that the artists were stabbed to death.

Except one person, who would know the truth about the stabbings only if they read the police reports—or if they were the killer.

Pepper thought about it, confirming to himself that person hadn't read the police reports.

The truth hit him like a sledgehammer to the chest.

"It's her," Pepper yelled from his knees. "Dayana's el Segador!"

CHAPTER THIRTY-SIX

Dayana appeared from behind a mausoleum about ten feet from Pepper. Her eyes were wide with surprise, but her face quickly changed to a piercing stare.

"What are you talking about, Pepper?" she said, her voice incredulous. "I shared everything with you. I trusted you with my life."

Pepper paused, getting a sick feeling in his stomach, to go with the pain in his ribs. *Am I wrong?* He hesitated...

"No, it all fits," he insisted. "Your rejected passport and exit visa, the other artists getting approval to leave Cuba while you were denied."

Dayana's lips curled into a sneer. "So now they're turning you against me too?"

But Pepper was just getting started. "You threw yourself on Alicia Arenas' body, covering yourself in blood to mask any DNA evidence. You called Guiteras instead of the general police emergency number, knowing you could manipulate him. But your big slip-up was talking about the stabbings. You knew every artist was dead before they were stabbed repeatedly in the back. All this week, you're the only civilian in Havana who described the murders to me that way. Only the killer and the police knew how the artists really died."

Pepper saw Guiteras and Beriev move into the open too, and they exchanged shocked glances.

"I can explain everything," Dayana insisted, reaching behind her back. Yet she pulled out a handgun, and her eyes were suddenly wide with fury.

Pepper, Guiteras, and Beriev scattered as Dayana opened fire.

Pepper dove behind a wide gravestone. *Now, that's a Cuban standoff,* he thought, trying to flatten against the ground. *Even the bystanders have weapons...*

"Dayana, stop!" Guiteras shouted, his voice trembling with emotion. "It doesn't have to be this way!"

Dayana responded by firing more shots, over and over.

Pepper pushed off the mausoleum and crawled directly away from where Dayana had been a moment before, trying to find refuge in the shadows and the maze of stone structures. His side was cramping and burning where he'd hurt his ribs, but he didn't think the gunfire had hit him.

Maybe if he distracted Dayana, then Guiteras or Beriev could take her down? He pulled his Sig Sauer, just in case they didn't.

"Why did you do it?" Pepper yelled to her, staying behind the stone grave.

Dayana laughed in the darkness. "You figured out I was el Segador, but not why?"

"I've caught lunatics before. They always have some brilliant excuse for what they did. But to me, crazy's just crazy." Pepper heard heavy footsteps to his right, so he crab-walked away to the left.

"I deserve my chance!" Dayana shouted. "I'm the best actor of my generation, but I'm chained here. They'll never let me go!"

Pepper heard another handgun fire from near where Guiteras

had been, and a bullet whizzed past Dayana, who ducked into the fading twilight's shadows and returned fire.

Pepper put his back against the nearest mausoleum, feeling like his heart was about to pound through his chest. Then he hunched down and jogged another stretch, positioning himself behind another mausoleum. His ribs burned in protest. Pepper heard several more shots ring out in the cemetery, but stayed out of sight behind the solid stone protection. He'd been shot before, as recently as last July. And it hurt like hell.

Pepper cupped his hands to his mouth. "I think you were just jealous!"

He heard movement to his right and ducked down farther. A handgun fired.

"I'm guessing maybe you killed Alicia Arenas by accident," he yelled. "Maybe you were drinking together, and your jealousy poured out and you argued about her abandoning Cuba. She didn't want to be involved with a movie adaptation of her book when leaving Cuba. Her mother told me so. I think you two argued. Maybe you hit each other. Somehow, she fell over the railing and died."

Pepper scurried behind the next mausoleum, then continued. "You panicked, took Hemingway's antique letter opener, and stabbed her dead body over and over. You wanted it to look like a stalker or a crazy person killed her, to deflect the PNR from the truth. But then some other artists from your *Vanity Fair* article got the same good news as Alicia. They got permission to go to America. Your application had been rejected and you must have been furious and jealous. Then, after a couple more dead bodies, you must have felt like that woman you played in the movie. You were enjoying the revenge, the total power. The total control."

"Marisol was right," laughed Dayana from behind cover. "Somehow you always get there in the end."

She shot at Pepper four times in a quick burst, striking the ground and stonework near him. And more shots came right after those, from different directions. Guiteras? Beriev?

Pepper pointed his handgun toward where Dayana had fired from, but didn't fire back. He felt a numbness growing inside, as the realization sank in that this woman he'd grown to care for had caused so much death and suffering.

Then Dayana broke into the open, running toward him. After a few steps she crumpled to the ground. She stood, then fell again.

At least one bullet must have hit her, thought Pepper. A dark stain of blood showed on her midsection.

Dayana lifted her handgun and laughed wildly. She pointed the handgun at her own temple. Pepper saw her finger move, heard a loud click, but heard no shot. Her finger moved again, another click, but no shot. She screamed.

She must have wasted her last bullets on Pepper.

Pepper slipped his gun into his pocket and charged forward to tackle her, but Guiteras was closer and leaped toward her first.

So when Dayana's handgun swung up and fired with a flash of flame, it was Guiteras who screamed with pain and surprise, falling back.

God, she'd faked it was empty! The damn actor even faked the damn clicks!

Pepper hadn't reached her before her weapon swung back toward him, but he dove to block her arm and her next shot went wild. He drove her to the ground, and the gun flew from her hand, disappearing into the shadowed grass.

She fought like a rabid animal, kicking and scratching and screaming. Despite his size advantage, he could barely subdue her.

"It's over," he yelled. "I don't want to hurt you. Stop fighting, Dayana!"

She kept bucking and thrashing beneath him. "Dayana?" She screamed, her mouth frothing with spittle. "My name's Maria!"

Pepper stared at her, dumbfounded as he continued pinning her in place. Did she think she was Maria, the murderous bride she'd played in her most famous film? Or another Maria, the character in *For Whom the Bells Toll*? Or was this just another of Dayana's performances, to build an insanity defense for her eventual murder trial?

Guiteras appeared at Pepper's side, his right arm and shoulder black with his own blood. But he shoved Pepper aside, his eyes filled with a mixture of anger and betrayal. "Call for help! Call for help!" he shouted at Pepper. With his good arm, the detective ripped off his shirt and pressed it against Dayana's stomach, trying to slow her bleeding while ignoring his own gunshot wound.

Beriev was kneeling beside Dayana now too, talking to her in Spanish, trying to calm her, while holding her closest hand firm against the grass.

Pepper already had his phone out and dialed 106. He had to admit—he did remember Cuba's emergency number when he needed to, but it still wasn't as catchy as 911.

Trying to enunciate in Spanish, Pepper told the man who answered to send police and an ambulance to El Cementerio de Cristóbal Colón. Then he repeated himself in English.

As Pepper put away his phone, he heard a groaning, echoing noise and felt wind rip through the acres of stone mausoleums, sounding like an immense animal's howls of rage. Hurricane Gussie, finally showing teeth again? Pepper swayed, fatigued and feeling a burning sensation cramping his ribcage.

He and Dayana locked gazes, but neither spoke words. Pepper's mind was a flood of questions, and feelings, and stunned disbelief. But words couldn't fix any of that now.

He thought back to when he first saw Dayana, when she'd slapped him at the club. He'd been just as struck by her wild beauty and passion. It was like he'd never had a chance to escape from her. But the secrets she'd confided to him about her dirt poor childhood, the bullying, her thwarted dreams to pursue acting, how much of it was real and how much was part of her act? Even after what happened, he was surprised to still feel a raw tenderness for Dayana. But were his feelings for her or the woman she'd played?

A police siren rose in the distance, harmonizing with the keening wind. There was nothing for Pepper to do but sit on a tomb with his head down and breathe as shallowly as possible, while trying to ignore the burning in his ribs and the cold, sick thoughts spinning around in his head.

CHAPTER THIRTY-SEVEN

Pepper got a few fitful hours of sleep at Casa de Vides, but woke early on Monday and immediately got up. He needed to catch the first flight he could find back to the U.S., then get his butt to Washington.

His taped ribs had made it hard to sleep. The doctor had told Pepper in excellent English that he had good news. His ribs were bruised, not broken. But they hurt like hell when he inhaled or moved his arms or shoulders.

He had almost passed out from pain when Angel hugged him last night. With his arm in a triage sling, Guiteras released Angel, Marisol, and Hector from the Zanja Police Station. He returned Hector's Cadillac too.

Because Angel and Marisol's door was closed, Pepper didn't have access to the kitchen without waking them. He waited in the living room. But a few minutes later, Angel padded out barefoot and joined him with bad news. José Martí International Airport was remaining closed indefinitely because of the high winds surrounding the broader path of Hurricane Gussie.

Pepper was stuck.

Every hour that ticked off the clock sounded like a nail being driven into the coffin of his FBI career.

Angel rejoined Marisol, who was now also awake, sitting up in bed in a long T-shirt. She looked fantastic, but she was upset.

"I just realized they took everything," she said.

"What?"

"The PNR. They gave me back my damaged phone, but they took every photo and piece of video off it. I texted Viktor. He says they seized every second of the footage he filmed for me on this trip. Everything Pepper did, everywhere he went. They even grabbed the buttonhole camera footage."

"Huh," said Angel. "They must want it as evidence against Dayana." He was surprised, but not upset at all. The opposite, actually. A lot of the footage had been taken during her faked disappearance. And Pepper hadn't signed on to star in her documentary about a serial killer running loose in Havana. He was probably already getting fired. The last thing he needed was video on social media about what he'd done unofficially in Havana.

"I'll never get it back," she said mournfully. "My project's dead."

Angel agreed silently. The Cuban authorities would lock away Dayana and any evidence as deeply as possible, then probably never admit that any of it had ever occurred. To protect the Cuban state.

"At least the serial killer got caught," he reminded her. "That's what you cared about most anyway, right?"

Marisol didn't respond.

That was the wrong response. "We need to talk," he said. The words came out like he was ripping them loose from his internal organs.

Marisol's posture stiffened. "What's there to talk about, Angelito?" She locked eyes with him and tried to smile.

Angel swallowed. "I told you when the el Segador chaos ended, we needed to discuss what you did. Your faked disappearance, the way you manipulated me and Pepper—everything you put me through."

Her mouth fell open and her hand flew to her neck. "We talked about that, and I already apologized. Multiple times."

"The thing is, I still love you. But I don't think I can ever trust you again."

"What?" she gasped. She placed her fists on her hips. Her face reddened. "Can't *trust* me? I explained everything to you, why I did it!"

Angel continued, now hearing his voice in his ears like someone else was talking. "That's what it comes down to. I thought you and me were the real thing, you know. And I was going to ... Well, it doesn't matter now. I love you, but without trust I just can't. And that's not something we can fix. I'm sorry."

Marisol shook, and she started crying. "You love me, but you're breaking up with me?"

"I'm sorry," Angel repeated. He felt sick about what they were giving up. But he knew deep down it had already been lost.

Angel stood to go, because there was nothing left to say. Nine months of dating down the drain. Another failed relationship. He would have bet everything that this time with Marisol was different. But it had been different in a way Angel could never have imagined.

Maybe he would give women a break for a while. Focus on his restaurant. Focus on himself.

Is there something wrong with me? he wondered as he left the bedroom, gently closing the door. But for once, he reminded himself, this breakup definitely wasn't his fault.

And then a thought made him laugh, despite his pain.

I may have bad luck with women, but at least Marisol didn't turn out to be the serial killer.

Pepper heard the story from Angel a little later. Marisol's tears turned to screaming, and then she stormed out of the casa in the roaring wind, carrying her few possessions.

"The crazy thing is, her plan actually worked," said Angel. "She tricked us into getting you down here to stop the serial killer. Which you freaking did!"

Pepper couldn't argue with that.

"Even crazier, she still wanted us to be a couple," Angel said, shaking his head. "Like all her lies and manipulations were justified in the end, so I should just put the whole thing behind me. I was going to ask her to marry me. Turns out, I didn't even know her."

"Sorry, pal," said Pepper. "That sucks."

"Mano, I apologize for dragging you into this nightmare."

Pepper shook his head. "Not your fault. But I'm sorry it's ending like this for you guys. Really brutal." He gave his buddy a hug. He wasn't surprised Angel had ended the relationship, and he believed it was the right move.

"I hope I can change my seat on the flight home," said Angel. "Or it's going to be a damn bumpy ride."

Later in the afternoon, Havana came out of hiding. The sun was out, and the air was fresh. Hurricane Gussie had spared Cuba a direct hit, sliding by at a distance that subjected the island only to heavy rain and sixty-mile-an-hour winds. By mid-afternoon, it had howled away into the Gulf of Mexico.

Around seven o'clock, Detective Lola Valdés phoned and asked Pepper if he would go for a walk with her along the Malecón seawall. Surprised, Pepper said yes.

They met there twenty minutes later. Valdés was wearing the same light green pants suit she'd worn when they'd met at the police station on Wednesday. But this evening she had her hair loose around her shoulders. She looked ten years younger. The detective was sneaky hot, Pepper thought.

A setting sun sent an orange blush across the harbor. The evening crowd was the largest Pepper had seen during his brief stay in Havana. Everyone wanted to get outside again, to meet up with relatives and friends. A rainbow of vintage American cars cruised past.

Pepper grinned at the sight. "They should film this for an ad campaign," he suggested with a smile. "Tourists would flood Cuba!"

She laughed. "This is my favorite place in the city," she said, looking up at him as they began strolling down the Malecón's concrete and stone promenade. "People fall in love here, they gather with their families and friends, they grow old here. I could never leave Cuba."

The tide was in and waves were smashing the seawall. Spray shot high and fell on people ahead of them, who roared with laughter. Pepper thought that on an afternoon like this, he couldn't think of a more beautiful place, full of happier people.

Valdés sighed. "Do you want to hear about Dayana?"

Pepper nodded. Despite her being a serial killer, Pepper was relieved that she hadn't died in the cemetery.

She kept her face averted toward choppy Havana Bay as they kept walking, and her voice was low and steady. "She's been answering our questions for over ten hours, and though every answer includes lies, I believe we've pieced together the truth."

Pepper held his breath, waiting.

"The first killing was accidental, or at least not premeditated. Dayana learned Alicia Arenas got permission to leave Cuba, so she went to confront her for betraying their country. They were both drinking in the tower and they argued. Alicia ended up going over the railing to her death. Dayana claims she never touched her, but . . ."

Valdés shrugged, then continued. "Dayana panicked. She staged the scene to look like a psychopath's work, stabbing Arenas' corpse with the letter opener and placing the Hemingway book. All improvised. Early the next morning, she made Viktor Beriev drive her back to the Hemingway estate for a fictional meeting with Arenas, so they could innocently discover the body together."

Pepper thought he understood. "So, alcohol-fueled rage and jealousy over Arenas' approval to go to America while Dayana's was denied."

Valdés nodded. "Another betrayal, like those Dayana had suffered since childhood."

"And the others?" Pepper asked.

"Similar story," shrugged Valdés. "As more artists from the *Vanity Fair* article won approval to go abroad, Dayana's jealousy consumed her. But each murder brought a growing sense of power and control, something Guiteras tells me Dayana had craved since her poor childhood."

"Crazy," said Pepper.

Valdés stopped walking. "Her endgame was just as crazy. Her plan was to frame Viktor Beriev as el Segador. She'd been manipulating Juan for months, flirting with him while pushing him to suspect Beriev. But she eventually admitted she put the Hemingway letter opener in Beriev's camera bag to frame him. She even confessed that last night in the gunfight, she hoped you or Guiteras would kill Beriev, and he would become the scapegoat for the murders. And she believed Cuban authorities would take pity on her and finally let her go become a Hollywood star. But she has been out of her mind the whole time."

Pepper shook his head, stunned by Dayana's deceit and desperation. His throat tightened, remembering how he had felt when he sang his song to her in the hotel suite bedroom, the chills he'd gotten when they harmonized together. And how he'd felt about the possibility of a future together.

But all along she'd been trying to use him as a pawn in her plan to pin the murders on Beriev. He clenched his fists as anger filled his veins. How had he been so easily fooled?

But as everyone had said all week, she was a hell of an actor.

They walked together for a while, not speaking.

"I have some good news for you," Valdés said, breaking the silence. "The airport is going to reopen in the morning. And we called airport administration and used our influence to get you on the first plane out."

Pepper was delighted. "Thank you!" he said. He'd been worried about that. After all the flight cancelations because of Hurricane Gussie, he'd expected he might wallow in standby limbo for days.

"Juan did most of it," she admitted. "I think to avoid saying thank you to your face. And to be honest, he enjoyed strong-arming the airport's officers. It helped him forget about the bullet wound in his shoulder."

Pepper laughed. Guiteras wouldn't be beating up anyone in the boxing ring for a while. "When you see him, give him a big, firm hug from me."

Valdés said she would drive Pepper back to his casa in her little Soviet–era PNR car, because she had a surprise for him. She refused to explain until they got there.

"A goodbye gift, and a surprise," she said, once she had parked curbside. "This is the gift. Open it."

She handed him a small brown bag. Inside he found a paperback copy of *For Whom the Bell Tolls*.

"Thank you," he said, touched that she'd bothered. He'd planned to read it again, after everything that had happened.

"Open it," she said.

Pepper flipped to the title page and saw she had written a note.

> *Cuba is a fine place and worth fighting for.*
> *Love,*
> *Lola Valdés*

And Cuba was, Pepper decided. He knew she was paraphrasing one of the most famous quotes from the book.

"Cuba is," he said, his voice choking a little. "And the world is too ... but I forget sometimes. So, thank you."

Her lips parted like she was going to say something else, but she stopped. Her expression changed and she said, "Now, Senōr Ryan, it is time for your surprise."

She made Pepper get out of her little car, and she popped the trunk.

He saw a stack of baggage.

"No way!" he said.

She laughed.

"Angel and Marisol's bags? How did you find them?"

She tossed back her hair and flashed him a big smile. "Good old-fashioned police work. We do that here too."

Pepper lifted out all the bags, then kneeled down and dug around in the backpack that he knew belonged to Angel.

He found the inner pocket Angel had mentioned. Inside, he felt something small and slippery, and pulled out a tiny velvet pouch. He opened it and removed a beautiful vintage diamond ring. Angel's dead grandmother's ring. In all the chaos of the past couple of days, he'd forgotten about the family heirloom.

Grinning, he held it up to show Valdés.

"Why, Pepper Ryan, we barely know each other," she laughed. "And you didn't ask my father's permission."

Pepper laughed too. He was so happy. He couldn't wait to see Angel's face.

An idea crossed his mind, and he said, "Actually, I have something for you too," he said. "Wait here."

He came back out a minute later and handed her the cast iron frying pan he'd gained during the La Guarida fight. "I don't think I'd get it through security anyway," he joked.

Valdés hefted the heavy pan, raised an eyebrow, then chuckled. "It will always remind me of you."

Then Pepper hugged the detective goodbye. Her embrace was stronger than he expected, and longer, too.

CHAPTER THIRTY-EIGHT

Pepper needed to be at José Martí International Airport shortly after dawn on Tuesday, and Hector insisted on giving Pepper a ride.

Angel's original flight home was on Wednesday and he hadn't been able to rebook. So he was staying behind for one more day, with a suitcase full of clean clothes to show off.

Quinto Chavez had called to insist on taking Angel and Hector out that night to thank them for their part in catching his stepsister's killer. No one had asked Quinto about some musty books that had disappeared from the Hemingway estate, so he was in a jovial mood. The jinetero had promised to show them the best of Havana, and Angel was excited to take him up on it.

Hector had washed and waxed his Cadillac convertible, but he said little when Pepper climbed in. He took Pepper by a scenic route through Old Havana, and they passed the dark, abandoned Plaza de San Francisco de Asís, where Marisol had faked her disappearance eight days earlier.

Hector turned on Elvis Presley at a medium volume and began crooning along to "Return to Sender." Pepper sang with him. He guessed that the young man was still embarrassed about informing to the police.

At the airport, Hector gave Pepper a hug goodbye. "Elvis is the king, but you..." said Hector. He shook his head, unable to speak further.

"*Gracias*, Hector, for everything. Elvis would be proud of what you did in the end. Let me know when you make it to Las Vegas. I want to see you perform."

Hector beamed, and his eyes shone with happy tears. "I've decided I don't need to go to Vegas to follow in Elvis's footsteps. I am going to ask permission to entertain patients at my hospital. Make them feel better with my singing and dancing! And I will keep driving tourists in my beautiful Cadillac, to show them the real soul of Havana."

That afternoon Pepper arrived at the FBI's headquarters in Washington, DC.

It was time to face the music.

He knew that he'd destroyed his FBI career. At the same time, though, he'd ended an exploitative visa-for-sex-and money scheme, and also caught Cuba's notorious serial killer. Worth fighting for, as Lola Valdés said, despite the professional asskicking he was about to receive.

The office of Edwina Youngblood, the Deputy Assistant Director of the FBI's Criminal Investigative Division, was cramped. The walls, too close.

She didn't invite Pepper to sit. Instead, she led him to a small interview room, of the type the FBI used to interview suspects. He noticed the two cameras high in the corners, covering the room. Did Youngblood want a record of his execution?

Pepper tucked his duffel bag under the table, wincing from

the sharp pain in his side as he sat down. His bruised ribs were a gift that would keep on giving for a few weeks.

Youngblood was a short, thin woman in her early fifties with jet black hair cut off sharply at her neck. The look on her face might have been intended as a smile, but looked more like she'd smelled something unclean.

"I hope your family emergency ended well?" she asked.

Pepper started to bullshit her, but then he stopped. He exhaled.

Then he came clean about everything. Marisol's disappearance, why Pepper had felt the need to go help his friend find her, how the case had escalated into an investigation of a serial killer, right up through the final confrontation and apprehension of Dayana in the cemetery.

Youngblood had her arms crossed and a scowl on her face as she listened to Pepper's story. Although, as a gentleman would, Pepper skipped the part about kissing the serial killer...

Youngblood didn't interrupt once. Occasionally, she unfolded her arms to make a note on a yellow legal pad. She scowled for forty-five minutes straight. Must be a new world record, even for Washington, DC.

"That's about it," he said. "But I wanted to apologize for not being straight with you while it was all happening. That wasn't right."

"I give you half a point for honesty," Youngblood said. "But what else did you come here to say? Are you here to tender your resignation from the FBI?"

Pepper's stomach tightened into a knot. "No," he said, softly but firmly. "I'm a good agent. I want to keep serving the Bureau."

"I'm glad you told me about Havana," she said. "Because I've already received several reports of your activity down there from the State Department."

Heather Wilder. No doubt she'd spread his name all over

Washington, as part of her efforts to get him the heck out of Havana before he nuked her visa scheme.

She glanced up at the camera in the room's corner.

Pepper wondered if that meant someone was watching them.

"Laurent Rappeneau was arrested this morning in Toronto, after he fled Cuba. But apparently one of his security employees has fully implicated Rappeneau in one murder, for the poet named Guillermo Infante. So Rappeneau is going to be extradited back to Cuba for prosecution."

Who would have sung first? Pepper wondered. *McDonald or Burger King?* Probably whichever goon the PNR started grilling first.

"Was Heather Wilder arrested too?" he asked.

"The diplomat?" Youngblood asked. "Why would she be arrested?"

Pepper stared at her. "For her scheme with Rappeneau to sell U.S. visas to Cubans for sex and money. She'd be criminally liable after Rappeneau had Infante murdered to shut him up."

"You didn't find any evidence that she received money, right?" she asked.

The question confused Pepper. "No, but it'll be there somewhere. She was in the scheme up to her nose. And I'm pretty sure her copy of *For Whom the Bells Toll* ended up on the poet's dead body."

Youngblood waved a hand dismissively. "Better that we don't worry about Wilder," she said. "Way above our pay grade. But hypothetically, if Uncle Sam ran a program to undermine Cuba by luring away its top artists, we'd never publicly admit it. The State Department would dismiss any rumors as Communist propaganda, right? So you should be more worried about your own actions."

Then she read Pepper the riot act. Listed the U.S. laws and regulations he'd potentially broken by going to Havana. Then the offenses under Cuban law that he, a federal special agent, had committed over the last week.

She went on and on, and Pepper didn't interrupt. She hadn't interrupted him, and he had no defense for his actions. He had been a reckless idiot again and deserved to be fired.

When Youngblood stopped talking, she studied him for the longest time. Maybe trying to incinerate him with her eyes. Then her eyes flicked again to the camera.

"When I think of the worst scandals in FBI history. J. Edgar Hoover. Whitey Bulger. Robert Hanssen. In every case, the cause was agents and officers who didn't follow the rules."

"Not corruption and stupidity?" Pepper asked.

Youngblood glared at him. "More like rule breaking and insubordination. Like you've exemplified this last week. So—"

Her cell phone buzzed. She answered it and mostly listened, then hung up. "I'll be right back," she said.

But she wasn't. Pepper sat alone in that uncomfortable chair in that small conference room for forty-five minutes. How long did it take to fire someone?

When Youngblood finally returned, her face was flushed and her eyes were tight. Maybe steeling herself for the ugly business of beginning his disciplinary process.

She sat down and loudly scraped her chair closer to the table. "You're the most headstrong, chaotic agent who's ever worked in my unit," she said. "It's probably best for the Bureau for your service to end right here."

Probably?

"I recommended terminating you, effective immediately. And my boss agreed."

Pepper's heart sank.

"But higher up the chain of command, someone didn't agree. They pointed out that you succeeded, and while the end rarely justifies the means—in this case they believe maybe it did. Even though your actions were totally illegal and outrageous."

She paused, but Pepper said nothing. He waited, his stomach in his throat.

Youngblood scowled at him. "I can't believe I'm saying this. But at this time the Bureau will not pursue any action against you for what you did this summer on Cape Cod, nor what you did during the last week in Cuba."

Wow!

Shock and relief flooded through him. "Th-thank you," he stammered.

"Don't thank me," she snapped. "I recommended referring your activity to Justice for a full review and prosecution. I believe you've committed several felonies, as well as acts disreputable to the Bureau."

Pepper didn't know what to say, so he said nothing.

"But I was overruled," she continued. "Apparently, you've developed a guardian angel within the Bureau."

Pepper liked the sound of that.

"Long story short," she said. "I've been ordered to give you a chance to salvage your FBI career. We have a specific high-risk assignment overseas that needs someone with your, ah, unconventional skill set. You'll work without direct Bureau supervision or support. No safety net. In other words, your sweet spot."

He was getting to like hearing her eat crow.

"I hope you understand this is your last chance," she said. "And you can't break *any* country's laws during your task. Am I clear?"

Pepper thought she was anything but clear. He was being offered a dangerous, secret assignment, but whatever you do, follow all the rules?

"Can you brief me on the details?"

She waved a hand. "You'll get that soon. For now, go home and heal whatever made you wince when you sat down. Your administrative leave will end with your new assignment in about two weeks. Someone will be in touch."

She stared at him and he stared back, unsure if she was finished.

"Why are you still sitting there?" Youngblood asked in a disgusted tone. She stood up. "I have a full plate of honest Bureau business to finish today. Dismissed!"

Pepper left FBI headquarters around four-thirty, feeling disoriented but with a spring in his step.

I wasn't fired!

When he reached the National Mall, he walked to the Lincoln Memorial Reflecting Pool. The place where his whole strange Cuba adventure began when he'd gotten Angel's panicked phone call. Pepper slowly threaded his way through the usual crowd of tourists and federal workers. His duffel bag was slung over his shoulder. He could have caught a cab, but he wanted some time to walk. Time to wrap his head around it all.

He wasn't fired. Even though his boss hated him.

He was getting a new assignment, a chance to redeem himself. He smiled, then stopped to buy a big, salty pretzel from a street vendor to celebrate.

The last week had been like a strange fever dream, especially the Cuban people.

Dayana, Valdés, Guiteras, Hector ... and all the others.

Pepper was proud that he'd stuck it out to the end in Havana. And proud that he'd shown up to face Youngblood's verdict on his FBI career. He still didn't know if his new assignment would be worse than getting fired, but at least he'd faced his mistakes honestly and head on. There was a freedom in that.

He knew he would never become a risk-averse desk jockey, like so many of the Bureau's employees. That wasn't in his DNA. But the FBI was a great place for him to keep on fighting the good fight his own way, as long as they let him.

Pepper munched his salty pretzel as he walked toward the Lincoln Memorial, where there would be a line of cabs waiting. He'd have a quick ride to the airport, a short flight to Boston, then a drive down to Cape Cod.

He was excited to get home. To rest, heal, and reflect. And soon he would receive the phone call about his mysterious new assignment.

Bigger and better things. A dangerous situation that was perfect for his unconventional skills, apparently with life and death consequences. Or maybe worse.

Pepper was already excited to go.

THANK YOU

Thank you for buying this book. Pepper Ryan and his friends (and some new enemies) will be back for more adventures soon.

If you liked this story, please write a short review for me on Amazon and/or Goodreads. I greatly appreciate any kind words, even one or two sentences go a long way. And as you may know, reviews significantly boost a book's visibility on Amazon.

To receive special offers, bonus content, and info on new releases, please sign up for my email list at:
  www.timothyfagan.com

If you have any comments, send me an email at:
  tim@timothyfagan.com.

I'm always happy to hear from readers and I try to answer every email I receive.

ACKNOWLEDGMENTS

Thank you to my excellent guides in Cuba, Dayron, Olga and Rocío, for helping me to explore Havana, Cojimar and San Francis de Paula, and to begin understanding the Cuban people, culture and history.

To my host Diamis, for providing an elegant and comfortable home base for my stay in Centro Havana.

To the Rafael Trejo Gym for granting me access to their unique training ground.

And to La Guarida paladar, where I had a world-class dinner. But Barack Obama ate there first.

However, the above-mentioned people (especially Mr. President) didn't contribute to, and aren't responsible for, any political facts or opinions expressed by me in this work of fiction.

Again, thank you to my excellent editor, John Paine, for his patient feedback and proofread that greatly improved the final story. To Elizabeth Coker for her *magnífica* review of certain Spanish words and phrases in this book.

Thank you to my first and best early reader, Karen Fagan. To my enthusiastic and thoughtful ARC readers: Erin Fagan, Matthew Fagan, Anna Fagan, Paul Donahue, Jim Fagan, Kate Taylor, Mary Fagan, Anney Ardiel, and Patrick Fagan. And to other loyal readers of the Pepper Ryan series who read, encouraged or pushed me along the way to get this book completed.

And to Damon, Alisha and the rest of the team at *damonza.com*, for their striking cover design, as always.

Readers of the Pepper Ryan mystery-thriller series know that sometimes Pepper takes a break from chasing baddies to perform as a singer and musician. Have you ever wondered what Pepper sounds like as a singer, or wanted to hear a song that he performed in one of his books?

I was curious myself.

So I spent some time at Zippah Recording Studio in Boston during the pandemic with one goal: to bring some Pepper Ryan music to life. I wrote the lyrics and the original melodies, then worked with some amazing talent in the New England music community to improve the songs to a level that Pepper would be proud of. It was an intimidating experience for me, but wicked fun.

One of those songs is "You Mystify Me" which Pepper sings to Dayana de Melina late one night in *Havana Fear*. If you'd like to listen to the country music studio recording of the song, search for "Pepper Ryan" or "You Mystify Me" on Spotify, Pandora and other streaming music sites. This song now has been streamed more than 40,000 times on Spotify alone, so thank you to all of Pepper's listeners!

And a huge thank you to the musicians, vocalists and producers who helped me bring to life Pepper's EP of four songs, titled "Cherry Sun". This includes Brian Charles, Paul Bohne, Annie Hoffman, Chris Anzalone, Jim Haggerty, Cody Nilsen, Houston Bernard, D.J. Charles, Davina Yannetty and Tyler

Simco—all among the brightest lights of New England's rich music scene.

It was a privilege to record at Zippah Studios in Boston, Massachusetts. The Pepper Ryan songs were mastered one night before the studio tragically burned to the ground in an eight-alarm fire. But I'm delighted to report that this studio has been reborn as Rare Signals recording studio in Cambridge, MA, where Brian Charles is again producing and engineering killer music.

And finally, thank you to all my readers for coming along on another Pepper Ryan adventure. Pepper hopes to see you again soon!

ABOUT THE AUTHOR

Timothy Fagan has always loved to read suspenseful books that make you laugh out loud in public. Now he loves to write them.

Timothy previously spent twenty years as an attorney and executive in the financial services industry, focusing on securities regulatory matters across North America, Europe and Asia-Pacific. He grew up in British Columbia, Canada and currently lives near Boston in Massachusetts, USA.

Havana Fear is the third book in the Pepper Ryan mystery-thriller series. The first in the series, *Killing Shore*, won the 2019 Best Thriller Award by Top Shelf Magazine.

Timothy also writes song lyrics in collaboration with musicians, including an EP of songs by virtual artist Pepper Ryan, available now on Spotify, Pandora and other music streaming sites.

For more information about Timothy Fagan, his upcoming books and other projects, please visit his website: *www.timothyfagan.com*.

ALSO BY TIMOTHY FAGAN

Have you read them all?

In the Pepper Ryan Mystery-Thriller Series:

1. Killing Shore

Pepper Ryan's Cape Cod homecoming takes a deadly turn when a Secret Service agent ends up murdered and an assassination plot is discovered before the U.S. president's vacation visit.

2. Kill Tide

A kidnapped girl. A terrified Cape Cod. And a police cadet in way over his head... The Pepper Ryan origin story: this prequel features 20-year-old Pepper Ryan trying to chase down a serial kidnapper, until his efforts backfire and the life-and-death stakes turn personal.

Visit an independent bookstore near you or Amazon.com to read more.

Made in United States
North Haven, CT
24 July 2024